VANISHED

USA TODAY BESTSELLING AUTHOR

T.K. LEIGH

Vanished

Published by Carpe Per Diem, Inc., 25852 McBean Parkway # 806, Santa Clarita, CA 91355

Edited by: Kim Young, Kim's Editing Services

Quotes from *The Walrus And The Carpenter* originally appeared in *Through The Looking Glass* by Lewis Carrol Copyright © 1871.

Cover Design: Cat Head Biscuit, Inc., Santa Clarita, CA

Image Copyright feedough

Used under license from iStock

BOOKS BY T.K. LEIGH

CONTEMPORARY ROMANCE
The Redemption Duet
Commitment
Redemption

The Possession Duet
Possession
Atonement

The Dating Games Series
Dating Games
Wicked Games
Mind Games
Dangerous Games
Royal Games
Tangled Games

ROMANTIC COMEDY
The Book Boyfriend Chronicles
The Other Side of Someday
Writing Mr. Right

ROMANTIC SUSPENSE
The Inferno Saga
Part One: Spark
Part Two: Smoke
Part Three: Flame
Part Four: Burn

The Beautiful Mess Series
A Beautiful Mess
A Tragic Wreck
Gorgeous Chaos

The Deception Duet
Chasing the Dragon
Slaying the Dragon

Beautiful Mess World Standalones
Heart of Light
Heart of Marley
Vanished

For more information on any of these titles and upcoming releases, please visit T.K.'s website:
www.tkleighauthor.com

VANISHED

How far would you go to protect the ones you love?
Lie for them?
Die for them?
Kill for them?

Rayne Kilpatrick has everything. A job she's dreamed of all her life. The perfect house. And a man she loves and is about to marry...

Until he never returns from a humanitarian mission.

Gone. Disappeared. Vanished.

When footage of his gruesome murder by an extremist group is broadcast around the globe, she wants the person responsible to pay. And she won't stop until he does.

Alexander Burnham has everything... Finally. A job he enjoys where he can actually make a difference in the world. The perfect woman who he's loved his entire life. And the most beautiful daughter a father could ask for...

Until he walks into her bedroom one morning to find it empty.

Gone. Disappeared. Vanished.

It's a race against the clock for Alexander to put the pieces together and find out who has taken his daughter.

As information comes to light, will he be able to bury the guilt of losing his fellow team member and focus instead on finding and saving his daughter?

To Stan & Harper Leigh. It's the little things in life…

PART I:
HONOR

*If a man injures his neighbor, just as he has done,
so it shall be done to him.*

~Leviticus 24:19

PROLOGUE

December 18 - 8:30 PM

Rayne Kilpatrick sat in the back seat of the black SUV, the windows tinted so no one could see inside. Night had fallen, the cloud-covered sky providing protection as she stared down a long driveway leading up to an enormous house in one of the wealthiest towns in the state. She could only imagine what a place like that cost.

"We'll wait for a few hours to make sure everyone's asleep, then you'll go in."

"Me?" She turned to the raven-haired man with olive-toned skin and an ethnic sort of ruggedness sitting beside her. His eyes were as dark as the moonless night, and just as unforgiving. "I thought…" Her knee bounced as she looked at the house, then the man, then the house again, sweat forming on her neck, despite the frigid winter temperatures.

Through a pair of binoculars, she saw a well-appointed fifteen-foot Christmas tree sitting as the focal point of the expansive living area, white lights twinkling against the windowpane. A young girl of no more than eight sat by the tree, smiling and laughing as she rolled around with a black-and-white spotted dog, a bit of gray fur peppering his face. Presents were piled high around the tree. Rayne could only assume most of them were for the little brunette happily playing without a care in the world.

"How did you…?" she continued, her eyes still glued to

the little girl. She seemed so content, so peaceful, so full of life. It reminded Rayne of her own childhood. She had been an only child, too, spoiled by parents who doted on her and gave her everything she could ever want…until she disagreed with the career they chose for her. She wanted nothing more than to have her own child whom she could love with every fiber of her being, but that dream had been cruelly ripped from her as quickly as the slashing of a blade.

"This is what you wanted, isn't it?" he replied snidely, his tone harsh, direct, abrasive. "You said you needed closure, to make him feel your pain."

She lowered the binoculars, opening her mouth slightly. Rubbing her clammy hands on the dark pants he had instructed her to wear, nausea settled in her stomach. Earlier today, this seemed like the only way for her to finally get what she had been yearning for since she lost her fiancé, but now, a fleeting moment of clarity had returned. This man had been one of Landon's best friends in the last several years of his too-short life. Would she betray him if she followed through with this? Would he love her any less?

"Don't tell me you're having second thoughts. If you make one wrong move, this plan will fall apart. I need you to keep it together." Reaching into a satchel, the man pulled out a small bag containing what appeared to be a disposable rubber glove. "I'll go in first and disable the alarm. His system is top-of-the-line. Unless you know what you're dealing with, you run the risk of setting it off."

"How do *you* know how to disable it? And what kind of system it is? And what is that glove for?" Rayne asked, leery, watching him handle it with extreme care. It seemed odd that, just this morning, he had encouraged her to finally take action so she could have the closure she so desperately needed. How did he plan this in the span of less than a day? Something didn't add up.

"Don't worry about any of that. All you need to know is if you do this, you'll finally find peace. The bastard responsible for Landon's death will finally know what it feels like to lose the one person who is *his* world."

"Peace," Rayne breathed. Closing her eyes briefly, she silenced the voices in her head screaming that it wouldn't work, that this was a horrible idea, that there was another way to ward off the demons that had been tormenting her since she stood over Landon's casket as it was lowered into the ground.

"Yes, Rayne." The man leaned toward her, cupping her cheek in his large hand. "Peace. Don't deprive yourself of this. Why should *he* have everything he's ever wanted when you've had all your dreams crushed because of him?"

As a lone tear cascaded down her cheek, he swiped it away with his thumb. He placed a gentle kiss where the tear had been. "Do this for you. And Landon. End your suffering. I can't bear to see you in pain any longer."

Swallowing the lump in her throat, she nodded, all sense of what was right and good leaving her when Landon's brilliant blue eyes flashed before her. She could almost feel the warmth of his embrace, the heat of his kisses, the electricity of his lingering touch. She didn't understand why life had to be so cruel as to take away the one person she had ever truly loved. He was her soul mate, her reason for breathing. She had nothing left to lose.

"For Landon."

"Good." He squeezed her arm, a cagey look crossing his face. The sincerity present moments ago had disappeared. Rayne wondered if she had imagined it. "Looks like it's bedtime."

Rayne turned from him and faced the house, raising the binoculars to her eyes. A tall, slender brunette ushered the little girl out of the living room, turning off a few lamps as she went. Rayne's heart dropped to the pit of her stomach when the woman peered out the window, her gaze stopping on the SUV parked over a football field away. The woman hesitated for what seemed like hours, but was only a second or two. Fight or flight kicked in. Rayne considered jumping into the front seat and speeding out of there. What if the woman came out and saw the two of them casing out the house? Would they be arrested? Would she be able to live with herself?

"*Let it rain*," she heard, the voice distant, dream-like.

"What did you say?" she said softly, swinging her eyes to the man beside her, wishing with everything in her that she could trade those stone-cold eyes for Landon's spirited gaze. It had been too long since anyone had said those three words to her. It was their thing. Whenever things got bad, Landon stood by her side. When her parents cut her off for dropping out of Brown so she could pursue her true passion in life, Landon simply whispered in her ear, "*Let it rain*." Rain brought new life, washing away everything else. It signified a new start, something she desperately needed.

"Nothing," the man answered, giving her a skeptical look. "Are you sure you're okay?"

Her racing heart slowed, her unease and anxiety regarding what she was about to do vanishing into thin air. She could feel Landon in that car, and he would want vindication for what happened to him, too. She needed to do this.

It was time.

He had to pay.

ONE

Twenty-Four Hours Earlier

December 17 - 7:00 PM

The rain fell like tiny knives against her skin as the wind howled and moaned on that dreary December evening. Everyone around Rayne ran in search of shelter from the wintry weather, but not her. She took her time, relishing each frigid step. The pain of the cold rain whipping against her brought her comfort. It was the only thing that reminded her she was still alive.

As time passed, she thought she would need this Thursday night ritual less and less. She had seen people come and go. Sometimes a familiar face would reappear during a holiday or particularly difficult week, but for most, the passing of time had healed their wounds.

Not Rayne.

For her, time was like a knife reopening scars that barely had a chance to heal. Most days, these meetings were the only thing that kept her going. If she could just make it to Thursday, she would be okay. She could step out of the darkness, if only for an hour.

Climbing the steps of the old stone church, she was met with warmth and light, which was at complete odds with the cold darkness that shrouded Boston. Her heels echoed on the linoleum as she walked through the bright lobby and made her way down the stairs to the basement, listening to the choir rehearse for the upcoming holiday services.

Silent night. Holy night.

All was not calm for Rayne.

Once upon a time, Christmas was her favorite time of year. Everyone always seemed to be a little bit happier, a little more forgiving. The movies, the cookies, the smell of roast turkey, the family gatherings. All year long, she looked forward to the magic and happiness in the air during the holiday season…until her life was turned upside down.

The joyful frivolity that accompanied this time of year now only reminded her of everything she lost and would never have again. It reminded her she would never see the joy in her child's eyes when he or she realized Santa and his reindeer had magically paid a visit during the night. It reminded her she had nothing. No reason to get up in the morning. No reason to go to her entry-level job a high school dropout could do. No reason to continue living her somber existence.

The aroma of stale coffee, baked goods, and lemon cleaner greeted her as she entered one of the basement meeting rooms. About a dozen people already perused the selection of sugary snacks or sat in one of the chairs, head down, avoiding eye contact as they tried to hide their tears. Rayne recognized about half. She knew some of their stories, but others hadn't worked up the courage to share their grief yet. She understood how difficult it was. It had taken her nearly four months to finally open up to this group of complete strangers.

Outside these walls, she barely spoke of it anymore. Her name had faded from the headlines and the requests for interviews had stopped. In the aftermath of the tragedy, the smiling, full of life woman she once was had been replaced by a withdrawn, grief-stricken stranger who simply went through the motions of what was expected of her. It was a good day if she remembered to shower. But inside these faded white walls, she could share her strife and heartache, even though this sympathetic group of people may never fully understand how broken she truly was. They were the only people who didn't judge, who didn't question why the events of a year ago still affected her.

Rayne poured herself a cup of obligatory coffee, then sat in her usual chair in the pre-arranged circle the facilitator said encouraged more open and honest discourse amongst the group. He must have been onto something. If Rayne had to stand up in front of a dozen people and share her struggles, she would have felt intimidated. This configuration of chairs was like a bubble. No one would judge her or anyone else while they shared the demons tormenting them.

She smiled a polite smile at a stocky, balding man a few chairs down. She hadn't seen him before and absentmindedly wondered what his story was. What heartache did he endure at this precise moment?

Over the months, she had become rather adept at guessing people's struggles. She was usually close, although sometimes a bit off on the details. She supposed this newcomer had just lost his wife sooner than anticipated.

Cancer, she mused to herself. *It's usually cancer.*

Sensing a presence next to her, she tilted her head, looking at her unexpected friend. Mark had been coming to these Thursday night meetings for almost as long as she had. He hadn't completely opened up about what brought him to that church basement every week, but based on hints he had dropped, Rayne surmised it had something to do with his sister. He spoke of his bereavement and how difficult it was to move on without closure. Rayne could only assume she had gone missing. Her heart went out to him living in a constant state of purgatory. She had been there…jumping up with each phone call, hoping it would be the one she waited for. During that one week, she clung to hope like a baby clings to a blanket. With each passing minute, she grew more and more despondent, struggling to come to terms with the likelihood that when the phone call did come, it wouldn't be the news she wanted to hear.

Unfortunately for Rayne, her phone call finally came in the form of a national television broadcast.

The country mourned with her. The President even ordered the flags to be lowered to half-mast for a week. But after that week, the story was forgotten. The nation went on to talk about the next hot topic of the day, and Rayne's loss was nothing more than a footnote in the history books.

History would repeat itself again. And again. And again. Rayne could do nothing to stop reliving that same agony day after day. Her coworkers tried to encourage her that life went on, but did it? She didn't see it that way. She had lost everything that cold, December day. Her heart. Her career. Her life. Now, all she had was her Thursday group session…and Mark. They used each other to cope with the torment of their lives. It wasn't healthy, but it was better than the alternative…for now.

"Earth to Rayne," Mark's deep voice whispered.

She snapped out of her memories, returning to the dismal present. His chocolate eyes were a cautionary mix of amusement and ire. It was the same expression he wore when he brought her to bed and they took out their rage through their distant act of intimacy.

"You okay?" he asked, eyeing her drenched frame. "You're soaked. Did you walk here from work?"

Rayne nodded, relishing the warmth emanating from the paper cup she held in her hands.

"That's what? Eight blocks? Why didn't you take the T?" he asked, referencing Boston's well-known subway system.

"Ten," she replied curtly.

"I stand corrected."

She turned the corners of her lips up, a polite gesture, then her face fell back to its normal position…blank, empty, haunting. She could sense Mark wanted to say something, but her closed-off expression warned him against it. They had shared their suffering, but nothing more. She willingly gave him her body, but not her heart. Not her soul. Never again.

"I get it's a difficult day for you, tomorrow being the anniversary of…" Mark trailed off, his voice consoling, laying his hand on her thigh.

She shot her eyes to him. In all the weeks they tried to dull the pain by finding solace in each other's arms, he had never touched her in public, apart from the occasional hug during the group meeting.

"I'm fine," she barked, pulling her leg away.

Mark sighed, running his large hand through his rugged, dark hair. "If you say so." He paused. "It's okay to feel vulnerable, ya know."

Rayne scoffed, rolling her eyes. "Stop with the psycho-babble bullshit. I hear enough of that from the guy who runs this meeting. I don't need it from you, too."

"Then why *do* you come here?"

Staring at the ceiling, the light panels in serious need of a good scrubbing, she closed her eyes, letting out a long breath. "To be with people who understand me, Mark. That's all. No one else does. But here, I feel like I belong, something I haven't felt since…" She trailed off.

In a bold move, Mark reached out and grabbed her hand, comforting her. For once, she didn't pull back. She let his warmth surround her. Hell, maybe he needed it as much as she did.

She stared into his eyes, a jolt running through her at the unexpected tenderness she saw there. Emotions weren't part of their arrangement. They had both loved and lost. Each knew the pain that accompanied such loss. It was foolish to willingly put yourself in that position again.

"I think we're ready to begin," a soothing voice announced, breaking their connection.

Mark cleared his throat, releasing his grasp on Rayne's hand as she readjusted herself, unbuttoning her jacket now that the warmth of the indoor heating had fought off the chill that had enveloped her when she first arrived.

The facilitator went through the typical motions of talking about grief, why they were all there, and that it was perfectly normal and healthy to mourn the loss of a loved one.

Too bad I don't feel normal, Rayne thought to herself.

Tomorrow would mark the one year anniversary of the day she lost her fiancé. They said each day would get better, that she'd think about him a little less, that she'd move on, but she hadn't. Talking about it didn't help anymore. She didn't know if anything would.

"The death of a loved one can be a life-altering event," the facilitator continued in the same pacifying tone that once brought Rayne comfort. Tonight, though, it only reminded her she still hadn't moved on from her loss. "While some of you may have initially felt grateful your loved one was no longer suffering, especially if you lost someone due to disease or old age, others may not have been ready for such a devastating event. Perhaps you lost a child."

He looked around the room. Many of the attendees had their heads lowered, trying to hide their tears. Sniffles echoed against the dusty linoleum, followed by the occasional sob.

"Perhaps the death was sudden or unexpected. Regardless of the circumstances, everyone in this room has felt the anguish of losing a loved one. You're all here to cope with what has become your new normal. It may not seem like it now, but you will soon begin to live again. Isn't that what your loved ones would have wanted?"

He made it sound so easy, like they would all forget their loss one day, the pain a distant memory. Maybe it was like that for some people, but for Rayne, her loss was too great. It wasn't just her fiancé she lost a year ago. It was her way of life.

A life she would do anything to get back.

TWO

December 18 - 3:15 AM

The sound of a pair of Salvatore Ferragamo wingtips echoed on the pavement as Alexander Burnham strode toward a rundown warehouse on the channel in South Boston…or, as locals called it, Southie. Glancing over his shoulder at his nondescript company SUV, he cocked his pistol, never knowing what kind of trouble would find him in this neighborhood.

A streetlamp flickered against the dark, rain-slickened pavement. The storm had taken a break, but the ominous clouds gave notice that it was just a short reprieve. Soon, the heavens would open up again, soaking the city with a layer of rain and perhaps ice as the temperatures plummeted. But now, just past three in the morning, the ground was still too warm.

An unexpected clanging of a metal object falling to the ground echoed through the night. Alexander surveyed his surroundings, searching for anything that struck him as suspicious. Everything about the area made his gut shout at him to go back to his car, that there was something disturbing going on. It wasn't just the rundown location, the dismal weather, or the abhorrent stench of rotten fish in the air. He sensed the reason for his brother-in-law's phone call in the middle of the night was not to tell him he would finally retire from the police force to come work for the private security firm Alexander ran with his brother, Tyler, since leaving the navy over fifteen years ago. Detective David Wilder had to have a damn good reason for pulling him out of his comfortable bed and away from his beautiful wife of nearly ten years.

It didn't help that Dave was a homicide detective with more years on the job than he cared to discuss. This only added to Alexander's unease and curiosity.

Walking along the perimeter of the warehouse, the air grew thick, the smell of fish and saltwater becoming stronger. Alexander had to fight back his gag reflex. Having grown up on the Connecticut shoreline, then spending the better part of a decade in the navy, he had lived most of his life by the ocean. Still, no amount of time spent near the water could make him ambivalent to the putrid funk of a fishing warehouse. As he covered his nose with a monogrammed handkerchief, all he could think was this was the perfect place to dump a body. The stench was so foul, a corpse would go undiscovered for days, weeks, maybe even months.

With each step he took, he considered several scenarios about why Dave needed to see him, each one worse than the previous. Alexander's line of work put him in contact with some of the most vile scum who would stop at nothing to harm the most vulnerable people. Mistakes could mean the difference between life and death. Lately, he'd thought more and more about the mistakes he had made and whether he could have done something to prevent them.

On the outside, he was the same Alexander he had always been…demanding, assertive, authoritative. But inside, all the bad decisions he had ever made nagged at him, haunting him, making him wonder if lives could have been saved had he acted differently.

He didn't know what caused it. Perhaps it was hitting forty just a few months ago. Perhaps it was because he finally had something more to live for…a loving wife and a beautiful eight-year-old daughter. Perhaps it was the approaching holiday season that made him conduct a yearly introspective, analyzing everything he had done in his life. All Alexander knew was, for some reason, he had been living with an inexplicable feeling of guilt for what seemed like months now. He kept thinking it would get better, but it never did. Now he wondered if that guilt had any correlation to the reason he was currently walking toward a rundown fish warehouse in an area of Boston he usually avoided like the plague.

Approaching the door of the building, a set of high beams shined on him. Instinctively, he turned toward them, shielding his eyes, and raised his pistol to the brilliant light before they shut off. It took a few seconds for his eyes to readjust to the darkness. Squinting, Alexander saw a familiar face through the front windshield of a tan sedan. He lowered his gun and returned it to its holster.

"Sorry about that, Alex," a tall man with a full head of gray hair shouted, jumping out of the sedan. "Department got me a new car and I'm still figuring out where everything is. Waste of taxpayer dollars, if you ask me. My last cruiser was running just fine." Dave rolled his eyes, approaching Alexander and holding out his hand. When he took it, Dave patted his brother-in-law on the back. "Thanks for coming."

"What's all this about? Why couldn't you tell me on the phone?" Alexander widened his stance, crossing his arms in front of his broad chest. Dave was easily at least six feet tall, but Alexander towered over him with his six-foot, five-inch frame. Dave was in good shape, but it was no match for the amount of conditioning Alexander received as a SEAL, which he still maintained to this day, nearly two decades later.

"I thought it would be better if you saw this one for yourself." Dave stared at him, his gaze almost apologetic, as if he were silently telling Alexander he was sorry for what he was about to show him.

With timid steps, Dave walked toward the open warehouse door. Alexander followed, the stench and unsettled feeling growing stronger with each step he took. The wind howled, the dampness in the air chilling him to the bone. The long trench coat he wore over his dark jeans and crisp button-down shirt did little to fight off the cold. He hugged the coat closer to his body, to no avail.

"I'll admit it, Dave," Alexander said in a deep, strong voice that always commanded respect. It masked the unease steadily building inside him. "I'm intrigued, albeit a little apprehensive."

Dave paused just as they crossed the threshold into what appeared to be a fish processing plant. Rows and rows of steel tables, a conveyer belt in the middle, lined the open space. Despite the workers' valiant effort in adhering to sanitary food preparation requirements, the amount of blood spilled from filleting what had to be thousands upon thousands of fish a day left its mark on the cement floor.

"I wanted to wait to call forensics until you were able to get out here." Dave met Alexander's eyes, a hint of remorse coupled with sympathy etched within his own gaze. "Out of respect, I… I just thought you should find out from me, see it with your own eyes, not hear about it on the morning news."

"Find out what?" Alexander asked, his heart rate picking up.

Taking a deep breath, Dave paused, then continued down the length of the warehouse toward stacks of metal barrels Alexander assumed were used to store fish. He hurried to catch up.

"When the call came in about an hour ago, dispatch sent

me since I was in the area on another case. A guy who works third shift phoned it in. Who knows how long the body's been here."

"Whose?" Alexander had a feeling his world was about to be turned upside down.

Dave met his eyes again, letting out a slow, protracted breath. The seconds stretched mercilessly as he grabbed the lid of a barrel and lifted it, Alexander's vision becoming a cloudy, slow motion scene typically used for dramatic effect in the movies. Except this wasn't a movie that would end, although he wished it would as he stared at the pale, lifeless body stuffed into the barrel.

Dave stepped back, giving Alexander space. "Mischa Tate."

Words escaped him as he struggled to keep his composure. This swollen face with ferocious bruises and lacerations bore no resemblance to the vivacious, energetic, gracious woman he knew years ago.

"How did you…?" He looked at Dave, swallowing hard as he covered his mouth with his handkerchief, the stench of death and decay so pungent, it was burned into his nostrils.

They say when one experiences a devastating event, their senses become heightened. They remember sounds, smells, feelings. Alexander had been through his fair share of traumatic events. He could remember exactly what he was wearing when told his childhood best friend had died. The smell of lemon cleaner and stale coffee would always be associated with the mixture of anger and despair running through him at that moment in time. The aroma of gunpowder and jet fuel would always remind him of the moment he received word his father had been killed on a job for the security firm.

Now, as he stared back at Mischa's face, her blue eyes

swollen shut, he would always equate this feeling of guilt with the stench of rotten fish, salt, and rain.

"Know it was Mischa?" Dave finished his question. Alexander nodded, unable to tear his eyes away from the remnants of Mischa's face.

During his time as a SEAL, Alexander had been deployed on some of the most intense missions imaginable. He saw the aftereffects of an IED. He witnessed things that would give most people nightmares for years. None of that compared to the bodily damage he now stared at, trying to keep his dinner from coming back up. Some would think things like this shouldn't affect him after all his years in the military, then running a private security firm. He wasn't a machine, though. He was a human with real emotions. He reacted as one would expect when staring at the tortured body of the sister of a former employee, friend, and fellow SEAL.

"I did a preliminary search and noticed this." Dave pulled on a rubber glove and extended her limp arm, using the flashlight of his cell phone to highlight a tattoo of Lady Justice on her wrist. "When you first introduced us, I remembered thinking how unique and haunting that tattoo was." He released her arm, then removed the glove.

Pulling his bottom lip between his teeth, Alexander struggled to look away from Mischa's face. He couldn't remember the last time he saw her. He kept meaning to call to see how she was doing, but life got in the way. Life had a strange habit of slipping out from beneath you when you were too busy to stop and take a breath.

"That's when I looked at her face again and realized who it was."

"What happened?" Alexander stepped back, straightening his spine.

"I won't have a definitive answer until the medical examiner does his exam and issues a cause of death. Right now, I'm operating under the assumption she's another victim of the Castle Island Killer."

Alexander nodded, staring at the barrel. At least every other day for the past month, a report of another murder appeared on the front page of the *Boston Globe*, the police attributing it to the Castle Island Killer.

"It fits his M.O. Assaulting the victim, killing her, then stuffing the body in a barrel and leaving it in this area of the city. The only thing giving me pause is that her throat wasn't slashed, unlike all his other female victims, and the physical assault appears to be substantially more severe and brutal. He may be progressing. Does she have any family or—"

"They were raised by their grandparents, but they died years ago," Alexander interrupted with a heavy sigh. "They have a few distant aunts and uncles, but no one who would care that she died. Landon was all she had left before..." He trailed off.

The fact he worked in a dangerous field was never lost on Alexander. Over the years, he had lost some of his best men on various assignments his company had been contracted to orchestrate and oversee. He took each one of those deaths personally, but none of them hit him as hard as Landon's. He wasn't just an employee. He was a friend, a brother in every sense of the word except blood. They could go months, even years without talking, then pick right back up where they left off, as if the passing of time had changed nothing. Their bond went back to the beaches of Coronado, where they were broken down and built back up as some of the most highly trained weapons in the United States military.

"Got it," Dave said quickly. Apart from the sound of

trucks beginning their early morning deliveries and seagulls squawking over the water, it was silent for a moment. Suddenly, Dave cleared his throat. "I have to ask."

Alexander shot his head up, knowing the question that was about to follow. He would ask the same one if he were running the investigation.

"Do you have any idea who—"

"Could have beaten this woman so badly as to be barely recognizable?" Alexander paced back and forth, the stink of the fishery no longer making him nauseated. "I have no idea. If I did, I'd—"

"When was the last time you saw her?" Dave asked, cutting him off.

Alexander stopped in his tracks, his face burning with guilt. An ache settled in his stomach as he remembered the promise he had made to Landon time and time again during their time together on the same SEAL team.

"If anything happens, promise you'll look after Mischa," Landon said.

"Nothing's going to happen to you, pussy," Alexander joked back.

"I know. If anyone's going to get shot, it'll be you," he sneered, jabbing Alexander in the shoulder.

They laughed nervously, although they tried to hide it. They had been trained to be dropped into any number of remote locations and take out some of the most dangerous threats to national security. Still, the anticipation never got easier, the adrenaline never going away. Would they come home in the passenger compartment or the cargo hold of the plane?

"But seriously, Alex," Landon pushed, looking him in the eyes. "I'm all she has. If anything happens to me, I need to know she still has family out there."

Nodding, he shook his friend's outstretched hand. "You bet. The only easy day was yesterday," he said, repeating a line they said to each other over and over again during their training days.

"Fucking A."

"The only easy day was yesterday," Alexander mumbled, returning to the present.

Failure was never something he coped with easily. Not acting a certain way could have disastrous consequences in the field. Why didn't he foresee that his failure to fulfill his promise to Landon would have those same disastrous consequences? Alexander had always thought his promise to Landon was an empty one, something one says to another before parachuting into some remote terrorist hotspot, not something he actually had to follow through with.

He kept meaning to call Mischa, but as the weeks turned into months and the months turned into a year, the time between phone calls had stretched until, one day, she was no longer a blip on his radar. He had no idea what was going on in her life. If she was dating anyone, if she was still trying to save the world one impoverished kid at a time. All he could think was this could have been avoided if he had just been true to his word, had taken his promise seriously. Instead, he had practically forgotten about the promise he made to the friend whose death made headlines exactly one year ago today.

"It's been a while," he admitted finally. Staring at the swollen eyelids hiding those same blue eyes Landon had, Alexander couldn't help but feel as if he had failed him all over again.

"Can you ballpark it?"

"At a holiday party maybe?"

"Recently?"

"Last year," he added in an uncharacteristic soft tone.

"Olivia kept pushing me to call and invite her to our house, but one thing led to another and it kept slipping my mind."

They stood in silence, staring into the barrel for what seemed like an eternity, regret swirling around Alexander's brain.

"Well…" Dave cleared his throat.

Alexander snapped his attention away from Mischa's face, her soft features now mutilated.

"My partner will probably be here any minute."

"And I probably shouldn't be here."

Dave nodded. "Slight breach of protocol for me to call *you* before the forensics team. I'll be sure to keep you posted."

Alexander shook his outstretched hand, then started back toward the warehouse doors, welcoming a breath of comparatively fresh air. Pausing, he looked over his shoulder. "And you'll let me know what the M.E. finds?"

"The second that report hits my desk, you're the first phone call I'll make."

"Thanks for calling me, Dave." He gave his brother-in-law an appreciative smile.

"You bet."

With a heavy heart, Alexander left the warehouse, walking in the brisk night air back to his darkened SUV. The rain had started once more, coming in at an angle, the cold drops stinging his face. Instead of running to the car to escape the elements, he slowed his steps, the icy droplets cutting through him like a blade. On a night like this, he'd normally want nothing more than to curl up next to his wife in their king-sized bed, a fire crackling in the hearth. But tonight, he couldn't gaze into her eyes and tell her what happened.

Tonight, he just needed to be alone with his guilt.

THREE

December 18 - 6:05 AM

Rayne collapsed on the bed in a hotel room overlooking the waterfront in Boston. Trying to catch her breath, she wiped sweat from her brow. She placed her hand on her chest, feeling the vibration of her heart thumping against her palm. She closed her eyes and lost herself in the rhythm. Listening to Mark panting next to her, his body warm, she drew in a long breath, the smell of sex in the air helping her forget, if only for a minute. Forget the feel of Landon's skin on hers, the heat in his eyes as he said he loved her, the itch of his five-day beard when he kissed her neck.

Landon had survived bullets, bombs, and a helicopter crash. He was deployed to some of the most dangerous parts of the world where his chance of survival was slight, at best. He had walked away from all of that with barely a scratch. The one assignment that was supposed to be safe turned out to be the one he'd never walk away from.

Rayne hated it. She hated herself for not worrying about Landon as much as she should have. She hated Landon's friend, Alexander, for breaking his promises to her. Above everything, she hated the people who took Landon from her. She wanted nothing more than for them to feel her pain, but knew that would never happen. She was left alone with her rage, unable to dispel it. The only thing that helped was the feel of Mark's slick skin against hers as they both worked through their pain and grief the only way they knew how.

Mark reached across the mattress, searching for Rayne's hand, squeezing it. She pulled away. She didn't mind the intimacy during sex. When she was finished, though, she didn't want to be touched or to talk. She just wanted to be left alone. Mark knew that. Why was he acting different now?

Draping the soft robe with the hotel's insignia over her body, she opened the sliding glass doors and walked onto the balcony, lighting up a much-needed cigarette.

"Want to talk about it?" Mark's deep voice came up behind her.

She whirled around, pulling the robe closer to her body, glaring at him. Regardless of the fact he was the one who paid for their hotel room every week, she hoped he would get the hint and leave while she took a minute to pollute her lungs with toxins.

She blew smoke in his face, studying his resilient expression. There had been a change in him over the past few weeks. When they first met, he battled his depression just as fiercely, if not more, than she did. His anger consumed him. Recently, however, there was a calmness about him. He smiled. He looked people in the eye. He no longer had that agitated expression on his face as if he were about to snap at the next person who asked how he was. Rayne noticed he seemed a bit more open and agreeable, a trait she now found herself envious of.

How come he *gets to move on while I'm stuck in this place? Will I be banished here forever?*

"No," she barked, spinning around to look at the city lights once more, everything twinkling in shades of red, green, and white.

Merry fucking Christmas, she thought.

"It might make you feel better." He approached her, leaning back on the railing.

She tried to ignore his proximity, his presence, his peace, growing even more irritated.

Sighing, she put her cigarette out, resisting the urge to use his arm to do so, and stormed back into the luxurious hotel room, searching for her discarded clothes. She had never taken Mark back to her place, and vice versa. What they had was superficial. Permitting him inside her home, allowing him a glimpse into who she was as a person, was too intimate. She didn't exactly live anywhere she'd be proud to call home anyway.

"I told you I don't want to hear any of that shit from you." She whipped around to face him. "And what's with the change in personality lately anyway? Four months ago, you were just as angry as I was. Hell, probably more so. Now, just like that, you're cured?"

"What can I say?" He shrugged. "Going to group therapy's been helping."

She eyed him for a minute. "Bullshit. I've been going to that same meeting for over six months now. The only peace it's brought me is knowing there are other people consumed by grief, too. Other people's pain is the only thing that gives me hope. But that hope is fleeting when, one day, they stop coming because they've been able to move on. They've been able to accept their new life, their new normal, but I'm still stuck in stage two. I've been angry for a year now. *One... entire...year.*" Her neck strained as she spit out her words. "Then, almost overnight, you're able to just flip the switch and find comfort in your anger and accept what's happened?" she scoffed, incredulous. "I don't buy it for a fucking second. Tell me what's really going on."

Mark studied her intently, in direct contradiction to the

empty gaze with which he typically gazed upon her. There was heat. There was electricity. There was life. She wanted that life, too. She was tired of being angry, of barely living.

"Please, Mark," she quivered, her voice almost inaudible. She felt weak, showing him a side of her she promised herself no one would ever see. She had been so strong for too long. She was willing to do anything to return to her old life.

Exhaling, he sat at the foot of the bed, patting it, gesturing for her to join him.

She took measured steps, keeping her guard up as much as possible. Her spine straight, she lowered herself onto the mattress, keeping her eyes fixed on him.

He scanned her face, a moment passing. Abruptly, he stood up. "Glass of wine?" He headed to the fully-stocked wet bar by the balcony doors.

"No, thank you." Truthfully, she had been craving some sort of drink since she left work earlier that evening. She didn't know what Mark wanted to tell her and she needed a clear head…or as clear as she could possibly have with all the anti-depressants she took.

"Come on," he pushed, pouring a robust red wine into two glasses and bringing them over to the bed. "Don't make me drink alone." He winked, holding a glass toward her. His chestnut eyes were alight with a rejuvenated energy.

Rayne wondered if it was the sex that had that effect on him or something else. His entire body buzzed with vigor and liveliness, something she hadn't felt in months. Hell, she couldn't remember the last time she smiled, apart from the forced smiles she gave her coworkers, assuring them she was okay. That couldn't have been further from the truth. She was anything but okay. She was sinking. Each day she woke up without Landon by her side, another weight pulled her deeper and deeper into the abyss.

With pinched lips, she swiped the glass out of Mark's hand and took a sip of the wine. It was heavy, just the thing to warm her chilled body.

"That wasn't so hard, was it?" Mark asked, lowering himself back to the bed, wearing only his boxers. He was a fit guy…his shoulders broad, his chest defined, his abs ripped. His naturally tan skin contrasted with the brilliant white of his teeth. On looks alone, he was any girl's dream, but he was as broken and angry as Rayne. At least he used to be. Now, she wasn't too sure of anything, making her even more upset. If he no longer shared her anger, what was she going to do? Knowing he was stuck where she was got her through most days. How could he move on and accept his new normal so easily when Rayne didn't see how she ever would?

"I'm pretty sure I shouldn't be drinking my pain away," she commented.

"There are other ways to deal with your pain," he replied guardedly, eyeing her.

"Oh yeah? And what's that?" she asked, drinking another hearty sip.

He leaned his forearms on his legs. Bowing his head, he seemed to weigh the pros and cons of what he was about to do, as if the moment were the point of no return. Rayne's interest piqued at the battle she could see raging in Mark's head.

"Her name was Sabrina. She had a smile and laugh that would light up any room."

Rayne surveyed his shrunken stature, the unfocused gaze, the trembling fingers. "Your sister?"

He shot his eyes to hers. "How did you—"

"Lucky guess. After months of going to grief counseling, you start to pick up on the little clues, I suppose."

Nodding, he faced forward once more, as if his story

were written on the wall in front of them. "She was two years younger and the most beautiful girl. Of course I'd say that. She was my sister. But she truly was. Once she became of dating age, she had an endless line of men interested in her. My father was a bit traditional and didn't permit her to date until she turned sixteen. She didn't mind. She wasn't interested in any of the boys who asked her out. She didn't want to waste her time on any man who couldn't measure up to her expectations." His laugh was subdued. "She was an old soul.

"One day, she met Benjamin, and her reluctance to date disappeared. They hit it off instantly. She was eighteen. He was a college graduate. Things were going good, so he asked my father for her hand in marriage. He agreed. Benjamin came from a very wealthy and well-liked family. He could provide for her. She'd be taken care of for the rest of her life. It was a good fit."

"But...," Rayne said, sensing there was more to the story.

"I think she got cold feet." He shook his head, running a hand through his hair. "She started disappearing from the house for hours at a time, then would come back with a made up story about where she had been. Worried she was starting to hang around with the wrong type of people, I followed her when she said she was going to the library. She pulled up to an alley, then knocked on a door. A man I recognized answered. He wrapped his arms around her waist and kissed her, but it wasn't just a friendly kiss. This was a kiss that didn't leave much to the imagination. I had always respected my sister...until that moment."

"Who was he?" Rayne asked, glued to Mark's every word. He had never opened up about what happened. Now that he was finally sharing his story, she couldn't get enough.

"His name was Omar. He was a year or two older than Sabrina and had a bad reputation around town. He had been arrested for a variety of things, mostly petty thefts and vandalism. He ran with people who were suspected of a bunch of violent crimes, although the police never had enough to make a case stick. They just brushed it all under the rug. I guess the law doesn't apply to everyone, especially the son of the police chief." He clenched his fists, drawing in a protracted breath.

"Did you confront her about it?"

"Of course I did," he responded in a curt tone. "But she brushed me off, telling me to mind my own business. I threatened to tell my father and Benjamin. She said to go ahead, that she was tired of living according to my father's rules. She said she wanted to make her own decisions, including whom she could date and love."

"What did she mean by that?"

"I guess she felt forced into the relationship with Benjamin." Mark shrugged, shaking his head. "I thought she was happy with him. We all did. Hell, she'd never have to work a day in her life if she married him. But Sabrina had a wild streak in her, and I think the finality of marriage to Benjamin brought it out. Still, I loved and cared about her. Instead of mentioning anything to my father or Benjamin, I kept what I saw to myself. I figured she'd eventually get over her rebellious phase." His chin quivered as he glanced at Rayne, unshed tears filling his eyes. "Maybe if I had said something..." His voice trailed off, the tears he had probably kept at bay for months, maybe even years, trickling down his masculine cheeks.

"One day, she was there; the next, she wasn't. She disappeared off the face of the earth. The police questioned everyone — me, my father, Benjamin, Omar — and they said there was no evidence of foul play. It was most likely just a case of a girl who wanted to get away."

"Without telling her family about it?"

"They refused to listen to our concerns that Sabrina wouldn't just pick up and disappear. I thought I was being helpful when I told the police what I had seen the day I followed her and our ensuing conversation."

"But it didn't, did it?"

He shook his head solemnly. For the first time in months, Rayne felt something other than anger. She felt sympathy. She had been there. She had begged Alexander to do everything within his power to find Landon before it was too late. If he had only listened to her and been proactive about finding out what happened, Landon might still be alive.

"With no physical evidence to the contrary, they closed the case. Disclosing our argument that day was just the icing on the cake they needed to move on to the next case, one that didn't name the son of the police chief as the main suspect."

"Mark," Rayne began, clutching his hand in hers, "I'm so sorry."

He shot his eyes to hers. "Everyone I spoke to brushed it off. No one understood what I was going through until..." He swallowed hard. "Until I met you." He cupped her cheek in his large, calloused hands.

For once, Rayne didn't brush him away. She melted into him, their bodies fusing through their shared heartache.

"Like you, I let my grief consume me. I was so angry, I wasn't coping. What made it worse was not having closure. If we knew what happened, I could learn to move on. Not knowing for years, well... That's a fate worse than death. Always jumping when the phone rings or there's a knock on the door, wondering if it's the news you've been waiting for."

"What's changed?"

"What do you mean?"

"Obviously something changed recently that helped you move past all this."

Drawing in a deep breath, he stood up and walked to the wet bar to refill his glass. A glow from the approaching dawn began to filter through the hotel room window, the city still blanketed in a sheet of gray.

Another miserable day.

Pacing, he eyed Rayne, unnerving her. She pulled her robe tighter, never feeling so exposed and vulnerable as she did at that moment. Mark's dark eyes penetrated her. Then he stopped, a bright smile crossing his face, lighting up his entire body. He buzzed with happiness. Rayne grew envious. She wanted to know the secret to moving on. She didn't care what it entailed. She couldn't go on like this anymore. Whatever Mark said he did to pull himself out of his grief, she would do. She had to.

"I knew I wouldn't survive if I didn't do *something* to cope with my grief."

"Which was…?" She raised her eyebrows.

Stopping in his tracks, Mark hesitated, unease covering his face. "I wish I could tell you," he admitted finally, lowering himself onto the bed again. Taking her hand in his, he continued. "I may be walking a fine line of legality with what I did. I'd hate for you to get wrapped up in all this, too. The last thing you need is any more pain in your life, especially when I can prevent it."

"What did you do?" she asked, her voice heavy with suspicion and intrigue.

"What any good brother would do. I found who was responsible for taking Sabrina and made them feel and understand my grief, my anger, my loss. For years, I was empty, thinking nothing and no one would ever be able to fill the gap left in my heart, but I was wrong. Finally confronting those responsible, making them understand my anger, healed me in ways I didn't think possible."

"Did you...?" Rayne trailed off, her mind racing with a thousand different scenarios of what Mark's words could imply. Did he kill Omar? Was someone else responsible for her disappearance? Did he find Sabrina?

"I told you," he said, his voice calm. "I—"

"I know. I just..." She took a deep breath, lowering her walls for a brief moment so she could begin to heal. "I want that, too, Mark. I need it."

"Then go after it. Get the closure you need."

Her shoulders shrinking, she pulled away. "It's not that simple. The people responsible for what happened to Landon live on the opposite side of the world," she scoffed. "What am I going to do? Head over to the Middle East and knock on every door until I find the right person? Great plan."

"There's another way to get the closure you want and deserve."

"I don't see how."

"From what you've talked about, it sounds like there's someone else who's *actually* responsible for what happened to your fiancé."

She narrowed her eyes at him, processing his words. "You don't mean..."

"I do," he responded gravely.

Rayne shook her head, feeling like she was in a fog.

"Remember how you felt when you were left without answers? I understand the hopelessness and desperation that invaded every inch of you. Most people have never been in that situation where they would give their life, their soul, *anything* just to have their loved one safe and in their arms. Until they experience that same anguish, they'll never truly feel and understand your anger."

"What are you saying?" Rayne asked, her heart thumping in her chest at his impassioned words.

"I think you know *exactly* what I'm saying."

Her jaw dropping, she stared at Mark, his eyes intense, focused, determined. She couldn't believe they were even having this conversation. Yes, she wanted closure more than anything, but at what cost? By harming one of Landon's best friends? She didn't think she could live with the guilt.

Standing up, she placed her wine on the dresser and found her jeans and sweater, frantically dressing. "You may be able to bend or break the law to get the closure you need, but I'm not," Rayne hissed, her skin prickling. "It's wrong. This man was Landon's best friend, not just a pawn for me to use to feel better."

"You're giving him more credit than he deserves. He doesn't give a shit about you! Why should you care about him?" He reached for her arm.

"No!" She spun around, freeing herself from his grasp. "I don't know what you did to get closure, and I don't think I want to know, but harming someone else just so I don't have to hurt anymore is *not* the way."

She stormed out of the hotel room and dashed down the hallway toward the bank of elevators, trying to shake off their conversation.

But she couldn't.

FOUR

December 18 - 6:30 AM

With heavy eyelids, Alexander steered his dark SUV onto a narrow road in a suburb twenty miles outside of Boston. Dense trees lined the street, hiding the large houses from view, ensuring the residents' privacy. While he missed the excitement and convenience of living in the heart of the city, it wasn't a place to raise a family. He wanted his daughter to experience the same things he did growing up…traipsing through a large back yard, building a snowman on those cold winter days, swimming in the pool to cool off in the heat of the summer. The sprawling estate in the heart of Dover where they now resided provided all that and more.

Despite the obscene size of it, they had decided on this house, thinking it would provide them ample space to grow their family of three. Melanie was now eight and, after two years in this house, it was still a family of three. Whenever they received a birth announcement from yet another friend or family member, the tension grew between Alexander and his wife. Neither one had summoned the courage to address the elephant that had been in the room for years now. That their prayers to add one more to their roster may go unanswered.

Navigating down the long driveway, the shingle-style colonial came into view, the overwhelming size serving as a bitter reminder of their small family. Olivia tried to fill the gaps by fostering rescue dogs from time to time, but it wasn't the same. No amount of paws could fill the void left in her heart…in all their hearts. Melanie no longer asked for a little brother or sister. Olivia would never admit it to Alexander, but he had overheard her whispers to Kiera, her best friend, that she felt as if she were a failure as a woman. Whenever Alexander had to get something out of storage and stumbled across all the nursery furniture they had saved from when Melanie was a baby, he couldn't help but feel as if he were a failure, too.

Slowing the SUV to a stop, Alexander stared at the stillness of the house during the early morning hour. A light drizzle fell, melting part of the blanket of snow that had fallen the previous week. A slight smile crossed his face as he recalled a recent conversation he had with his daughter. They were decorating the Christmas tree, which seemed to become more and more difficult every year due to their cat, Nepenthe, taking up residence in the branches the instant the tree arrived. When he asked Melanie what she wanted for Christmas this year, she said all she wanted was for it to snow since that was what the reindeer and Santa were used to.

He gazed down at her, growing nostalgic as the little girl continued placing decorations on the tree, their dog, Runner, behind her every step of the way. Alexander was more than aware this may be the last Christmas Melanie believed in Santa.

When Olivia and Alexander were expecting her, people told them time and time again to cherish the early days, despite the lack of sleep, because they grew up so fast. Nothing could have been more true. In the blink of an eye, it seemed like their little girl had become a little lady. In just a few years, she would be a teenager, trading their time together to go shopping with friends. Growing up was inevitable, but Alexander would give anything to keep her young and innocent for just a little while longer. He witnessed the cruelties of the world almost daily. He didn't want Melanie exposed to any of that.

When a light flicked on in one of the second-floor windows, he could almost feel Olivia's warmth as she woke up. He had spent the past few hours formulating what he would tell her when she asked why he had to leave in the middle of the night. It wasn't the first time he had done so and it wouldn't be the last, but this was different. How could he look in his wife's eyes and tell her it was just another case? Nothing could be further from the truth.

Driving the SUV up the remainder of the cobblestone path, he pulled it into the large garage and stepped out. Walking into the kitchen through the garage entrance, a low light illuminated the large, open space. Alexander made his way to the counter and popped a pod into the one-cup brewer. The early hour and lack of sleep were starting to catch up to him. He considered crawling back into bed, but knew his mind wouldn't let him sleep…not until he had more answers.

The past few hours, as he drove around listlessly, he kept telling himself this wasn't his fault, that he couldn't possibly have foreseen something like this happening to Mischa of all people, a woman who, much like her brother, dedicated her life to making other people's lives better. Still, there was a nagging feeling buried deep within that had he stayed in touch with her, things may have been different.

Watching the dark liquid trickle into his mug, the aroma of coffee finding its way to his senses, Alexander contemplated who could have been responsible for Mischa's death, each thought more hopeless than the last. From what he knew, which wasn't much, she didn't have any enemies. She lived a simple life. Granted, it had been almost a year since they last spoke. Still, nothing about the woman he remembered would make him come to the conclusion this was anything other than an unfortunate, brutal murder at the hands of a local serial killer. Still, something about it didn't add up, particularly after receiving additional information from Dave. The extensive bruising, the restraint marks on her wrists and ankles, coupled with the lacerations on her face, neck, arms, and torso raised Alexander's suspicions that Mischa had been targeted specifically. This wasn't just an instance of her being in the wrong place at the wrong time, as they believed to be the case with the rest of his victims. This looked personal.

"Hey," a soft voice murmured as a slender arm wrapped around his midsection, bringing him out of his cloud of remorse.

He turned around, a calm washing over him for the first time all night when he gazed at his rock, his life, his everything. Olivia's five-foot, nine-inch frame was dressed in a long, silk robe, the ivory color a stark contrast to her olive-toned skin. Her curly, dark brown hair was disheveled, and Alexander wanted nothing more than to get lost in her to forget about the past few hours.

"Hey," he breathed, pulling her close.

This was what he needed, her warmth enclosed in his arms. He kissed the top of her head, inhaling the heavenly aroma of vanilla. Despite their nearly decade-long marriage, he found himself falling in love with her all over again each and every day — with her smile, her laugh, her spirit. Until Melanie was born, she was the only girl he had ever loved. He didn't think it would be possible to love another human as much as he loved Olivia, but he was wrong. Olivia was his heart, but Melanie was the blood that kept it beating. She was his reason for wanting to be a better man.

"Late-night emergency?" She leaned her head against his chest.

"Mmm-hmm," he answered, closing his eyes as he lost himself in her embrace. He refused to let go, her devotion to him giving him strength. Rocking from foot to foot, they swayed to the music only they could hear, moving in unison, the tempo in their heads identical, regardless of the stiff silence in the room.

"What was it this time?" She tilted her head back, wrapping her arms around his neck, playing with a little tuft of hair that had grown over his collar. He had meant to make time for a haircut, but work was busy lately. Olivia didn't seem to mind, though. She said she liked when his hair grew out a little because it reminded her of the unkempt, disheveled hair he sported when they started dating.

He stared into her beautiful brown eyes, his gaze raking over her soft complexion. Luckily, Melanie had inherited all her mother's traits — her thick, dark hair, her high cheekbones, her passion for music and animals. But there was no denying their daughter had inherited Alexander's eyes, the green as vibrant as freshly cut grass.

"A dead body in Boston," he murmured.

"What?" Olivia gasped, stepping away from him, studying his face.

His late-night emergencies typically had to deal with complications at one of his company's overseas operations — an explosion in an oil field in the Middle East, a car bomb in Turkey, an attack on a camp in Sudan. Something that never truly hit close to home. It was different this time. The target wasn't a government contractor doing a dangerous job he signed up to do. The victim was someone who, at one time, was family to him…to all of them.

He nodded, his gaze somber. A heaviness set in his chest, the weight of knowing this could have been prevented returning with a vengeance. For a brief moment, as he lost himself in the love and reverence of his wife, he found peace with his newfound knowledge of Mischa's death. In Olivia's arms, the tragedy and cruelty of the real world disappeared, even if for just a minute, and he would give anything to go back to that bubble.

"Who?" she pressed, a slight quiver in her chin as she searched his eyes for an answer she probably wasn't prepared for.

With a heavy heart, he whispered, "Mischa Tate."

Olivia closed her eyes, a short breath escaping her lungs. "Oh, Alex," she murmured, shaking her head in a way that made him think she wasn't surprised by the news. "How?" Craning her neck, she searched his eyes.

"I don't know with any certainty. Dave called and asked me to come down to a fish processing plant in Southie, almost in Dorchester."

"Southie?" Olivia asked, turning and handing him the cup of coffee that had finished brewing before preparing one for herself. She must have known by his tired, scratchy voice and barely open eyelids that he needed coffee like he needed air. "Why would Mischa be in Southie?"

He shook his head. "Last I heard, she had a townhome in Arlington."

Olivia nodded. "It's right down the street from Mo and Kiera's new house," she said, referring to two of her good friends.

Alexander scrunched his eyebrows. "You've been to Mischa's?"

She spun around and opened the refrigerator door, searching for some milk. "I passed the street sign a few months ago when I went to see Kiera. I remember thinking I knew that street name for some reason. like I knew someone who lived there. It drove me crazy for weeks." She closed the refrigerator door, poured milk into her mug, then raised it to her lips, leaning against the elaborate marble countertop. They had cost a small fortune, but Olivia had fallen in love with them. Alexander spared no expense when it came to his wife. "When I was putting together a list for our Christmas cards, I noticed Mischa's address and saw it was that street."

She smiled, her eyes looking everywhere but at Alexander. He tried not to think too much into it, but he couldn't ignore the feeling that Olivia was hiding something from him.

"What was the cause of death?" she asked when he remained silent, studying her. When her eyes finally met his, he could tell she struggled to reel in her emotions. Mischa had been like a sister to them at one time, especially once Landon began working for the security company. It wasn't until his death that they grew apart. Landon was the glue that bound them together. Alexander lost more than just one of the best friends and employees he ever had. He lost himself.

"Dave won't know until they conduct the official autopsy, but based on the fact that she was beaten to death, stuffed into a barrel, then left somewhere in Southie, he thinks she may have been another victim of the Castle Island Killer."

Olivia pulled her lips between her teeth. "Who?"

"Castle Island Killer. Apparently, it's one of Dave's open investigations. It's been going on for the last month or so. Bodies have shown up in the South Boston area every few days, the first one around Castle Island. The victims cross every ethnicity, gender, and age group. There has been no common denominator in how his victims are chosen. The men are killed with a bullet to the head, and the women's throats are slashed. All of the bodies are shoved into a barrel. This time…" He drew in a long breath. "Her face was barely recognizable from all the bruising and swelling."

Olivia covered her mouth, a few tears falling down her cheeks.

"It most likely wasn't a quick death. Mischa probably suffered for hours…" He trailed off, closing his eyes to regain his composure. It didn't matter how much training he had undergone throughout his career. Nothing could prepare him, or anyone, for the death of a loved one. "There was no quick bullet to the head or slash to the throat. She probably fell in and out of consciousness for hours, maybe even days, as she fought against horrendous pain, her brain swollen from multiple blows to her head. Dave promised the second the medical examiner completes his autopsy report, he'll provide a copy to me. Until then, it's all just speculation based on an initial exam."

Shaking her head, Olivia kept her mouth covered. "How awful," she said in a small voice. She wiped at her cheeks as Alexander brought her into his arms, trying to offer her comfort. He would do anything to shelter her from such horror.

"Ugh! Are you two kissing again?" a sweet voice squeaked. Olivia pulled back slightly, but Alexander kept her close, lost in her eyes.

"We are, and you're next, munchkin!"

After placing a kiss on Olivia's lips, Alexander broke his hold and rushed toward Melanie, scooping her into his arms as she squealed with delight. He knew it was only a matter of time until she pushed him away and barely looked up from texting with her friends. Thankfully, today was not that day. He was still her fun dad who took her and her friends camping and taught them survival skills, much to Olivia's dismay. Who took her to Hawaii when she showed an interest in learning to surf. Who made her pancakes every Saturday morning.

"Stop it!" Melanie squealed, her voice echoing in the cavernous kitchen. Runner's barking only added to the ruckus.

Alexander needed this after the night he had. He needed to feel a sense of normalcy, a connection to the people he cared about most.

"Put me down!"

Her giggles warmed his heart. He hoisted her over his shoulder, carrying her like a sack of potatoes. Her legs kicked, her laughter increasing.

"Dad! Stop! I'll have Runner go after you!"

"That dog doesn't even chase the cat these days," he replied, spinning around, her brown curls flying. His eyes locked on Olivia's as she shook her head, laughing.

"You're going to make her sick, then *you* can clean it up."

Grinning, he slowed his steps and lowered Melanie back to her feet, holding her steady while she regained her balance.

"Pancakes, Daddy?" she asked once she was no longer dizzy, her eyes hopeful.

"It's Friday. A school day."

"No, it isn't!" she replied excitedly, jumping up and down. "It's the first day of Christmas break!"

"Already?" He looked at Olivia, who just shrugged. He had been so busy at work, it didn't even dawn on him it was just a week before Christmas. He wondered what else he had dropped the ball on. "When I was your age, we were in school up until the day before Christmas Eve."

"Blah, blah, blah," Melanie joked, mimicking a mouth opening and closing with her hand. "And walked uphill both ways. In the snow."

"Shoeless," Olivia added, her voice light.

"With no cell phone!" Alexander smiled.

"What?" Melanie gasped. "You didn't have a cell phone when you were growing up?"

Alexander shook his head. "Or an iPad."

"Wow," she replied in faux amazement. "How did you survive?"

He tousled her hair. "Barely."

"So… Pancakes, Daddy?" she asked again.

He looked at the time, then Olivia. He hated disappointing his daughter, but Mischa's death lay heavy on his mind and he needed some answers. True, his brother-in-law was one of the best homicide detectives around, who wouldn't stop until he found the killer, but Alexander couldn't sit back and do nothing, particularly with his gut telling him Mischa wasn't just another victim of the Castle Island Killer, as the evidence would lead everyone to believe.

"Melanie, sweetie," Olivia began, noticing his apparent unease. "Daddy has to go into work today." She opened her arms and Melanie ran into them.

"I promise we'll make pancakes tomorrow," he offered in consolation.

"And go ice skating?" she added excitedly.

"The lake hasn't frozen over yet, munchkin. It's not safe."

She frowned.

"We'll find something else to do. Maybe your mother will take you to the skating rink today, and we'll go sledding tomorrow, if you'd like."

She nodded vigorously, giving him a wide, toothy grin. Running from Olivia, she flung her arms around him. "Love you, Daddy."

"I love you, too, little nugget."

"I'm not little anymore."

"You'll always be little to me."

FIVE

Droplets fell from the sky as Rayne climbed the steps from the Park red line station onto the street. She didn't know what possessed her to get off at this stop. It wasn't close to where she lived or worked. Not anymore. But after running out on Mark, she was consumed with her past.

On autopilot, her legs carried her the few city blocks toward the storefront that had been a second home to her for the better part of a decade. The city was just coming to life, the illumination from the streetlamps replaced by the rising sun hidden behind an endless sky of clouds. The sidewalks were slick with a combination of rain and melted snow, a brown slush highlighting hundreds of footprints.

The smell of sugar and coffee made its way to her senses and she stopped, staring into the large window. A few familiar faces stocked the display cases with freshly made doughnuts, cakes, cookies, and other specialties of the house. She wondered if they still used her recipes, even after she had been ousted from her own bakery. These four walls had been her dream since she could remember, although her parents never supported it. They had a plan for her, too — Brown, law school, then become a partner at her father's law firm.

When she dropped out after her first semester to follow her dream of becoming a pastry chef, her parents were horrified. Refusing to let anyone stand in her way, she moved out with barely a penny to her name. Her hunger to succeed, to prove her parents wrong, was the driving force she needed to be the best. She studied under the most notable pastry chefs in the world, honing and perfecting her skills over the years. She worked long hours and holidays, trying to save enough money to see her dream come true. Finally, after years and years, she had her very own pastry shop in the financial district of Boston, the perfect location to cater to tourists and the young professional crowd alike.

One day, she was on top of the world, thinking she finally had everything she'd ever wanted.

The next, she'd lost it all.

She could still remember what she was doing when she received the phone call that changed everything.

One Year Ago

"Is the cake ready for the Vandekamp retirement party?" Rayne's bubbly blonde employee, Lillian, asked, bursting through the swinging doors to the kitchen of the bakery. Rayne liked to think it was where the magic happened. Ever since her nanny taught her how to whip up a cake or her famous bread pudding, she knew what she wanted to do. She wanted to be a pastry chef. From sunrise to sunset, she was covered in confectioner's sugar, flour, chocolate, and whatever other ingredients were necessary for her sweet concoction of the day. It made her feel alive. Every morning, she smiled happily at all the suits heading to their jobs, a scowl on their faces. She truly felt blessed to have a career she enjoyed.

"Just putting the finishing touches on it right now," Rayne said in an even tone, mirroring the steady hand with which she piped frosting onto the cake. She stepped back, admiring her handiwork. It was a masterpiece.

Once she'd learned Mr. Vandekamp planned to move to South Carolina where he would spend most of his days hitting balls on the golf course he would soon live on, Rayne's creative juices had begun to flow. Soon, she had constructed a cake to replicate a golf bag, complete with cookie clubs.

When she first opened the bakery, she stuck to what she was comfortable with — cannolis, cupcakes, tarts, eclairs, and the like. But as the bakery's reputation grew, she stepped out of her comfort zone, designing and constructing spectacular cakes from practically nothing. The joy on her clients' faces when they came to pick up their orders was priceless.

"They're going to love it," Lillian said, admiring her work.

Looking at her, Rayne smiled. "I think so, too. Help me box it up."

"You got it."

"Rayne?" a voice bellowed over the commotion of clanging metal and people shouting orders.

"Yes?" she answered, not looking up, keeping her attention entirely devoted to securely boxing up the cake so it arrived at its destination undamaged.

"You've got a phone call."

"Take a message, Alberto," she instructed, glancing at a short, dark-skinned man.

"I tried. He said it's urgent."

"Who?"

He looked down at a napkin he held. There was probably something scrawled illegibly to everyone except Alberto on it. "Alexander Burnham," he responded in a thick Spanish accent. "He said he's your fiancé's boss."

Rayne inhaled a quick breath, her stomach rolling. She stared at Alberto, unsettled thoughts circling through her head, then snapped out of her daze.

"Alberto, can you help Lillian finish boxing up this cake and get it into the client's car?"

"You got it, el jefe."

On unsteady legs, she headed toward her office. Normally, she would laugh at Alberto's nickname for her, but something about Landon's boss and friend calling her didn't sit right. Sure, he had occasionally called to check in with her, as he promised to do while Landon was on assignment in Afghanistan for his security firm, but he never insisted on speaking with her.

She had been with Landon for over fifteen years. He was a SEAL when they began dating, although she simply thought he was a lieutenant in the navy at the time. The first few times he said goodbye before heading overseas, she worried she'd never see him again. But as the years went by, it just became a part of life. When Landon told her he had left active duty as a SEAL to take a special assignment for the private security firm, she was thrilled, knowing he'd no longer be in harm's way. She had spent their months of separation putting her efforts into the bakery and planning their wedding slated for the following September, not to mention preparing for the arrival of their son, the result of the two weeks he'd spent visiting back in August.

Now, the unease she hadn't felt since the early days had returned.

Closing her office door, she sat behind the desk, staring at the black phone like it had a contagious disease. Chills ran through her as she reached for it with cold fingers and picked up the receiver.

"Alex?" she answered, trying to mask her nerves.

"Rayne," he replied in that familiar deep voice, a hurriedness in his tone. "Have you spoken to Landon recently?"

Furrowing her brows, she tried to calm her racing heart, her mind spinning a mile a minute. She thought back to the past week. She had been so preoccupied with the upcoming holiday season, working nearly sixteen hours a day at the bakery, it hadn't dawned on her that Landon hadn't called Sunday evening, like he usually did. That was four days ago. It had been eleven days since she'd spoken to him. What had happened in the past eleven days to bring on this phone call?

"No...," she said timidly, swallowing back the ache in her throat, her air passage tightening. "We usually speak every Sunday evening at seven. The bakery's been slammed with holiday orders. It didn't even phase me when I didn't hear from him."

Alexander let out a barely audible sigh. Rayne could picture his normally intimidating physique sinking. She bit her lip, her pulse quickening.

"There's been an attack," he said in a soft voice.

"An attack?" she squeaked out, feeling dizzy, hot, and cold at the same time. "When?"

"I'm still trying to find out the details and narrow down a timeline. When I didn't hear from him during our normal check-in time, I started asking around. I called a friend who's deployed over in Kabul. He said he had heard rumblings about a bombing of a school or something fifty miles out of town."

"I don't understand," she interrupted, holding on to all

the hope she could. "How is this relevant to Landon? Where was he stationed?"

"Rayne," Alexander continued, his voice sincere. "Landon wasn't on the front lines of anything. It was more of a humanitarian mission, but even so, it was still dangerous. Many locals don't like the presence of westerners, especially when they believe we're interfering with certain customs."

She shook her head, her stomach churning with each word Alexander muttered. "Where's Landon, Alex?"

"I don't know. My friend owed me a favor, so he agreed to take his unit to where Landon was stationed and check it out for me. When he got there…" There was a heavy pause.

"When he got there what?" she pushed, her voice growing louder and more unsteady.

"There was nothing left. The building had been reduced to rubble."

Gasping for air, she felt the room spin as her world fell apart. This couldn't be happening. They were supposed to get married. She was carrying his child. They were supposed to live happily ever after in their beautiful house and raise their son together.

"There was evidence of only one body in the vicinity. They assume it was the bomber since she was wearing a backpack that appears to have been the origination point of the explosion."

Rayne's mind raced. Did Landon escape with his life? Surely, even in an explosion, there would have been some sort of evidence of a body, wouldn't there? She prayed that was the case. That he had gotten out and was just laying low, trying to determine his next move. He was a former SEAL, after all. He had served over a decade in some of the most dangerous places in the world before taking this job.

"They're trying to determine a precise timeline and who's responsible," Alexander continued. "The initial guess is a suicide bomber, but they usually target large groups of people out in public. This was a building in the middle of nowhere. Even if everyone perished, it would have only killed a dozen or so people."

"What was Landon doing for your company?"

"Rayne…" He paused. "As much as I want to tell you, Landon's life may be in jeopardy because of his assignment. I can't do the same to you."

"You think Landon was targeted specifically?"

"I do."

"By whom?"

He hesitated. "I don't know. I'm afraid I won't have any answers until I can get feet on the ground over there and push people to start talking."

She nodded, closing her eyes as tears trickled down her cheeks. *He's not dead*, she reminded herself. It was the only hope she had.

"Rayne?"

"Yeah?"

"He's okay. I know it. He's one of the bravest, smartest men I've had the good fortune of knowing. I promise I'll bring him home to you."

Placing her hand on her protruding stomach, she put all her faith into Alexander's words. It was all she could do.

Present Day

"Here ya go, Miss," a man dressed in a long trench coat and expensive-looking shoes said, summoning Rayne back from her memories. She snapped her head up, her gaze lingering on his debonair smile, blond hair, clear blue eyes, and sexy five o'clock shadow. Her expression flat, she stared at him for a brief moment. When he gestured toward his outstretched hand, she glanced down, unsure how to react to the five dollar bill he held out to her. She returned her eyes to his.

"'Tis the season, isn't it? Just promise you won't buy drugs or booze, okay?" He shoved the bill into her hand, then disappeared around the corner.

She gazed at the green bill, Abraham Lincoln looking back at her, a smug expression on his face. She raised her head and stared into the bakery's window, able to make out her reflection. Her red hair was disheveled and appeared as if it hadn't been washed in weeks. In truth, she wasn't sure when she had last showered. She wore a torn jacket and old scarf that had seen better days, but were gifts from Landon during their time together. She simply couldn't get rid of them or stop wearing them, no matter how decrepit they were.

She was still stuck in that time of her life, wishing she could rewind the clock to the weeks before her world turned upside down and ask Landon to come home for the holidays. After receiving that dreaded phone call from Alexander, she had remained a nervous wreck most of that night. Every buzz from her cell phone made her leap to check whether Alexander was calling with more information. Instead, she heard nothing from him or Landon. Hours turned into days as she waited, trying to distract herself from thinking the worst by pouring all her energy into her work. She spent days in the worst kind of limbo imaginable. She prayed Landon was okay.

Her prayers were never answered.

Instead, a week before Christmas, she had found out

Landon's fate with the rest of the nation on the six o'clock news. She thought it was just a cruel nightmare, that something so horrific couldn't be real. Most of the following week was a blur as she remained curled up in her bed, barely sleeping, eating, or moving. She couldn't remember how, but she somehow made it to Landon's funeral, where they lowered an empty casket into the ground.

A month later, she began having contractions at only twenty-five weeks and was rushed to the hospital, scared and confused. Even then, she held on to hope that the memory of Landon would survive through their son.

"I'm sorry," the doctor had said when he returned after whisking the baby away to the operating room. "The duct between the two major blood vessels near his heart didn't close properly. We did everything we could, but his heart wasn't pumping enough blood."

She still remembered holding the small, lifeless body that barely weighed two pounds, tubes and wires, the remnants of the hospital's efforts to save his life, still taped to him. In an instant, all hope she would be able to move on from Landon's tragic death vanished. Her grief consumed her. Air filled her lungs and her heart continued to beat, but she wasn't living. Most days, she could hardly muster up the strength to get out of bed. Sleep eluded her. Every time she closed her eyes, she saw the grainy video broadcasting Landon's final moments on this earth, coupled with the blueish newborn baby she never even heard cry.

As the weeks passed and she was unable to bring herself out of her deep depression, her bakery was on the verge of going under. She had no option but to sell the business to an interested buyer. In the span of less than three months, she had lost her entire world — her fiancé, her bakery, and her son. She had nothing left to live for. She became an empty shell of a woman. There were many nights she considered raising a blade to her flesh, stopping when she saw Landon's sad eyes flash in her mind. It was at times like these, when she felt most vulnerable and ready to end it all, that his presence surrounded her, urging her to continue.

As she walked down the aisle of the local liquor store on a sunny afternoon in May, a flier stuck between a shelving unit and the dirty linoleum floor had caught her attention. She picked it up and read the advertisement for a grief counseling meeting held at a local church every Thursday night. It listed the five stages of grief, and Rayne wondered where in the spectrum she fell, doubting whether talking to a group of complete strangers about what she was going through was even worth her time.

Then Franki Valli's "Can't Take My Eyes Off You" came through the overhead speakers. For the first time in months, Rayne smiled. She closed her eyes, basking in the memory of Landon bellowing those lyrics to her on his last night of liberty all those years ago when they first began dating. Despite his horrendous singing voice, which made it perfectly clear to everyone listening in the bar that he was tone deaf, she fell for him even more. Hearing that song again had made Rayne think Landon was there, urging her to try to move on from her pain and grief. Landon had his life cruelly extinguished. He would have wanted her to look at every day as if it were a gift, and she had hoped assimilating herself with others who were going through the same thing would help her get on the path to living again.

But as the weeks turned into months, she had trouble doing that, plummeting lower and lower into the abyss of her anger. The woman staring back at her now, holding a crumpled five dollar bill, her red hair ratty, her eyes sunken, her skin pale, was a complete stranger to her.

"*He* did this," she muttered somberly, fighting a thousand conflicting emotions. Yes, she wanted nothing more than for Alexander, or *someone*, to suffer for what had happened to Landon, but would she really feel any better if she were the one wielding the blade, so to speak? Would she finally have closure?

She shook her head, pocketing the five dollar bill and shuffling down the street. Mark was stronger than she was. He wanted revenge and went after it. What would Landon have wanted her to do? She knew the answer to that. Despite his hard exterior, Landon spent his life making the world a better place for everyone else. He was a trained killer, yet each life he took hit him hard. "It's for the greater good," he had said time and time again. There was no greater good here. No matter how much anger and pain she still felt, she simply couldn't hurt anyone, especially Landon's best friend. After all, *he* didn't kill him.

Her head hung low and she hugged herself to stay warm in the frigid early morning temperatures as she trudged along the city streets. A wetness splashed the left side of her body and she stopped, lifting her head slightly to see a yellow cab speeding down the street.

Glancing at her surroundings, she laughed at the irony of it all. She wondered if she subconsciously found her way here, or if Landon's spirit was trying to tell her something. She had walked this path on many occasions and could blindly navigate the few city blocks between her bakery and the building that housed the security firm for which Landon had worked. She considered turning around and going back the way she had come, but something pushed her forward.

She continued down the street, lowering her head once more to fight off the bitter wind whipping around her. She didn't even need to look up to know she was walking past the large glass doors of that familiar skyscraper. There was an inviting warmth about it.

Her heart thumped in her chest as she faced the revolving doors, staring into the lightness and bustle of the lobby. People rushed through, scanning a keycard at a security turnstile before heading toward a massive bank of elevators that serviced all twenty-nine floors of the building Alexander Burnham owned. The top few floors housed the security company, the rest of the floors being rented by various businesses. Knowing how pricey the lease was on her small bakery, her head spun just thinking about the amount of money Alexander received every month in rent alone, while she struggled to rub two pennies together.

She considered walking through those large revolving doors and going up to see Alexander. At least once a week following the funeral, he had shown up on her doorstep to check on her, but she was never able to muster enough strength to let him in the house she once shared with Landon. She was surrounded by memories everywhere she turned. She couldn't face a living, breathing reminder of everything she had lost.

Maybe she was now standing in front of this building for a reason. Maybe being around someone who knew Landon as well as, if not better than, she did was precisely what she needed to move on.

She had hoped that sharing her grief with others every Thursday night would help, but it didn't. It had been an entire year and she still felt the same…stuck in a rut. Maybe it was because she hadn't shared her grief with someone who could truly understand. No one in the support group could truly sympathize with her pain because they didn't suffer that same loss. The only person who could truly understand was Alexander, the same man Mark insisted was the cause of it.

About to step toward the revolving doors, she was caught off guard when a large body bumped into her from behind. She stumbled, catching herself, and stared at the tall, intimidating figure rushing past her, not even offering an apology. He barked orders on his phone, the designer coat and shoes he wore making it clear he was in charge. He pushed through the doors and into the lobby, then turned around and their eyes met.

She inhaled a quick breath as she stared into that vibrant green hue. From behind, he looked like every other corporate executive in the city, apart from the height, but those eyes were unmistakable, the green as clear as shimmering emeralds. She held his gaze through the glass doors, almost sensing a hint of recognition. Then, in the blink of an eye, he snapped out of his trance. Spinning around, he carried on with his phone call, continuing through the lobby.

Her heart deflated. He recognized her. She saw it in his eyes. But instead of approaching her, he simply ignored her, his phone call obviously more important than a thin, haggard-looking, thirty-something woman standing in front of his building.

Struggling to fight back tears, she turned, clutching her jacket against her as she walked the busy city street, fighting the crowds of professionals descending upon the city the Friday before Christmas. Everyone seemed happy, which made Rayne even angrier. All of these people would go home at the end of their day to a husband, a wife, a daughter, a son. They would sit in their living room and watch the lights of their tree twinkle. They would bake cookies and laugh. They would watch Christmas movies together in preparation for Santa's big night.

The farther she walked, the angrier she became. In a flash, everything had changed. Seeing how normal

Alexander was made her irritation grow to a height it had never been before. She wanted to scream at the top of her lungs. Her chest clenched and she became short of breath. Her face grew heated, despite the frigid temperatures, and she felt as if her legs were about to give out beneath her. She supported herself against a brick wall, but no one paid her any attention. Why would they? They probably thought she was just a homeless drug addict. And wasn't she?

She had lost everything. Her home. Her career. Her family. She now lived in a small, barely habitable studio apartment in Dorchester. In a year's time, she had fallen so far from where she once was, but Alexander hadn't. If anything, he was even more successful, having even more than he did this time last year. He hadn't suffered like she had. And she hated him for that.

Mark was right. She needed to make someone else feel her pain, and that person was Alexander. He may not have been the one who took Landon's life, but his inaction made him just as culpable. It was time he finally felt the same pain Rayne had endured since watching Landon's casket, filled with nothing but memories, be lowered into the ground.

SIX

Swirls of blue mixed with purple ingrained in Alexander's mind as he tried to remember where he had seen those eyes and that face before. She seemed so familiar, yet a complete stranger at the same time. Her red hair appeared weighted down by dirt. Her skin was pale, her face gaunt. Her hollow eyes were devoid of almost all emotion. Despite the emptiness, he sensed something in those colorful eyes. Hope maybe? He'd racked his memory, trying to place where he had seen her before, but came up short. Years in the security field taught him to never forget a face, and hers was completely unfamiliar, despite the nagging in his head that he should know her.

"The background checks you asked for, sir," somebody said, bringing him out of his unease as he strode down the hallway of his company's building located in the financial district of Boston.

He looked up to see Martin, his right-hand man, standing just outside his office door, his posture taut, his expression all business. Alexander had known him almost his entire life. He had been his father's go-to guy before Alexander took over the company nearly two decades ago. Still, he could probably count on one hand the number of times he had seen Martin display any sort of emotion. He was professional to a fault.

He handed Alexander a small folder as he walked into his

office. Alexander took his coat off and tossed it on the loveseat.

"Anything stand out to you?" he asked, perusing the contents of the folder as he lowered himself to the couch opposite the loveseat. Propping his legs on the coffee table, he loosened his tie and unbuttoned his suit jacket, trying to focus on what Martin was saying, his mind still elsewhere. Haunting purple eyes flickered on the pages in front of him, a ghost of his past sent to remind him of all his failings, as if Mischa's death wasn't reminder enough.

"She lived what appears to be a simple life," Martin began, summarizing what he'd found in the few short hours since Alexander had ordered him to the office early to dig up everything he could on Mischa Tate. "Other than her brother and her being taken away from their parents at an early age and raised by their maternal grandparents, nothing stands out that could indicate a motive or who could be responsible for her murder." He paused, his expression grave. "Your brother-in-law may be right, sir. She may have simply been in the wrong place at the wrong time and tragically became another victim of the Castle Island Killer. Simpson was able to access the police files on those deaths."

"And?"

"From what you told me about everything, it fits. The only thing that's off is the cause of death. Everything else is the same."

"So it could very well have been a copycat who tried to cover his tracks by following the Castle Island Killer's M.O." Alexander looked at Martin hopefully. He didn't know if he could sit idly by and come to terms with the idea that Mischa was just a random victim. He had a feeling in his gut there was more to it, and his gut was usually right. Hell, his instincts had saved his life on more than one occasion.

"It's a possibility," Martin agreed, albeit reluctantly. His expression remained respectful and serious, despite thinking his boss was looking for something that wasn't there. He would never say it, though. A Marine veteran, Martin respected the chain of command.

Alexander continued sifting through the papers in the short file — immunization records, school transcripts, bank statements. He hoped something would stand out to help prove his theory that this was the work of a copycat. The police seemed pretty certain that wasn't the case, but if he didn't explore the possibility, there was a chance Mischa's killer would never be brought to justice. Then he'd be letting Landon down all over again. He couldn't have that on his conscience.

"I have Simpson running more checks to see if he can uncover anything else that wouldn't turn up in an initial record check—"

"You mean *sealed* records?" Alexander raised his eyebrows.

"He does have a particular set of skills. I think that's why you hired him."

Alexander smirked. "That's a nice way of saying he's a great hacker."

"Your words, sir. If he finds anything, I'll be sure to bring it to your attention. Should I have your assistant bring you a coffee? Or would you rather have your privacy?"

"Coffee would be great. Thank you, Martin, and keep me updated. Dave said he would call if anything turns up, so make sure he's put through. If anyone else calls, tell Amy you'll handle it yourself."

Martin nodded, then left the office, closing the door behind him. After just a few moments of flipping through the papers, a court-ordered termination of parental rights caught Alexander's attention. Perhaps that had something to do with what happened to Mischa.

Just as Alexander settled in to devote his full attention to the report, there was a slight knock. The door opened and a tall redhead scurried into the office.

"Good morning, Mr. Burnham. I wasn't expecting to see you today. I thought you would be out of the office until after the New Year." She carried a tray containing a cup of coffee and a chocolate hazelnut pastry he treated himself to every morning, setting it down on the table in front of him.

"Yes. Well, something has come up that couldn't wait until then."

"Understood." She took a notepad out of her suit jacket and began scribbling notes with a pencil. "Martin's already instructed me that, unless your brother-in-law calls, he'll handle all your business today. Is there anything else I should be made aware of?"

"No, Amy. That's all for now. Thank you."

"You're welcome, Mr. Burnham. Just holler if you need anything." She gave him a cordial smile before spinning on her too-high heels and walking out of the office.

Taking a sip of his black coffee and a bite of his danish, he returned his eyes to the folder in front of him, reading through the court order terminating Landon and Mischa's parents' parental rights, granting full custody to their maternal grandparents. No other details were given, but from their time on the same SEAL team, Alexander knew Landon and his sister had survived years of neglect by two parents who had grown addicted to crack during its rise in popularity. Malnourished and dirty, Child Services finally intervened after the house was raided by the police.

Their grandparents had been beside themselves when they learned what the two kids, neither being more than eight at the time, had been through, taking custody of them while their parents served their time in prison for neglect, child endangerment, and a myriad of drug offenses. Mischa was too young to truly remember any of it, but Landon did, which probably shaped him into the man he had become.

Other than the events of her early years, the rest of Mischa Tate's life seemed rather boring, at least on paper. She was a model student, achieving mostly As and Bs throughout her schooling. She went into the Peace Corps just after high school, spending two years working with infants and pregnant women in Namibia. Landon talked about her often during his SEAL days, always bragging about something she was doing.

After her time with the Peace Corps, she easily gained employment with the United Rescue Mission, a non-governmental organization based out of Boston whose purpose was to offer aid and assistance to those displaced by war, natural disaster, or persecution. She had visited some of the most dangerous places in the world, putting her own life on the line to offer safety to those at risk, before being promoted to the position of executive director approximately five years ago.

"I suppose she must have rubbed off on Landon," Alexander mused to himself, remembering his friend's own mission to save the world, one poor soul at a time.

The next few hours ticked by as he tried to get in touch with people who knew Mischa during her time in the Peace Corps, then the agency she had worked for, hoping something would stand out to explain a motive for her murder.

He could hear Olivia's voice in the back of his mind, trying to persuade him that Dave was a seasoned homicide detective who would know a copycat when he saw one. Alexander knew it was a long shot, but the guilt that consumed him for not fulfilling his promise to Landon all those years ago ate away at him. He had to operate under the assumption this wasn't just a senseless random act of violence against a beautiful, young woman.

After speaking with several of Mischa's employees and acquaintances, Alexander was back to square one. It sounded as if she was extremely well-liked. He considered perhaps she had become a target because of her high-level position, but the more research he did on the organization, the less likely that seemed. It was a smaller agency with a paltry budget that relied mostly on donations and a meager amount of government grants. Her salary as director was barely enough to pay her bills. It wasn't exactly anything that would put a target on her back.

A knock on the door startled him, pulling him away from the normal and rather mundane life of Mischa Tate.

"Sorry to interrupt, sir," a tall, wiry man with spiky blond hair and dark-framed glasses said, entering Alexander's office.

"What is it, Simpson?" he asked. "Did you find anything else?"

"Not really. I ran credit reports and got bank statements going back over ten years. This girl was kind of boring. The deed to the townhouse she bought several years back was in her name alone, so it doesn't appear there's a boyfriend or anyone else in the picture. With nothing else to go on, I went ahead and did some preliminary background checks on her brother to see if anything stood out. It might take me a little longer to get everything together on that end because of his time as a SEAL and all—"

"That's not necessary, Simpson," Alexander interrupted, grabbing the file he held out to him. "He was an employee, so we probably have all his information on record somewhere."

He shook his head. "That was my first thought, too, but it was apparently never done. There's no record of it anywhere."

Alexander narrowed his eyes. "That's a bit odd." He shrugged. "It's possible I never requested it since he was a good friend. It probably just slipped my mind."

"Yes, sir. Nonetheless, I'll start looking into his background to see if anything there may shed some light on what happened to his sister."

"Thank you."

Simpson nodded and retreated from the office.

"Simpson," Alexander called out as he was about to disappear down the hallway.

He popped his head back in. "Yes, sir?"

Alexander sighed. "What do you think?"

"Sir?" he responded, straightening his posture.

"I'm sure you've seen the news reports on her death, how the police think she's another victim of the Castle Island Killer."

He nodded.

"What do you think?"

Simpson shifted nervously on his feet. He had worked for Alexander for over ten years. He was the friend of a friend of one of his agents, who had used Simpson in the course of an investigation the company had been hired to conduct. Simpson possessed a rather specific set of computer skills that had proved useful in solving the case, and were still useful to this day. He could hack into even the most rigid computer systems without leaving a trace. Because his background was vastly different than the typical person he employed, Alexander valued his opinion.

"I don't know, sir. The police have a good point. She was dumped in the same area of Boston in a barrel similar to the ones used in the other murders." He shrugged. "The police never released any information regarding the victims' fingernails being ripped off, yet Mischa's were, too. So if it *is* a copycat, as you want to believe, it had to be someone within the police department who had access to all the intricate little details on their investigation and was able to replicate it perfectly."

"Or someone with the skills necessary to access their records." Alexander raised his eyebrows.

Simpson shoved his hands into his pockets. "That's true."

There was a brief silence as Alexander considered his opinion. Everyone seemed to be thinking the same thing… everyone except him. It was too much of a coincidence that her body turned up on the one-year anniversary of her brother's death. There had to be something more to it.

"With all due respect, sir," Simpson said, breaking the silence. "Maybe you're too close to the investigation. You could dig for days, even weeks, and not find what you're looking for. Maybe instead of operating under the theory this is a copycat who targeted Ms. Tate, you could use your resources to help find the Castle Island Killer."

Closing his eyes, Alexander nodded. "I made a promise to Landon I would always watch out for her."

"I'll do everything I can to help you, sir, no matter which path you choose."

"Thank you, Simpson."

"Yes, sir." He turned and disappeared into the hallway once more.

Left alone with a nagging doubt about whether or not he was on the right path, Alexander began flipping through Simpson's latest investigative efforts. He wasn't prepared to be confronted with a photo of himself standing with Olivia, Mischa, Landon, and Landon's fiancée. They were at a fundraising event for Mischa's agency. Her blonde waves were styled in a way that made her look like a 1930s movie star, her red lips glistening against her smooth, pale skin.

Turning away from the photo to avoid being faced with the memories, he glanced out the large windows of his office. Dusk had fallen over the city, bringing a subtle glow to the room. His eyes drooped from the lack of sleep last night. He threw the file on the coffee table, turning on the large television screen mounted on the wall directly in front of him.

The voice of a local news anchor with a non-regional dialect blared as she spoke about a gruesome murder in Southie. His eyes glued to the screen, Alexander lay back on the couch and kicked off his shoes just as Mischa's smiling face flashed on the screen. At least they hadn't shown any of her autopsy photos.

He closed his eyes, an odd feeling of déjà vu washing over him. He had sat in this same office, his eyes glued to the exact same television, as he watched Landon's brutal murder with the rest of the world.

SEVEN

"Any word yet?" Martin asked, snapping Alexander out of his unease regarding the past week.

"Not yet." He let out a slow breath, focusing his attention on the handful of television screens mounted on the wall across from the desk. Each was tuned to a different news station as he waited for any new information about the story that broke over a week ago…an explosion at a building outside Kabul where an American private security company had reportedly been operating a clinic. So far, no further details had been leaked, but Alexander knew it was only a matter of time. Reporters were a vicious breed, pit bulls to the end. Once they sunk their teeth into a story, they never let go. Soon, they'd find a weak link who would disclose what his company was really doing over in Afghanistan…interfering with centuries of tradition, at least in some people's opinions.

"I should be there," Alexander muttered, scanning the screens.

Ever since learning about the explosion, his stomach churned with uncertainty. It took everything inside him to fight his gut response to hop on the first military transport flying over there to figure out what happened and where Landon was, but he knew it would be futile. There was protocol in place for how to proceed in the event something like this should happen. Perhaps Landon was waiting to call until he knew it was safe to do so. But as the hours turned into days, he couldn't help but think the worst…that the threats Landon had received on an almost daily basis had been realized.

Regret ate away at him, unable to get past his last conversation with Landon. He hadn't thought twice about what his friend had asked of him, but it was now at the forefront of his mind. He had an awful premonition all of this could have been avoided if he had just done what Landon requested, regardless of the consequences.

"And do what? Bang on every door, asking if they've seen him? Westerners aren't exactly liked by everyone. Not to mention…" Martin stepped toward him. "No one's supposed to know the medical clinic is just a front for what you're really doing over there."

"I know," Alexander sighed, leaning back in his chair and propping his designer shoe-clad feet on the desk.

His surroundings were a far cry from the barren and meager environment in which he had first met Landon… wearing their navy-issued boxer briefs, standing at attention as they listened to their instructor call them pansies and remind them that, in just a matter of days, their numbers would dwindle. Their friendship had survived Hell Week, deployment, and years of little to no communication after Alexander left the navy and Landon remained. They had shared parts of themselves with each other, things they never told another person. In anticipation of embarking on yet another covert mission under the cover of night, they'd made promises to each other. Alexander hoped he wasn't letting his friend down.

"Rayne keeps calling to see if I've heard anything,"

Alexander continued. "I don't want to lie to her, but what can I do? I keep assuring her he's okay, that he's just adhering to standard protocol and will call when it's safe to do so. Part of me wants to admit it's not looking good, that he should have called by now to let me know he's okay. I can't help but—"

A flash on one of the television monitors caught his attention and he snapped his head up. "Breaking News" ran across the screen in bright, bold letters before cutting back to the same anchor. Alexander hoped for news about Landon, but had a feeling if there were any developments of which he was not aware, it wouldn't be anything good. Like dominoes falling, each of the other stations the television monitors were tuned to also flashed a "Breaking News" title. His stomach rolled.

He grabbed one of the remotes on his desk, not caring which monitor it controlled. It didn't matter. They all seemed to be reporting the same story. A weighty voice, mixed with a touch of compassion filled the silence. People often remarked they remember exactly where they were and what they were doing when Kennedy was shot or the Twin Towers fell. This was his Kennedy assassination. This was his 9/11. The start of a series of events that would slowly unravel the pieces of his seemingly perfect life.

"Breaking news tonight out of Afghanistan where we've been closely following the explosion at an American-operated medical clinic, and the search for the missing staff and patients. Last Sunday, just before noon local time, what is believed to be a suicide bomber stepped up to this building, located approximately fifty miles outside Kabul, and detonated a crude cell phone bomb." A photo of the remains of a nondescript one-story clay building appeared on the screen. All that was left was the foundation and a few wall fragments.

The rest had been reduced to rubble. *"No bodies have been recovered, except for that of the bomber, so it is believed all staff and patients were able to escape."*

Tapping relentlessly on the desk in front of him, Alexander sat up in his chair, his attention glued to the screen. He knew the news wouldn't be good, but he couldn't help but hold out hope for a happy ending.

"Over the past week, there's been much speculation about the cause or reason for this attack. Experts have weighed in, some calling it just another unfortunate incident in an area riddled with violence. Although the bomb was crudely made, which gave rise to many opinions that this was simply an isolated event, we can now say with certainty that isn't the case. This was a planned act of terrorism against an American company whose entire purpose overseas is to help those in need."

Alexander stood from his desk, crossing the room toward the large television screens. He could faintly make out Martin's voice in the background, probably trying to get to the bottom of why they were learning about all this by watching the national news, not through their contacts and connections in the intelligence field.

"Just moments ago, we received a videotape from an extremist group we're just now getting word about, I.U., or Islamic Union, claiming credit for the bombing, as well as the abduction of one of the key staff members of the clinic, a man they claim to be Landon Tate, a former Navy SEAL now working for Burnham and Associates, a private security firm based out of the States, but whose presence is known across the globe."

"Shit," Alexander muttered.

As with most of the humanitarian work his company did, he preferred to keep it secret. On paper, the clinic was run by one of the many "shell" corporations his company had set up to keep the security side of the business separate. He didn't want someone to target any of the clinics, camps, or aid stations set up to help those in need simply because of its connection to the company's military contracts. It would have taken some serious digging or some very loose lips within his management team to connect his company to this clinic.

"It's normally not our policy to broadcast such videos, but little is known about this group just yet. We felt it necessary to warn the public about the potential new threat we face as a nation. What we're about to show you is very graphic, so if you're particularly sensitive or have little ones in the room, you may want to change the channel. It has been edited, but it still may be a bit too violent for some viewers."

The camera cut from the reporter to a fuzzy homemade video. The room was all white with low ceilings. A lone green flag with a large white circle in the middle and Arabic symbols scrawled beneath it hung on the wall. Alexander's chest rose and fell with increased frequency as he searched his brain for any memory of seeing that particular flag before. He didn't recognize it as the official flag of any nation he had ever heard of.

He swallowed hard, a sour taste in his mouth. The sound of a door opening echoed, like footsteps on a creaky floorboard, and five figures dressed all in black with their faces obscured, save for their eyes, entered, pushing a tall, muscular man before them, his arms bound in front of him and a blindfold over his eyes.

Alexander fought with everything he had to remain impassive as he looked at his employee, his team member, his *friend* clad in a bright orange jumpsuit, the little skin visible bruised and bloody. All he could do was pray Landon's fiancée wasn't watching the same newscast at this moment. He felt nauseated and lightheaded thinking about Landon and what he was going through for all to see. If Rayne was watching, he couldn't imagine how she was coping with it.

One of the nondescript figures removed Landon's blindfold and forced him to kneel in the center of the room, the five men standing in a straight line behind him. Alexander had seen such a display before. He always felt bad for the man in the orange jumpsuit, and for their wives and kids, if they had any. But his sympathy was always short-lived. Within a day or two, he would forget the name, the person becoming one more among many who had fallen victim to this war on terror. Some were military. Many were not. Seeing Landon in the same shoes many strangers before him had walked made Alexander sick. Staring into the eyes that got him through so many rough patches during his time as a SEAL, it felt as if a heavy weight was crushing his chest, his lungs unable to draw in enough air.

He fought back the dizziness running through him, focusing solely on the mission, as he had been trained to do. This was different, though. He wasn't on assignment, fighting not only for his life, but the lives of the rest of his team. Instead, he was in his cushy office wearing a designer suit that cost more than most enlisted men made in a month, watching a real-life horror story unfold before his eyes. There was no mission. If there were, he had abandoned it, leaving his team in peril. For what? To follow protocol? Fuck protocol. The old Alexander would have followed his gut, not the rules.

He wanted to look away from the television, but was glued to Landon's blue eyes staring directly at the camera… at him. Taking a deep breath, Landon lowered his head and studied a piece of paper he held in his bound hands, hesitating. Pulling his bottom lip between his teeth, he subtly shook his head.

One of the men stepped forward, hitting him in the back of his head with the butt of an automatic rifle. Landon grunted through the pain, taking a moment to recover and compose himself. He mumbled something in a language Alexander recognized as Pashto, then looked back at the camera.

"*This is a message for every American.*" His voice cut through the heavy silence. He blinked slowly. His body appeared frail, a shell of his former self. Like Alexander, Landon had been trained to withstand days of physical and mental torture, but he was only human and had his limits. Alexander didn't even want to consider what Landon had been forced to endure that had brought him to this point. Even so, he stared directly at the camera, his voice as strong as ever.

"*You think you're so powerful, so smart, that your way of life is the only way. You are wrong. You come into our country and impose your western ideals. You thought you were untouchable, that you would be victorious. The mighty Allah has shown us your weakness. We have existed for thousands of years without your intervention, and we will exist for thousands of years after you've all been exterminated. We are the chosen ones. You can keep interfering with our traditions, but it will be met with the same end. The Islamic Union will do everything within its means to continue striking down every rat who stands in its path. My blood...*" Landon paused, closing his eyes briefly as one of the men stepped up behind him, a long blade in his hand.

Alexander brought his hand to his mouth, his heartbeat echoing in his ears. The *tick-tock* of the clock on the wall seemed to be amplified a thousand times as his surroundings swirled into a twisted rabbit hole. He knew what was about to happen. Still, as much as he wanted to, he couldn't look away. He owed Landon that much. He needed to remain as courageous and brave as his friend was in the face of a grim and sadistic end.

Landon licked his lips, his eyes narrowed. If he were

afraid, he did a good job of covering it up. *"My blood is the price I must pay to atone for my sins and the sins of my brethren."*

The executioner raised the blade, gripping it with both hands, a macabre baseball bat to end Landon's life. Then the screen went black.

EIGHT

Present Day

December 18 - 10:15 PM

Blinking his eyes open, Alexander was frozen in place as he stared at the white ceiling fifteen feet above him. He hadn't thought about that day in months. He tried to not blame himself for what happened to Landon. At first, it was difficult, especially when he had to look into Mischa's eyes at the funeral and offer his apologies for not doing more.

"You can't blame yourself, Alex," Mischa had responded consolingly, the epitome of strength and grace, even when saying goodbye to the only family she had left. *"This isn't your fault."* Standing on her toes, she had wrapped her arms around him, offering him the comfort he should have been providing her. He had closed his eyes briefly, allowing himself to mourn with Landon's sister. As he pulled back, he caught Landon's fiancée's blank stare, her purple-blue eyes vacant.

Alexander shot up on the couch. Grabbing the file Simpson had given him off the table, he fumbled through it, the memory of those eyes intermingling with his unusual encounter earlier this morning. Frantic, he threw photo after photo onto the couch, the floor, the coffee table, desperately searching for the one he had been looking at before he dozed off. Hearing paper crinkling, he looked beside him to see the corner of a photo sticking out from beneath him. Hurriedly, he jumped up, papers scattering like leaves. Grabbing it, Alexander zeroed in on the other woman beside Landon… Rayne, his fiancée of over five years and girlfriend for even longer.

Her deep red hair contrasted with her creamy white skin. She was tall, slender, happy. Her eyes were remarkable, unforgettable…shades of blue mixed with lilac. They shimmered and gleamed, so alive.

As Alexander stared at the photo in front of him, Rayne's features began to fade. Her clean skin was replaced with a weathered appearance and large bags under her eyes. Her face showed signs of significant weight loss and perhaps even drug addiction. Her hair was no longer lustrous and full, but wiry, frayed, and tired. Those eyes that once were so full of life and whimsy were empty, cold, unforgiving.

"Why didn't I see it sooner?"

Dashing to his desk, he grabbed his cell and searched through his contacts, praying he hadn't deleted her information for some unknown reason. When he finally found her name, he breathed a momentary sigh of relief, waiting as the call connected. He paced in front of the windows, the Boston sky a murky mix of rain, ice, and snow. The meteorologist on the local news had said this was just the warmup. By Sunday evening, the forecast was for up to two feet of snow to cover the city.

As Alexander made a mental note to make sure his driveway would be plowed, the line picked up without ringing, a recording announcing that the phone number was no longer in service.

"Shit," he mumbled before turning to his laptop. It could have just been a coincidence that a woman he believed to be Rayne stood outside his building this morning, but something about today being the anniversary of Landon's death, coupled with Mischa's suspicious murder, made him think that wasn't the case. In less than twenty-four hours, he'd crossed paths with two of the most important people in Landon's life — his sister and his fiancée. Alexander refused to believe it was simply a coincidence.

He navigated toward his search engine of choice to see what hits came up on Landon's fiancée, then paused, fumbling for her last name. He stared at the white screen, the bright letters of the search engine's logo mocking him. He should have remembered. He had been trained to recall random combinations of letters and numbers, security codes, bank account numbers, license plates. Why, when it came to someone who was once a close personal friend, was he drawing a blank?

His fingers hovering over the keyboard, he stared at the twenty-six letters of the alphabet, hoping something would come to him. "Rayne, Rayne, Rayne." He repeated her name over and over, wishing he had used her real last name in his phone contacts instead of Landon's. "Kilpatrick!" he shouted, as if Landon were in the room, introducing him to his girlfriend for the first time.

He hastily typed her name and the search engine came back with a few hits, mostly articles about the bakery that had made her a rising star in the Boston culinary scene. There were a few photos of her from Landon's funeral, wearing all black, the bump beneath her dress visible. A renewed sorrow formed in his heart when he recalled the weeks following Landon's death.

He had tried to check on Rayne repeatedly to see how she was doing, but she never answered the door. Soon, his visits grew more and more infrequent, stopping altogether when she hadn't answered her phone or door in over a month. He assumed she was simply busy with the bakery again.

It wasn't until several weeks later that he learned the bakery was in trouble and about to go under. He had tried to get in touch with her once more, but she never returned his phone calls. When he went to her house, a complete stranger answered the door, saying she no longer lived there. Wanting to help, not knowing how, he had one of his subsidiary companies purchase the bakery from her at a price far over market value to give her some sort of financial security. As far as he knew, his subsidiary still owned it.

Staring at the search results, he realized he had hit a dead end and would need someone with skills far more advanced than those he possessed to track her down. He grabbed the receiver of his office phone and punched in a few numbers.

"Simpson," Alexander said when he picked up, surprised he was still at the office at this late hour. "Stop what you're doing. I need you to hunt down an address for a Rayne Kilpatrick. Text me the minute you have it. I'm heading out."

He hurriedly grabbed his coat and left his office in a complete state of disarray. He had come in today, neglecting his family, to try to look for proof that Mischa wasn't just another victim of the Castle Island Killer. Instead, he now found himself trying to track down yet another ghost from his past. He didn't know why he needed to get in touch with Rayne so badly. Maybe he felt as if he could have prevented Mischa's death and hoped to atone for his guilt by making sure Rayne was okay. Maybe their paths had crossed again for a reason. Maybe he simply needed reassurance that none of this was his fault, hoping he could get that from Rayne. The reason no longer mattered. He just knew he needed to find her.

"Where to, Mr. Burnham?" a voice bellowed behind him as he strode down the hallway. Alexander turned around to see Martin running to catch up.

"There's something I have to do, Martin. Take the rest of the night off. I'll let you know if I need anything."

Martin immediately slowed his steps, a look of confusion and disappointment falling over his serious face. He typically always accompanied Alexander wherever he went, partly out of safety and partly out of convenience. But this was something Alexander felt he needed to do on his own. He could sense Martin was on the edge of insisting he come along, as he had in the past, but something about the personal events of the past twenty-four hours must have given him pause.

"Yes, sir."

Alexander opened his mouth to explain what was going on, but stopped himself. Spinning around, he continued down the hall, about to walk through the security door that blocked the public's access to most of the offices.

"And Alex?" Martin called out.

Alexander whirled around, surprised at his sudden familiarity. It didn't matter that Martin had watched him grow up from the little boy who played with G.I. Joes, to a pimply adolescent, then a know-it-all teenager. When Alexander had become his boss, all informality ceased and Martin insisted on calling him Mr. Burnham.

"Yes?" Alexander looked into his eyes.

"Be careful," he admonished, his tone soft and sincere, at complete odds with the serious and business-like expression he normally wore. "I respect your desire to keep what you're up to a secret, but remember that secrets took your father from you." He narrowed his gaze.

"My father died protecting the identity of someone," Alexander argued, his ears reddening from Martin's comparison between the two men. Alexander refused to believe he was anything like his father.

"No." He took a step toward him. "Your father died because, just like you, he thought he didn't need any help. Don't go down the same path he did." Martin turned and walked back into his office. Alexander simply stared at the vacant space, wondering if he was, in fact, making the same mistakes that led to his father's untimely death.

NINE

December 19 - 6:00 AM

Alexander stepped out of his dark SUV onto the cracked pavement, staring at a three-story brick building that looked like it would fall over if he breathed on it too hard. Sirens blared in the distance, and the stench of garbage singed his nostrils. As a train drew close, he glanced over his shoulder to see the tracks just a hundred yards from where he stood. There was a small park across the street, the swing set in serious need of repair. He hoped no children actually played there.

Another sleepless night had come and gone as he drove around the city, waiting to hear from Simpson. He had visited Landon's grave, a lone American flag and wreath marking the resting place of a casket filled with only memories. He had driven past Mischa's townhouse in Arlington, flowers and candles lit in memoriam filling her small front yard. He drove by the house in Revere where Mischa and Landon lived the first several years of their lives. It looked like every other house in the working-class suburb of Boston. Two stories. Yellow aluminum siding. Gray shingle roof. But inside those four walls lived the ghost of a little boy forced to become a man at an early age, which molded him into the determined leader Alexander met during SEAL training… or, as it was more commonly referred to as, BUD/S.

As the hours passed, he thought about Landon and the bond they had formed over the years. He thought about

Mischa and all the good she had done in the world. He thought about Rayne, hoping she had finally found peace after Landon's death, but fearing she hadn't. Mostly, he thought about his father. Martin's warning played on repeat as night gave way to dawn. Alexander wondered whether he had a point, whether he was following the same path as his father. He didn't want to think that was the case, but he really didn't know his father that well. When he was growing up, his father had let his work consume him and was barely home. Alexander had made a point to always be there whenever Olivia or Melanie needed him, working from his home office many times instead of making the commute into the city. He wanted to believe he always put them first.

Except for yesterday morning, a voice in his head reminded him.

Closing his eyes, he rubbed his temples. "That was different," he said to himself.

A truck zoomed by, slamming down into a pothole before continuing its journey up the road. Alexander snapped out of his thoughts, staring at the brick building once more.

Squinting, he noted a faded 301 painted on the mailbox, then double-checked the text from Simpson to verify he was in the correct place. It had taken him a lot longer to track down an address for Rayne than either one of them had anticipated. From what he was able to find out, she had been evicted from her rental house around the same time she lost the bakery. Alexander had assumed she would have been able to live quite comfortably for several years on what the bakery sold for. Looking at the decrepit building, though, all he could think was she must have spent the money on drugs. It was the only explanation that made sense. The address on her bank account and driver's license was a mailbox service in downtown Boston. Simpson was able to hack into the employee database at the cellular phone company she currently worked at to obtain her physical address.

Checking his watch, Alexander saw it was now six in the morning on Saturday. He shook his head, rubbing his hands over his weary face. He should have been home with his arms wrapped around his wife. Instead, he stood in front of a rundown apartment building in Dorchester. Why? Was it guilt? Remorse? Maybe this was his penance for years of shortcomings.

He climbed the steps and pressed the buzzer for Rayne's apartment. He had a feeling she was awake, despite the early hour.

The sound of wood scraping on wood caught his attention. He turned his head to his left.

"The fuck you want?" a voice asked groggily. A black man poked his head out of the window, his eyes heavy, teeth in serious need of dental work. "You a cop? If you are, you have to say so."

"I'm not a cop. I'm looking for the woman who lives in unit 2A. Her name's Rayne."

"Who?"

"Blueish-purple eyes. Red hair."

"Oh, you mean Snow White?"

"Snow White?" Alexander repeated, raising his eyebrows.

"Only white folk in the building. Actually, she's probably the only white folk in the entire neighborhood. You ain't exactly in Beacon Hill, mister. So tell me what you want with Snow White, then be on your way."

"It's personal," he responded, fighting his instinct to reach into his coat and place his hand on his pistol, just in case.

"Well, mister, she ain't home. Even if she was, it's a

Saturday morning, and the only people knocking on doors before the sun's up are cops or someone up to no good. Since you said you ain't a cop, that leads me to believe you're no good, so why don't you get on your way."

Pinching his lips together, Alexander knew enough not to push the man. Neighborhoods like these stuck together. He was the outsider. He guessed Rayne was, too, at first, but it sounded like that wasn't the case anymore. She was one of them. It gave Alexander hope to know she had at least one person looking out for her, despite her squalid surroundings.

"Okay." He reached into his pocket. A familiar clicking echoed, and he looked up to see a revolver pointed at his chest. "Whoa, whoa." He held his hands up to show the man he had no weapon. "I was just reaching for a business card."

"What the fuck do I want your business card for?"

"To give to Rayne," Alexander responded in a steady tone. "I also wanted to give you a little something for your troubles," he added, hoping his good faith gesture would make this man a bit more cooperative. "And for your discretion."

The man nodded. Alexander slowly reached into his jacket, placing a business card and crisp one hundred dollar bill on the window sill.

The man eyed it with skepticism. "That real?"

"My father taught me to never play jokes on a man holding me at gunpoint. So yes, it's real."

Studying him for a second longer, the man finally lowered his gun. "Your daddy sounds like a smart man…a lot smarter than you coming into this neighborhood in your shiny car. You don't belong here, so why don't you get. I'll make sure to give Snow White your card. After that, whether she calls ya or not is up to her. And I don't want to see you standing at this door again, ya hear?"

"You have my word," Alexander replied, giving him a sincere look before turning and heading back to his car.

He had done all he could. He would try to be patient and give Rayne the weekend to reach out to him, then he'd pay her a visit at work. He knew he should be focusing on finding Mischa's killer, but he needed to know Rayne was okay, that the only remaining family Landon had wouldn't fall through the cracks, too.

TEN

The house was tranquil in the early morning hours of Saturday, just like it had been the previous day. But this morning, Alexander carried a weight with him. Ghosts of his past, which he hadn't thought about recently, had reappeared almost overnight. He wondered whether there was a reason, or if it truly was just a coincidence. He contemplated whether they were trying to teach him some grand lesson about being a better person, about not letting his work consume him, like it had his father. He felt like Ebenezer Scrooge in *A Christmas Carol*, except his ghosts came in the form of his own subconscious.

Maybe it was the same with Scrooge.

Regret can torture a man, rip him open and bleed him dry for the world to see. In the end, only he could pick up the pieces and put himself back together in the hopes of learning from his past. Alexander had made his fair share of mistakes in life and, over the past twenty-four hours, he'd been forced to come face-to-face with many of them.

A thousand what-ifs ate away at him. If he had done one thing differently, if he had picked up the phone, if he had made more of an effort, if he hadn't allowed the comfort of being the one signing the paychecks to bewitch him into staying out of the field, maybe things wouldn't have turned out the way they did.

He pulled his car into the garage, then entered the house

with light steps, not wanting to wake anyone. As much as he wanted to take a shower and get back to the office to keep digging around into Mischa's life, he needed to put his family first today. It was something his father never did and, after Martin's word of warning, Alexander wanted to make every effort to ensure he hadn't already made that mistake. It didn't matter that his father had saved many lives by putting his work first. Years of animosity toward him due to his absence and neglect had ruined whatever relationship they had. Alexander shuddered at the notion that Melanie would someday see him the way he viewed his own father.

As he made his way through the kitchen and toward the formal living room, inhaling the pine tree aroma that reminded him of the holiday season, a welcome feeling of serenity washed over him. A fifteen-foot Christmas tree, surrounded by mountains of presents, sat in front of the large bay window. Several ornaments lay scattered on the floor, most likely the result of Olivia's cat deciding they were more useful as toys than decorations. After the past few days, he wanted nothing more than to be surrounded by the love of his family, something he should have done yesterday instead of rushing off to the office, just like his father did so many times when he was growing up.

The floorboards of the century-old house creaked below Alexander's feet. He tried to lighten his steps, not wanting to wake anyone. Saturdays in the Burnham household were generally reserved for sleeping in, then lounging in bed with his wife, daughter, and dog while they watched whatever movie Melanie wanted. Lately, she'd been on a *Frozen* kick, like every other little girl in the country. Alexander could probably recite the entire movie from memory.

Walking into the formal entry rotunda, he stopped abruptly. An extravagant, yet modern chandelier hung from the vaulted ceiling, the landing of the second floor following the circular shape. Several feet below the chandelier sat a large round table where Olivia displayed a new floral arrangement weekly. Cursing the cat under his breath, he made his way to the table where it looked like Nepenthe had pushed the wreath-shaped centerpiece to the floor. Flowers were all out of place, petals scattered, but it wasn't ruined.

Squatting down, Alexander picked up the wreath, shaking his head when he noticed several framed photos knocked off one of the small entryway tables, as well. He placed the centerpiece back where it belonged, fixing a candy cane and pine cone that were askew, then continued up the winding staircase to the second floor, leaving the broken photos for the time being.

The *tick-tock* of the antique grandfather clock in the foyer echoed against the high ceiling, the sound finding its way to the second floor as Alexander walked down the hallway. A purple stuffed bear sat in the corridor. Smiling, he picked it up, then paused outside a white paneled door, placing his hand on it.

Slowly turning the knob, Alexander pushed the door open and snuck into the large square room filled with toys, books, and games. The walls were a shade of yellow Melanie had chosen when they first moved here a few years ago. It was warm and inviting, the one room of the house where there were no rules, where imaginations could run wild. One day, this room was Camelot. The next, it was Emerald City. Then it would be Wonderland. Alexander never knew what world he'd be entering when he stepped over the threshold. Melanie was always full of surprises.

He padded across the plush carpet, making sure to side-step some sort of arts and crafts project Melanie was apparently in the middle of that lay on the floor. He glanced at the wall above her bed. In just a few years, she'd probably want to replace the Dr. Seuss art hanging there. Instead, there would be a poster of some boy band she'd swoon over as she gossiped on the phone with her friends. Adolescence was coming like a freight train, and he couldn't do anything to stop it. All he could do was treasure the time he had with her while she still believed Daddy was her hero.

He lowered himself onto the edge of her bed, trying to make sure the sudden weight didn't disturb her. Placing the bear beside her, he leaned down, pulling the fluffy comforter away from her head to give her a kiss. He swiftly shot up, his pulse skyrocketing as he stared at a lumpy pillow where Melanie's sleeping form should have been. Ripping the covers from the bed, alarm bells went off as he stared at more pillows, giving the appearance someone was lying there when it was distressingly empty.

He dashed from Melanie's room toward the master suite on the opposite end of the second floor. When they first moved in, Alexander had been uneasy that her room was so far away, but she picked it out as hers, wanting to be able to wake up in the morning and look at the lake on their property. Plus, it gave him and his wife some privacy. Now, a troubled feeling settled in his stomach, heat rolling through his body.

Entering the master bedroom, he prayed Melanie had simply crawled into bed with Olivia in the middle of the night, although she hadn't done that for quite some time. He stepped closer to the bed, his eyes falling on Olivia's sleeping form. Melanie wasn't there.

The ache in his chest grew as he ran out of the room. The dog glanced up briefly from his bed in the corner, then returned to snoring. Frantic, Alexander tore through every room on the second floor, searching for any sign of Melanie.

Each was dark, as unused as they were the day they moved in.

"No, no, no, no," he murmured, storming through the hallway and down the stairs. He hoped he was simply overreacting, but given the strange events of the past twenty-four hours, he had a feeling something terrible had happened.

"Melanie!" he exclaimed as he searched the first floor, opening every door, all the rooms empty and devoid of any sign of his daughter. "Where are you? The fun's over. You're worrying Daddy!" He strode back to the center of their home, the living room. He glanced out the rear windows at the massive, snow-covered lawn. If she were a few years older, he'd think maybe she snuck out with her friends, but he knew that wasn't the case. There was no way she could have left the house without the security system remotely alerting him to it. Still, he couldn't leave any stone unturned.

He darted out the back door, running toward the guest house located by a small lake on the rear of their property. He hoped she hadn't ignored his warnings and decided to go for an early-morning skate on the ice that still hadn't frozen completely.

Cresting over a small hill, his eyes settled on the lake. Topped with a thin layer of ice and a light dusting of snow, it appeared as undisturbed as it had the previous day. Turning around and gazing back at the house, he looked over the snow-covered grass. Apart from his, there was no sign of footsteps in the white powder. He struggled to breathe, his world spinning around him as he called out Melanie's name over and over, to no avail.

In the stillness of dawn, his voice echoed against the void, no sign of life, apart from the occasional squirrel or bird that had yet to fly south for the winter. Refusing to think the worst, he raced back inside, a knot forming in his throat when he entered the living room. The house was as still as it was when he arrived home this morning. His eyes fell on the broken frames and scattering of flowers in the entryway.

With slow steps, he walked into the rotunda and toward the front door, picking up one of the photos. He should have known the disarray wasn't because of the cat. He ran his fingers over the black-and-white photo, his heart aching as he stared at the image of Melanie and Olivia rolling around on the sand at their beach house this past summer. He could see himself just off to the side, files scattered around him as he spoke on the phone, completely ignoring his family…just like his father.

"Alex!" Olivia said, her voice fraught with worry.

He spun around to see her rushing down the steps, her gaze lingering on the broken frames and disheveled floral arrangement. Her face was ashen, her chest heaving as she frantically tried to tie her long silk robe around her body, her fingers fumbling with the sash.

"What's going on?"

"It's Melanie." He pushed past her, refusing to believe his worst nightmare had come true. "She's not in her room." With hurried steps, he searched the bottom floor again, wondering how she could just disappear without anyone hearing anything. It was completely absurd to think that three people needed a house this big. There was too much space, too much distance, too much opportunity for something like this to happen.

"What do you mean?" Olivia asked with a quiver in her voice, her eyes glued to Alexander as he searched every nook and crevice for any sign of his little girl. With each empty room, the ache in his heart and throat grew more pronounced. "She *has* to be here," she cried, following him up the stairs.

Methodically, he walked through all the rooms on the top floor again, checking the closets, looking underneath the beds, pulling back the drapes. All he kept thinking was this couldn't be happening, that she'd jump out and surprise him any second. The seconds turned into minutes, the minutes into almost an hour with still no sign of his little girl.

The truth of the situation washed over him like a storm as he pulled his phone out of his pocket. The sound of toys clattering together caught his attention. He headed down the hallway, hope building in his chest as he turned the corner. Olivia sat in Melanie's room, dumping out bins full of toys, which she probably hadn't touched in months, if not years.

Deflated, he went to her. "Olivia," he said in a calming tone. The nagging voice in his head told him this never would have happened had he come home last night. He didn't know what *this* was yet, but he couldn't ignore his gut telling him Melanie had been taken. The bear in the hallway, the floral centerpiece knocked to the ground, the broken picture frames on the entryway table... All signs of a struggle.

"Olivia," he called out again as she continued ripping through Melanie's room. "Please, Olivia. Stop." His voice was forceful. He hated to see her hurting like this, knowing he should have been here to prevent it. "Please," he added with a tremble, placing his hands on her arms to stop her from continuing her futile search. This all seemed like a bad dream, like he was watching a movie of someone else's tormented life.

"She *has* to be here!" Olivia wailed, pushing against him and sliding down the wall next to the window. She pulled her knees to her chest and buried her head against her legs. There was no way to know precisely how long Melanie had been gone. Each second counted, and Alexander wanted nothing more than to use every resource and skill he possessed to find the person responsible. But he couldn't leave his wife to cope with her pain alone.

His head hanging, he took measured steps and lowered himself to the ground beside Olivia, wrapping her in his arms. He pulled her close and kissed the top of her head. The faint scent of vanilla made its way to his nose, placating his own fear and turmoil for a brief moment. Their relationship had been fraught with ups and downs from the very beginning, the result of them both being strong-willed and stubborn. But no matter the obstacle, no matter the hurdle, they survived. They found strength in each other. Yes, Olivia needed Alexander to get through this horrific tragedy, but he needed her just as much.

"We'll get through this, love," he assured her, his voice barely audible. "I promise you. I'll call the police and get Martin out here immediately. It could be nothing. She may just be hiding," he added, his words unconvincing. Despite not wanting to think the worst, in his heart, he knew his little girl had been taken.

"I was having trouble sleeping without you, so I took some cold syrup." She lifted her head, meeting his eyes. She bit her lip, her chin quivering. "I never should have. If I hadn't, maybe I would have heard—"

"Shh." He hugged her tighter. She wasn't the one to blame here. If anyone was, Alexander felt he needed to shoulder that burden. On their wedding day, he vowed to protect his family, to always put them first. Looking around Melanie's vacant room, a dozen different scenarios about where she was and who could be responsible circling through his head, he realized he had turned into his father.

"Don't think about any of that." He kissed her head once more, feeling so violated at the notion that someone had come into his home, into his sanctuary, and took his world. The dread and unease he had felt since pulling back the comforter on Melanie's bed quickly turned to anger. His body tensed. His jaw clenched. The vein in his neck pulsed. His voice turned into an animalistic growl.

"I'll find her, and when I do, whoever took her is going to pay for what they've done."

ELEVEN

December 19 - 9:30 AM

Alexander's head was cloudy as his house became a beehive of activity. Martin had arrived almost immediately and began touching base with the parents of all Melanie's friends, getting word out that she was missing. Police and crime scene techs swarmed the formerly quiet house, snapping photos and dusting for prints, while Olivia and Alexander answered question after question. He grew irritated as the seconds ticked by and the questions became more and more ridiculous. He was wasting precious time when he could be out there trying to find his daughter. He kept glancing at the front door, waiting for her to magically reappear. He knew she was gone, but that didn't stop him from checking each room in his house over and over again.

"Sorry to interrupt," a man said, approaching where they stood in the formal living room speaking to a local detective. Alexander looked up, observing he was of average height and build, had short, sandy hair, and the expression on his face was a dead giveaway for someone in law enforcement. Alexander had been around it his entire life and could pick a cop out of a lineup. "My name is Agent Moretti." He flipped open his wallet and showed his ID and badge. "I work for the FBI out of the field office in Boston. When the local LEOs got the call about a possible missing child, they notified our office since the FBI has a bit of expertise in this area, and due to the probability this will turn into a media frenzy since you're a high-profile target."

"High-profile target" was all Alexander heard, as if saying it were his fault Melanie was in this dangerous situation. Crossing his arms over his chest, he widened his stance and peered down at Agent Moretti. Alexander was used to being the one asking questions and calling the shots. The combination of his tall, muscular body and his decisive demeanor intimidated most people. However, it seemed this agent was not most people. He didn't draw back or blink. His eye contact and stature remained steady, unwavering. There was a smugness about him. He'd barely spoken a word to Alexander, but he already didn't like him.

"How can we help, Agent Moretti?" Olivia asked, stepping in front of Alexander. She placed a hand on his arm, silently telling him to play nice for the sake of their daughter.

"I overheard you talking about your security system here."

"Yes," Alexander replied, taking charge, ignoring the agent's pompous demeanor. He had to remind himself this agent was here to help, that the FBI had a great deal of expertise in finding missing children. He needed to put his ego aside for a minute and answer every question. It might just bring Melanie back.

"Like I was telling the detective here…" He gestured to the local police officer he had been speaking with before Agent Moretti interrupted. "Everyone who lives here or has access to this house has their own unique code they enter on a keypad before placing their thumbprint on the pad. The code and thumbprint must match before anyone can enter. A keypad and scanner are located at every entry point to the house — the front door, rear door, and garage. When the system is armed, all the windows have sensors that will trigger the alarm if any amount of pressure is applied."

"I noticed a few small cameras mounted at various points on the exterior of the house. I assume this is all part of your system?"

"Yes."

Agent Moretti jotted a few notes in his pad, nodding. "Sounds like quite the setup," he mused.

Alexander didn't respond. He didn't appreciate Moretti's backhanded accusation that even the best security system around wasn't enough.

"Well, I suppose there's no such thing as being too cautious in your line of work."

"What does all of this have to do with finding my daughter?" Olivia interrupted. She shifted from foot to foot as she kept glancing at the large clock hanging on the wall. Alexander knew what she was thinking. Melanie had been gone for hours and it seemed as if nothing was getting done, that they weren't moving fast enough.

"I understand how difficult this is for you, Mrs. Burnham," Agent Moretti began in a tone that was borderline condescending.

"Don't give us that speech," Alexander shot back. He imagined Moretti had given the same one to countless other families desperate for answers, grasping at any bit of information in the hopes of finding their loved one. He wondered how many of the cases Moretti worked on had a happy ending. "Just tell us how you intend to find our daughter."

Flipping his notepad closed, Moretti shoved it into his jacket pocket. "I've called in the rest of the regional CARD team."

"CARD team?" Olivia asked, her brows furrowed.

"Child Abduction Rapid Deployment team," Moretti

answered, meeting Olivia's concerned eyes. "I'm leading them. The rest of my people will be on-site within the hour. In the meantime, I'm trying to gather as much information as possible to get a jump start on finding your daughter." He turned to face Alexander. "Now, these exterior cameras of yours… Do they record?" He raised his eyebrows.

"Yes."

"Can we take a look at the footage?"

"One of my men has been going through it all morning. He hasn't found anything yet."

"Nevertheless, I'd like to take a look at it."

Alexander widened his stance and glared at Moretti. It was ludicrous to think this FBI agent would be able to see something in those video feeds he or his employees couldn't. They had advanced training far beyond anything they taught at the academy.

"Need I remind you that, if need be, I can get a court order for it. It's in your best interest to cooperate with this investigation. I wouldn't want word to get out that the father of a missing girl refused to cooperate with the FBI. I don't think it would be very good for your public image."

Alexander's nostrils flared at his insinuation. "This way," he answered with a clenched jaw, leading Agent Moretti out of the living area and down the long corridor toward his private home office.

"Sir," Martin said as the two men entered the circular room, large windows overlooking a massive expanse of Alexander's snow-covered property. An oversized cherry-wood desk sat in the center, built-in bookshelves boasting a wide variety of hardcover books behind it. Placed on end tables beside a large leather sofa were photos of Alexander throughout the years — with his family growing up, high school graduation, in his navy whites, in some desert in the

Middle East, with Olivia and Melanie. The photos showed the progression his life had taken from a troubled boy, to a SEAL, then to a man who finally had everything…until it was ripped away from him last night.

"I'm still going through all the footage," Martin explained. "I haven't found anything yet. Since we don't have a precise window, it could take some time."

Nodding, Alexander said, "Martin, this is Agent Moretti from the FBI. Agent Moretti, this is Martin. He works for me."

"Pleasure to meet you," Martin said, extending his hand.

"Likewise." Moretti took Martin's outstretched hand. "If you don't mind, I'd like to take over from here. Thank you," he said in dismissal.

Alexander opened his mouth, about to chastise Moretti for ordering his employee around, but stopped. It was becoming more and more difficult to be cooperative. He had to keep telling himself to play along with Moretti's game in the hopes of finding Melanie.

Meeting Martin's eyes, Alexander nodded. "Go check on my mother and Olivia. Make sure they're okay."

"Yes, sir." He stood from the desk and walked out of the office, Agent Moretti watching him every step of the way until the click of the door sounded in the silent room.

Moretti pivoted and looked at Alexander with an arrogance he would have given anything to smack off his face. Alexander didn't want to read too much into it, but he couldn't shake the feeling Moretti enjoyed some sort of sick satisfaction from ordering Alexander and his employees around.

"Let me ask you," the agent started, meandering through the office as if it were his and Alexander were an unwelcome guest. "You're a pretty high-profile guy. You work in a kind of business where it's probably easier for you to make enemies than friends."

Alexander remained silent, neither agreeing nor disagreeing with his assessment.

Moretti picked up a small, silver-framed photo of Melanie on her first day of kindergarten a few years ago. She wore a frilly, pastel-striped skirt with white tights, a pink t-shirt, and purple Converse. Her curly brown hair was pulled into two pigtails high up on each side of her head, and she was grinning a brilliant, toothy smile.

For the first time since realizing she was missing, Alexander felt her absence. He had been in work mode all morning, trying to fix what had been done. Now that he had a minute, the reality that Melanie was gone started to sink in. She wasn't simply over at a friend's or in school. She had vanished into thin air. A pain unlike any other settled in his chest, and Alexander tried to keep from breaking down in front of the agent.

"Piss anyone off lately?" Moretti asked.

Taking a breath, Alexander pinched his lips together, seething. "Agent Moretti," he began in a steady voice, "with all due respect, that's not really any of your fucking business."

"With all due respect, Mr. Burnham, it *is* my business. Everything about you is my business right now. Your daughter is missing."

"And you think *I'm* to blame?" His voice grew louder, his ears turning red.

"I didn't—"

"Don't you think I've thought about that? Fuck! All morning, that's *all* I've been able to think about! Since the day Melanie was born, I've been worried sick someone who's been on the receiving end of one of my company's contracts would be pissed off enough to hurt her, and me in the process. That's why we moved out of the city. That's why we have more security measures in place than most politicians and diplomats, for crying out loud!"

Alexander ran his hands through his hair, tugging at it. He wasn't thinking clearly. He felt the weight of the world on his shoulders — the guilt, the blame, everything. Reaching into the holster under his blazer, he pulled out a pistol and raised it.

Moretti's eyes widened as he quickly reacted, drawing his own weapon. For the first time, Alexander saw something other than the sanctimonious, judgmental expression on the agent's face. As they stood just a few feet apart, their guns pointed at each other, he saw a hint of fear and uncertainty.

Shifting his aim, Alexander fired the weapon over Moretti's shoulder, hitting the window behind him. Moretti flinched, instinctively covering his head.

"You see that?" Alexander roared.

Moretti spun around, looking at the pane of glass, a bullet lodged in it.

"Bulletproof glass!" Alexander bellowed, taking several cautious steps toward Moretti. "Bulletproof *fucking* glass in a house where I'm supposed to raise my daughter!" His voice turned despondent, a lump forming in his throat. "Because of me, she doesn't get to live a normal life. So, to answer your question... Yes, I've pissed off a lot of people. The list of possible suspects in my head is a mile long, and every single one would have enough training and expertise to carry out this kind of thing. So if you don't mind, instead of answering pointless questions, I'd like to get out there and find my daughter!"

"Everything okay in here?" Martin asked, peeking his

head into the room, a few officers behind him with their weapons drawn.

"Yes. Everything's fine." Alexander didn't look his way, keeping his eyes narrowed on Moretti.

"Agent Moretti?" one of the officers asked.

Several intense moments passed, amplified by the ticking of the clock on the wall. Moretti appeared relatively unfazed by Alexander's emotional outburst. Alexander knew his type. Hell, he *was* his type. Controlled. Scrupulous. Attentive. Typically devoid of emotion…except when it came to those he cared about and loved. Alexander's normally hard exterior had cracks only Olivia and Melanie could seep into.

In his professional life, no one questioned him. He ran his company as he saw fit. What he said was law. But here, in the office of his house, Agent Moretti glaring at him with a look that confirmed his original suspicion that Melanie's disappearance was all his fault, Alexander felt weak. Worse, he felt just as guilty as the man who actually took his daughter.

"Everything's fine, gentlemen," Moretti finally answered.

"Yes, sir." Martin hesitated, then closed the door to the office, leaving the two men once more.

"Let's look at the camera feed." Agent Moretti interrupted their stare down.

"Fine."

Both men put their weapons in their holsters and walked to the desk. Alexander sat in the chair, his eyes scanning the camera feeds on his laptop. Sensing a presence over his shoulder, he glanced behind him to see Agent Moretti hovering, his eyes focused on him and not the laptop screen.

"My company provides security services for a variety of clients," Alexander explained, trying to clear the tension. If he didn't know any better, based on the agent's demeanor, he'd think *he* was a suspect. "We have a patent on our own top-of-the-line security system, which is what's been installed here. Security cameras are wired directly into the house's electrical, but there's also a battery backup that will automatically switch on in the case of a cut wire or loss of power. The cameras operate independently of the alarm system, so even if that goes down for any reason, the cameras still run. Clients can log in at any time from wherever they are to see real-time video feeds. We maintain a server containing all archived video feeds that can be accessed upon request."

"And that's what we're looking at here?" Moretti asked, eyeing Alexander as if he were waiting for him to snap again.

"Yes. This is all the exterior cameras from last night, starting at eighteen hundred hours."

"And where were you last night?"

After a brief moment of hesitation, Alexander admitted, "At my office working on a few things."

"What specifically?"

"As I'm sure you can understand, the nature of most of my business is classified." Refusing to turn around, Alexander continued staring at the laptop screen, keeping his eyes peeled for anything unusual.

"I can certainly appreciate that," Moretti offered, "but it could be relevant to your daughter's disappearance. Do you typically work late, especially on a Friday? My office was pretty much a ghost town yesterday afternoon."

"Something came up that required my immediate attention."

"So you stayed late?"

"Yes," Alexander answered with a clenched jaw.

"Leaving your wife and daughter alone in this big house?"

"I leave them nearly every day when I go to work," he

responded, struggling to control his temper. "I get called in at odd times on a regular basis. This was no different."

"Hmm." Agent Moretti paced behind him, studying the books on the shelves. "I'm sure the CARD team is on scene as we speak, probably going through a timeline of the past twenty-four hours with your wife. I just hope both your story and hers match up."

"What are you saying?" Alexander spun around in his chair, his nostrils flaring. Heat flashed through his body at the agent's insinuations. In missing persons cases, usually those closest to the victim were suspected. No one was ruled out, even parents, but Alexander couldn't imagine how any parent could cause their own child harm.

"Mr. Burnham, it's been my experience that what the lay person believes to be an insignificant detail, such as what one was working on at the office, could be the clue needed to find and bring home a loved one." His eyes narrowed. "And isn't that what you want? Don't you want to find your daughter?"

"Of course I do!" Alexander roared. "What kind of question is that?" He shot up from his chair, towering over Agent Moretti by a good six inches.

"Then prove it," he hissed, standing his ground. His fierce expression unwavering, he glared at Alexander, leaning into him.

Clenching his fists, Alexander fought the urge to take his aggression out on him and use him as a punching bag. Agent Moretti had a disdainful attitude toward him and he had no idea why. But what if Moretti was right? What if Melanie's disappearance was connected to Mischa's death? Alexander didn't see how, but the more time they wasted arguing, the less time he would have to find his daughter.

Sighing, he lowered himself back into his chair, returning

his attention to the security camera feed. He pressed a button on the keyboard to speed the video up.

"Just before three Friday morning, I got a call from my brother-in-law."

"Detective Wilder, correct?"

"There are two Detective Wilders," he reminded Moretti.

"One being your sister. She retired from the police force, didn't she?"

"How do you seem to already know so much about my family?" Alexander asked, a bit wary.

"I take every case I get called on very seriously. While the local LEOs were looking through your house for physical evidence, I was doing my research on your family to see if anything in your history stood out. Based on what I was able to ascertain, I'm in complete agreement with your earlier assessment. You've made quite a few enemies."

"Dave Wilder is my brother-in-law," Alexander answered, ignoring Moretti's last statement. "He's the lead homicide detective for the city."

"And what did he want so early?"

"He asked me to meet him in Southie."

"Such a shame to leave your comfortable house in Dover for the slums of Southie, don't you think?" There was a hint of venom in his tone.

"I've been to worse places during my time in the navy, making barely three grand a month after I first enlisted."

"But you rose in the ranks fairly quickly, didn't you? If I'm not mistaken, you were a commander when you left, weren't you?"

"And in what branch did you serve?" Alexander spit out.

"I went into the police academy right out of college. I'm still paying back those student loans. I didn't have the money to just pay for college up front." He glared at Alexander before continuing. "Now, why did Detective Wilder ask you to meet him in Southie?"

"He wanted to show me something."

"And what was that?"

Alexander hesitated briefly, reluctant to get Dave in trouble for his breach of protocol. However, the game had changed. If this information helped find Melanie, it was a chance he had to take.

"A body was found in an old fishing warehouse."

"Why did he call you about it?"

"Because it was a friend. Mischa Tate." His solemn voice wavered slightly as he recalled staring at the badly bruised and barely recognizable face of his friend's sister.

"I heard about that on the news. Another one of the Castle Island Killer's victims, right?"

"I suppose, except Mischa didn't exactly fit the profile. Something about the entire situation seemed off to me. I couldn't help but think it was a copycat, even after Dave assured me there were details of the case not shared with the general public that Mischa's body had." Letting out a breath through tight lips, he shook his head. "I wanted to believe him, but I couldn't, so I went into the office yesterday to see what I could dig up. Like you, I like to do my research. I spent hours poring over every detail of Mischa's life, looking for something that could point me in the right direction."

"Is there anyone who can vouch for your whereabouts?"

He flung his eyes to Agent Moretti, fire in his gaze.

"I apologize, Mr. Burnham. It's protocol. We have to account for the whereabouts of everyone close to the girl."

Running his hand over his weary face, he nodded. "My secretary could, as well as my, well…Martin."

"Martin? The fellow who was just in here?" Agent

Moretti took out his pad and began scribbling in it. "What's his relationship to you?"

"I've known him practically my entire life. He was my father's right-hand man when he was alive. After his death, Martin stepped in to temporarily run the company before I decided to leave the navy and take over."

"And how did Martin feel about that?" His interest piqued, he put his notepad back into his pocket, his attention devoted to Alexander once more. "It must have been difficult for him to hand things over to you, don't you think? Hell, if I had been working for someone for years, essentially being groomed to run things, and someone who never exhibited any interest in having anything to do with the day-to-day operations suddenly came back and took over, I might get a little upset. In fact, I'd be fucking livid."

Alexander opened his mouth, bewildered at how this agent seemed to know all the tiny details of his life. Things very few people knew.

"Like I said, I did my research on you." He gave a contemptuous smile.

"Martin's not like that," Alexander explained. "He never wanted to run the company. He just stepped in for the time being while my mom convinced me that my father wanted the business to stay in the family. Martin was the only one who *could* fill my father's shoes at the time. He was the only one who knew where all the bodies were buried, so to speak. To this day, he's still the only one, besides me and my brother."

"So you and your brother both run the company now, correct?"

"More or less. We have different skills. Tyler is more interested in expanding our humanitarian presence in areas that need help..." Alexander trailed off, thinking how much his brother reminded him of Landon. They both bent over backwards to help some of the most vulnerable people in the world. Tyler devoted endless resources to people whose countries had all but forgotten about them. Landon opened Alexander's eyes to the potential impact his company's vast resources could have. Now, Tyler carried on that legacy.

"It's a bit ironic, isn't it?" Agent Moretti cut through his thoughts.

"What's that?"

"Some of the people you try to help could be running from the very same armies your men have trained."

"We never get involved in areas of internal conflict," he insisted. "We provide resources *after* armed conflict to help stabilize the region."

"That may be true, but your company's contractors have trained armies in Afghanistan, Iraq, and Africa, just to name a few. There's always conflict."

"What does any of this have to do with finding my daughter?" Alexander asked, losing the little patience he had left.

"It could all be related. Now back to your, well…Martin. What's his official title with your company?"

"Operations Vice President."

"And what does that entail?"

"Everything, really. Whenever I need something, he's the person I go to."

"Including a ride?"

Alexander shot his eyes to him. "What do you mean?"

"Operations Vice President sounds like a rather embellished title for someone who seems to be just a chauffeur. To go from being interim president of the company to driving around the new president must have been difficult."

"He's not just my chauffeur," Alexander hissed. "If he

were, do you think he'd be the only one who knows *everything* about the company? He's the only one who has full access to everything — files, cases, even this house! He's more than just my driver. He's more than just my right-hand man. Martin is *family*. When I came back to take over the company, Martin showed me the ropes. He helped mold me into the leader I am today."

"Still…" Moretti shrugged. "Sounds like he could be hiding some resentment. I know I would be."

"Thankfully, with all due respect, Martin is a bigger man than it sounds like you are, Agent Moretti."

"I suppose you're right," he retorted, everything about him condescending. "So your secretary and Martin could both vouch for your presence in your office from the time you arrived until the time you left?"

"Yes. Well, not the whole time. My secretary left at five. I fell asleep a little bit after that. I was tired from having been up most of the night. When I woke up, it was after ten."

"At which point you decided to continue working instead of come home," he said, very matter-of-factly.

"Yes," Alexander agreed, bending the truth. He did go back to work. That he left the office to search for another ghost of his past was none of Moretti's business.

"And what time did you arrive home?"

"Around seven this morning."

"Did you notice anything out of the ordinary?"

"Not at first. I parked my car in the garage and entered the house through the kitchen."

"The entrance from the garage has the same security as the other exterior doors, correct?"

"Yes. It has the same keypad and thumbprint scanner as the other doors. The house was quiet. There were a few ornaments scattered on the floor, but that's usual around here. We have a cat who thinks Christmas ornaments are toys."

"My ex-girlfriend had a cat. I'm convinced the thing tried to kill me in my sleep on a nightly basis."

Alexander gave him a congenial smile, not surprised he was single. He pictured him treating everyone with the same respect he gave him, which was none.

"Anything else appear out of place?"

Nodding, he continued recounting the morning's events. "If you recall, just past the living room is a large rotunda entryway. Olivia always keeps a floral arrangement on a table in the center. It was knocked onto the floor, as were some of the pictures from the smaller entryway table. As I headed up the stairs, I saw Melanie's bear in the hallway outside her room."

"And none of that raised any red flags with you?" he asked, lifting an eyebrow and cocking his head.

"It wasn't until I pulled the covers back on her bed and saw it was empty that I put two and two together. Until that point, I just thought our cat had decided to cause a ruckus and that Melanie had left her bear in the hallway. She's a typical eight-year-old who tends to leave her things all over the house."

"And your wife didn't hear anything?"

"This house is over eight thousand square feet. It's not her fault she didn't hear any sort of commotion," Alexander said defensively. He didn't want to say anything about Olivia taking some cold syrup to help her fall asleep. Then Moretti would pry into why she had trouble sleeping to find another reason this was all Alexander's fault.

"When you realized Melanie was missing, what did you do?"

"After searching every inch of this property, I called Martin."

"How did he react when you told him what was going on?" Agent Moretti asked, his intrigue increasing.

Alexander eyed him with renewed skepticism. "Why does it matter?"

"Humor me." He smirked.

"I didn't tell him at first. I just told him I needed him to come over to the house right away."

Standing back, Moretti widened his stance, crossing his arms in front of his chest. "I thought you told him everything, that he was your 'right-hand man'? If he's your sole confidant, why didn't you confide in him immediately? Wouldn't you want him to do everything he could to help find your daughter? Why did you keep that information from him all the time it took him to drive over here?"

"Because!" Alexander slammed his fist on the desk, his face flaming. All his training to remain calm and focused during interrogation-type settings had been forgotten. This wasn't just him keeping information out of the hands of the enemy. This was so much bigger. His entire world was at risk and this agent was doing nothing, except making everyone seem like a suspect when the real culprit was out there somewhere with his daughter. With each breath Alexander took, he feared Melanie could be taking her last, and the lack of action on Agent Moretti's part frustrated him to no end.

"Because saying it out loud would make it seem real! Because I should have been home last night instead of chasing down a theory on a case that may turn out to be completely pointless! Because I know it's my fault Melanie's gone! So, if you don't mind, I'd like to look through these camera feeds to see if we can find something!"

Alexander's voice rang out in the room for what seemed like an eternity, then a heavy silence settled between the two men. Agent Moretti remained standing over his shoulder as Alexander continued scanning through the camera feeds. He tried to unclench his jaw and relax his shoulders, but he couldn't.

"My apologies, Mr. Burnham. I didn't mean anything by—"

"Yes, you did," Alexander shot back. "I don't need you reminding me of what I already know."

He kept his eyes glued to the laptop screen, watching the time code on the camera feeds race by. He had scanned through hours of footage with no sign of anything suspicious. Every so often, a raccoon would scurry across the cobblestone driveway. The only sound in the room was that of Moretti's heavy breathing, coupled with the occasional throat clearing that grated on Alexander's nerves. Each one was a little louder, a little more obnoxious. Just as Alexander was about to lose it and kick him out of the room, there was a subtle knock on the door.

"Come in!" Moretti called out, as if it were his office.

Alexander turned to glare at him, then something on the screen caught his attention. If he hadn't paused the video when he heard the knock, he probably never would have noticed it. He had been focused solely on looking for some dark figure approaching one of the entrances. What he failed to take into account was the probability that this was a very well-thought-out plan requiring months of preparation.

A man wearing an FBI jacket, jeans, and glasses peeked into the room. "Agent Moretti."

Alexander looked up briefly before returning his attention to the screen in front of him, trying to hide his interest. He caught his lip between his teeth, rewinding the camera feeds in slow motion to see if his hunch was right.

"Yes. What is it?" Alexander overheard Moretti inquire in the background. His attention remained fixed to the laptop screen, continuing to rewind and fast forward through the camera feed, jotting down the time code displayed. *00:12:36. 00:17:50. 00:23:04. 00:28:18.*

"Five minutes and fourteen seconds," he whispered.

Starting at just before midnight, there was a skip in the video every five minutes and fourteen seconds. During each of those five minute intervals, a raccoon ran across the driveway at the same exact place. He didn't think it possible, but someone was able to manipulate the video feed to set it on a loop. There were only two or three people who could even log on and access the server.

"We've been in touch with the tech team at Mr. Burnham's security firm," the agent told Moretti. "They've granted our team access to the system information from last night to see if we can find anything suspicious."

"I already checked the system myself," Alexander interrupted. "There were no entries at all. The system logs every time someone uses their unique code and fingerprint to enter."

"In cases like these, where the victim usually knows the suspect, we like to control everything," Moretti explained. "Someone may have been able to pull this off because they had access to your system and were able to manipulate it." He turned back to the agent. "What did you come up with?"

"It took a bit of digging. There were a few entries over the past twenty-four hours, but nothing after eighteen hundred hours last night, which is about the same time Mrs. Burnham confirmed she arrived home with her daughter after taking her ice skating. We looked into the database that logs all these entries to see if there were any irregularities."

"And were there?"

"At first glance, no."

"But you found something, didn't you?"

The FBI agent looked at Alexander, hesitating briefly, then back to Moretti. "Yes. We found evidence that an entry into the house had been deleted from the system. At approximately thirty-three minutes past midnight this morning, someone gained access to the house through the front door. The code and fingerprint used belonged to one Leroy Martin."

TWELVE

December 19 - 10:15 AM

In a daze, Alexander walked calmly and deliberately down the long corridor to the living room. He wanted to believe it was just someone trying to point the finger at Martin, but how could he argue with the fact that his code and thumbprint were used to gain entry, then deleted?

His footsteps seemed to thunder in his head, the sound of hurried voices in the living room like crashing waves against the shore. Agent Moretti's words echoed in his mind as he struggled to think clearly. What if he was right? What if Martin *was* bitter when Alexander left the navy to take over the company? Did Martin really view everything Alexander had as something that should have been his? For the past several years, he had encouraged Alexander to spend more time with his family and away from the office, saying he didn't want his work to consume his life like it had his father. Alexander had refused over and over again, thinking he was needed. Maybe this was Martin's final play in getting Alexander to step down.

The living area was still buzzing with activity, but now there were even more people here. The uniform of the day seemed to be a navy blue jacket, "FBI" in big, bold letters on the back. Some agents snapped photos of every square inch of the house. Others hovered over a large table in the dining area, staring at a map. Alexander's eyes zeroed in on Martin standing in the corner, his arms wrapped around his mother, offering comfort.

Heat rose in his body at the duplicity of it all. There *he* was, acting as if he were truly upset by Melanie's disappearance, when all the evidence pointed to him being the one responsible for it. Alexander's heart pounded when he saw him place a reassuring kiss on the top of his mother's platinum hair. All he could think was how he had been duped… how they all had. He put his trust in him, like his father had, but when Martin realized he'd never run the company, he decided to hit him where it hurt…by taking his daughter, then probably demanding a hefty ransom.

Alexander strolled casually toward the fireplace, all the stockings hung by the chimney with care. His eyes caught Melanie's name on her stocking just to the left of where the man he had trusted with his life stood, acting as if nothing were wrong. Rage filled him. His vision became cloudy, his throat grew dry, his heart pounded in his ears.

"Mr. Burnham, sir," Martin said, noticing him enter the living area. He stepped toward Alexander. "Is everything all right?"

Alexander snapped at the fake worry etched on his face. Martin had him fooled. He had them *all* fooled. Reeling back, he delivered a powerful left hook to Martin's jaw, knocking him to the ground. Alexander vaguely heard his mother screaming at him that he'd lost his mind, but he ignored her. His head was a complete haze. He'd reverted back to his training. Shoot first, ask questions later.

"Where is she?" he demanded, his eyes wild, vicious, untamed.

"Where is who?" Martin responded, holding his jaw, caught off guard.

Alexander pressed his shoe against Martin's throat,

getting a twisted satisfaction out of watching him struggle for air as he grasped his leg. His face turned a shade of purple and red as he fought for every breath. Officers and other law enforcement officials attempted to disengage Alexander, but he remained steadfast. Their interrogation methods would be completely inept against someone like Martin, who had been trained to withstand some of the worst situations imaginable and still not disclose any information. He would keep them running around in circles, chasing down every false lead, while Melanie remained lost. Alexander couldn't let that happen.

"Melanie!" he roared through the lump in his throat. Every inch of him ached from not seeing it all sooner. "Your code and thumbprint were logged in when you came here last night! You tried to erase your tracks, but you failed to realize that nothing online is ever truly erased. *Where…is…she?*"

His chest heaved as he stared into Martin's frightened and confused dark eyes, looking for a sign that proved he betrayed him, as all the evidence led him to believe. He was torn between wanting to do permanent damage to Martin for destroying his family and wanting to stop the pain he was causing him. Something about this didn't seem right.

"Why would I take her?" Martin strained with labored breaths, his voice barely audible. "I've treated her like I would my own granddaughter. Do you think I haven't been affected by her disappearance? Because I have, Alex. All morning long, all I've thought was that I could have done something to prevent this from happening. The pain you're feeling, that Olivia's feeling, that your mother's feeling…" Martin gasped as Alexander let up the pressure against his throat slightly, still keeping him trapped to the floor. "I feel it, too."

Alexander didn't know what to think, what to believe, his emotions at war with his rationale. He knew Martin. Hell, he was a better father figure to him than his own father was. Martin had put his life on the line countless times to save Alexander. If he truly wanted to take over the company, why would he have done that? Still, Alexander couldn't ignore the hard evidence — the entry code, the thumbprint, the manipulation of the records.

In a swift move, he grabbed Martin by the throat, picked him up, and pinned him against the wall, pulling his gun from his holster and holding it against the man's head.

"Don't give me that sob story," he ground out. "You were pissed when I came back and took over my father's company, the company he had pretty much groomed *you* to run. You must have been planning this for months, maybe even years. Wait until I was distracted, take Melanie, cover your tracks, then demand a hefty ransom in exchange for her safe return, all because you felt cheated out of my father's company. I never thought you'd be capable of such deceitfulness and spite, but I guess I was wrong about you."

"Alex!" a stern voice yelled.

Alexander snapped out of his hate-filled trance and looked at his mother, her dark eyes begging him to be reasonable. But all reason had left him the minute he walked into Melanie's empty bedroom. He needed answers, and he didn't care what he had to do to get them, including actions of questionable legality.

"I was nowhere near here last night!" Martin explained. "You can waste all the time you want blaming me, but it won't bring Melanie back."

"Then where were you?!" He pressed his gun harder against Martin's head, completely ignoring the officers who now had their weapons pointed at him. They could threaten to shoot him all they wanted. He wasn't going to let up until he had answers.

Opening his mouth to respond, Martin scanned the room and hesitated, as if he were trying to figure out his story.

"*Tell me!*" Alexander bellowed, imploring him to come forward with an alibi. This man had stood by his side through everything. He had lost his daughter this morning. He didn't know if he could handle losing Martin, too.

Martin swallowed hard, uncertainty in his gaze. Alexander pinched his lips together, his breathing labored, the gun in his hand like a ticking time bomb. His nostrils flaring, he begged, "Please, tell me."

"He was with me!" Alexander's mother, Colleen, answered, catching him off guard.

He shot his eyes to her as she approached them, her murderous expression making him feel like a four-year-old little boy instead of the forty-year-old man he was. Mothers had a habit of doing that. He could face some of the most vile and dangerous men who walked the earth, but put him in an interrogation room with his mother and she'd have him singing like a canary in a coal mine in a matter of seconds.

"Ma?" Struggling to hide his confusion, Alexander focused on his mother's eyes as she placed her hands on his biceps, trying to placate him.

"Martin was with me from around eleven last night to just after seven this morning."

Alexander's lips parted as he looked from his mother to Martin, then back at his mom again. He stepped back, lowering his pistol.

"What was he doing with you last night?"

"I don't kiss and tell, dear," she answered sarcastically. "I'm not so sure you'd be interested in the details."

Alexander shot his eyes to Martin, who was readjusting his suit and rubbing his neck. He felt a pang of guilt when he saw the red bruise beginning to form. Martin shrugged, his expression offering him a silent apology.

"Wha…? I mean, how…? I mean…" Alexander slumped onto the couch, defeated. As much as he didn't want to believe Martin was the one behind Melanie's disappearance, at least it was *something*. Now all he had was the knowledge that whoever did this was sly enough to obtain Martin's security code and thumbprint to gain entry into the house.

"He wanted to tell you years ago, but I wouldn't let him," Colleen explained.

"Years? This has been going on for…" He shook his head.

"He's always been a good friend of the family," she continued. "After your father passed, I found myself missing him more than I thought I would. In his line of work, I knew the probability of me outliving him was very high, but when I heard he was killed… I don't know." She sighed, joining Alexander on the couch, grabbing his hand in hers. "I got through the funeral being the strong woman everyone thought me to be. But when the dust settled and I was surrounded by Thomas' ghost, I guess I just wanted to be able to share my pain with someone. Leroy and I, well… We mourned your father together. When I finally moved back to the Boston area after Melanie was born, what started out as a friendship based on shared grief blossomed into something neither one of us expected."

"I'm sorry I never said anything, sir," Martin offered in his normal, curt tone, his voice a little scratchy. "I assure you my relationship with your mother has never interfered with my ability to carry out my responsibilities and it never will."

Alexander nodded, still in a daze as he processed this new information and how he'd never put the pieces together before. Shaking his head, he wrapped his arms around his mother.

"I'm happy for you, Ma." Kissing her platinum hair, he pulled away and stood up, approaching Martin. "For both of you." He offered his hand to Martin, who shook it. "But if you hurt her," Alexander said in a low voice, gesturing to where he just had Martin pinned to the ground, gasping for air, "that was just a taste of what you can expect to see from me."

"Sir," Martin nodded, then broke his composure briefly and gave Alexander a small smile.

"Mr. Burnham," Agent Moretti interrupted. "If you two are done sorting this out, I'd like to get back to the investigation since Martin apparently has an alibi." He looked at Martin. "We do need to speak to you about how someone could have obtained your security code and thumbprint."

He stepped forward. "I'm more than happy to answer any of your questions."

"I can also have my tech guy help with that," Alexander offered. "He may be able to shine some light on the safeguards in place in our computer systems."

"I would certainly like to speak with him, as well." He pulled out his notepad again. "What's his name?"

Alexander narrowed his gaze, cognizant of Moretti's thinking. "Jamie Simpson, but I wouldn't waste your time investigating him. Yes, he has the expertise to hack into even the most stringent computer systems, but he has no motive. Plus, he was at the office all night working on a few things for me."

"That may be so," Moretti said, "but I'd like to be the judge of whether or not he had anything to do with this. If what you say is true, I'm sure we can quickly cross him off our list. In the meantime, the rest of the CARD team is setting up the command center at an elementary school just down the street. They're already combing through hundreds of tips received from the amber alert. We have local agents going door to door, asking if anyone noticed anything suspicious last night."

"Door to door?" Alexander interjected, his voice rising. "That's your solution to finding my daughter? Asking people if they've seen anything suspicious? I thought the FBI was supposed to be experts at this type of thing!" He paced the room, tugging at his dark hair. He knew all these things were important, but he wanted answers. He wanted to know they were close to finding Melanie.

"Mr. Burnham, I assure you, we're exploring every avenue possible. Based on what we know so far, this was a meticulously planned abduction. To that end, I've been in contact with your publicist. We've agreed to go ahead with a press conference this afternoon. Both you and your wife will be present. Many times, it's the public's assistance that helps solve these cases, but we need to give them a reason to tear themselves away from their smart phones and keep their eyes peeled for your little girl. We need to make the public think of Melanie as their daughter, too, so they feel vested in her safe return."

"That's it? That's your genius plan? Have the public do your job for you?"

"Mr. Burnham—" Moretti began.

"Do you think that will work?" Olivia interrupted, squeezing Alexander's arm. When he shot his fiery gaze to hers, she gave him a pleading look. Reluctantly, he bit back his temper.

"It might. It might not," Moretti answered truthfully,

causing Alexander's frustration with him to rise. "But, right now, we need to try everything to find your daughter."

"Do whatever you want," Alexander barked, "but while you and your team waste time going door to door and setting up a command center, I'm going to do what *you* should be doing right now instead of drinking my coffee…and that's finding my daughter."

He grabbed Olivia's hand, pulling her toward the garage. He didn't want to be in that house anymore, the memories of Melanie ripping him open. Her soul was carved in the wood frames. Her laughter was in the nails that held it together. Her spirit was in the air he breathed.

"Mr. Burnham, I must insist you stay out of the investigation," Agent Moretti ordered. Alexander spun around to face him, his eyes narrowed. "You're personally involved and can't possibly act with a clear head, which could not only endanger your life and the lives of all the law enforcement officers here who are *trained* to find missing children, but it could put your own daughter's life at risk. Your best course is to remain out of sight and out of the way. All we need is for you to attend the press conference. Let your wife do all the speaking. She's a much more…likable person than you are. Hold her hand. Rub her back if she cries. But under no circumstances should you conduct your own investigation."

Alexander took several slow steps toward him, glowering. "I'll play your little game, Agent Moretti, but there's nothing you can do to stop me from doing everything within my power to find my daughter. You're right. I *am* personally involved. Sometimes the only time you can get things done is when the stakes are high. And the stakes have never been higher, so I suggest you stay out of my way." He turned away from him, pulling Olivia with him.

"I can have you arrested for interfering with an ongoing police investigation!" Moretti called after him.

"You'd get crucified by the media!" he shouted over his shoulder. Pausing, he faced him once more. "I can just see the headlines. *FBI Agent Jails Kidnap Victim's Father.* I'm not so sure the boys in blue need any more bad publicity these days. Don't interfere with my work, and I won't interfere with yours."

Moretti opened his mouth to respond, then snapped it shut.

"That's what I thought." Alexander spun around again, grabbing Olivia's hand and heading toward the garage.

"If you find anything, you'd better tell me!" Moretti shouted, his authoritative tone waning as he made one last stand.

"Likewise," Alexander said, having no intention of following through on his promise. He couldn't quite pinpoint what it was, but something about Agent Moretti and his vast knowledge of his family's history didn't sit well with him. Like the agent said, everyone's a suspect until proven otherwise…including Moretti.

"Alex, slow down!" Olivia ordered as he pulled her out of the house and through the garage. The large door was open, letting in the frigid winter air, while crime scene techs searched for evidence Alexander was certain they'd never find. Moretti was right. This was a thoroughly planned abduction. Whoever took Melanie wouldn't mess up and leave fingerprints or a hair fiber behind.

Finally able to breathe again for the first time since entering the house this morning, Alexander stopped and drew Olivia into his arms, hugging her tight. He needed to feel something real, something tangible in a world that seemed to turn on its head in the matter of just a few hours.

He kissed the top of her head, burying his face in her dark curls. Ever since the reality of what happened set in and their house became flooded with law enforcement, Olivia had been surprisingly composed. She had remained focused, just as Alexander had, worried that one missed detail could mean the difference between finding Melanie and having to watch the sun fall this evening, praying she survived the cold night wherever she was. Now that they were alone and away from judgmental eyes, they could finally let go. They had been through many ups and downs over the course of their relationship, but through it all, even when the outcome looked bleak, they always found their way back to each other.

But never before had they faced a storm of this magnitude. Alexander feared their love wouldn't be strong enough to survive the clouds shrouding their world with darkness.

A sob reverberated in the still air and Olivia clutched onto Alexander's back, squeezing with all her might. Her tall, slender body trembled uncontrollably, the flashing lights of the police cruisers an ominous background to her breakdown. Alexander wanted nothing more than to let out all the emotions he'd been forced to bottle up all morning, but he remained strong, being the rock of support Olivia needed.

He wished he could say something that would assure her everything was going to be okay, but it would just be an empty promise. He had no way of knowing whether everything would work out. But he did know he was going to do everything within his power to fix this.

"I'm going to find her," he mumbled in a soft voice, swallowing the lump in his throat. "I promise you, love."

She pulled her head away from his chest and tilted it back, her brown eyes wet with tears. "How, Alex? How are

you going to find her?" She covered her mouth as she struggled to breathe through her heavy cries.

"I don't know," he answered honestly, comforting her the
only way he knew how…within the shelter of his arms. "But
I'm not going to leave any stone uncovered."

She pulled away from him, wiping her tears. "The FBI
thinks it could have a connection to one of your company's
contracts. Do you—?"

"I'm not ruling anything out," he replied. "As much as I
don't want to give that man any credit, it's a very strong
possibility. I've pissed off a lot of people…" He closed his
eyes, letting out a breath as he considered the monumental
task of narrowing down precisely who could have done this.
"Some of them certainly have enough training and resources
to be able to orchestrate something like this." He held both
her arms, staring deep into her brown eyes.

His voice grew louder, more assured. "I don't want you to
worry, Olivia. I have just as much training and resources
available, without the bureaucratic red tape the FBI has to
deal with. I *will* find our daughter and bring her home, and
when I do, we'll never have to worry about anything like this
happening again. I promise you."

He released her and stepped toward the SUV, opening
the passenger door.

"Maybe I should stay here," she said, pulling her bottom
lip between her teeth as she looked between Alexander and
the door to the house. "Just in case she…" Her breath
hitched.

"Martin and my mother will take care of things around
here. I already lost half my heart today. I'm not going to lose
you, too," Alexander said forcefully, his voice almost a growl
before his expression grew tender, loving, reverent.
Approaching her, he cupped her cheek. "I don't know who

took Melanie or why. I failed her by not being here when I should have been. I won't fail you, too." He placed a soft kiss on her nose and helped her into the SUV, then ran around to get behind the wheel.

A heavy silence fell between them as Alexander drove down the long, tree-lined driveway and out the front gate, the police lights disappearing behind them. Olivia reached across the center console, resting her hand on his jean-clad leg, squeezing gently.

"Please don't blame yourself for this," she said, her voice no louder than a whisper.

"I don't know if I can do that," he answered, keeping his eyes glued to the road as the miles flew by, both of them probably thinking the same thing... Melanie could be anywhere.

THIRTEEN

No matter how hard Rayne tried, she couldn't get warm. Rubbing her arms, she glanced around the two-story house where they were now holed up, the walls barren, the ceiling showing signs of water damage. Her eyes settled on Mark sitting at a table in the dining area. He appeared so relaxed, leaning back in his chair, his feet propped on the table, flipping between all the national news networks as they broadcast the same story…the abduction of the daughter of the man who owned one of the largest and most successful private security firms in the world.

Rayne should have felt a rush of satisfaction when the reporters commented about the irony of it all. Here was a man who was in the business of keeping people safe, yet he couldn't extend that luxury to his own daughter. She should have felt thrilled that she finally did something to make the man responsible for Landon's death feel the pain she'd endured for a year now. She should have felt at peace.

But she didn't.

Her stomach churned every time she glanced at the television and saw a photo of the girl they now had locked away in the cold, damp basement of wherever they were. Mark had it all planned out, down to having somewhere to keep the girl. Rayne's suspicions that he had been wanting to do this for quite some time continued to mount with each passing second. He knew everything about Alexander and his family. He knew where they lived. He knew all the details of their security system. He knew how to access the online database and manipulate it. He even had the code and fingerprint to gain access to the house. It was as if he had been planning on doing this no matter what, so why did he need her?

She felt duped and betrayed. She thought he truly understood her pain and grief. Instead, Mark used that to his advantage, preying on her vulnerability.

"Will you sit down already?" Mark said, breaking through the stiff silence. "You're making me nervous."

Rayne continued pacing. "You *should* be nervous! Don't you feel just a hint of remorse? That what we did was wrong?"

"You mean what *you* did," he said in a condescending tone, picking up a newspaper and flipping through it. The Mark sitting at the table as if he didn't have a care in the world seemed like a completely different person. Rayne began to wonder if she really knew him at all. "I only got you inside the house. Anything you did there is all on you."

Over the past few hours, as she waited nervously for him to announce their next move, jumping out of her skin every time the sound of police sirens approached, she had heard him quietly talking on his cell phone in a language she couldn't quite place. Ever since she'd met Mark, Rayne had thought he was second-generation Greek, as he had led her to believe. He had olive-toned skin, dark hair, dark eyes, and no accent. Now, it was all different.

"Which never would have happened if you didn't push me," she retorted. "Why did you care so much? What could you possibly gain out of me doing this? I've seen Alexander in action. He won't stop until he's turned over every rock, searched every abandoned warehouse, questioned every person who has any connection to him and his family. We may get away with this for a little while, but not for long."

"I don't need that long," he said in a sinister voice. "Just enough time to get back what he has no right to."

"What do you mean?" Rayne asked, furrowing her brow as a heaviness set in her chest. Her limbs felt like they were chained to the floor, a weight preventing her from moving.

"Exactly what I said," he responded, barely looking up. "He's wronged countless people over the years. It's my job to make it right."

"Why did you even involve me? It sounds like you were going to do something like this anyway."

He glanced up. "I needed someone who had been in that house before and knew exactly where the girl's bedroom was. Sure, I could have done it myself and figured it out, but as you saw tonight, the less time it took, the more likely we were to get away. And look at us! No one has a clue. Thanks to you, we were in and out of there in less than five minutes."

Rayne crept toward him, the room spinning around her. "You *used* me," she declared, hurt, upset, and frustrated, but more at herself for falling for this kind of trap.

She caught her reflection in a cracked, dusty mirror hanging on the wall. She should have known Mark wasn't who he said he was. How could someone as attractive as he be drawn to her? Her appearance had deteriorated over the months, the woman staring back at her a shell, physically and mentally, of who she once was. She had no redeeming qualities. She treated Mark like crap, yet he still came back to her over and over. She should have known he had an ulterior motive.

"No more than you used me to try to forget about your

dead fiancé. It's been a year, Rayne," he hissed with venom in his tone. "Move on. He's not coming back."

"You can't compare the two!" she shrieked. "I used you for sex, to forget for a minute, not to commit a felony!" Her lip trembled, wishing this were all just one big nightmare. How could she have been so blind? She was smarter than this. Landon had taught her to be extra cautious. He liked to see the good in people, but he also said the devil often disguised himself in sheep's clothes. She should have seen the signs earlier. Mark always seemed more interested in Landon and his line of work than her own past. At first, Rayne thought he was offering her a shoulder to cry on, allowing her to reminisce about the times she had shared with Landon. Now that she knew the truth, that he used her to commit this horrible crime, it all made sense.

"You're just feeling a bit of remorse. It's completely normal after your first time. I was paranoid after my first time, too." He got up from the chair, slowly approaching Rayne.

She gaped at him, shocked that he could talk about this so nonchalantly, as if it were no big deal. She wondered how many other felonies he had committed.

"You need to stop sweating the small stuff and look at the bigger picture here." He placed his hands on her arms and met her violet eyes. "You can finally make peace with Landon's death."

"But his daughter…," she pleaded softly. "She did nothing wrong. Why does she have to suffer?"

"An unfortunate casualty, but they need to be motivated to return what's been taken. If we didn't do this, they'd never see all the wrong they've done. They'll never think twice about changing their ways."

"What did he do?" Rayne asked, intrigued by the passion in Mark's voice.

"I've seen countless families torn apart. I don't have to explain to you how difficult it is to sit down to dinner and see an empty chair at the table." He grabbed her hands in his. His expression softened, his eyes pleading. Mr. Hyde had transformed back into Dr. Jekyll. "Yes, I lied to you, Rayne. I'm sorry I wasn't transparent with you from the beginning. I knew who you were. I followed Landon's story on the news. I kept tabs on you. I'd observed you from afar and knew you wouldn't talk to me if I just showed up on your doorstep, so I decided to go to the same grief counseling session you'd been attending. At first, my goal was just to find out more about Alexander Burnham. After all, you were engaged to his friend. Then something unexpected happened," he said, his voice becoming soft as he gazed upon her with all the tenderness and warmth Landon used to.

"What's that?" she whispered, a lone tear falling down her cheek.

He sighed, his taut stature relaxing. A smile spread across his full lips. "I fell in love."

"You what?" Her voice rose in pitch. She searched his eyes, unsure what to believe. This was a man who had admittedly used her to further his own personal vendetta. Could she really believe that he loved her? She didn't know, but dammit if she didn't miss the feeling of bliss that went with being loved.

"I don't expect you to believe a word that comes out of my mouth," Mark said, reading her mind. "I wouldn't after everything I put you through. But you need to know you're loved, especially after all these months of thinking no one could ever care about you the way Landon did. I never had the pleasure of meeting him, but the way you've talked about him, I know he must have been special. I don't expect you to return these same feelings, but I thought, after everything you've been through, you deserved to know you're valued." He reached out, swiping at the tear falling down her cheek. "That you're loved, Rayne."

"I don't know what you want me to say," she responded, trying to regain her composure.

The ache she had been living with grew dull for the first time in months. Maybe she was stuck in a rut because she refused to believe she deserved to move on. Perhaps Mark was right. Perhaps she *did* deserve to know her life still had value.

"I don't know what to think right now," she admitted. Thoughts swirled in her head, some shouting at her that this was just another one of Mark's lies. She knew she shouldn't trust him, but part of her wanted to be loved again. Love was like a drug, and Rayne was an addict who had gone so long without experiencing that unmistakable rush of euphoria, she was more than happy to overlook all of Mark's faults.

"I know. I get it. And to prove I mean what I say…" He took a deep breath, taking her hands in his. "If you want to turn me in, I'll take the fall for all this. Your name will never come up. Here." He released his hold on her hands and grabbed a cell phone from his pocket. "Go ahead and call it in. Right now. I'm willing to go to prison for the rest of my life to prove my words are true."

She raised her eyebrows, staring at the smart phone as if it contained the launch codes for several destructive missiles. Rayne wanted to do what was right. Overwhelmed with hatred for everything that had been taken from her, she'd acted impulsively when she agreed to take the girl. Now, in the light of day, regret churned in her stomach. She thought she'd feel better knowing she hit Alexander where it hurt, but she didn't. Guilt for hurting one of Landon's friends consumed her. She feared her conscience would never be clear unless she did something to make it right.

Torn, Rayne glanced around the room. Her gaze settled on the television and she stared, listening intently to the reporter talk about a press conference scheduled in an hour's time where both Alexander and Olivia Burnham would appear to discuss their missing daughter.

"How about this?" Mark said, noticing her rapt attention on the report. "Why don't you go to the press conference? Look into Alexander's eyes, see if you still feel the same remorse. If you do, go ahead and turn me in. If not, well, we'll get back to work."

"And if I turn you in?"

He shrugged. "No hard feelings. And, I swear, your name will never come up."

"You would do that for me?"

He smiled at her, drawing her into his arms. "I told you, Rayne. I love you. That's what people who love each other do. They put their loved one's needs ahead of their own." Cupping her cheeks, he brought her head toward his, kissing her forehead.

She closed her eyes, relishing in Mark's proximity. The heat was so much more charged, more intense.

"Now, you'd better get going."

A chill replaced the warmth and she opened her eyes to see Mark heading toward the window and peering out at the street. She had a strange feeling that if she walked out that door, she'd never see him again. She didn't want to leave, but she needed to be at that press conference. She didn't know why. All she knew was something inside her pulled her toward Boston City Hall that gray Saturday morning. Maybe she needed to see their pain, know that Alexander was suffering just as she had. Then he'd understand.

Retreating to the couch, she grabbed her coat and pulled it on, searching for her backpack. She could have sworn she dropped it beside the couch when they walked into the house in the middle of the night. Now, it was nowhere to be found.

She retraced her steps, checking the bathroom and bedroom, banging drawers and cabinets shut in her futile search. She stormed back into the living area and ripped the cushions off the couch.

"What's wrong?" Mark asked, turning around.

"I can't find my bag. It was right here. I put the scarf Landon bought me in it, and now…" Her voice grew frantic. "What if I left it at…?" She trailed off, the thought of having left her bag at Alexander's house churning her stomach. It wasn't because it could have been connected to her. It was because one of her last gifts from Landon was in it.

"Relax, Rayne." Mark approached her, rubbing her arms. "You fell asleep. I wanted to keep it in a safe place, just in case."

He disappeared up the stairs as Rayne tried to steady her nerves. A wave of relief washed over her when he returned with her bag in his hands, the scarf from Landon peeking out of the front pouch.

"Better?" he asked, handing it over.

"Much," she said, taking it from him and slinging it over her shoulder.

"There's something in there for you, but promise me you won't peek until after the press conference and you've made up your mind."

"What is it?" she asked, intrigued. It had been so long since anyone had given her a gift.

"You'll just have to wait to find out." He winked.

Allowing a small smile to form on her lips, she nodded, then headed toward the door.

"Oh, and Rayne?" She looked over her shoulder at him. "No matter what you choose, I'll still love you."

Bathed in the warmth of his words, she beamed at him, then continued toward the back door, ignoring the cries for help emanating from the padlocked basement.

FOURTEEN

"Are you going to get that?" Olivia asked Alexander as she paced in front of the floor-to-ceiling windows in his twenty-ninth floor penthouse office, looking down at the Boston city streets below.

The phone had been ringing almost constantly since they arrived a half-hour ago. The story of Melanie's abduction had hit the mid-morning news at both the local and national level. Alexander's publicist handled all the requests for an official statement, but that didn't stop acquaintances and work colleagues from calling him to personally offer their condolences and assistance. World leaders, diplomats, politicians…some of whom were on his list of possible suspects. Each took him away from what he needed to focus on. After the tenth call in so many minutes, he simply ignored his phone, allowing it to ring over and over again. It was better than sitting in an uncomfortable, awkward silence.

"No, I'm not." He looked up and met Olivia's eyes briefly. His focus shifted to the large expanse of the city visible behind her, the office and everything in it disappearing.

Helplessness washed over him as he stared at the large buildings and multitude of maze-like streets. His daughter could be anywhere, and he didn't even have so much as a small lead as to her whereabouts. He had scratched out a list of about a dozen people who he believed had the motive, means, and wherewithal to carry out such a crime, digging into their records to see if anything popped up. He had Simpson looking into whether he could track where Martin's log in to the system came from last night, but it would take some time. Other than that, he was at the mercy of Agent Moretti and the CARD team's investigation. If Moretti had made any progress, he wasn't sharing the information with Alexander. Based on their conversation earlier in the day, he figured he was probably the last person Moretti would call.

"Can you at least turn the ringer off then?" Olivia huffed. "It's driving me crazy."

Reaching for the phone on his desk, he slid the ringer off, silence falling over the room once more.

"Thank you." She let out a breath, crossing her arms over her stomach. She rubbed her biceps, warming herself, despite the fact his office felt like a sauna. Roaming the large space, she stopped and peered at framed photos hanging on the wall of Alexander and various diplomats as if she had never seen them before. It was clear she was trying to think of anything other than their missing daughter. Alexander doubted that was possible.

Sighing, he returned his tired eyes to the file in front of him, scanning the dossier of a former drug lord the DEA had contracted his company to track down and dispose of by any means necessary. A local liaison, who ended up being dirty, gave the drug lord a heads-up, but not before Alexander's agents destroyed all his cocaine processing houses and coca plants. Millions and millions of dollars of product had been incinerated in the Colombian night air. The man was eventually put on trial and imprisoned, but had recently been granted parole, the circumstances behind it still vague. Even so, he was no more or less capable of pulling this off than every other person on Alexander's list of suspects. Sure, he had the motive and means to do this, particularly because kidnapping seemed to be this cartel's specialty, but it didn't fit. Alexander's gut told him he didn't do it. Granted, he had lost what most people would consider a small fortune, but he had taken a page out of Pablo Escobar's playbook and had buried the equivalent of the operating budget of a small country all over the place. Losing a hundred million dollars was just a drop in the bucket to this guy.

"What's all this?" Olivia interrupted.

"What's all what?" Alexander replied, not even looking up. He couldn't afford to waste a second of time.

"All these papers," she answered in an even tone, masking any trepidation or unease she felt about Melanie's disappearance.

Alexander raised his head to see her flipping through the folder containing all the information he had been going through yesterday.

"Background checks on Mischa," he answered through the pang of guilt in his chest.

"You never did invite her to Christmas, did you?" Olivia inquired in a non-accusatory tone, but he couldn't help but hear the unspoken allegation in her voice.

"I meant to, but…"

"I know. Life got busy." She cast her eyes back to the papers, the rustling the only sound in the too-quiet room. "One holiday goes by. Then another. Then it's been a year. At that point, it'll just seem strange to call out of the blue. I'm guilty of it, too." Her voice grew soft as she ran her fingers across the photo of Mischa, then Rayne. "Not anymore, though," she added in a whisper.

"Not anymore," Alexander repeated, then hesitated, feeling as if he needed to be completely honest with his wife regarding the past twenty-four hours. "Olivia…," he began.

"Yes?" She looked up.

"You remember Landon's fiancée, right?"

"The redhead. Rayne. This woman, correct?" She held up the photo, pointing to a beautiful, exuberant woman who appeared to not have a care in the world.

He paused briefly as he stared into those haunting lilac eyes. "I saw her yesterday."

Olivia scrunched her eyebrows. "Where?"

"Here," he answered. "Except I didn't realize it. I walked right past her as I headed into the building, but I didn't recognize her." He closed his eyes, warding off the guilt eating away at him. Lately, he had been carrying too much responsibility on his shoulders for what happened to Landon, and now Mischa. Was it his fault Rayne had spiraled downward, too? "She's thin, pale, almost looks like she came from a homeless shelter, which would probably be a step up from the squalor she now lives in."

"You've been to her house?" Olivia stepped toward him, glued to his every word.

Alexander nodded slightly. "When I finally realized who she was, I tracked down her address to the slums of Dorchester. As if losing her fiancé wasn't bad enough, she lost everything else, too." Shaking his head, he let out a slow breath. He closed his eyes, pinching the bridge of his nose. "When did I become like this?" He looked at Olivia, pain in his eyes. "When did I become my father? How did I let that happen?"

"What do you mean, Alex?" She walked toward him. "Where is this coming from?"

"Just something I've been thinking about the past few days," he admitted with a sigh. He rubbed his temples, then met her eyes. "Until Dave called me down to that fishing warehouse in Southie, it had been months since I'd even thought of Landon or Mischa…or Rayne."

"You're extremely busy, Alex," Olivia offered in sympathy.

He let out a humorless laugh. "That's the same thing my mother used to tell me when I asked why Dad was never home. He let his work consume him. Looking at everything that's happened the past few days, all I can think is I've done the same thing. If I had been more involved, maybe Mischa would still be alive and Rayne wouldn't be living—"

"You can't beat yourself up over this." Olivia grabbed his hands, kneeling in front of him. "You are *not* your father. Do you work a lot? Yes, but I know it's because you care about what you do. You work hard so all your employees can provide for their families."

"But I couldn't even take the time to make sure Landon's fiancée was provided for?" He raised his eyebrows.

"Alex, you did everything you could to make sure she'd be okay. You said so yourself. For weeks after the funeral, she wouldn't allow you in to even check on her."

"I could have pushed harder. I could have forced her to let me in. I guess I thought since I paid all that money for the bakery, she'd be okay."

Olivia stood up and leaned on the corner of the desk, her brows furrowed. "How did she end up living in Dorchester with all the money you gave her?"

Alexander shrugged. "I have no idea. I checked her bank accounts and she barely has twenty dollars to her name. She works, but her pay isn't much more than minimum wage.

There's no record of her *ever* depositing the proceeds from the sale of the bakery."

"Did you mention any of this to Agent Moretti?"

"What? All this about Rayne?"

"Yeah. Maybe there's a connection. It's a bit curious that Rayne suddenly reappears in your life, after a year of intentionally shutting you out, just hours after her fiancé's sister is found brutally murdered and just before your own daughter…" She turned her head, unable to say the words. She took a steadying breath, then met Alexander's eyes once more. "I just think maybe whoever did this might be closer to the family than we want to believe."

"Maybe," Alexander said, humoring her. "Or maybe she was trying to come to terms with Mischa's death, as well. She may have simply been revisiting the past and that's why she was standing outside this building. I'm not so sure they teach Computer Hacking 101 in culinary school," Alexander added, trying not to sound too sarcastic. Olivia was simply trying to offer a fresh perspective, but being able to manipulate the company's online database, not to mention break through its firewall and various other security protocols, as well as have enough knowledge to somehow secure Martin's thumbprint required advanced training. While it had been a year since he had last spoken to Rayne, he simply couldn't see her being able to pull something like this off.

"I know, but—"

"Excuse me, Mr. Burnham," a voice said, interrupting Olivia. "Mrs. Burnham."

Simpson hurried into the room, carrying what appeared to be a rather large accordion file, placing it on the desk. Olivia took this as her cue to get up and head back to the sitting area of the office. Alexander felt a hint of remorse that he shot down her theory that Rayne could have been behind Melanie's disappearance, but so could countless other people who would actually be able to carry out something like this. While Rayne may have had the motive, she was lacking in the other criteria. Still, he made a mental note to dig a little more into her background.

"I'm sorry it took so long, but here's everything you requested on Vincent Moretti."

Alexander raised his eyebrows. "This is his file?"

"Yes, sir. Well, his is relatively small. Model student all through high school. Went to a community college for two years, then transferred to a state school. Studied criminology, then went straight into the police academy. He graduated at the top of his class and worked as a beat cop before being promoted to a detective in the Family Justice Division. He was only there for a short period of time before being recruited by the FBI. All this before turning thirty. Pretty impressive, if you ask me."

"Right." Alexander eyed him. "Then what's the rest of this?"

Simpson paused for a beat. "Turns out Vincent Moretti's father used to work here."

Alexander's eyes widened. "For the company?"

"Yes, sir. In this office, as a matter of fact."

"I don't recall anyone with the last name Moretti working here. Was it before my time?"

"He was here for a few months after you took over. And you wouldn't recall anyone with the last name Moretti. Vincent took his mother's maiden name when his parents divorced approximately eighteen years ago. His father's name was Joseph Mulligan."

Alexander flipped through the papers on his desk,

allowing the information to soak in. "That name sounds familiar," he commented. While he liked to think he knew everyone who worked for him, it simply wasn't possible. The company had offices all across the country and around the world, hiring hundreds of people from administration to field agents.

"He was shot approximately six months after you took over. He was on his way to his son's baseball game and was gunned down. A mob boss had put a hit out on him to prevent him from testifying in conjunction with one of his cases here. I'm still digging for details. Suffice it to say, Mulligan never made it to the baseball game."

Alexander leaned back in his chair, staring at the ceiling. Everything began to make sense. "So *that's* why this guy hates me. He thinks it's my fault his dad died. The second he got to my house, he acted like he had a permanent stick shoved up his ass." Returning his attention to the papers in front of him, he flipped through them before eyeing the time.

"Thanks for this, Simpson. I'll let you know if I need anything else."

"Certainly, sir. I understand how it looks as if I could be involved, considering how your system was hacked into. Like I told Agent Moretti, I'm more than happy to answer any questions and have an independent analyst go through all our computer systems."

"I appreciate that, Jamie," Alexander responded. "I could be wrong, but my gut tells me you're not the type to do something like this."

"Yes, sir." Simpson nodded, heading toward the door before facing Alexander once more. "Oh, and there's one more thing I probably should point out."

"What's that?" Alexander asked, getting up from his

chair and organizing all the scattered papers on his desk. He opened the drawer and placed the file in it.

"Vincent Moretti minored in computer science. Before he was put on the CARD team, he was in the Cyber Division."

Alexander slammed the desk drawer closed.

FIFTEEN

Alexander rushed into the conference room in City Hall, Olivia eyeing him with concern as she struggled to keep up with his long, determined strides. During the short drive there, he had refused to say a word.

With fierce eyes, he scanned the large room, the smell of coffee and doughnuts making him nauseated. Several FBI agents and other officials were assembled, many of them discussing the upcoming press conference and what information should be released. But Alexander was only looking for one person.

"Mr. Burnham." Agent Moretti glanced up at him briefly, ignoring his rabid demeanor, then returned his attention to a group of agents, all of them looking over a stack of papers he held in his hand.

"When were you going to tell me?" Alexander bellowed.

The room went still. His face grew red as he yanked at his tie. His wild eyes, disheveled hair, and scruffy chin gave him a crazed appearance, like a man at the end of his rope. Olivia pulled on his arm, giving him a questioning look, but Alexander didn't budge, his eyes remaining zeroed in on the agent.

Moretti remained hunched over the table, flipping through a file for a protracted moment, then faced him with an annoyed expression.

"Tell you what?"

Alexander stood tall, widening his stance. "Did you not think I'd look into your background? I found out about your father. I get it. You don't like me because you think it's my fault he was shot. So… What? You use all the training you've received on the CARD team and working cybercrimes to take my daughter, then be the first on scene to steer me in the wrong direction? You made me accuse my right-hand man, all the while standing by, knowing he wasn't the one to blame! Why?"

"Alex…" A hand grabbed his arm. He glanced at the short, graying blonde woman standing to his left, a questioning look on her face.

"Your brother doesn't know what he's talking about," Moretti said defensively to Carol, then faced Alexander. "I understand how stressful this situation can be, but throwing baseless accusations around will not bring your daughter back."

"*Baseless?*" Alexander retorted. "You had the motive and means to carry this out! So tell me, Vincent Moretti. Where were you this morning around 12:30?"

He shook his head, avoiding Alexander's eyes, his face growing flush. "I don't have to answer that," he hissed through clenched teeth, then turned around, walking away.

"Why? You think you're above the law?"

"*I am the law!*" Moretti shouted, spinning back toward him, leaning his hands on the table as he took a defensive stance. "And it's something I'm damn proud of! I've had to work for everything. *Everything!*" He slammed his fist on the table. "I didn't have the luxury of simply being handed a multi-billion dollar company! And you think I'd jeopardize my career over my distaste for you?" He narrowed his eyes at Alexander, the animosity he had toward him painted in every crevice on his face. "I wouldn't give you the satisfaction," he sneered. "I'm going to find your daughter, regardless of my feelings toward you. My reputation is worth more to me than that."

Alexander stared at him for several long moments, absorbing his words. He couldn't put his finger on it, but he had a feeling he wasn't getting the whole story.

"Alex, listen to him," Carol begged, tugging on his arm and bringing him out of his thoughts. He met her green eyes. "Remember what's at stake here. You need to focus on doing everything you can to help find Melanie. Okay? Starting a fight with the lead on her case isn't the way to do that. Stow that famous Burnham temper of yours for a minute and learn to work with him."

Glaring at Moretti, Alexander nodded reluctantly. "Fine."

He allowed Carol to lead him and Olivia toward a corner where his mother, brother, and Dave were assembled. He shook his head. Unable to bite back what he wanted to say, he spun back around.

"I'm sorry he died, but *I* didn't pull the trigger." He pointed to his chest, then at Moretti. "You of all people should understand that."

"You think I blame you for his death?" Moretti glowered at him. "I'm not that naïve," he scoffed.

"Then why all this hostility toward me?" Alexander asked, baffled. "I haven't done anything—"

"*Bullshit*," Moretti roared, standing tall once more. "Bullshit, Mr. Burnham. You pretend to care about your employees, but all you see are dollar signs. My mom left my dad because he was always working…for your *father*. She gave him an ultimatum — his family or his career. I guess it's not a big surprise which he chose. At least he was still making good money and had no trouble paying those alimony and child support payments. Until he died, that is. And you…," he sneered, a disgusted smile crossing his face as he scowled at Alexander with venom in his eyes, "with your flashy cars and designer suits… You denied my mother any death benefits because they were no longer married at the time. You didn't care that she could barely make ends meet without those alimony and child support payments. So, to answer your question, *that's* why I don't like you. Ever since my mother was forced to sell the house she raised me in and move us to a one-bedroom apartment, I was determined to do everything in my power to make a better life for myself and for her."

Alexander was dumbfounded. The man Moretti described sounded like a horrible person, not like the man Alexander thought he was. He prided himself on caring about his employees, paying them what he believed to be a very generous salary. Was he really as self-centered as Moretti made him out to be? He couldn't remember making a decision to deny death benefits to the family of one of his employees. He never got involved with those types of things. That was what his lawyers were for.

"Agent Moretti, I'm—"

"Stop," he declared, holding his hand up. "I don't want to hear your apologies. You might feel bad for a minute, but it won't change what we had to go through. I had to watch my mom struggle to work three jobs just to make ends meet and put me through college. I'm a better person because of it. Honestly, I'm the FBI agent I am today because of what you put us through. Yes, I'll do everything I can to bring your daughter back home safely, but that's only because I can't bear the thought of anything happening to a child, no matter who her father is. Got it?"

"Got it," Alexander murmured, speechless. He

wondered how many other people he had screwed over. How many other families had been torn apart because of his failure to take an interest? The more he looked at himself from an outsider's perspective, the more he believed he *had* turned into his father. A man who put his own needs first. A man who worked so much, he barely spent any time with his family. A man who didn't offer any apologies until it was too late. He didn't want to think that was what he had become, but how could he not when all the signs were there?

"Hey." A tall man, bearing a striking resemblance to Alexander, approached him, dragging him away from Moretti.

"Tyler… Hey," Alexander replied, his head still in a fog.

"How ya holding up?" he asked, giving Alexander a longer than usual hug. Despite the nine year age difference between the two men, Alexander felt closer to his younger brother than most people, and not just because they ran the security company together. They had been through so much over the years, Alexander couldn't help but feel as if he had a role in the man Tyler had become, and vice versa.

"Good," Alexander answered.

Tyler pulled back and muttered, "Liar."

Alexander forced a laugh and nodded, glancing over his shoulder at Moretti and the frenzied atmosphere surrounding him. Helplessness crept into his veins. He had never felt more useless than he did at that moment. It seemed everyone there had a job to do. He had a job to do, too, one he felt completely inept to actually carry out. He knew how to survive in the wild for extended periods of time. He could take out a target with his sniper rifle at nearly 2,000 yards. He could hold his breath underwater for close to two minutes without releasing a single bubble. But he had absolutely no training, other than his gut, that would help find his daughter.

"We're all here for you, Alex," Carol's husband, Dave, said, extending his hand to him, bringing his attention back to his family. He shook his hand, finding it hard to believe that not even forty-eight hours had passed since Dave asked him to meet him at a fish warehouse in Southie. That seemed like an eternity ago now. "Whatever you need, it's yours."

"Thanks for being here." Alexander pulled back, feeling everyone's eyes on him — Olivia's, his mother's, his sister's, his brother's…hell, even all the agents' and police officers'. Maybe they all knew he was responsible for Melanie's disappearance. Were they whispering amongst themselves, theorizing that had he been home, had he not put his work first, had he not turned into his father, Melanie would still be safe?

"Do you have a minute?" Dave interrupted Alexander's unsettled thoughts. He gestured toward an empty corner of the room.

"Sure," he answered, curious, following him.

"I know Mischa's murder has probably been the furthest thing from your mind," he started in hushed tones, "but it looks like your gut may have been right."

He raised his eyebrows. "What do you mean?"

"I got the final autopsy report back. On the surface, everything about the case fit the Castle Island Killer's M.O. Beaten. Stuffed into a barrel. Left in Southie. Fingernails ripped off. The only thing that didn't fit was the cause of death. His other victims either had their throats slashed or a gunshot to the head. But not Mischa. We thought maybe he was progressing his kills, but the coroner thinks something's off, especially when he studied Mischa's bruises more closely." He opened a folder and handed Alexander two photos.

"This is a close-up of one of Mischa's bruises," he explained, pointing to one of the photos. "And this is a close-up of one of his other victim's bruising. Do you see the difference?"

Alexander squinted, wishing he had brought his reading glasses with him. He couldn't see what Dave referred to. They looked practically identical. Sure, there was some discrepancy with the discoloration, but nothing stood out as being off.

"I didn't, either," Dave assured him. "There's a redness to the bruises here." He pointed to the photo of the other victim. "And if you look close enough, you can see the imprint from where a fist made contact with the victim's ribs. That's not the case here." He placed the image of Mischa's bruise on top. "This is the same exact part of Mischa's body, but the imprint is scattered, almost jagged. After doing an internal exam, seeing chips of missing bone fragments, the M.E. opined these bruises were not the result of a normal beating. It was something much worse."

Alexander met his eyes and swallowed hard. "What?" he whispered.

Dave paused for a beat, licking his lips. "Based on the appearance of the bruises and the restraint marks he found on her wrists and ankles, the M.E. believes Mischa was stoned to death."

"Stoned?" he repeated in disbelief.

"I thought it was an antiquated method of execution, but after doing a bit of research, I found some cultures still use it. There have been deaths in the Middle East reported as recently as just a few months ago attributed to an honor killing."

"Honor killing?" Alexander swallowed hard, holding onto the table to steady himself as he felt the room spinning around him. His eyes glazed over. It was useless to ignore the connection between Landon's role in the security company and Mischa's death. They had to be related. If they weren't, it was one hell of a coincidence.

"I've reached out to the agency she worked for to see if this has any connection to her job there. Maybe she pissed someone off. Who knows?" Dave shook his head, shrugging. "I hoped we'd find *something*, but that angle doesn't seem to be working out. The agency's been very forthcoming with all their records. Mischa's never even been to the Middle East. Before she was promoted to executive director, most of her fieldwork was concentrated in Africa and South America."

"So you have no leads?" Alexander exhaled, running his hands through his hair.

"We're looking into a few other things. The plant where her body was dumped recently installed security cameras. It's not the best system and leaves plenty of blind spots, but we're taking a look at the footage to see if we come up with something."

"You'll let me know if you do?" Alexander asked, even though he was pretty sure they wouldn't find anything. That would be too easy, and nothing about the events of the past few days made him think finding Mischa's killer would be easy.

"Of course." Dave closed the folder, turning as a tall brunette dressed in a dark pant suit approached with Shannon, Alexander's publicist.

"Mr. Burnham," the suit began. "I'm Agent Long. I'm part of the CARD team under the direction of Agent Moretti." She held her hand out to him and he shook it. "I've just been speaking with your publicist about how this press conference will proceed. We'd like to go over a few things with you and your wife before we get started." She headed toward the end of the conference table and sat down, opening a file. Alexander met Olivia's eyes and gestured for her to join them.

"My wife, Olivia," he said to Agent Long when she approached, and they exchanged pleasantries. Then he pulled out a chair for Olivia.

"I've spoken to Agent Moretti and he's expressed a few concerns." Shannon looked directly at Alexander. "He's of the opinion that Olivia should do most of the talking since she's the mother." She paused, allowing that to sink in. "However, I disagree. We could face serious backlash if you remain silent. The media is already in a frenzy with this story, speculating as to who could be responsible. They've been digging up everything about both you and Olivia, along with your friends and families. Unfortunately, nothing is out of bounds for some reporters." She rolled her eyes, then her expression grew serious once more. "The last thing we want to do is give the media a reason to think *you* have something to do with Melanie's disappearance," she said to Alexander. "Be warm."

"I'm—" Alexander interrupted, only to have Shannon shoot daggers at him. She had been his publicist for the better part of the past decade. She prided herself on knowing more about him than even he did.

"Be compassionate. Engaging. Do whatever you need to so you don't come off like an arrogant man who can buy his way out of anything. Your money won't bring back Melanie. This is about her and appealing to the public's sympathy. Remember that." Shannon's voice was firm as she stared Alexander down.

He hated being told what to do, but this was why his publicist had the position she did. She knew exactly how to handle the press, how to read them. As much as Alexander didn't want to think he needed someone to tell him how to act, especially when his daughter's life was at stake, he was willing to listen…for Melanie's sake.

"Understood?" She raised her eyebrows.

Alexander nodded. "Sure."

"Good. Now, I've taken the liberty of writing a few paragraphs for each of you." She pushed a few papers toward Alexander and Olivia.

"I won't be needing this." Alexander said immediately, pushing the papers back to Shannon.

He could tell Agent Long was biting her tongue. She could talk until she was blue in the face, but he wasn't about to get up there and read a prepared speech about how special his daughter was. This needed to come from his heart, not the brain of a woman whose job was ensuring his public image remained positive. He didn't care about any of that right now. All he cared about was getting his daughter back.

"I don't, either," Olivia said firmly, following Alexander's gesture.

Shannon looked at Agent Long, who narrowed her gaze at them.

"Mr. Burnham," the agent began, "I know you've been on the receiving end of the firing squad in the past, but this is different. This is personal, so the reporters may get personal in their attacks."

"I believe it may be best that we don't give them anything *to* attack you with," Shannon urged, looking between Agent Long and Alexander. He had a feeling Shannon was simply following the wishes of the FBI in trying to convince him to read a prepared statement they had approved. "Which is why I think you both should stick to the script I've prepared for you."

"With all due respect, Miss Walsh," Olivia piped up,

staring at Shannon, "Agent Long." She turned her attention to the FBI agent. "I agree with my husband." She reached next to her and grabbed Alexander's hand, a show of solidarity. "I understand your reasoning and rationale, but Melanie is *my* daughter. I'm not going to get up in front of a crowd of reporters and the public with some generic and half-hearted plea to bring her home safe. Whoever took her may be listening or watching. This may be my only opportunity to talk directly to him. I'm not going to waste it."

"Very well then," Agent Long said with a sigh. "If we can't persuade you otherwise…"

"You can't," Olivia barked, narrowing her fierce eyes on both women, almost willing either of them to try her patience.

"Agent Moretti will open the conference with information he is comfortable releasing to the public," Shannon explained. "Then the two of you will speak." She glanced at Agent Long. "Your mother, brother, and sister will also be up there with you. We need to make you relatable here, Mr. Burnham, so showing you with your family will help toward that end. Then the FBI will answer questions from the press for a few minutes. Some of these questions may be directed to you, as well. Regardless of what you're asked, always bring it back to the reason for the press conference…to beg for the public's help in finding Melanie."

"Any questions?" Agent Long looked at Alexander and Olivia.

"What precautions have you taken for security?" Alexander asked firmly.

"Precautions?"

"Yes. As your Agent Moretti aptly stated earlier this morning, we are high-profile targets. I know it's unlikely, but

I need to know precautions have been taken to ensure everyone's safety."

Agent Long opened her mouth, then glanced up.

"Security measures are in place," Moretti's voice boomed, approaching them. "Plainclothes agents will be strategically placed throughout the crowd, ready to respond, if needed. Several agents will also be on the makeshift platform with you and your family to get more of a bird's-eye view of the crowd. If there's anything suspicious, we'll know."

Alexander eyed him, not feeling reassured, but at least it was something.

"Now, are you ready?" Moretti raised his eyebrows.

Alexander looked at Olivia and squeezed her hand. "Yes." He just wanted to get the press conference over with so he could get back to finding his daughter. He didn't see how any of this would help, but he knew he had to address the public about what had happened.

"Good. Follow me."

Agent Moretti led Alexander and Olivia out of the conference room and toward the elevator. After riding down to the lobby, they emerged out the front doors and climbed onto a makeshift stage that had been hastily erected for the event, joining Tyler, Carol, Dave, and Colleen, as well as several FBI agents.

A hush fell over the substantial crowd as Agent Moretti stepped up to the podium, his voice reverberating through the speakers, echoing against the tall buildings surrounding them in the government center area of Boston. The press was positioned up front, the flash of cameras going off constantly. The sun peeked through the clouds, but there was still a damp chill in the air.

Alexander zoned out as Agent Moretti rehashed the

details of Melanie's disappearance. His brain was being pulled a thousand different directions. Who took Melanie? Who was responsible for Mischa's brutal death? What was the reason for Rayne's sudden and unexpected reappearance in his life? It all seemed so odd, so peculiar, that he couldn't help but wonder whether it was all connected.

Scanning the faces in attendance, Alexander took inventory. Some of them were familiar, others not. The flash of cameras was almost blinding, black dots obscuring his vision. Each flash was like a gun going off in the night, protecting someone who didn't deserve it. Unable to see any potential threat through the blinding lights, he felt exposed. Sweat prickled his neck, each sound amplified ten-fold. He loosened his tie, his breathing becoming labored and shallow. Stretching his neck from side to side, he tried to get rid of the tension, but nothing worked. His adrenaline spiked as he struggled to get a good bearing on his surroundings. An unsettled feeling that they were all sitting ducks formed in the pit of his stomach.

With every flash, Alexander grew more jumpy, unable to brush off his fears…until Olivia's voice rang out from the speakers. He looked to his side where he thought she had been standing, the space now empty. Instead, she stood at the podium a few feet in front of him, her voice wavering slightly, but still strong. He focused all his attention on her instead of the burgeoning crowd.

His momentary panic waning, he could finally breathe again. Olivia was the eye in the storm of his life, the compass pointing him north, the lighthouse guiding him to safety. Together, they could get through anything. Apart, they would cease to exist.

"Most little girls dream of the day they'll become a mother," she began with a quiver. "They push their little dollies around in a miniature stroller. They give them bottles. They nurture them. All of this to prepare for what many women believe to be their sole purpose in life."

She took a deep breath, glancing down before returning her attention to the rapt crowd, many of them holding signs with Melanie's photo on it, praying for her safe return. Alexander had never been one to pray or even follow any sort of organized religion, but he was thankful for their prayers. He was willing to try anything in order to hold his daughter again.

"But not me," Olivia confessed. "I always thought there was something wrong with me. Why didn't this motherly urge ever hit? I thought maybe as I matured, as I grew older, the bug would finally strike. Even when most of my friends were getting married and starting a family, I didn't feel happy for them. In fact, I was sorry for them. Sorry they couldn't just pick up and go to whatever tropical destination they wanted at a moment's notice. Sorry they couldn't go to happy hour after work. Sorry they couldn't sleep in on a Saturday.

"Then I met someone…" She glanced over her shoulder at Alexander and held her hand out. He took a few steps and clutched onto her outstretched hand, joining her at the podium. "And everything changed." Her eyes remained locked with his. "I fell in love."

A warmth spread through him, filling his heart, his pulse becoming steady and calm, a welcome moment of peace. She stood on her toes and placed a delicate kiss on his lips. Cameras snapped, but he tuned them out. The only thing that mattered at this moment was his devotion to his wife.

Smiling, she gave him a comforting look, then turned back toward the crowd. "My love for Alexander Burnham was and still is so strong, so special, so unique. He brought out feelings I never knew existed." She paused, clutching onto the podium as she closed her eyes, trying to steady herself.

"But the love I have for my husband is *nothing* compared to my love for my daughter." Several tears escaped her eyes.

Alexander leaned down, kissing the top of her head. He hated to see her hurting like this. She didn't deserve to live through this kind of pain. Nobody did.

"I'll never forget how I felt leaving the hospital with her in my arms." She wiped her cheeks, then placed her hand over her heart, letting out a shallow sigh before refocusing her attention on the audience.

Alexander hated to admit it, but Agent Moretti was right. The crowd was on the edge of their proverbial seats, hanging on to each and every word Olivia spoke. They were able to see bits of themselves in her. Those who were mothers nodded in agreement, wiping their own cheeks, unable to imagine being in her shoes.

"I was so nervous. I worried I would mess up, wouldn't know what to do. I remember staring into the car seat, which I wasn't even sure we had installed correctly, at this tiny human who depended on me for everything. I couldn't believe the hospital would just let us take her home without some sort of test." She paused, allowing the crowd to respond with polite chuckles. "I didn't know if I was up to the task of being a mother. Well, as it turns out..." She glanced at Alexander, then back at the crowd. "I was."

A small smile crossed her face. "I've achieved a lot during my time here on this planet. I graduated at the top of my class in college. I've traveled and seen the world. I helped start a fitness center where, to this day, we try to improve the lifestyles of thousands of people. But all of that pales in comparison to what I believe is my greatest accomplishment, and that's being Melanie's mom."

She opened a folder on the podium and took out a large 8x10 photo of Melanie. She was smiling wide, displaying a few missing teeth. Brown curls cascaded down her shoulders, framing her face.

"This is Melanie Sarah Burnham," Olivia said with a strong voice, cutting through the audience. "She loves dogs, pancakes, and the Red Sox. She still believes in Santa Clause and the Easter Bunny. For her birthday this year, she asked everyone invited to her party to bring unwrapped toys she could donate to kids less fortunate who have never received birthday presents. A girl after my own heart, she saved a fawn with a broken leg that was found on our property. After searching for its mother, to no avail, she cared for and nursed the fawn back to health before releasing it back into the wild. And this was when she was only six years old.

"She wants to be a veterinarian when she grows up. Or president. Or an astronaut. It changes every day." A slight laughing rippled through, and Alexander glanced down at the assembled crowd. Some had trouble keeping their own emotions at bay. Chins trembled, lips pinched together, unbridled tears escaped watery eyes.

"Before I had a baby, I would hear reports of a missing child and feel a pang of sympathy for what the family was going through, but I would move on and forget the face and name when a different story came on. That all changed after I had Melanie. Whenever I heard any story involving a child, all I could think was, 'What would I do if that were Melanie?'" She paused, gripping the podium as she closed her eyes, drawing in a slow breath.

"Never in a million years did I think I would be up here, begging for the public's help to bring my baby home," she choked out. "We've become the story that, years ago, I would listen to, then forget." She shook her head, her words barely audible through the lump in her throat. "This time, I can't forget. I'm living a nightmare. Every second that passes, I lose another sliver of hope that we'll find her. I beg you. Look at this face." She held up the photo of Melanie again. "Memorize the eyes. The nose. The smile. Please, help bring our baby back home."

Sobs wracked through her as she buried her head in her hands, her body trembling. Alexander pulled her into his arms, wishing he could erase her pain, that he could turn back the clock and prevent this from happening. He held her close, not wanting to let her go, as photographers captured her very public breakdown with the intention of showing it on the five o'clock news just to score higher ratings. He wanted to rip those cameras out of their hands. He hated that the press could be so insensitive they'd want to capitalize on what would be one of the most difficult moments of a person's life. The media couldn't possibly fathom what they were currently going through. Alexander doubted any of them even had a spouse, let alone a daughter. This was just another job to them. Go listen to another poor family talk about their missing daughter and beg for the public's help in finding her. All they cared about was taking enough photos and shooting enough footage to make the boss happy before it was time to clock out.

Colleen approached, pulling Olivia into her arms and ushering her away. Alexander gave her an appreciative smile before turning to the vast collection of microphones set up on the podium, scanning the crowd for anything that appeared suspicious, an occupational habit.

Moretti had stationed what he referred to as "plain-clothes agents" amongst the crowd to keep an eye on everything. Alexander could pick his "undercover" agents out of a lineup, and not just because he recognized them from the briefing room prior to the press conference. They were dressed all in black and wore dark sunglasses, despite the relative lack of sun. They stood out like a baby in a bar at last call.

Refocusing his attention on the reason he stood in front of this crowd of relative strangers, Alexander gave them a solemn smile. "When I was seven, I put bubblegum in my best friend's hair. When I was ten, I broke the window in my bedroom and lied about it. When I was sixteen, I stole my father's shiny new sports car and took a girl to the movies. I told her I was a sophomore in college, not a sophomore in high school. You can imagine the sting of her hand across my face when she found *that* out." The crowd chuckled.

"When I was twenty, I killed a man." The audience grew silent, their former light expressions turning serious, intrigued. "I didn't know his name. I didn't know if he had a wife, a family. All I knew was I had been given orders and my job was to carry them through to the end." His voice remained even, calm, unwavering, as if speaking of something as mundane as the weather.

"I felt no guilt or remorse for what I did. It was necessary for the greater good…our freedom. I couldn't tell you how many people I killed during my enlistment in the navy. I've made quite a few enemies over the past twenty years of my life. I've taken lives, destroyed families, all for what I thought to be a noble cause…ensuring our safety from foreign and domestic threats. Now, I fear that someone I've wronged has decided to get back at me the only way they know how…by hurting me where it counts."

He drew in a breath, closing his eyes briefly. When he opened them again, he scanned the crowd, unable to make out any distinct faces through the camera lights and black dots obscuring his vision.

"I wish I could stand here and tell you I'm a good person who doesn't deserve this, but I can't. I probably *do* deserve this…"

Out of the corner of his eye, a short figure wearing a tattered overcoat caught his attention, a ghost of his past. Despite the faded Burberry scarf covering her signature red hair, he knew who it was this time. It wasn't just someone who looked familiar. She had come back.

It took everything he had not to jump off the platform and run to her. His gut shouted at him that she was the missing piece of this huge, convoluted puzzle he couldn't put together.

As she walked through the crowd, she kept her eyes downcast, only looking up every so often to avoid running into anyone. Most people barely even noticed her, and those who did seemed to turn their noses up in repulsion, as if she didn't belong there.

Alexander felt a nudge and snapped his head to his left, seeing Moretti furrowing his brow at him. He gave the agent a reassuring look and returned his attention to the crowd.

"I may deserve this," he continued, glancing at Moretti briefly, then facing front once more, "but Melanie doesn't. Melanie is everything I'm not. She's caring. Kind. She gives and gives until she has nothing left. I've woken up every day since she was born wondering what I did in my life to deserve a daughter as beautiful on the inside as she is on the outside. This morning, I've been forced to do quite a bit of soul-searching. I know I'm not a good man. I've done bad things for what I believed to be good reasons. I've ignored friends and family who needed me because I was too busy working. I've been selfish. But Melanie has done nothing wrong, apart from the unfortunate circumstance of having my DNA running through her. If whoever took her did so because of something *I've* done, your issue is with me, not Melanie. Please…"

He scanned the crowd, his eyes locking with Rayne's. He felt compelled to speak directly to her for reasons he couldn't quite explain.

"It's cold. It's wet. They're forecasting a Nor'easter to hit us tomorrow evening, dropping over a foot of snow. All I can think is that my little girl is somewhere out in the cold. I beg all of you. If you know anything that could help, no matter how small or insignificant you think it is, please call the tip line the FBI agent provided earlier. We can't find Melanie without you."

Silence rang out as Alexander narrowed his gaze at Rayne. Peering into her haunting eyes, his suspicions mounted with every passing second that she might know something. Just as he opened his mouth to speak one last time, so did she, her voice strong and tenacious, at complete odds with the frail and broken woman looking back at him.

"I took her!"

Everyone turned toward her, photographers snapping photos incessantly as FBI agents sprang into action. Rayne straightened her back, her chin held high, paying no attention to the commotion around her.

Alexander glanced at Olivia, who seemed just as surprised as he did, despite her earlier speculation. They never expected someone they considered to be almost family at one time to do something so harmful, so hateful, so devastating. Rayne, of all people, should have understood how soul-wrenching and torturous it was to be in a state of constant purgatory, not knowing whether or not your loved one was still alive, every minute that passed with no answers another coal on the fire.

"Rayne?" Alexander asked, his voice almost inaudible as he stepped away from the podium. "Why did you take her? Where is she?"

"I thought it was the only way!" Rayne answered, her voice frantic. Her eyes grew wide, her expression agitated. There was a wildness about her that was completely at odds with the calm, lively woman Alexander remembered her to be when she was still part of their lives.

"What do you mean?" He stepped toward the stairs, hearing Moretti issuing orders to his agents in the crowd who were having difficulty reaching her through the blockade of reporters and their equipment.

Shaking her head violently, she let out a loud sob. "I've been so angry and it just hurt too much. It took finally meeting someone who had been hurt like me to realize that this needed to happen, that you needed to feel my pain, too! I can't—"

With a flash, a deafening boom filled the air, a brilliant blaze rushing over the crowd before everything went dark.

PART II:
HONOR

Honor: /noun/
Chastity or purity in a woman.

SIXTEEN

Three Years Ago

"I can assure you, gentlemen," Alexander said to the two men clad in dark suits sitting across from him. "I am personally involved in every job the company takes on. Even though I may assign another highly-trained agent to oversee the operation, I always make sure I'm fully apprised of all the details, regardless of how small." He smiled his million-dollar smile at them.

This was the part of owning the private security firm Alexander loathed…wining and dining potential and current clients. He had seen his father in action over the years, always the charmer. The man had loved the satisfaction of knowing he could land a multi-million dollar contract, then plan some sort of clandestine operation that would go off without a hitch…all before he had his morning coffee. Because of his father's training and tenacity, the company he built was the most well-respected and sought-after private security firm in the country, if not the world. Alexander had agents on various assignments in practically every state and across the globe…some for private individuals, others as government military contractors. He had hoped the days of the hard sell would be behind him. He didn't feel the need to sit here and give the same sales pitch these guys had probably heard over and over again. The company's record spoke for itself.

"And that's why we always come to you first, Mr. Burnham," one of the men answered. "With your brother taking on a leadership role within the company, we just want to make sure nothing's changed. No offense, but he doesn't exactly have the same background as you or your father."

"That may be true." Alexander took the tumbler in his hand, bringing the expensive scotch to his lips. If he had to sit and give these men the same song and dance, at least he could reward himself for his pain and suffering with some good scotch. "But I can assure you, even though Tyler may not have been a SEAL, like me, or an operative for the CIA, like my old man, he still has a military background. He may not have run the beaches of Coronado, but there's no one else I'd trust to help run my father's company. Even though I have men with that specialized training it appears you think necessary who have been working for the firm for decades, I still value my brother's skill set above them. He has something the military can't teach you. A great instinct."

"We didn't mean any offense," the other gentleman said.

"None taken."

"We just aren't too familiar with your brother."

"And you weren't familiar with me, either, when I took over the company after my father's death, yet here you still are, even thirteen years later."

"That may be true; however—"

"Gentlemen, I hope you don't think it rude of me to say, but—" A buzzing on the table interrupted him. He glanced at his phone to see a blocked call coming through. Returning his attention to the two men who were his father's first clients when he started the company, Alexander continued. "I have ten-figure contracts with the U.S. government. Your fifty thousand dollar job isn't going to make sure I can pay my employees for one more day. I'll forever be grateful to you for taking a chance on my father and his vision, but you know damn well there's no one who will do a better job. You can stop with all these baseless concerns and just let us handle your security detail like we always have, or you can go find someone else and hope they'll provide the same services for that small of a fee." His gaze burned through them. "I'll let you talk it over while I take this call."

He got up from the table and stepped away. Rubbing his temples, he headed into the bar area of the restaurant and took a breath.

"Burnham here," he answered, keeping his eyes trained on the men at the table. While what he said was true, that this contract was small peanuts compared to most of the jobs the company had been hired on, Alexander didn't want to lose them as clients. He wanted people to still respect the company, even with his brother joining him at the helm.

"Alex," a voice practically shouted from what sounded like a construction zone. The connection was sketchy, the banging of hammers amplified over everything else.

"Who's this?" he asked, covering his free ear to try to hear better.

"It's Landon."

"Landon?" He shook his head, as if he were imagining things. "I thought you were overseas. I ran into Rayne a few weeks back and she said she wasn't expecting you home for at least four more months."

"I am," he replied, then paused.

Alexander sensed something had to be wrong if Landon called him out of the blue like this. They hadn't spoken in months, maybe even a year. Alexander knew how difficult it was to find time to make a call while on deployment, particularly if Landon was on a classified mission, which he probably was, considering he was still on active duty with the

SEALs. Whatever the reason for the phone call, Alexander had a feeling it was important.

"I need your help."

"*My* help?" Alexander raised his eyebrows, intrigued.

"I wouldn't ask if it weren't important," Landon declared in a hurried tone. "There's this girl—"

"A girl?" He couldn't mask his disbelief. "You call me after we haven't spoken in who knows how long to talk about a girl? What's going on in…wherever you are?"

"It's not what you think. It's just…" There was a heavy sigh. "We need to do something about what's happening." His tone was frantic, the urgency with which he spoke increasing with each word. "There's just so many of them. For every one reported, there are at least a hundred who go unreported."

Alexander listened, his mind spinning. He scanned the restaurant, but he wasn't really paying attention to his surroundings. For all he knew, he could have been right next to Landon. He had known him since they reported to BUD/S training. They connected immediately. Being put through the most rigorous mental and physical training did that. There were times they both wanted to quit, but they refused to let each other ring that bell. In the field, they had run operations together seamlessly. Alexander could always tell just by looking at him or listening to the tone of his voice when something was serious. This was another one of those times.

"Slow down, buddy. You're not making any sense. What are you talking about?"

"I've tried to get the military to do something about it, but they keep saying the rules of engagement forbid us from intervening."

"And the same would apply to me as a government contractor, so I—"

"Your company has provided security and staff for shelters and refugee camps in the past, right?"

"Yes, but—"

"I'll take the job," Landon interrupted.

"What?"

"Every time we talk, you keep begging me to leave the navy and come work for you. If you do this for me, you have my word. I'll go into the reserves, effective immediately, and work for you. Hell, I'll even spearhead this."

"Spearhead what exactly? What precisely are you asking me to commit my company to?"

Landon let out a sigh. "You need to see this with your own two eyes. Words alone won't do the problem justice." He paused. "Do you think you can hop on the next military transport to Kabul?"

Alexander stiffened, caught off guard by Landon's unusual request. More intrigued than surprised, he glanced around the upscale restaurant, the dull murmur of meaningless conversations broken by the occasional clanging of a dish or wine glass. It all seemed so superficial. Here he was, dressed in a suit that cost more than most people made in a year, schmoozing another set of clients for the business.

When he had agreed to take over the company, he was well aware that this was part of the job. Lately, though, he felt as if he had been spending all his time sitting in an office or a restaurant like this, meeting with clients. He missed the thrill of the unknown, the adrenaline of being in the field. He wanted something more, something different.

Something about that moment, the unhappiness he had been feeling toward his chosen career path, coupled with the frantic and excited tone with which Landon spoke made Alexander believe this was exactly what he needed.

"I'll be there." He hung up and strode out of the restaurant, leaving his clients sitting at the table. He hadn't felt this alive in months, maybe years.

Twenty-four hours later, Alexander emerged onto the dusty tarmac in Kabul, Afghanistan. Assaulted by the hot, relentless sun, he remembered the first time he had stepped foot in this country, not knowing whether he'd be returning home in the passenger compartment or cargo hold. It didn't matter. Back then, he had nothing to return to anyway.

"Alex!" a voice bellowed as he walked toward the administration building.

He looked in the direction of the voice and smiled, approaching his old friend and teammate. He pulled him in for a quick hug, then stepped back.

"I half expected you to walk off that plane wearing a suit." Landon grinned, crossing his arms in front of his broad chest. "I've only seen you a handful of times over the past few years, but you were always wearing some suit made by a guy whose name I could hardly pronounce and would probably never be able to afford."

"You will if you hold up your end of the bargain and come work for me," he reminded him, raising his eyebrows.

"First things first. You never know what we'll come across in our travels, so let's get you geared up." Landon started toward the administration building on the base.

Alexander ran to catch up, fighting off the wind. "Where exactly are we going?"

"A hospital about a hundred miles from here," he shouted over the roar of a helicopter.

It felt oddly strange to be back on a military base in this

country. If it weren't for the stark desert surroundings, Alexander wouldn't have believed he was anywhere other than the United States — palm trees waving in the wind, the sun shining brightly as birds chirped in the distance. But once they left the secured fences surrounding the military installation, both men now sporting bulletproof vests and helmets, that all changed. Kabul was a city like any other, but the violence it saw over the years had left its mark. Some neighborhoods had been reduced to rubble and never rebuilt. The area wasn't as dangerous as it once was, but Landon was right. It was best to always prepare for the worst.

"Want to tell me why you had me come all the way out here?" Alexander shouted over the loud engine as Landon navigated the all-terrain vehicle down a sandy path. They had left the crowded city behind and were now surrounded by nothing but desert and mountains.

"Like I said over the phone, words can't adequately describe this. You need to see it with your own eyes to fully understand how important it is that something is done. The military can't do jack shit about it...or so I'm told." He rolled his eyes, then glanced at Alexander. "But *you* can. You're a civilian with too much money. You can use that money for good."

Alexander stared at Landon, whose blue eyes were hidden behind his dark sunglasses. The sandy hair peeking out from underneath his helmet was lighter than Alexander recalled, probably from being deployed here for who knows how long. Studying him, Alexander thought how much Landon had grown and matured since their days of drinking beer together while on leave fifteen years ago. He had never heard him speak with such passion and zeal, even when he talked about Rayne, his fiancée. He knew this had to be important. Landon wouldn't ask him to jump on the next military transport out here if it weren't.

"You certainly have me intrigued," Alexander mused.

"Good." Landon gave him a look, then turned his attention back to the road.

After a bumpy two-hour drive, which was hell on Alexander's back, Landon finally pulled up to a small tan building in a remote village. There was a line of people out the door. Women held crying children. Old men looked like the next breath they took might be their last.

"Medical care leaves much to be desired here," Landon explained, turning off the engine.

"Where are we?" Alexander asked, staring at his surroundings in bewilderment. He couldn't imagine anyone living in such deplorable conditions. Many of the buildings were made of clay, the tin roofs rickety.

"A medical clinic."

"*This* is a clinic?" he said in shock, looking back at the line of people snaking out of the building.

"Yup," Landon replied curtly, then jumped out of the ATV.

Alexander followed him past the line and into the building. The smell of urine and death surrounded him, a lone fan the only means of lowering the temperature and circulating the air.

"As you know, the military does what it can, but it's not our place to provide medical care to the people here. At least that's what my commanding officer tells me."

"And he's right," Alexander responded in a stern voice, then relaxed his expression. "I've never known you to be such a softie."

Landon glanced over his shoulder. "Maybe I've grown

wiser over the years. Maybe I want to finally do something that makes a difference."

"You don't think you make a difference?" Alexander shot back, crossing his arms as they came to a stop. "You're a SEAL, for crying out loud," he whispered. "You go into areas most other military forces run from. You can't say——"

"I know. I know. I just…" He sighed, removing his helmet. Alexander did the same. He had forgotten how much he hated those things. "I don't know. Maybe you're right. Maybe I *have* grown soft. Or maybe this isn't what I'm meant to do. Maybe God has a different purpose for me."

"And you think opening up a medical facility with my help is that purpose?" Alexander tilted his head, raising his eyebrows.

"No. Not a clinic." Landon grinned slyly.

Alexander narrowed his eyes. "Then what?" He had assumed this was about using his vast resources to provide medical care to those in need. Now he had no idea what to expect.

"Come here." Landon gestured down a short corridor that was abuzz with medical personnel and patients trying to be seen, some of them begging and offering bribes. "There's someone I want you to meet."

Eyeing him, Alexander followed him down the narrow hallway, trying to swallow back the bile rising in his throat from the putrid stench. Hospitals always had a strange smell to them, but nothing like this. He couldn't wrap his head around the fact that this was somewhere people went in order to receive medical care. The tile looked like it hadn't been cleaned in years, and he was pretty sure there was a combination of blood and feces smeared on the walls.

"As you can see," Landon explained, leading Alexander through the crowded hallway, "most hospitals here are so poor, the only thing they can offer a patient is a bed and perhaps a staff member to check in on them once a day. If the patient has no family, there's no one to pay for medications or food. They're lucky if a worker can spare a minute to change their clothes or sheets."

Alexander looked around at the cots in the halls, wondering if any of the people lying on them were still alive.

"I brought Fatima here after my unit found her a few weeks ago."

"Fatima?" Alexander asked.

"That was before I knew how hospitals worked," Landon continued, ignoring Alexander's question. "I thought she'd be taken care of, protected…until I stopped by a few days ago and found her lying in a pool of her own waste. She could have been dead." He paused, swallowing hard, then looked at Alexander. "Please understand. I'm not blaming the doctors or nurses. That's just the way things are here. The staff is doing everything they possibly can with the limited resources available to them. In this culture, the family unit is the one expected to nurture and take care of each other. As long as the family unit is intact, the system works. But when the patriarch of your family wants you dead—"

"Wait… What do you mean?" Alexander interrupted, giving Landon a questioning look. He had a feeling he knew what his friend was talking about. He had spent enough time here to know that some antiquated traditions still existed, despite their government's efforts to paint their culture in a positive light.

"*This* is what I mean," he replied, pulling back a simple white curtain, revealing a face Alexander imagined was beautiful at one time. Now it was marred with scars, wounds covered in bandages, fresh blood leaking through. He couldn't imagine one's own family abandoning someone in such a state.

"Why?" he asked in disbelief, his voice almost a whisper. He had no idea how this woman could still be alive, although it appeared as if she were holding on by a thread.

"Why has no one come?" Landon replied passionately. "Why would someone do something like this to their own flesh and blood?"

Alexander nodded, swallowing hard.

"Because, according to her family, she's an adulterer. She's brought dishonor to her family, and the only way to bring it back is by—"

"Killing her," Alexander finished.

"Most of the residents of the village we found her in refused to talk. However, I was able to piece together her story from a handful of people who shared what they knew. About two months ago, she arrived with a man. I assume it's the man whose decapitated body was found next to her. Apparently, just a few days before we found her, two older men came looking for her. The story the villagers were given was that it was her father and her husband. They estimated both men to be in their seventies. This girl probably isn't more than twenty, yet she was married to a man in his seventies?" He raised his eyebrows.

"So you think she ran away from an arranged marriage?"

"I'm pretty sure." Landon shrugged. "All I know with certainty is these two men, one of whom claimed to be her father, tied her to a chair and pelted her with rocks and stones for God knows how long. The only reason she's alive right now is because they probably thought she was dead. It was by pure luck we ran across their two bodies."

"And the man she was with?"

"Was hardly a man. He was probably only eighteen

himself. He was stabbed repeatedly, then beheaded. The scarring on his wrists and legs led us to believe he was restrained and forced to watch them torture Fatima first."

He grabbed her lifeless hand in his, squeezing it. "She's just one of who knows how many girls. The doctors say she was lucky to have survived such an attack." He looked at Alexander, his eyes bold, a storm raging within. "*Lucky*," he emphasized, then looked away, his vision focused solely on the bruised and scarred body lying on the small cot. "Most girls don't walk away from this kind of attack. The government usually doesn't get involved, either, especially in the more rural Pashtun areas."

"Why not?"

"From what the staff here has told me, many of the local officials choose to honor the Pashtunwali, an ancient tribal code prevalent in these areas. Advocates have worked tirelessly to overturn such an antiquated system, but it still exists, probably because there have been little to no repercussions to those who violate the law by adhering to this tribal code. A man can kill his daughter for bringing dishonor on the family and be lauded a hero, not arrested as a monster."

He swung his eyes to Alexander. "Many of these girls have no option but to stay in an arranged and abusive marriage. If they run, they fear they'll be killed by the very people who should protect them. They have no one to turn to. Some brave women *do* decide to run, even though they know death will more than likely be their punishment if they're found. They'd rather die than live another day subjected to sexual and physical abuse."

Alexander swallowed hard, listening to Landon's impassioned tale. He had seen some of the horrors of the world. He knew this sort of thing happened. Still, he couldn't understand what would cause anyone to act in such a way, especially to their own family. He had a daughter whom he loved more than life itself. He would do everything in his power to protect her and keep her safe from harm, including laying his own life on the line. The idea that a father would intentionally harm, maim, and even kill his daughter because she may have acted in a way he didn't approve of was beyond him. Yes, this was a different culture, but certain social mores should transcend cultural and ethnic lines, including ensuring the safety of your loved ones.

Staring at the bloody bandages, Alexander gripped the side of the cot. "What can I do?" he asked, heat building in him the longer he stared at the bruised and beaten woman.

Landon turned to him. "For starters, you can help get Fatima transferred to a hospital in Kabul where she'll receive around the clock medical care. I tried to arrange it on my own, but my military salary doesn't exactly leave my bank account overflowing with zeros."

"Consider it done," Alexander answered without a moment's hesitation. If he could pay for medical care for every woman who found herself in this position, he would.

"There's more," Landon continued, an uncertainty in his tone. He paused briefly and drew in a breath. "We can help Fatima get the medical care she needs, but what happens when she's released from the hospital? What about the rest of the girls who are in danger of meeting the same fate? What if we can prevent this from happening to other women?"

"I'm listening." Alexander crossed his arms over his chest.

"We can open up a shelter for women here."

"We?"

"Well, technically, your company would. I know you

already have several security contracts over here, so it won't be like you're going into a completely new region."

"Yes, but…" Alexander ran his hand over his face, thinking of the logistics of getting involved in a humanitarian project of this scale. Yes, his company had provided security for government-run shelters and camps, even orchestrating the occasional food drop, but he'd never tried to do something like this on his own before.

"I'll run it for you," Landon interrupted. "I'll take care of hiring the local medical staff, coordinating with the Ministry of Women's Affairs, and ensure the safety of everyone who comes through that door. All you have to do is pay for it."

"Oh, is that all?" Alexander chuckled, wondering how much something like this was going to cost.

"Come on, Alex. This is serious. I'm ready to walk away from the only life I've ever really known to start something completely new. I just…" He let out a long breath, glancing down at Fatima, then back at Alexander. "Haven't you ever thought about whether all the sacrifices you've made have been worth it?" he asked in a soft voice.

"What do you mean?"

"I don't know." Landon shrugged, running his hands through his hair, which could use a good trim. "I always thought I'd feel proud of myself for risking my life and being dropped into these random places in the middle of the night to carry out covert assignments. The number of dangerous men we've captured or killed in the name of freedom… You'd think I'd feel a sense of pride in that, and I guess I do…to a certain extent."

"But…"

He gave Alexander a hard stare. "Haven't you ever felt like there was something missing? That no matter how much you love your friends and family, it's just not enough?"

"Maybe." Alexander broke his eyes from Landon's. It was as if his friend could read his mind. Lately, he'd certainly felt dissatisfied with his own career, like he was just a glorified secretary, sitting behind a desk and meeting clients. He wanted something more. "I've been a civilian for over a decade now, so maybe I'm too far removed from it to give you a good answer."

"You've been a civilian, but you've still been in the game." Landon raised his brow. "You may not wear the uniform anymore, but you've trained private military forces all over the world. What would make you sleep better at night? Knowing you're sending some of your teams in to do a random extraction the U.S. government refuses to give you details about, or relocating a woman so she no longer has to live in fear that her abusive husband will find her and her children?"

"They're both part of my job, so—"

"What do you want Melanie to remember you for?"

The question punched Alexander in the gut. He was more than aware the security company had been involved in some more questionable operations. Was Alexander proud of everything he had done in his past? Of course not, but that didn't mean he wasn't a good man.

"Don't you want her to be able to tell all her friends how her daddy stood up for something he disagreed with and used his vast resources to prevent it?"

Pulling his lip between his teeth, Alexander shook his head. He closed his eyes and pinched the bridge of his nose. What *was* his legacy? What would he tell Melanie when she asked why he had gone to "that desert country", as she had grown to call any of the Middle Eastern countries? Would he be able to look her in the eye and tell her it was nothing important? Could he lie to her, then go on as if he didn't just make a conscious decision to send a young girl, as well as many others who could be in her same position within the next week, to her death? What if that were Melanie? Wouldn't he want someone to help her?

If it were five years ago, he'd insist on a business plan, needing to know the precise dollar amount he'd be investing before making a rash decision. Melanie changed all that.

"I'll do it," he murmured.

A brilliant smile crossed Landon's face. He pulled Alexander in for a quick hug, his stature relaxing, as if a weight had been lifted off his shoulders. "I'll submit my resignation papers today."

"Welcome to the company, Landon," Alexander replied, pulling away from him.

"And all it took to get me to finally agree is what will probably be a multi-million dollar investment in a women's shelter in Afghanistan. I'd call that a bargain."

Alexander rolled his eyes. "You would," he shot back sarcastically.

On its face, opening a women's shelter in Afghanistan sounded relatively innocuous, but he spent time here during deployment, then in conjunction with various contracts his company had secured with the U.S. government. He knew all too well that many Afghan people saw the presence of westerners as an assault on their own culture. They would not take kindly to any establishment where the sole purpose, according to them, was to interfere with age-old customs, no matter how gruesome and barbaric they were.

"I know what you're thinking," Landon cut through Alexander's thoughts, noticing the troubled expression on his face. "Trust me. I'm fully aware of what I'm getting myself into here. I know it could be dangerous for all involved, but I already have a plan. One of my buddies who works for NCIS made a few phone calls and put me in contact with a case worker at the Ministry of Women's Affairs. She and I have already discussed at length the effectiveness of the shelters currently open in combatting this. Generally, it's the ministry's goal to reunite the family unit after mandated counseling. Unfortunately, she fears some of these women are forced out of the shelter too soon."

"So what makes you think our shelter will be any different?"

Landon's lips slowly curled into a mischievous smile. "Because, for all intents and purposes, it will be exactly what you thought. On paper and from the outside, it will operate as a state-of-the-art medical clinic. No one will know it's actually a women's shelter. My contact at the ministry will refer cases to us that she believes to be in greatest need of our intervention. Women the ministry's pushing to be reunited with their families. Women who, if they return home, are at risk of meeting the same fate they're trying to escape."

Alexander rubbed his temples, his head spinning. He didn't know if it was the lack of sleep, the unforgiving desert heat, or the death surrounding him, but he felt completely drained.

"So... Not only do you plan on opening a women's shelter no one is supposed to know about, but you're also going to hide women so no one knows they're even there?"

Landon grinned. "Sounds about right."

"I don't know," Alexander began, thinking of a hundred different scenarios where this could all go wrong. He should have known there was more to Landon's plan than he had originally let on. That was how it always was with him.

"I know how it sounds, but if I don't do this, I'll always wonder whether I could have prevented another unmarked shallow grave. Please, Alex," he begged.

Alexander let out a long breath, staring into Landon's eyes. He knew nothing he said would convince him the risk of something happening to him and everyone else was too great. If he didn't finance this venture, Landon would find someone else who would. When his friend wanted something, he didn't stop until he got it.

"Just be smart," Alexander said finally. "I don't want to get a phone call saying you'll be coming home in a wooden box."

Landon gave him a look that said he was up to something. "Smart is my middle name."

SEVENTEEN

Present Day

December 19 - 12:48 PM

It all happened so fast. One minute, Olivia was staring into the eyes of the woman who took her little girl. A woman she once considered to be a friend before she cut everyone out of her life. A woman Melanie trusted and played make-believe with.

A woman *Olivia* trusted.

The next minute, she was forced to the floor of the makeshift platform as it collapsed, a sound unlike anything she had ever heard filling the air, almost sucking the oxygen from everything around her. An inferno rolled over her, forcing her to recall all the Sundays she had spent in church growing up. The priest had warned his parishioners to follow the Bible or they'd spend eternity in hell.

If there was a hell, she was currently in it.

As the heat on her skin waned, she glanced up, unable to see Alexander through the smoke and utter pandemonium that had enveloped City Hall Plaza. FBI agents had sprung into action, uniformed officers running toward the smoke billowing thirty yards in front of her as everyone else tried to run away.

"Mrs. Burnham!" a muffled voice called out.

Every sound seemed to be dulled, as if it were all a

dream. But if this *were* just a dream, Olivia's head wouldn't have been throbbing like it was. This was real. Something horrible had happened when, for a brief moment, she felt something she hadn't all morning…hope. Hope that she was about to get her daughter back.

Looking at the blood-covered faces and unconscious bodies lying in front of city hall, she feared the one woman with answers would no longer be able to provide those.

"Come with me."

Disoriented, Olivia slowly turned her head toward the sound as a woman in a navy FBI jacket helped her up. She had no idea what happened, but was pretty sure even the FBI agents swarming the area were just as confused, trying to piece everything together.

Olivia snapped out of her daze. "My husband!" The reality of the situation hit her like a truck as she struggled against Agent Long, who was trying to usher her to safety. "I need to find my husband!" She looked toward the spot she had last seen Alexander before it all went to hell. There was no sign of him.

"*Alex!*" she screamed, fighting with everything she had. She needed to see him, needed to feel him, needed to know she hadn't lost everything.

"Mrs. Burnham, please!" Agent Long begged, using all her strength to pull her from the collapsed stage and toward flashing lights.

Smoke billowed around her like a cheesy haunted house during Halloween. It almost seemed like a scene out of one of those "end of the world" movies. She had never seen anything like this before.

"We need to get you to safety. We'll find your husband, but you need to get checked out by the paramedics and stay out of the way so we can get to the people who *do* need help. Okay?"

"But my husband…," she cried, her body growing weak, exhaustion setting in.

Sirens blared in the distance as firefighters in full gear rushed past her. She glanced over her shoulder at the confusion enveloping City Hall Plaza, praying Alexander was simply being who he was. That he rushed off to find the woman who had taken their daughter. She refused to consider the alternative. That he was one of the bodies lying on the pavement, bloodied and lifeless. Her husband was too strong, too resilient, too determined. She couldn't stomach the thought of seeing him in any sort of vulnerable state. That wasn't who he was. He was a fighter. Deep inside, she knew it would take a hell of a lot more than whatever had just happened to take her husband from her.

"I'll go and look for him myself, but it's too dangerous for you," Agent Long assured her. "There are people who are seriously injured and need medical attention. Paramedics need to be able to get to them as quickly as possible. We can't have anyone in the way."

"But…" She looked into the young agent's deep blue eyes, pleading. She couldn't think clearly. All she knew was that her daughter had been taken from her, and now her husband was missing in a cloud of smoke and flames, people with gashes on their heads, arms, and legs limping toward safety. What if Alexander was injured and on the brink of drawing his last breath?

"If I have to lock you in the back of a cruiser so I know you won't interfere, I will." She raised her eyebrows, her formerly docile and easygoing mannerisms replaced with a fierce and stern expression. Despite her light, airy voice, motherly demeanor, and contagious smile that made Olivia think she moonlighted as a Disney princess, she came to the conclusion that Agent Long wasn't someone to mess with.

Drawing in a breath, Olivia reluctantly nodded and allowed Agent Long to lead her toward a handful of ambulances several blocks away. A sense of familiarity washed over her when she saw Alexander's mom sitting on a stretcher beside Tyler, who fussed over scratches and cuts on her face.

"Olivia, dear," Colleen said in relief when she entered the area.

Olivia let out a sob and walked toward her mother-in-law. Colleen shook Tyler off her and stood, reaching her arms out toward Olivia.

"Colleen," Olivia breathed. "Thank God you're okay."

"Of course I am," she said, still the same spitfire, regardless of the situation. Olivia supposed she'd have to be after having been around this kind of thing nearly her entire life. She had been married to a navy pilot turned CIA operative, who then went off and started his own private security company. She probably lived every day wondering if her husband would come home at night, much like Olivia used to until she grew complacent that nothing would ever happen to Alexander.

Now, given the events of the past twenty-four hours, she wasn't too sure.

"And I'd appreciate it if my darling boy would stop making a fuss over nothing. It's just a few scratches." Colleen glared at Tyler, who had resumed his attempt to apply a bandage over a deep gash on her forehead.

"It's not just a few scratches, Ma," Carol interjected, Dave nodding.

"Paramedics are a bit short-handed, so I'm helping out," Tyler explained. "Ma wouldn't let any of them treat her anyway. She made them all leave to go help people who actually needed it, according to her."

"And do you blame me?" Colleen shot back, gesturing toward City Hall and the pandemonium surrounding them.

A sense of comfort wrapped around Olivia as she listened to their conversation. She needed this. She needed some sense of normalcy. The overbearing, protective son. The level-headed daughter. The feisty, spunky mom. This was her family, and she needed them more than ever right now.

"I suppose not," Tyler mumbled.

"What do you think caused all this?" Olivia looked at the worrisome expressions on their faces. They didn't have to ask her where Alexander was. They all knew. No matter how dangerous the situation, he ran toward it, not away. He was brave, strong, and sometimes a bit reckless, especially when it came to his family.

"My guess is a bomb," Tyler said softly, still diligently patching up Colleen's face.

"A bomb?" Olivia's eyes widened. Her heart dropped to the pit of her stomach, thinking Boston had enough tragedy with bombs to last a lifetime. The city didn't need another catastrophe to mar it.

"I could be wrong, but I don't think this was just the result of some gas main explosion."

Olivia met Tyler's green eyes, the shade identical to her husband's. The two men were almost mirror images of each other, with just a few differences. Both were tall with dark hair, strong jaws, and piercing green eyes. But Alexander was slightly more muscular and looked more distinguished than his brother. Even though he was now over thirty, Tyler had retained a sort of boyish look about him. Where Alexander had some harder, more defined facial features, Tyler's were soft.

"Have you been able to get in touch with your wife?" Olivia asked. "Let her know you're okay?"

"I can't," he sighed, placing the pack of bandages into the first aid kit and stepping away from Colleen.

"Standard protocol after any sort of suspicious explosion," Dave explained. "You don't want another bomb going off, so you take the cell towers offline in case that was a trigger."

Hearing Dave talk about the possibility of another bomb made Olivia dizzy, her knees growing weak. They were in a secure area, but what about everyone still in the vicinity of the initial blast? What about Alexander? Her stomach churned as she peered down the street toward City Hall Plaza and the flashing lights of over a dozen ambulances, bomb squad trucks, and fire engines.

"Don't worry," Carol said, approaching Olivia and wrapping her arm around her shoulders. "He's fine. He's probably just doing what he does. He's just being Alex."

Olivia pulled her lower lip between her teeth and chewed on it, an old nervous tick. She didn't know how long they expected her to wait, but she needed to do *something*. Fearing all of this was just a way to distract the FBI from finding her daughter, she grew even more anxious that Melanie was slipping further and further away.

She swallowed through the lump in her throat, her gaze shooting up and down the block, frantically searching for some sign of her husband. Her legs felt like jelly, heat rushing to her head. She was tired and achy, running on pure adrenaline. She wanted to wake up from this nightmare, to hold both her husband and daughter and never let go, never take them for granted again.

"It'll be okay," Tyler said, pulling Olivia against his chest.

As she tried to find comfort in Tyler's encouraging words and reassuring arms, she almost swore she heard Alexander's voice calling out to her. It was muffled, like a dream.

Then it grew louder, more distinct. She spun from Tyler toward the source of the voice. Her eyes set on a tall figure dressed in a deep gray suit emerging from a cloud of smoke.

Letting out a sob, she darted from the medical tent and leapt into Alexander's arms, his familiar warmth surrounding her.

"You're okay," she cried, tears pouring down her cheeks as she held onto him, never wanting to let go. Relief washed over her, the unease and fear that she had lost Alexander leaving through each unbridled tear. "One second you were with me; the next, I was alone. I…" Avoiding his eyes, she placed a hand over her panicked heart. "I tried to go find you, but they wouldn't let me. The whole time, all I could think about was—"

"Shh," Alexander soothed, running his hands up and down her back, kissing her forehead. "It's okay. I'm okay. Nothing bad is going to happen to me. I promise."

"But what if it does? I can't—" She shook her head, burying it against his chest once more, and drew in a long breath, finding comfort in his familiar musky scent. It brought back so many memories of their years together — the ups, the downs, and everything in between. No matter what, Alexander Burnham had always been at her side, supporting her, loving her.

"Olivia, look at me." His voice was firm and forceful, yet serene. This man was a walking contradiction, and Olivia loved everything about his duplicitous nature. "Please, love. I need to see those beautiful brown eyes of yours."

She melted into a puddle at his term of endearment. It

didn't matter that they had been together for over a decade. Hearing his voice sent shivers down her spine. So many of their married friends struggled to keep the flame alive. Theirs only grew stronger with each passing day.

Pulling her head away from his chest, she met his gaze.

"I'm sorry I scared you." He wiped the tears from her cheeks. "I was on autopilot. Once the worst of the blast died down, I glanced behind me to make sure you were okay, then ran off to look for—"

"Did you find her?" Olivia interrupted, her eyes growing wide, her lips parting. She searched his face, desperate to hear that Rayne had survived the blast and was in custody, answering questions.

That she had told them where Melanie was.

That this nightmare was almost over.

Her heart fell when he hung his head.

"She didn't make it."

Olivia pinched her lips together, fighting back the helplessness washing over her. They were within arm's reach of finding Melanie, but the hope had disintegrated in the blink of an eye. She felt cursed, as if no matter how hard they tried, no matter what they did to find her, it wouldn't matter. Whoever was behind this would have the upper hand. She tried to stay positive, to ward off the negative thoughts circling her head, but it became more and more difficult.

"Melanie's never coming back, is she?" she blurted out in resignation.

"Don't think like that." Alexander brought her back into his arms. "You need to stay positive. We *will* find her," he declared, even though Olivia was certain it was just as difficult for him to remain optimistic. She was usually the assured and hopeful one, not Alexander. He was pragmatic and realistic to a fault. "This is just a tiny setback. It happens. We had no idea who was behind any of this before the press conference. Now we at least have something."

"We do? How?"

"We're going to sift through Rayne's life with a fine-toothed comb to see if anything falls out."

"Do you think that will work? That you'll find Melanie that way?"

He ran his hand through his hair. "I don't know, but I have some of the best men working for me. They could probably find Jimmy Hoffa's body if they really wanted to."

"I'm sorry, Mr. Burnham," a female said, out of breath. They turned to see Agent Long come running up. "Agent Moretti needs to see you right away at the FBI field office."

Alexander turned to Olivia, letting out an irritated sigh. "Stay here with Tyler, okay?"

"Actually, he needs both of you. This involves your wife."

"My wife?" Alexander furrowed his brows.

"What's going on?" Olivia asked, nerves settling in her stomach as she glanced between Agent Long and her husband. She wondered how much digging the FBI had conducted into their backgrounds, whether they had found something she didn't want them to know.

Something she didn't even want Alexander to know.

"He ordered me not to say anything, just to bring both of you back…in handcuffs, if necessary." She raised her eyebrows, looking directly at Olivia.

Shaking off her unease about what they may have found out, Olivia held her head high, giving the appearance she had nothing to hide.

Alexander's grip on her waist tightened. She glanced at his reddening face, the telltale sign he wasn't too happy. He was probably itching to get back to the office and see what he could dig up on Rayne. When every second counted, this felt like it could be another waste of time.

"His words, sir, not mine," Agent Long added.

"Fine," Alexander muttered through a clenched jaw.

"If it makes you feel any better, it's about a new lead."

EIGHTEEN

"Mr. And Mrs. Burnham," Agent Moretti greeted Alexander and Olivia when they stepped into a large conference room at the FBI's Boston field office. A pristine white table sat in the center of the room, a half-dozen agents congregated around it, some of them talking in hushed tones amongst themselves. There was a hurried sort of buzz in the room, and Olivia grew hopeful there had been a major break in the case, despite the setback they had just experienced.

"You had *one* job to do! *One!*" Alexander roared, cutting him off, taking Olivia completely by surprise. "If you can't even ensure the safety at a goddamn press conference, how am I supposed to believe you when you say you'll do everything to find my daughter? The one lead we had is now dead! Gone! Because your agents couldn't get to her in time!"

"No one could have foreseen something like this happening!" Moretti responded, his voice raised. His white suit shirt that was once crisp and clean now bore several new stains — black, brown, red. Looking into his weary eyes, Olivia could tell everything weighed heavily on him. Despite the rough start he and Alexander had gotten off to, she wanted to believe this man would be true to his word and work tirelessly to bring their daughter back home. It was all she could do.

"It's your *job* to foresee something like this happening and prepare for it, no matter how little the probability may be!" Alexander continued. "In this day and age, can you really stand there and tell me the FBI doesn't train all its agents to plan for this kind of attack and how to counteract it? All of this…" He gestured to a television monitor on the wall broadcasting the news story, "is on your head."

Olivia glanced at the screen, her jaw falling. On ground level, it was hard to fully understand what had happened. Now that she was looking at aerial footage of the plaza, she couldn't help but gawk at what appeared to be a large black crater-like hole a few hundred feet from the steps of City Hall, almost exactly where Rayne had been standing. She wondered how anyone could have walked away from that, but she knew some had. According to Agent Long, there were only five confirmed deaths and a dozen or so injuries that required hospitalization. The rest of the crowd had miraculously escaped relatively unscathed.

"I realize that, Mr. Burnham, and I take full responsibility for what happened. I am just as frustrated as you are, and you better be *damn* sure I intend to do everything within my power to find the bastard who's responsible. Now, there have been a few developments I want to discuss with you and your wife. Please, have a seat." He gestured to two chairs at the far end of the table, almost directly across from where he sat at the head.

Alexander glared at him for a prolonged period of time, his chest heaving. Olivia tugged on his arm, encouraging him to play nice.

"Need I remind you that time is of the essence here."

With a tense jaw, Alexander lowered himself into a vacant chair, his fierce eyes remaining trained on Moretti's every move.

"It's my understanding that Ms. Kilpatrick is an old friend," Moretti continued after a pause.

"How did you…?" Alexander asked, raising his eyebrows. Olivia grabbed his hand beneath the table, squeezing it. He shot his eyes to her and she gave him a look, urging him to be cooperative.

"I've been cursed with an eidetic memory. I saw her name while I was doing my research on you earlier this morning. Once I see something, it never leaves here." He tapped the side of his head. "It's ruined more relationships than I care to talk about. When was the last time you saw Ms. Kilpatrick?"

"Yesterday," he responded firmly.

Moretti narrowed his gaze. "Yesterday?"

"I didn't realize it was her. She doesn't look like she used to. She was standing outside my office building as I was running in. I hadn't seen her in close to a year. She shut us out after the funeral."

"Funeral?" Moretti raised his eyebrows. "Whose funeral?"

"She was my friend's fiancée," Alexander huffed, annoyed. "He died a year ago while on assignment for my company. I assume she blames me for his death and decided taking my daughter was the only way to get back at me."

"And your friend's name?"

"Landon. Landon Tate."

"Any relation to the Mischa Tate who was found murdered?" he asked with a smug expression on his face. It was more than apparent he knew exactly who Landon was and his connection to Alexander and Mischa.

"He was her brother," Alexander shot back.

"Have you found out what caused the explosion?" Olivia asked, trying to break the tension. She knew discussing

Landon was a hot-button issue with her husband. The guilt he felt for not doing more in the days following his disappearance still ate away at Alexander, regardless of how well he tried to hide it.

"The local bomb squad is working with the FBI in analyzing the device," Agent Moretti explained, finally breaking his eyes away from Alexander and addressing Olivia.

"Device?" Alexander asked.

"Yes. They're still trying to piece it together, but it looks like what caused this was a rudimentary explosive designed to have a small blast radius. They're still going through all the debris, but based on the parts found at the blast seat, they're guessing C4 with a cell phone trigger." Agent Moretti paused, glancing out the windows, then back at the room again, taking a deep breath. "There's more." His expression turned grave. "They were able to pinpoint the epicenter of the blast to where Ms. Kilpatrick was standing. They believe she was carrying the explosive in her backpack."

Olivia shook her head, glancing at Alexander as he seethed. "Why would she do something like that?" she inquired.

Moretti sighed, his expression weary. "We're looking into that as we speak. I have quite a few questions I'd like to ask the two of you, since you knew her, but all that needs to wait."

"Wait? Why?" Alexander shot up from his chair, his voice rising. "That woman confessed to taking our little girl, then went and blew herself up! I'm pretty sure that takes precedent over anything else right now."

Ignoring his outburst, Agent Moretti remained calm, all eyes in the room on him. He pulled a smartphone out of his pocket and placed it on the table. "It's our belief she didn't blow herself up, that she was working with a partner. This message was left on the tip line around the same time as the explosion."

"Message?" Olivia grabbed Alexander's hand, pulling him down into the chair.

"Unfortunately, in high-profile cases like these, we don't have the manpower to answer each call individually. The tip line gets flooded with a combination of well-meaning citizens and complete idiots searching for their fifteen minutes of fame. It's our experience that if someone has to sit on hold for a prolonged period of time, they'll hang up, so we set up a messaging system for people to leave information." He tapped the screen of the phone. An unfamiliar voice with an accent filled the room.

"It's funny, isn't it? You pretend to live such noble lives, but you're no better than anyone else."

There was a pause. Olivia could hear her voice echoing in the background, amplified by speakers. She remembered those words. No more than a few hours ago, she had spoken them during her plea to the public to help find her daughter. Whoever made this phone call was at the press conference.

"Is that—"

Agent Moretti raised his hand.

"I've taken something. Yes, you may think I'm a bad man for putting this little girl in harm's way or for trying to make it look like your precious little bodyguard did it, but you're not without blame. You brought this upon yourself. You are in possession of something that doesn't belong to you, and unless it is returned, you will never see your daughter again."

The buzz in the background sounded through the phone once more. This time, it was Alexander's voice ringing through, strong and powerful. Olivia inched forward in her seat, staring at the phone. She knew what was going to happen. Rayne was about to interrupt Alexander, then the explosion would rock the plaza.

"Tonight, Olivia will bring me ten million dollars in cash in one of the company's armored SUVs. She will come alone, or the girl dies. If I so much as sense any law enforcement tail, the girl dies. I will call Olivia with more information this evening, at which point she will have approximately one hour to drive to the specified location. Olivia will then exit the vehicle and bring me the keys. Once I've left with the armored vehicle, she will wait exactly fifteen minutes to call for someone to pick her up. Then I will release the girl to you. If any of these steps are not followed, the girl dies…just like your friend, Rayne, is about to."

Almost instantly, a thunderous explosion could be heard before the message cut off, silence filling the room.

Olivia couldn't move from her chair, a heavy weight keeping her glued to it. Who was this person? What was his connection to Rayne? What did he think they had taken from him?

"No," Alexander's authoritative voice declared, breaking the silence. "Absolutely not. We'll find him another way." He placed his hand possessively on Olivia's leg, squeezing it as if she'd disappear if he let go. "You said this message was left on the tip line. Don't you keep a log of where the calls originate?"

"We do," Agent Moretti assured him. "Unfortunately, as I'm sure you could probably predict, this was from a prepaid cell phone. I have agents combing the area to see if he dumped it after the explosion. They're also canvassing local convenience stores to see if anyone suspicious came in and bought a prepaid phone. However, I'm not putting a lot of faith in uncovering anything that way."

"I don't care how many convenience stores you need to go to in order to track this guy down. Olivia is *not* going to a ransom drop!"

"For once, Mr. Burnham," Moretti responded, his calm voice at complete odds with Alexander's anger, "I'm in complete agreement with you."

"She… Wait… What?" He jerked his head back, stammering. Several other agents appeared just as surprised with this turn of events.

"Sir, with all due respect," one of the junior agents piped up. He didn't look like he was old enough to be in college, let alone have graduated from Quantico. "We don't have any other solid leads. This is our—"

"I didn't say we *weren't* going to do the drop, Agent Gibson," Moretti responded, then looked at Olivia. "We'll simply find a way to do it without putting Mrs. Burnham's life at risk."

The room erupted in chatter, all the agents throwing out ideas to make the plan work. They were all talking about Olivia as if she weren't even in the room, as if she didn't have a say in what happened to her own daughter. She had enough of their game, of having every course of action decided for her.

"I'll do it," she declared loudly, cutting through their voices. The room grew eerily silent as everyone looked at her.

"No, you will *not*," Alexander insisted, his teeth clenching, his jaw tight. He glared at her, giving her a demanding look, but she brushed him off. He could be the one in charge and giving orders at work, but when it came to their family, they were equals. She had a say, too.

"I don't need you telling me what I can and can't do, Alex." She stood up, leaning into him. "This isn't just some game. There's a life at stake here! Our daughter's!"

"And there's another life at stake here, too! Yours!" He raised himself from his chair, towering over her. "It's too risky to send you in," he continued. "Not to mention, the way he's got this planned, there won't be time for a proper sweep prior to the drop. Hell, we won't even know the location until an hour beforehand. It's too dangerous."

"It's too dangerous *not* to do this!" she exclaimed. Holding her head high, she addressed the room of trained agents. "Melanie is *my* daughter. That man on the phone…" She gestured to the center of the table where Agent Moretti's phone still sat. "He's capable of God knows what, and if you think I'm just going to sit back and let you make a risky situation even more so, you're out of your minds. Sure, I don't have a badge. I didn't graduate from…" She waved her hand in the air, continuing, "wherever the FBI graduates from. I never served in the military or went through any special ops training. But I have something no one else in the room has… a mother's instinct. That's something that can't be learned. So you can sit here and discuss a plan all you want, but I'm making that drop. I'm not going to give that bastard any reason to harm my baby, and if something happens to me, so be it." She sat back down in her chair, crossing her arms in annoyance.

The room was still as the agents analyzed the situation, probably trying to come up with a way to talk her out of it. None of that mattered. She'd made her decision, and nothing they could say was going to stop her.

"Mrs. Burnham, I don't think—"

"Agent Moretti," Agent Long interrupted, giving Olivia a quick, reassuring glance before returning her attention to Moretti, "I agree with Mrs. Burnham. I can appreciate the risk involved, but I agree she needs to do the drop. He seems to harbor unfettered animosity toward the family. I believe he won't even think twice about carrying through with any of his threats if we don't follow his order that Mrs. Burnham do the drop. That's what he requested and that's what we should give him."

"Yes, but…" Alexander started, pinching the bridge of his nose, squeezing his eyes shut.

Olivia looked at him, able to see the weight of the world on his shoulders. She hated putting him in this position. She hated thinking of him waiting once she received information about the drop. She could picture him pacing back and forth, every second stretching as he waited to hear from her. She had just been in those shoes, nervously waiting to find out if Alexander was okay after the explosion. It was only a matter of minutes, but it felt like an eternity. Her heart ached for him, but this was something she had to do…for Melanie.

"We will do everything we can to make sure nothing happens to Mrs. Burnham," Agent Long insisted.

"But he said no police presence," Alexander argued.

"Once we receive the location, we'll strategically place a few unmarked cars with plainclothes agents in the vicinity, just in case something were to go wrong. We'll blend in so as not to raise suspicion."

"I want to be there," Alexander demanded, firmly grasping Olivia's hand. "If my wife is putting her life on the line, I need to be nearby. Not to mention…" He shot his eyes toward Moretti. "You assured me nothing would go wrong at the press conference and look what happened. There's no way in hell I'm going to just sit by and let my wife do this and not be there."

Agent Moretti shook his head. "You're too recognizable."

"He goes," Olivia pushed, observing the worry on Alexander's face. His eyes were heavy with exhaustion, his face seeming to have aged beyond his years. He was still as handsome as ever, but she could tell all the not knowing and "what if" scenarios swirling around his head were getting to him. The least she could do was give him this.

Turning back to the assembled agents, she added, "If I'm going, so is Alex. If he were in my shoes, I'd want the same. You said you'll have plainclothes agents in unmarked cars. If this guy's been following the case, as I'm sure he has, he'll be able to pick any of you out of a lineup. I'm sure you'll want to be there, correct, Agent Moretti?" He simply nodded. "Then Alexander gets to be there, too. He's the only one in this room I trust with my life."

NINETEEN

Alexander didn't know how long they would have to sit in the living room of his house, surrounded by FBI agents and call tracking equipment, waiting for the phone to ring. He wondered whether this was all part of this guy's plot to sabotage the ongoing investigation. It felt like everything else had stopped as they waited. He knew that wasn't the case since he was there when Agent Moretti barked orders to FBI agents and local law enforcement officers, telling them to pull everything on Rayne, search her home, and question her co-workers. Still, it seemed like the FBI was putting all their resources into being able to apprehend this guy or, at the very least, get Melanie back at the ransom drop.

Minutes dragged by, dozens of sets of eyes watching Alexander's every move. Friends and family had congregated in their house as a show of support. It sounded ungrateful, but he wished they weren't there. He didn't want an audience for whatever was about to take place.

"I'll be right back," Olivia announced, getting up from the couch.

"Where are you going?" Alexander looked at her.

"To use the little girl's room," she answered, her voice empty. She didn't even look at him. She simply walked away.

Ever since leaving the FBI office downtown, Olivia had seemed distant. Alexander could normally tell exactly what she was thinking, but not this time. What she was about to do was either incredibly brave or monumentally stupid. The entire house was on edge. According to Agent Moretti, the FBI was working tirelessly to comb through Rayne's personal life to see if they could find anything that may indicate who had taken Melanie. They had just completed their search of the building she lived in, not finding so much as a grocery store receipt. Alexander wondered how the FBI reacted to the "doorman" of her building.

His legs bouncing, Alexander scanned the large living room, the scene like a macabre Rockwell painting. Tyler sat on the loveseat with his pregnant wife, Mackenzie, their little boy, Charlie, playing with a bunch of toy cars at their feet. Carol was on the floor with him, trying to keep his innocent mind off the reason they were here, redirecting him every time he asked if Melanie could come and play. They had just celebrated his second birthday, and he was too young to fully understand what was happening. Alexander had to swallow back the lump in his throat every time his nephew asked when Melanie was going to be home.

Not soon enough, he thought to himself.

The sound of a phone ringing echoed through the air. Everyone looked up from their respective conversations. Disappointment showed on their faces when it was just another agent's phone. Frustrated with the entire situation, Alexander got up off the couch, wanting to escape the hushed voices and sympathetic eyes. He felt like an intruder in his own house.

Heading out of the living room, he passed the kitchen, his mother busy making trays upon trays of her famous lasagna. Apparently, she planned on feeding a small army. Alexander didn't say anything, though. This was her coping mechanism, but eating was the last thing on his mind, as was probably the case for most everyone else there.

He continued down the hallway, looking at the photos hanging on the walls. Each of them told a story. Melanie's first Red Sox game. Her first trip to Walt Disney World. Her first T-ball game. For a man who, at one point, never wanted a wife or kids, they had become his world.

Coming to a stop at a black-and-white canvas, Alexander ran his hand over it. The photo had been taken when Melanie wasn't even a day old. She lay in a custom-made pink blanket, his hand resting on her stomach, as if protecting her from this strange new place in which she found herself. She was so small, so vulnerable. He remembered looking into her eyes and finally feeling as if he were whole.

Melanie was everything he never knew he always needed.

Placing his hand on the wall to steady himself, he bit his lip, fighting back the emotions wanting to break free. Out of nowhere, whispered voices cut through the silence, snapping him out of his memories. Creeping down the hallway, he turned a corner into an alcove leading to Melanie's playroom, seeing Olivia and Martin in deep conversation. They simultaneously shot their heads toward him.

"Sir," Martin said in greeting.

"Everything okay?" Alexander asked with a furrowed brow, curious as to what they could have been discussing. Olivia appeared jumpy, as if she just got caught with her hand in a cookie jar. Then again, she had been fidgety all day.

"Certainly," Martin answered. "I was just reassuring Mrs. Burnham that she's doing the right thing by making the drop. That what she's doing is a brave thing, but she has nothing to worry about." He looked between Olivia and

Alexander. "If you'll excuse me, I'll give the two of you some privacy. I'm sure you're both tired of constantly being under the FBI's watchful eye. Take a few minutes for yourselves." Martin gave Alexander a look he couldn't quite explain. Remorse? Apprehension? Perhaps a bit aloof? "Try to find some sort of normal amidst the turmoil. If you need me, I'll be in the kitchen, trying to convince your mother that four trays of lasagna are more than enough for the handful of people here." His normally resolute expression softened when he spoke of Alexander's mother, then he turned and left.

Once Martin disappeared from view, Alexander peered into Olivia's eyes. He wished he knew exactly what was going through her mind. Was she nervous about what she had committed herself to do? Worried? Afraid? Her eyes didn't give anything away.

Taking her hand in his, he led her down the hall, stopping outside a rounded oak door in the style of the late nineteenth-century house.

"Alex, no…" She began to pull away from him, but he tightened his grip, narrowing his eyes at her.

"Just humor me, love." He gave her a pleading look, telling her he needed this as much as she did.

Letting out a sigh, she stopped fighting him. He gave her an encouraging smile, then opened the door. He flipped the switch, light spilling through the room. Relief washed over him, the tension that filled his body throughout the day slowly leaving with each step they took inside their own little oasis within the chaos.

Framed prints of some of their favorite musicians hung on the walls — The Beatles, Prince, Billy Joel, The Eagles. All the classics. Several guitars sat on their stands against one wall. On the opposite wall, a couch and loveseat made up a sitting area. In the center of the room was the focal point…a stunning baby grand piano. Its beautiful music filled the room on a daily basis, except today. This was the first day since Alexander could remember that he didn't hear the familiar sound of a hammer hitting strings. It had always brought him joy. He needed to feel that again. He needed to feel something other than anger and heartache.

"Play something for me," he whispered into Olivia's curls, nuzzling her neck.

"I… I can't, Alex." Her voice was barely audible as she stood frozen in place, staring at the piano.

"You need this, Olivia." He ran his fingers down her back, wanting her to feel some sort of love in a world that didn't seem real.

"I don't know if I can."

"Please," he murmured against her skin. "For me. I need this, too."

Spinning around, she met his eyes. He knew he was asking a lot of her, considering the mark Melanie had left on this very room, how pronounced her absence had become in the last few seconds. They needed this time to themselves, their own way of praying for the safe return of their daughter. Some people went to church. Some found God in nature. Music had always been a big part of all their lives. This was their sanctuary. Their refuge. Their temple.

Taking her hand, Alexander led Olivia across the refinished hardwood floor and pulled out the piano bench. She looked at him, unshed tears glistening in her eyes. He squeezed her hand, hoping to give her some of his supposed strength. He refused to let her know he felt anything but strong at that moment.

Drawing in a long breath, she closed her eyes, then lowered herself onto the bench, placing her hands on the cool ivory keys. Alexander sat beside her, needing to stay by her side. He didn't know how much time passed as they sat in the still room, the ticking of the clock like an unyielding metronome counting down to zero hour. Just when he didn't think Olivia would actually play, the sound of the piano filled the room, soft and low, almost timid. He placed his hand on her leg and their eyes met.

It was just as difficult for Alexander to listen to this song as it was for Olivia to play it, but they needed to do this. This was Melanie's song. The song she always begged Olivia to play for her. The song she always sang as she danced through the house. The song Olivia used to sing to her when she was just a baby. It brought Melanie comfort in those early days. Now, it made Alexander feel oddly at peace.

Olivia's voice reverberated against the walls, the tone sweet and measured as she sang the first verse of the song Judy Garland made legendary. Alexander closed his eyes, losing himself in the music. For the first time all day, he let himself feel Melanie's absence. He could almost hear her laugh as she spun and twirled around the room, dancing to "mommy's music", her sweet, innocent voice shouting "again, again" after Olivia had finished one song.

He glanced at his wife as she sang the bridge at a languid tempo, her voice becoming strong and impassioned. A memory rushed back, hitting Alexander hard, leaving him almost breathless. They were still living at Alexander's penthouse on the waterfront in Boston. Olivia had turned his music room into a playroom for Melanie. He was sitting on the couch and Olivia lay on the ground, a play mat and various toys scattered around her as she played with a babbling Melanie. At the time, she wasn't yet one. She had been taking a few uncoordinated steps here and there, but still hadn't been able to master the art of walking.

He could almost hear the muddled cheers in his mind that erupted from both his and Olivia's mouth when Melanie took that first unassisted step, then another, and another, babbling "Dada" as she stumbled toward Alexander, her arms outstretched.

She was always a daddy's girl, he thought to himself.

He lowered his eyes back to the black and white keys that had become blurry through his tears, the memory of Melanie taking her first steps making his heart ache. He feared that, no matter what he did to get her back home, it wouldn't be enough. Nothing had gone right since this all started. Now he was at risk of not only never seeing his daughter again, but also losing his wife. He ran his hands through his hair, tugging at it, the pain of everything almost unbearable.

When a glimmer caught his eye, he shot his gaze to a sterling silver frame sitting on the corner of the piano. Melanie couldn't have been more than a week old at the time. He sat in a glider, a little bundle wrapped in a pink blanket in his arms. His forehead was pressed against the baby's, her body tiny compared to his tall, muscular frame. Alexander was grateful Olivia had captured the moment. In all the months of her pregnancy, it had never sunk in that he was about to be a father. Even after she had given birth, it still didn't seem real, complications with labor and delivery preventing a true celebration. But once they were released from the hospital with this human who now needed comfort, food, and changing around the clock, it finally set in.

Alexander had never dreamt of starting a family and being a father. He didn't exactly have the best relationship with his own father when he was alive. He had no desire to repeat the cycle of disappointment. But in that moment, his life changed. He was so moved with a love he had never experienced before, he couldn't imagine life without the small bundle in his arms.

Now, she was gone.

Tears fell down his face more steadily. He tried to hide them from Olivia. He needed to keep himself together. He couldn't fall apart in front of her, not when she was about to put her own life on the line.

Consumed by the pain that had been eating away at him all day, he didn't notice when the music stopped. In an instant, two arms were around him as he struggled to hold himself together.

"I'm sorry," Alexander whispered, clearing his throat, wishing there were something that could take this pain away. He raised his hands, about to wipe his cheeks, but Olivia grabbed his arms, preventing him from doing so. She peered into his eyes. He could see his own pain staring back at him.

"Don't be sorry," she said. "As much as you want everyone to believe you are, you're not a stone wall incapable of feelings. You're hurt. You're angry. You're lost. Don't bottle it up, Alex."

He shook his head and looked away, hating that something as innocuous as a song, a series of notes and rhythms strung together, could be the thing that broke him.

"I need to keep it together. It's the only way—"

She grabbed his face, forcing him to return his teary eyes to her. Smiling, she kissed his cheek.

"A wise man once told me it's okay to show weakness." She winked, reminding him of something he had told her time and time again. "You can't carry the weight of this alone. Let me help shoulder the burden. You can't save the world all on your own, ya know."

"You can't, either."

"We'll see about that." She smirked, lightening the tension.

"I'm sorry, Mr. Burnham," Martin interrupted.

Olivia and Alexander looked up to see him standing just inside the room, a grim expression on his face. Her body went rigid, and Alexander grabbed her hand, squeezing it.

"The call just came in. He's asking for Mrs. Burnham."

Alexander looked at her, her eyes wide, then addressed Martin. "We'll be right there."

"Certainly," he replied, retreating and closing the door behind him, giving them one last minute of privacy.

Alexander didn't want to leave this room, but he knew every second counted. There were a thousand things he wanted to tell Olivia in case something went wrong. That he was grateful for everything she'd given him. That he couldn't imagine anyone else he'd want to share his life with. That he loved her.

Love seemed like a completely inadequate word to properly convey how he felt about Olivia. Four letters strung together were insufficient. He doubted there was a word in any language that would do his feelings for this woman justice.

Without saying a word, she stood up and headed toward the door. Alexander hesitated for a minute, watching her walk away. He prayed it wouldn't be the last time. He planned to do everything in his power to make sure it wasn't, but what if that wasn't good enough?

"Olivia," he called out, taking purposeful strides toward her.

"Yes?" She turned around.

Before she could react, he held her face in his hands and pressed his lips against hers. Her body grew taut, then melted into him.

Through that kiss, he gave her everything he had. Every forgotten apology. Every missed opportunity. Every fight. Every reconciliation. Every up. Every down. Every smile. Every tear. Every day he waited for her to finally walk into his life. He gave her every piece of himself, hoping it would give her the strength to survive this, although he doubted she needed it. His wife had proven to be braver than most men he fought overseas, and he couldn't be more proud of her.

Pulling back, she peered into his eyes. "What was that for?"

He ran his hands through her hair, a mixture of emotions flowing through him. "I had to, just in case——"

"Shh…" She placed a finger over his lips, silencing him. "You have nothing to worry about. Nothing's going to happen to me, Alex."

Dropping his head, he simply nodded, wishing he could ignore the unsettled feeling in his gut that something horrible was about to happen.

TWENTY

Walking down the hallway, hand in hand with Alexander, the sound of frenzied activity greeted Olivia's ears before they even stepped foot into the living room. Agent Moretti barked orders at everyone in sight, all of them jumping to action, typing furiously on laptops or making phone calls. Agents murmured in the background that the call was untraceable, that it would take weeks to pinpoint the origin because of the number of satellites he used. Olivia grew more nervous.

The clicking of her heels on the wood floor caught Moretti's attention and he looked up immediately.

"Mrs. Burnham…" He rushed toward her and placed his hands on her shoulders, staring into her eyes. "Do just what we discussed earlier. Agent Long will be right next to you and will help with what to say, if you need it. We're still working on a profile of this man, but we believe he has specifically requested to deal with you simply to upset your husband. He wants to get to him any way he can. He's arrogant and thinks he's untouchable. He chose to take your daughter from your home, making it look like the man you both trust more than anyone else was responsible, instead of abducting her from somewhere with much less security. He thinks he has the upper hand, that he's succeeded in making you both feel completely vulnerable and exposed. You need to act as if that's the furthest thing from the truth."

"But it—"

"Just trust me," he said slowly. "I know it sounds like we're playing a dangerous game, and we are, but this is the only way we can learn more about him. By catching him off guard, by making him think his actions haven't had the desired effect."

"I'll be right next to you the whole time," Alexander encouraged, placing his hand on the small of her back.

"He's going to try to upset you," Moretti continued. "That's what he wants. If he veers off-topic, don't respond. Just try to get him back on course. All we need to know is where he wants you to make the drop so we can get Melanie back. Ready?"

Olivia didn't know how to answer. She didn't know if anyone could ever truly be ready for what she was about to do. This phone call would set into motion a chain of events that would be completely unstoppable once it began.

She drew in a deep breath and nodded, then followed him toward the formal dining area where all the equipment had been set up. On shaky legs, she took a seat next to Agent Long. Alexander sat beside her, squeezing her hand.

A younger FBI agent with dark-framed glasses met her gaze across the table and raised his eyebrows, mouthing, *Ready?* She nodded once more. He pressed a button, then nodded at her.

"Hello," Olivia said, trying to mask her nerves with a steady voice.

"Oh, Mrs. Burnham," a man with an accent she couldn't quite place answered. It sounded Indian or perhaps even Middle Eastern. Based on the bomb detonated during the press conference earlier, she guessed it to be the latter. "So nice of you to finally join us. I was beginning to think you weren't ever going to come to the phone, which would have been quite tragic for little Melanie."

Olivia opened her mouth, a fire building deep in her stomach as she listened to this monster speak her daughter's name. He didn't deserve to even say her name, let alone be in her presence.

When a hand touched her bicep, she whipped her head to her left. Agent Long gestured toward the legal pad in front of her.

Reading it, Olivia struggled to calm her temper, forcing herself to do just that. She needed to play the part this waste of space wanted her to play.

"I have the money you requested. Where do you want me to make the drop?"

"Ah, do you now? I'm actually rather surprised at this. You must be quite resourceful, Mrs. Burnham… I'm sorry. Do you mind if I call you Olivia? I'd much rather prefer that."

Agent Long scratched on her pad, but Olivia ignored it, following her gut instead.

"If we're exchanging pleasantries, what should I call you?"

She could feel Agent Long's eyes burning through her, but brushed it off. She didn't want to follow some dumbed-down script. There was no guarantee this man would be true to his word and return Melanie once they paid him the money he demanded. Olivia wanted to try to get as much information from him as possible so the FBI could track him down.

"Oh, Olivia—"

"Mrs. Burnham," she hissed back. "I didn't agree that you could call me by my given name, not until I know yours."

There was a pause on the line and her heart raced, waiting to hear dead air any second. Maybe she should have listened to Agent Long and not been so impulsive.

"Very well then," he said finally. "You may call me Maleek."

"Is that what everyone calls you?"

Agent Long placed her pen on her pad, irritated.

"Nice try, Olivia. I will tell you my legal name is Maleek, which is what I would like *you* to call me." His voice had an almost sinister quality to it. Mix that with the obvious contempt he had for her, it took everything Olivia had to remain calm.

There was a flurry of activity around her, everyone in the room using all available resources to see if they could find out anything about someone with the first name Maleek.

Olivia looked at Agent Long, unsure of where to steer the conversation now that she had his name. She circled something on the pad and Olivia nodded.

"Okay, Maleek. Like I said, I have the money you requested. Tell me where to go."

"A little short on patience this evening, aren't we, Olivia?" he replied smoothly, as if he didn't have a care in the world…as if he weren't currently holding her little girl hostage. Her sweet, innocent little Melanie, who still believed reindeer could fly and a fat man could slide down the chimney to leave her presents. Her green-eyed angel, who still called out to her mommy when she wasn't feeling well. Was she calling out to her now, wondering why she wasn't rushing to her? Wondering why she had let this complete monster take her?

Her throat grew dry, her entire body tensing. Flashes of her happy, carefree little girl were interspersed with her cries for help, cries that went unanswered. She closed her eyes, her chest rising and falling in an increasingly faster and irregular pattern. She felt like she couldn't breathe. Couldn't move. Couldn't speak. She was blind with anger, outrage, a hatred unlike any she had ever experienced before.

A squeeze on her thigh snapped her out of her rage. She looked to her right, meeting Alexander's green eyes. He didn't need to say a single word. In that one look, he told her everything she needed to hear. That she could do this. That she was strong. That he would be at her side until it was over. That he would find who was responsible and make them suffer…

Except Olivia had a feeling she was the one responsible for this.

"No, not short on patience," she responded, "but you sounded rather anxious on the message you left earlier."

Maleek sighed. "Well, I do suppose 'The time has come,' the Walrus said, 'to talk of many things. Of shoes, and ships, and sealing wax, of cabbages, and kings.'"

He paused. Olivia could imagine a smirk on his mysterious face. "'And why the sea is boiling hot,'" she continued, finishing the stanza. "'And whether pigs have wings.'"

"Ah, Olivia. You know one of my favorite poems."

"It's fitting you quote *The Walrus and the Carpenter* to me, isn't it? A twisted tale of a monster who lures a dozen innocent babies away and feels no remorse whatsoever."

"You know something, Olivia? We're not so different, you and I."

"I don't even know you," she spat. "But, I can assure you, we couldn't be *more* different."

"You think so, do you? That's true. *You* may not know *me*, but *I* know *you*. I've been watching you for some time now, Olivia." His voice was calm, even, collected. An unwanted chill ran through her. She had no idea who this man was or what he looked like, but just from his menacing tone alone, she felt as if he were able to see into her soul. All her pain. All her happiness. All her secrets. He knew it all.

Olivia glanced at Agent Long, not knowing how to respond. She shook her head, indicating she wanted her to stay quiet.

"You believe it's okay to break the rules for the greater good, just like your husband, who I'm sure is sitting right next to you, having difficulty controlling that famous temper of his."

Olivia faced Alexander. He gritted a smile at her, encouraging her to keep going, despite the personal attacks.

"Am I right, Olivia?" Maleek asked.

She swallowed hard. "I haven't broken any rules." She was confident even a complete stranger could hear the uncertainty in her tone.

"Oh, I find that hard to believe. We all do. Some are bigger than others, having consequences that are hard to imagine. And why do we do that? Why do we stray from social norms and mores?"

Olivia stayed mute at his apparent rhetorical question. Her skin flamed. It felt like the walls of the dining area were closing in on her, every set of eyes focused on her and the conversation she was having with a complete stranger. Her secrets and faults were laid bare for all to see. Every wrong, every mistake, every slip of the tongue were plastered on her face.

"Because we *believe* in something. In a cause, if you will, Olivia. We believe so strongly in it, we're willing to break the rules, and even a few laws, to further that cause."

Her face flushed, heat coursing through her body as her mind reeled. Her lungs tried to fill with the oxygen they needed to function, but no matter how many deep breaths she took, it wouldn't satisfy them. The room spun around her as she wondered if this man, this complete stranger, knew her secret. When she caught Martin's gaze from across the room, he gave her a reassuring look.

"What is it you believe in that could possibly justify you taking my daughter?" she asked, praying her voice masked the panic coursing through every inch of her body. She knew this conversation would be analyzed under a microscope by the FBI agents listening in. It was only a matter of time before they put the pieces together.

"Retribution," he barked in a clipped tone. "Honor. Justice." There was a pause, then he spoke in a subdued voice again. "I believe there's someone at your front door. You'll find what you're looking for in there, as well as proof I'm not messing around. See you in an hour, Olivia."

"Wait!" she exclaimed, jumping up. "You didn't tell me where!"

She listened for a response, but heard only dead air, followed by the doorbell. Everyone snapped their heads toward the entryway, the extravagant chandelier hanging from the high ceiling overhead casting an ominous light below.

Alexander bolted from his chair and darted toward the front door.

"Mr. Burnham, wait!" Agent Moretti called out, chasing after him. "I don't think—"

"What?!" He spun around, his eyes wild with an emotion that was much more than anger or rage. The look on Alexander's face was one Olivia had never seen. This was a man at the end of his rope. A man who was done playing games. A man who was ready to go into battle for the ones he loved. "You don't want me to answer the door to my own house? Well, thank you for your concern, Agent Moretti, but I can handle whatever this is."

Before Moretti could respond with some half-assed justification to mask his need to always be the one calling the shots, Alexander jumped the few steps up to the entryway landing and pulled open the front door.

Olivia inched toward the foyer, trying to peek beyond the open door at whomever was outside. He wore a navy blue cap, pants, and a matching jacket with the name of a courier service displayed prominently on the chest.

"Sign here," the man said in a disinterested voice with a heavy Boston accent. His lack of enthusiasm was a marked contrast to the intrigue and nervous energy contained within the four walls of the house.

Alexander closed the front door, then turned to face the crowd that had assembled in the entryway, a square box in his hands.

"It's for you." He stared blankly at Olivia. All eyes went to the box he carried as worried thoughts ran through her head, particularly after the events earlier in the day.

"Do not open that," Agent Moretti ordered, walking toward Alexander, keeping his eyes on the box. "Gibson, go question the courier for any information he may have. I'll get the bomb squad out here as soon as I can."

"It'll be at least twenty minutes before they get here!" Alexander yelled in frustration as Gibson dashed out of the house. "You heard him! She has exactly one hour to get to wherever she needs to make that drop! It doesn't take a genius to figure out *he* sent this! It may be a clue as to where Olivia needs to go because he certainly didn't tell her on the phone. He has no reason to send a bomb, not when he knows Olivia has the money he thinks we owe him! So, if you don't mind, I'm going to open this. Time is running out."

"Mr. Burnham, sir...," Agent Moretti continued, rushing toward Alexander, his arms outreached as if about to wrestle the box from his grasp.

"Now this I'd pay to see," Martin mused in Olivia's ear. She glanced over her shoulder to see him standing next to Colleen, her mother in law's eyes concerned, his formal and serious with a touch of sarcasm. "Ma'am," he added.

Returning her attention to her husband, Olivia gasped when Alexander drew a three-inch blade out of his pocket with incredible speed just as Moretti was inches from him. Moretti stopped, holding up his hands. Alexander held his gaze, a somewhat mischievous expression on his face, and Olivia began to think he'd snapped from the weight he had been carrying. Then he grinned, sliding the knife under the tape securing the box, everyone holding a collective breath... except for Alexander and Martin. They both knew the chances of this guy sending a box containing some sort of explosive was slim. Olivia tended to agree with them, but there was still a part of her that held on to that fear.

Alexander pulled open the flaps of the box and blinked, rubbing the back of his neck.

"What is it?" Moretti asked.

Shaking his head, Alexander's eyebrows furrowed. He reached into the box and pulled out a stuffed penguin.

Olivia's hand flew to her mouth, covering her quivering chin, as she let out a slight shriek.

"Mrs. Burnham?" Agent Long approached and placed her hand on Olivia's arm in a show of compassion. "What is it? What's wrong?"

"That penguin..." Olivia swallowed hard. "Melanie..."

"Go on," she pushed.

"I take Melanie ice skating at the indoor rink in Newton at least once a week." She looked down at the penguin in Alexander's hands. "They have one of those claw games. You know, the one where you pay a quarter or something and try to maneuver the claw around to grab the prize you want. That penguin's been in the machine for weeks now. *Weeks*! And Melanie's been trying to grab it since she saw it. It didn't matter to her that she has a room full of stuffed animals. She wanted the thrill of mastering that claw game."

"You took her there yesterday, correct?" Agent Moretti asked, pulling his notepad out of his pocket and scribbling in it.

"Yes. In the afternoon."

"And did she play the game then?"

Olivia nodded. "After she skated. She was with a few of her friends from school and they all tried. I was talking with their moms and..." She trailed off, staring into space.

"What is it? Do you remember something?" Alexander asked, taking a few steps toward her, still holding the penguin.

Olivia grabbed it from him, inwardly laughing to herself. It was such a small thing. Black and white with a yellow beak and orange feet. It had a goofy smile and a silly red bowtie.

"I noticed a man standing off to the side, watching them. As a mother, you're always on the lookout, sometimes to a fault, for anyone who seems to take an unusual interest in your child. This guy looked normal enough, dark hair, dark eyes, but something about his expression rubbed me the wrong way...until I saw a little boy, probably the same age as Melanie, run up to him and give him a hug." She shrugged. "I guess I was just a little on edge after hearing about Mischa..." She grew quiet and took a quick breath.

"What? What is it?"

Her eyes raced back and forth as she tried to recall every-thing about yesterday — the smells, the cold, the crunch of the snow beneath her feet, singing with Melanie in the car as they left the skating rink.

Olivia straightened her spine, snapping her head back to Alexander. "I saw him leave without the boy. He was alone. And..."

"Yes?"

"He was carrying this penguin."

TWENTY-ONE

The house erupted with commotion, the noise amplified by the high ceilings in the formal entry. Alexander felt like this was just one giant game of cat and mouse, like this guy, Maleek, was simply trying to distract them from finding and bringing Melanie back home.

"We'll get a sketch artist down here immediately," Agent Moretti said, nodding to one of the other agents before turning to Olivia. "Do you think you can describe what he looks like?"

In a daze, she nodded.

"There isn't time for that!" Alexander roared. "Remember, we have one hour. *One*! And all he sent was that damn penguin!" He gestured to the stuffed animal in Olivia's hands, then looked back into the box. A white envelope taped to the bottom caught his eye.

"It's the ice rink," Olivia mumbled. "It's got to be. There's no other possible explanation. This penguin…" She held it up. "Melanie's been trying to win this damn thing at the ice rink for weeks now. Part of me thinks he knows that, that he was watching the whole time, but I was so absorbed in my own little world, I didn't notice him."

Alexander gave her a reassuring look, letting her know he was in agreement with her, then turned his attention back to the envelope in the box.

"Send the advance team to the rink to see if anything

looks suspicious," Agent Moretti ordered one of his agents. "Anything at all. Be vigilant, but smart. We need to make it appear as if Mrs. Burnham will be alone, so you must blend in." There was a pause. "What is it?"

Alexander looked up to see Moretti staring at him, his brow furrowed. "There's something else."

"What?"

Alexander held up the white envelope, his pulse quickening. Moretti reached for it, but he pulled it away. This was personal, not something he wanted Moretti to see and analyze, then bag into evidence. As much as he didn't want to open it and confirm his suspicions, he knew he had to.

He slid his finger under the flap, Olivia's gaze locked with his, and tore the envelope open, pulling out a folded piece of white paper. All eyes were on him, the room silent once more as everyone waited. Pinching his lips together, he unfolded it, every beat of his heart echoing in his ears. No parent should ever have to see what he was looking at.

"What is it?" Olivia's voice cut through the space.

He closed his eyes, barely able to even say the words. "Proof of life."

Alexander returned his eyes to the paper, struggling to keep it together as he stared at a photo of Melanie. She wore her pink Snoopy pajamas, her hair in two messy braids, missing her left sock. She held up a newspaper. Looking closer, he saw it was today's edition of the *New York Times.* She sat with her back straight, her legs crossed in front of her. To the left of her was that damn penguin.

Alexander studied the background and her surroundings to see if anything stood out to indicate where she may be. A small, boarded up, barred window was directly behind her. It looked cold and dirty, the walls cement. She could have been in any basement anywhere.

"We're going to get her back," Agent Moretti said softly over Alexander's shoulder as he continued to stare blankly at the photo. Was she okay? Was she cold? Was she hungry? Would she ever forgive him for letting this happen to her?

Alexander straightened his back, clearing his throat. "We're running out of time. What's the plan?" He faced Moretti, all business once more.

"Everyone has been briefed on what their roles are. Agent Long will get Olivia ready. We're going to put a wire on her, just in case."

"In case? In case of what?" Alexander shot back.

"Everything and anything," Moretti answered calmly, as if this were just another day in the office for him. Then he spun on his heels and headed back into the dining area.

Alexander opened his mouth, his temper rising. Olivia caught his eye and gave him a look of warning. Reluctantly, he bit back his remark, not wanting his ego to stand in the way of getting his daughter back. True, he had advanced training in battlefield tactics, taking the enemy by surprise, hand-to-hand combat, freeing himself from a wide variety of restraints, hot-wiring a car, and high-altitude parachuting, just to name a few. But he wasn't an expert in civilian kidnapping cases, not like Agent Moretti claimed to be. As much as it pained him, Alexander had to allow him some slack, on a very short leash, to run the investigation.

Olivia grabbed his hand and followed Moretti toward a team of agents assembled around the large dining room table, frantically typing on laptops.

"What are they doing?" Alexander asked, peering over the agents' shoulders at the computer screens.

"Looking at satellite images of the ice rink," Moretti answered. "This is a tough situation because the rink is open right now, but he's specifically demanded there be no police presence. This is certainly a safety risk to everyone there, but if we were to evacuate, he may grow suspicious and leave. We're not even sure exactly where he'll be anyway."

"Yes, we are," Olivia piped up, glancing over her shoulder. She had her back to everyone as Agent Long taped a wire to her chest.

Alexander hated everything about this. He had seen his wife in many different situations in the past, but never would he have imagined he'd be watching an FBI agent tape a wire onto her body.

"He'll be at the crane machine."

"And where exactly is that located in the skating rink?" Agent Moretti asked, everyone's eyes on Olivia.

"In the snack bar."

"Is it visible from outside the building?" he pushed.

She shrugged. "I don't know. I never really thought about it, but…" She trailed off, looking into the distance. "It could be, at the right angle." She closed her eyes and raised her hands in front of her, as if imagining she were at the rink, not in her living room swarming with FBI agents. "You walk into the building. To the left is the skate rental booth. Just past that are all the restrooms and locker rooms. To the right is the snack bar. The crane machine is pretty much right at the entrance to the snack bar. Then there's a bunch of tables in front of the counter." She opened her eyes. "It's possible it could be visible from outside."

"That's not good enough for me, not when there are civilian lives on the line," Moretti stated. "I'm going to send some undercover agents inside."

"But he said—" Olivia began.

"We'll make it look like they're on a date or something," he assured her. "They'll be roaming the area, looking for anything suspicious. Under no circumstances are you to look to either of them for guidance. Don't even make eye contact with them. The second you pull into that parking lot, he'll most likely be watching you to make sure you've followed his instructions. Don't give him any reason to think you haven't. He'll pick up on it. The best thing we can do is give him a false sense that he got away with the cash, then bring him down. And believe me, we *will* bring this guy down, but we need to do so with your daughter's safety in mind. Now, unless you have any more questions or concerns, it's imperative that we all get in position before the drop." He turned to Alexander. "We'll give you two a moment alone."

He removed his holster in an attempt to look less like an FBI agent and more like a regular civilian. Pulling a thick ski jacket over his button-down shirt, he kicked off his loafers, put on a pair of work boots, then walked toward the front door.

"Okay. You're good to go," Agent Long said, stepping back from Olivia, allowing her to button her blouse. "Agent Moretti will be able to hear everything that is said, but won't be able to respond. We find people in your shoes are less likely to act in a way they shouldn't if they don't have someone else's voice in their ear. It's all right if you look nervous, he'll expect that, but remember what Agent Moretti said. Under no circumstances should you look around for any of the other agents or your husband. They'll be there keeping an eye on everything, making sure no civilian is harmed, but you can't let on they're there. Okay?"

Olivia closed her eyes and inhaled a long, steadying breath, then nodded. "Got it."

"Good luck. I'll see you when you get back." She smiled, then headed toward the kitchen where Alexander's mother was still cooking. He had a feeling she wasn't going to leave that room until Melanie was home. She had already sent Martin out at least once to get her more supplies.

Once the FBI had cleared the room, Alexander turned to Olivia, a jittery feeling in his limbs. "Ready?"

"Would you think less of me if I said no?" She tilted her head back and met his eyes.

Exhaling, he pulled her against his body and wrapped her in a strong embrace. He breathed her in. Her eyes. Her smile. Her trust. Her loyalty. Her stubbornness. Her love. She rested her head on his chest, placing her hand right beside his heart.

"Thump-thump." She tapped out the rhythm with the words. "Thump-thump."

"What are you doing?" Alexander asked. He was more than aware Agent Moretti could hear everything they said through Olivia's wire, but he didn't care. He needed this time with her. He would regret it if he treated this as just another op.

"Memorizing your heartbeat," she murmured. "That way, I can take a piece of your heart with me in case…"

"Hey." He grabbed her chin, forcing her to look him in the eyes. "Nothing's going to happen to you, Olivia. We've been through a lot together."

Biting her lower lip, she nodded, her eyes remaining locked with his.

"And we made it through it all. You and me…" He clutched her cheeks and drank her in, imprinting every dip and curve to memory. The feel of her smooth skin. The heat of her body. The fire in her eyes. "We're survivors, Olivia. Even when the odds were stacked against us, even through all the bumps and hiccups along the way… And that's all this is. Just another bump in the road. We'll get through this one, just like we've gotten through everything else. Together."

Leaning down, he lowered his lips to hers and left her with an unhurried kiss. It was soft, simple, delicate. There was no moaning, tugging, or groping. There didn't need to be. There were "I want you" kisses and "I love you" kisses. Then there were kisses they'd always remember. This was one of those. A kiss that said everything they may never again have the chance to say to each other.

"You need to get going," he said with a quiver, pulling away from her.

Closing her eyes, she nodded, taking a moment for herself. Reluctantly, she grabbed the keys to the armored SUV and started to walk away.

"I'll see you later," she murmured over her shoulder.

TWENTY-TWO

December 19 - 6:15 PM

As Alexander sat in the rundown old station wagon he was pretty sure was around when Gordie Howe played for the Hartford Whalers, he remembered why he hated surveillance so much. He had to hand it to Moretti, though. No one would suspect the FBI would use this heap of metal to conduct surveillance. Hell, there was no way this car could even muster the horsepower to apprehend a suspect in a high-speed chase.

Moretti cranked up the receiver, the sounds of the ice rink filling the car. Four footsteps, a drag, then four more footsteps.

"She's pacing," Moretti observed.

"Wouldn't you if you were in her shoes?" Alexander pulled his jacket closer, able to see his breath as they sat in the cold, dark car. The night was still, a starless sky over them…the calm before the storm that was expected to drop several feet of snow on the state, which would start in just a little over twenty-four hours. Alexander prayed Melanie would be home by then.

"I suppose."

Alexander kept his eyes trained forward, looking for anything that appeared suspicious. It had been over twenty minutes, but no one matching Maleek's description had entered the rink or approached the dark SUV containing the cash. They were taking a risk even being here, but letting

Olivia do this alone was not an option. The parking lot was relatively full of cars of all different types, from the typical Mercedes and BMWs to the more economical Fords and Hondas. It was a Saturday night a week before Christmas and the ice rink was filled with kids of all ages enjoying time with their friends…just like Melanie should have been doing.

The sound of Olivia's shoes were like the ticking of the clock, bringing them closer and closer to zero hour. Every second that passed, Alexander's heart rate increased, his muscles growing more and more taut. He hated all this waiting, not knowing what to expect. He recalled what one of his BUD/S instructors had said. *"There are no unpredictable situations. Read the clues and you'll know what to expect."* But he was out of his comfort zone this time. There was something about this ransom demand that hadn't sat well with him from the start, and it had nothing to do with sending Olivia to do the drop.

Read the clues, Alexander thought, replaying the past few days' events in his mind.

Mischa's murder. Rayne's reappearance. Melanie's empty room.

They had to be connected, but how?

The explosion. The message left on the tip line. Ten million dollars.

For someone who appeared to have done his research on Alexander and his family, this guy should have known that ten million dollars was just a drop in the bucket for him. Hell, he had that amount of cash available through his security company. He called it their "rainy day fund". He didn't like to call it what it really was — a stash of unmarked, non-consecutive numbered bills to be used in case any of his operatives were abducted while on assignment. He never had to use it…until today.

Alexander furrowed his brow and glanced at Moretti, who appeared incredibly relaxed. "Doesn't something about this seem fishy to you?"

"What do you mean?"

Alexander shook his head. "This guy seems to have had his eye on me for a while now. He knew how to manipulate my home security system, making it look like Martin was responsible for Melanie's disappearance. He's done everything to ensure he can't be found and nothing traces back to him. Sure, he gave Olivia a name, but based on everything else, I can pretty much guess your men haven't been able to pull anything up on any Maleek. Am I right?"

Keeping his eyes trained forward, Moretti nodded. "Nothing to match the brief description your wife was able to give us. We've checked with Homeland Security, but I don't expect anything to come back. As you probably saw back at the house, we tried tracing his phone, but he bounced the signal off dozens of satellites. It would take our tech team days, if not weeks, to pinpoint the source."

"Then answer me this. Why would a guy go to such lengths to cover his tracks, but make no mention of unmarked, non-consecutive bills for the ransom? That's Ransom Demand 101, if you ask me. Your team logged all the bills."

"And marked a few of them with a GPS tracker," Moretti added. "He didn't say we couldn't." He shrugged.

"Exactly my point. And why demand Olivia use one of my company's armored SUVs? He must know we'd be able to track it."

"Maybe he knows how to disable the GPS."

When the footsteps keeping time in the car stopped, Moretti and Alexander straightened, their eyes glued to the large glass doors of the skating rink.

"What is it?" Moretti whispered. "Can you see anything?"

Squinting, Alexander tried to make out what was going on. "I think she sees something in the snack bar area," he answered, observing his wife's back facing them. She was oddly still.

Agent Moretti got on his communication device. "What's going on in there?" he asked the agents working surveillance inside.

"A teenager wearing a red polo shirt with the skating rink's logo is approaching," an agent Alexander recognized to be Gibson replied in a low voice. "I assume he works here."

Alexander craned his neck, struggling to see Olivia's tall body through the fogged-up window. He could faintly make out her red-belted coat and wavy brown hair.

"He's handing her a piece of paper," Agent Gibson observed.

Alexander inched toward the edge of the seat, ready to spring into action at any moment.

"It could be nothing," Moretti murmured.

"Or it could be someone Maleek sent," Alexander retorted, thinking this teenager had gotten instructions from someone to approach Olivia, then hand her that piece of paper.

"He's walking away," Gibson said hurriedly.

Alexander kept his vision trained on the front doors, waiting for Olivia to leave the keys somewhere, then walk out. Instead, she glanced over her shoulder, seemingly directly at the car he sat in, then headed farther into the ice rink.

"What's going on?" Alexander shouted, his pulse quickening.

"She's heading around the rink toward the locker rooms," Gibson's voice cracked over the receiver.

"Follow her," Moretti ordered. "Under no circumstances are you to let her out of your sight. Do you understand?"

"Yes, sir."

"Is there a back entrance to this place?" Alexander asked Moretti, his mind spinning. Something didn't add up.

"Yes," he answered calmly. "The locker rooms each have exterior entrances for use during hockey games. The other team has had eyes on it while we watched the main entrance. Aside from a few random cars driving around the building, looking for parking, they've noted nothing suspicious."

Shaking his head, Alexander threw open the door to the car, cursing under his breath.

"Where are you going?!" Moretti bellowed as Alexander took off sprinting. "You're going to blow our cover!"

"This isn't a ransom drop!" Alexander couldn't believe he didn't see it all sooner. "This is another abduction!"

The pavement was slick from the rain and ice, but it didn't slow him down. He bolted across the large parking lot, passing row after row of cars. He gritted his teeth, thinking about all the happy families enjoying time together on a Saturday night while he was trying to bring his family back together. Moretti's footsteps sounded behind him in the distance, but Alexander was on autopilot.

The lights of the parking lot grew dim as he raced around the right side of the building, running faster than he had in years. Just as he turned the corner to where the locker room entrances were located, a dark compact car drove around the opposite corner and stopped. Alexander hid behind a dumpster, peering past it to keep an eye on the sedan. The driver was shrouded in darkness, his face protected by the night. He looked down, as if checking his watch, then glanced back to the locker room entrance.

Alexander held his breath as Olivia exited into the crisp night air. The front passenger side window of the sedan lowered and Olivia ducked, as if speaking to whomever was behind the wheel. If this were simply a ransom drop, she could just hand the keys through the window and walk away. Instead, she reached for the handle of the back door, about to pull it open.

Only thinking of keeping Olivia safe, Alexander rushed toward her, his weapon drawn. His heart raced, his entire body heating from the adrenaline coursing through him. His legs felt weighted down, the distance between him and the sedan seeming like miles instead of just a few yards.

"No!" he bellowed. Olivia snapped her head in his direction, taking a step back in surprise. He threw himself toward her, pushing her away from the car, as the squeal of tires reverberated through the cold night air. Aiming his weapon at the back of the car, he fired a few shots, staring at the license plate as it disappeared around the corner.

Repeating the combination of six numbers and letters in his head, he holstered his gun, spinning toward Olivia. She stared at him in confusion, disoriented.

"What did you do that for?" she shrieked. He could see her terror and panic as she searched his face for an answer. "He has Melanie. He was going to bring me to her!"

Alexander grabbed her face between his hands and gazed deep into her eyes, resting his forehead on hers. "No, Olivia. He wasn't. This was all a setup."

"A setup? He said—"

"I should have seen it before," he interrupted. "I was so caught up with finally having some answers, I overlooked one rather important detail."

"What?" she asked in a grim voice.

"His ransom demand. This guy took every precaution imaginable from the beginning, even being so bold as to make it appear Martin had taken Melanie. It makes sense he wouldn't want us to use the ransom to find him, too, doesn't it?"

She nodded. "Yes, of course, but—"

"The cash," Alexander said hurriedly as FBI agents began swarming the area, Moretti bellowing orders. "He never asked for non-consecutive, unmarked bills. He didn't care about the money because he had no intention of taking it *or* returning Melanie. This was his way of drawing you out alone so he could…" He trailed off, grateful the light had come on before it was too late. If a few more seconds had passed, he shuddered to think what would have happened had Olivia gotten into that car.

"But what could he possibly want with me?" she asked, biting her lip.

Alexander shook his head, still as dumbfounded as ever about what was going on. It was now past six at night. Melanie had been missing all day, and they were still clueless about why she was taken or where she could be.

"I don't know, love. It's probably just another way to try to get to me."

"Who?" she quivered.

He ran through the list he had made in his head of everyone he had pissed off in his life. It wasn't short by any stretch of the imagination, but not one person on it stood out. He had thought this was about money. They all did. His firm had worked hundreds of cases for private citizens and very large corporations where they recovered stolen cash and goods. They had been responsible for people losing their jobs, their livelihoods. Some even lost their families as a result of the investigations. But now he knew he had it all wrong. This clearly wasn't just about money. Maleek was after something else. But what? He absently wondered whether it was connected to Mischa's death and Landon's time in Afghanistan, but he couldn't be sure of anything. Until he knew for certain, everyone was a suspect.

"I don't know," he admitted. "But we have a description and a name. You're going to sit down with a sketch artist so we can blast this guy's face all over the country. In the meantime, we'll do our best to track him down with what information we *do* have."

"And what's that? This was our one shot at finding Melanie, but we're now back to the same place we were before!" she said, fighting back tears.

"No, Olivia. Now we have a plate number. Even if he ditches the plates, he's got a busted tail light."

A look of understanding washed over her. "So *that's* why you intentionally missed. I thought you were slipping. Even *I* could have made that shot." She smirked, lightening the intensity momentarily.

"As much as I would have loved to put two in the bastard, he may be the only one who knows where Melanie is."

"We'll find her, right?" Olivia asked, looking up at Alexander through wet eyes.

Wrapping his arms around her and staring at the black sky, his mind went to dark places thinking of Melanie alone and scared. "Of course we will."

TWENTY-THREE

"**D**oes this look about right?" a young man named Robert asked, flipping his tablet around and showing Olivia the final version of a sketch they had been working on.

He had asked questions about so many intricate details regarding Maleek's appearance — the shape of his eyebrows, the fullness of his lips, the curve of his chin, the darkness of his eyes. After over an hour of sketching and re-sketching, Olivia now stared back into a pair of two-dimensional eyes that espoused evil and superiority. It was as if he were here with her, laughing at her, mocking her. They finally got it right.

All she could do was nod at the sketch artist, who didn't look a day over eighteen, even though he hinted he had been with the bureau for close to a decade. He was extremely talented, able to translate Olivia's lackluster description with ease, guiding her every step of the way.

"Great," he responded, punching a few buttons on his tablet.

Olivia marveled at how technology had evolved over the years. She had expected him to show up with pencils and an art pad. Instead, he was armed with a large tablet and stylus pen. With the click of a button, his rough sketch was distributed to every law enforcement agency in the state, as well as the rest of the country. It, along with the car description and plate number Alexander had provided, was added to the **BOLO**, the law enforcement term for "be on the lookout". Still, Olivia had her doubts whether anything would come of it. Alexander had assured her he was working other angles, unbeknownst to the FBI, but refused to tell her what they were. Part of her began to think he simply said that to assuage her fears. The other part of her was terrified of what he would find if he dug too deep.

The house that, just hours ago, had been a flurry of activity in preparation for the ransom exchange was now quiet. Moretti thought Maleek would make contact with her again, but the call never came.

After several hours, most of the FBI agents decided to relocate to the command center down the street from their house. It was nice to have some privacy again, but with the lack of activity and noise, it felt as if nothing were being done to find Melanie. Olivia prayed she was still okay, that Maleek hadn't carried out any of his threats. While she hated the FBI's presence in her house, their absence terrified her. With them here, she was an eyewitness to the frenzied pace at which they moved to find her daughter. Phones constantly rang, people appeared at their door with more files, more computers, more everything. Now, it was eerily silent. No longer surrounded by chaos, she felt more alone than she could bear.

"Mrs. Burnham?" Robert's voice cut through her thoughts and she glanced up, dazed. She didn't feel like herself. She felt like an outsider watching the drama unfold as a strange family navigated through a horrible tragedy.

"Yes?" Olivia heard herself say. It didn't sound like her voice. It was distant, alien, obscure.

"Thanks for your time tonight, ma'am." He stood from the chair across from her and collected his things. "If you think of anything else that could help with his description, please call." He handed her a simple white business card, the FBI's logo dead center. "It's my understanding Agent Long will be staying here with you to keep you apprised of the investigation?" He raised his eyebrows.

Olivia nodded. After most of the agents and officers had dispersed, Agent Long stayed behind, informing the family she would be camping out at the house until the investigation came to an end. Olivia wondered whether that was the real reason for the agent's presence. It was just as easy to keep them updated on any developments via phone. Still, it gave Olivia some sense of security, regardless of how fleeting it truly was. She had always felt secure and protected by her husband. His need to keep her safe was one of the things she fell in love with before she even realized it. His loyalty. His protectiveness. His willingness to risk his life for hers. All reasons she fell madly in love with this man when she had avoided love for so long.

But all that had been destroyed in the blink of an eye. She no longer felt as if her home were an impenetrable building where they could live out their happily ever after. A black cloud hung over the house, under her skin, in her soul. The void left from the absence of laughter and little feet running down the halls made her ache with a pain she couldn't describe.

"I'll let you get some rest," Robert said.

Olivia simply stared blankly at him. He paused for a moment, probably waiting for her to say goodbye, but she had no words left. The helplessness she had avoided all day as they were swept up in the whirlwind of the investigation crashed over her.

She stood from the couch, leaving Robert standing there, and walked out of the room.

"Olivia, love," Alexander called after her, excusing himself from the hushed conversation he had been having with Martin as they toiled over his laptop, probably trying to find Maleek before the FBI did.

She stopped as she approached the ornate staircase, the focal point of the grand entrance to their extravagant house. Yellow police tape roping off the table and broken centerpiece caught her eye.

It took some convincing on Alexander's part for the FBI to allow them to stay when the house could be considered an active crime scene. Olivia understood the FBI's need to maintain the integrity of the evidence, but this was their home. She refused to allow anyone to chase her out.

She turned to face her husband, concern and worry etched on his strong face.

"What can I do?"

Alexander always had a way of asking the right question. He knew not to ask what was wrong or if she was okay. Those questions could be answered without words. Instead, he asked the question she needed at that moment.

Approaching him, she ran her hands through his dark hair. "You're already doing it, Alex." She placed a soft kiss on his lips, trying to hide her true anguish. He had enough on his plate at the moment. He had the resources and ability to track down their daughter. Olivia, on the other hand, felt completely useless, like she had nothing to offer. Even worse, as she had watched Alexander do everything within his power to find Melanie throughout the day, she kept thinking about Mischa. She'd barely had time to mourn her death before her world was tilted on its axis.

"You look exhausted. Why don't you go upstairs and lie down?" he suggested. "I'll come get you if I find anything."

Olivia nodded, allowing his promise to bathe her with a

modicum of comfort. She wanted to ask if he had heard anything more from Dave about Mischa's case, but stopped herself. What kind of grieving mother would she be if she didn't devote all her anguish, heartache, and tears to her missing daughter? One wrong move and the media would crucify her.

"I love you, Mr. Burnham." She placed a lackluster kiss on his lips before heading up the staircase, which was lined with framed photos of their family. They were so happy, so peaceful, so secure. They would never have that again. Even if they found Melanie and she had been spared any physical scars, the psychological ones would never vanish. Olivia was living proof of that. She'd suffered a traumatic event in her early years, having witnessed her own mother's death at the age of six. To this day, even over thirty years later, it still haunted her. She had done everything in her power to shield Melanie from enduring anything like that in her life. She'd failed her.

Stepping onto the second floor landing, Olivia continued down the corridor, the sound of voices fading. The hallway was practically pitch black, another reminder of Melanie's disappearance. She breathed life into the four walls of this house. Without her, there was no energy. There was no heartbeat. There was no soul.

Most nights, her laugh could be heard throughout the halls as she played make-believe or chased Runner. Olivia normally looked forward to the nights Melanie planned to sleep over at her cousin's or a friend's house so she could have a moment of peace and quiet with her husband, a rarity most of the time. Now she craved to hear her daughter's infectious giggle.

Olivia slowed to a stop outside a door blocked with yellow police tape. They had been warned, rather strongly, by Agent Moretti not to cross any of the areas they had marked off. There was a chance they may need to comb the areas again for any evidence that had been overlooked the first time they thoroughly examined each and every nook and cranny of this room. What she was about to do could compromise the entire investigation, but she was no longer concerned with that. She was desperate to feel her daughter's heart, hear her pulse, revel in her spirit.

Ducking beneath the police tape, she turned the knob and entered Melanie's room. The space seemed different now. This was no longer home to a fearless girl who had more love for Olivia than she deserved. This would now become a place of nightmares for her daughter. Would she ever be able to sleep in this room again? Would she ever want to sleep alone? Would she ever feel safe?

Olivia struggled to come to terms with what Melanie's life would be like if she survived this. She hadn't done anything to deserve this. Alexander wasn't without his faults, and neither was Olivia, but Melanie was so young, so pure, so innocent. Now, at far too young an age, she would be jaded by the cruelties of the world.

Would she ever see her smile again?

Would she ever hear her carefree laugh?

Would she ever feel her unconditional love as she flung her arms around her?

Bleakness invaded Olivia right down to her marrow as she fell onto Melanie's unmade bed. Sheets that were once warm from her presence had grown cold, and Olivia could no longer keep it in. She wasn't just watching a made-for-TV movie about a successful, semi-famous family losing their daughter. She was living the nightmare, wishing with everything she had that this would all be over soon, that it wasn't real.

"*Wake up!*" Olivia screamed, slapping her face as relentless tears streamed down her cheeks. She curled into a ball, the torment growing inside her becoming unbearable. It felt like someone was ripping her open with sadistic apathy, the pace languid and sluggish, taking pleasure from each strained breath she struggled to capture. Her skin prickled with the heat of a thousand branding irons. No matter how loud she screamed, it wouldn't dull the pain.

"*Wake up, Olivia!*" she bellowed again, louder and more desperate. Nothing worked. No matter what she did, no matter how loud her cries, nothing would wake her from this nightmare.

Sobs wracked through her body as she fought for air. She tried to gain control over her body and tears, but it was useless. She was no longer in command of her own destiny. Even the seemingly innate task of inhaling and exhaling had become arduous and complicated. Melanie was her lifeline, her reason for living. Without her, Olivia's heart gave out, her lungs refused to work, her body shut down.

Suddenly, a pair of familiar, strong arms cradled her, lifting her off the torturous bed, cocooning her in a shelter only they could provide. They comforted her sobs, giving her exactly what she needed. She cried into her husband's chest, a hundred tears falling for every regret. No words were spoken. Lowering himself to the floor and leaning against the wall, Alexander simply held her in his lap, wiping her tears, providing her with warmth in this cold, hateful world.

She didn't know how many minutes ticked by as he remained there, silently assuring her with his presence that they would get through this, that everything would work out. Still, she knew they would never be the same. This had shaken their family to its core. There was no returning to the way things were before.

Olivia cried harder.

She cried for all the time she should have spent with her daughter instead of working tirelessly for one charity or another. She cried for all the times she told her no when she should have said yes. *Yes, we can have pancakes for dinner. Yes, we can go feed the ducks at the pond. Yes, we can make Christmas cookies in July.*

Exhaustion set in as her cries subsided and she closed her eyes. The last thing she saw before drifting off was Melanie standing alone in a dark room, a blank expression on her pale face.

TWENTY-FOUR

December 19 - 11:15 PM

Alexander tried to remain completely still as he held Olivia in his arms. She looked so peaceful as she slept, her chest rising and falling evenly. The anguish that had consumed her when he first found her in Melanie's room had all but disappeared. Now, she was finally resting, able to keep her worries and fears at bay, if only for a minute.

Moretti would lose his mind if he knew they were both in here, but that was the least of Alexander's concerns at the moment. Olivia needed this. She had held her head high all day, showing great strength. But everyone had their breaking point, and she had reached hers.

"Do you remember our first night in this house?"

Her voice cut through the silence. Alexander looked down to see her studying his face. He wondered how long she had been awake.

Kissing the top of her forehead, he tightened his hold on her as they sat on the floor, Alexander's back against the wall. "I do." A nostalgic smile crossed his face. "There was a mix-up with our furniture delivery. Instead of staying at Ma's for the night, Melanie convinced us to camp out here, so we put sleeping bags in front of the fireplace."

She nodded. "We roasted marshmallows and told scary stories."

"And you told her your idea of 'roughing it' was a hotel with no room service."

"Now every time we stay in a hotel, she asks if we're 'roughing it'." She let out a small laugh as they recalled some of the happy times they'd spent in this house.

All married couples hoped the good times outnumbered the bad, and Olivia and Alexander had been blessed for that to be the case. Just like everybody else, they'd hit a few bumps in the road along the way, but those had been few and insignificant in the grand scheme of things. They'd been fortunate enough to be happy, healthy, and safe…until now.

From the very beginning, Alexander knew both his current position and his status as a discharged SEAL could potentially put all their lives in danger. He had considered walking away from everything the day Melanie was born, but he liked knowing he had a purpose, that people needed him. It didn't occur to him his family needed him more than his employees ever would.

Waves of regret washed over him. He didn't know where he went wrong, how he didn't realize he had been making the same mistakes as his father…the very ones that drove him away.

His phone buzzed, bringing him back from his thoughts, and he pulled it out of his pocket. Reading the text Martin had sent, he tried to hide his disappointment from Olivia.

"What is it?" she asked.

"We got a hit on the plates of the car. Came back to a stolen vehicle out of Peabody. It was found ditched near Boston College."

Nodding, she snuggled against him once more. "You always knew it was probably a dead end," she assured him with a heavy sigh.

"I know, but it didn't prevent me from hoping," he responded quietly.

"Me, either."

They continued to sit in the stillness of Melanie's darkened room…Alexander with his back against the wall and legs stretched out in front of him, Olivia curled in a ball on his lap. This was the first time in weeks, maybe months, they had a moment to themselves. He hated that their daughter's abduction was the reason. They had both been so busy… Alexander with the company, and Olivia with all the charities she was on the board of. When they did have time together, they always spent it with Melanie.

Since the very beginning, Olivia had been insistent on raising Melanie with minimal outside help. With the wealth they had, most would assume they'd have a full-time nanny, but Olivia refused. It takes a village to raise a child, and they'd been fortunate to have a village at their fingertips. Still, life changes after having a baby. Moments alone are rare and valued…like this. Just them. The more he thought about it, though, that wasn't necessarily the case. Alexander felt Melanie's spirit surrounding him. Her energy. Her enthusiasm. The eyes that always looked at him as if he were her hero.

"Thank you, Mr. Crenshaw, for taking the time to tell us all about working in finance," Melanie's teacher said, clapping in a way that encouraged the rest of the class to follow her lead. Doe-eyed with brunette hair cascading to her mid-back, she barely looked like she could have been more than a day out of high school, yet here she was, instilling knowledge into Alexander's little girl.

He glanced around the classroom as he sat in front of a few dozen desks arranged in a circle. It was a far cry from the classroom he remembered from his school days. Then again, he went to public school. His father's company didn't take off until he was a teenager, and even when it did, his parents didn't let that wealth go to any of their heads. Nothing changed, except they were able to take more vacations, drive nicer cars, and not worry about how to make the money stretch to pay all the bills.

The decision to enroll Melanie in private school didn't come easily. Alexander wanted her to have the same kind of upbringing he did, but his need to keep her safe outweighed all that. The other students here were the sons and daughters of politicians, CEOs of Fortune 500 companies, and anyone else wealthy enough to spend more on a year of first grade than most paid for their freshman year of college.

"Next, we have Melanie's dad here to talk about what he does for a living. Class, give Mr. Burnham a warm welcome." She clapped, the rest of the class following her lead.

Alexander looked at the group of students, Melanie standing out with her wide grin and proud eyes. Standing up, he adjusted his tie and made his way to the center of the room, sitting down in the chair.

"Thanks for being here today, Mr. Burnham," Miss Killingly said, sitting in the chair next to his. "We've been learning about different careers and jobs over the past few weeks. Melanie has told the class you're a veteran."

Alexander turned his attention to the group of six-year-olds in front of him, a sudden bout of nerves overtaking him. He had no problem being put on the spot in meetings, confrontations, or interrogations, but there was something uninhibited about children. They asked whatever came to mind. They hadn't yet grasped the concept that there was a time and place for everything, that certain questions just weren't asked.

Based on the previous few parents who had been in the proverbial "hot seat", Alexander knew he could expect anything and everything from these kids. Melanie's teacher certainly encouraged them to ask questions and learn. He had a feeling they would have a lot to ask him. In the grand scheme of things, the other parents worked relatively mundane jobs — real estate investors, hedge fund managers, stockbrokers. Alexander doubted they'd ever had a bullet fired at them, let alone shot a gun.

"Yes," he answered. "I joined the navy when I was eighteen."

"You didn't go to college?" one of the kids asked.

"Thomas," Miss Killingly scolded. "Remember what I told you about not speaking unless you are called on."

"I'm sorry, Miss Killingly." He raised his hand. Alexander nodded at him to go ahead. "Did you go to college, Mr. Melanie's dad?"

"Burnham," Miss Killingly corrected.

"Mr. Burnham," Thomas said, grinning.

"I went to college for a semester, but decided I wanted to serve my country instead. At first, I had planned on going back after leaving the navy, but I became an officer, then went to BUD/S training."

"Why don't you explain to the class what BUD/S stands for, Mr. Burnham," Miss Killingly encouraged.

"It's Basic Underwater Demolition / SEAL training."

Hands shot up all around him. Alexander nodded to a little girl with perfect blond curls.

"You trained seals?" Her eyes were wide and innocent, and she could barely contain her excitement. All the students were on the edge of their seats, honestly believing he was a seal trainer.

"No," Alexander replied, trying not to laugh.

Miss Killingly gave him a grateful smile. Teachers were so underappreciated. This moment reaffirmed that belief. She dealt with the absurd on a daily basis, keeping her composure when Alexander was sure she wanted to laugh at some of the crazy things these kids said.

"A Navy SEAL is a special type of seaman. That's what people who are in the navy are called...seamen." Alexander thanked his

lucky stars this was a class full of six-year-olds and not sixteen-year-olds. That sentence would have had a completely different reaction if the latter sat before him.

"That's right, kids," Miss Killingly said. "Do you remember when we talked about 9/11 and the bad man responsible for that?"

They all nodded.

"Well, it was a team of Navy SEALs, like Melanie's dad, who captured that bad man so he wouldn't do something like that again."

"Oh," several of the kids said, a look of understanding crossing their faces, although there was no way they could truly comprehend exactly what that meant at this age.

"So you killed that bad man?" the little boy named Thomas asked.

"Thomas," Miss Killingly berated. "Remember to wait until you're called on."

"It's okay," Alexander said. "No, I didn't kill that bad man. I left the navy more than a decade ago to take over my father's private security firm."

Hands shot up all around, and he nodded to a sandy-haired boy sitting in the front row.

"Have you ever killed someone?"

He rubbed his hands on his pants and turned his eyes to Miss Killingly. She gave him a look, as if saying he were on his own.

"My team had been responsible for taking down numerous threats to the safety of our country. When I joined the military, I took an oath to do everything in my power to protect this country. I still keep that promise, even to this day."

"I want to be a seal trainer when I grow up," Thomas said, a look of awe on his face.

Alexander smiled, scanning the intrigued faces in the classroom, catching Melanie's eyes. She had a look of pride on her face. He hoped the day would never come that he did something to make her resent him.

Alexander's phone buzzed in his pocket, startling him. He blinked, reacquainting himself with his surroundings. He glanced down to see that Olivia had fallen back to sleep. He must have dozed off at some point, too. He had been running on maybe five hours of sleep over the past three days and his limbs ached from exhaustion. His back throbbed from falling asleep in such an uncomfortable position. After everything Olivia had been through today, she deserved better than sleeping on the floor.

He gingerly extracted himself from her and stood before picking her up and cradling her in his arms. Heading toward the door, he pulled it open and carefully ducked under the yellow police tape, then padded down the long corridor and into their master bedroom. The bed had been left unmade, everything precisely as it was the last time he stepped foot in this room...before he realized Melanie had been taken. It was like it had been frozen in time, a moment of their history he would do anything to change.

Olivia stirred slightly when he placed her on the bed and pulled the duvet over her. A small moan escaped her lips as she nuzzled into the warmth of the silky sheets and down pillows, comforting her, regardless of how short-lived the relief was. Alexander paused and gazed upon his wife lying in the bed they had shared for years. Too many nights, he'd worked late in the office and came home after she had fallen asleep. There was nothing like waking from a dreamless sleep to the feeling of his wife and daughter, who had found her way into their bed at some point during the night, snuggled next to him. He had taken those moments for granted.

Never again.

When this was all over, he wanted to give his wife and Melanie something he'd yet to provide them with...a normal life.

He placed a soft kiss on Olivia's forehead and retreated from the bed, allowing her this time to sleep and forget about the reality of what had happened twenty-four hours ago.

Stepping into the hallway, he pulled his phone out of his pocket and saw a missed call from Simpson. A momentary flash of hope filled him. He'd been having Simpson do everything he could to keep tabs on the FBI's investigation. Alexander was more than aware that Moretti probably wouldn't share everything with him, but Simpson would, and he had the talent to access the FBI's computers without their knowledge. Most of his other agents had the brawn and training from years of military service. Simpson had never worn a uniform of any kind. Alexander often joked that he was born with a computer glued to his hands. He knew more about firewalls and secure IPs than most people could ever fathom. He truly was the brains behind the security firm.

Dialing his number, he waited for the call to connect. Simpson picked up almost immediately.

"You called?" Alexander muttered quietly as he headed down the stairs and toward the east wing of the house where his office was located.

"Sorry for calling so early, sir, but this couldn't wait."

"What is it?" He glanced at his watch and saw it was after five in the morning. He wondered if Simpson ever slept. He kept stranger hours than Alexander did. Regardless of the time of day, Simpson answered whenever he called, sounding as if he were wide awake.

"I've been keeping an eye on the FBI's investigation into…" He cleared his throat, "well, everything."

Alexander knew this was his way of trying to avoid saying Melanie's name. Aside from Martin and Tyler, Simpson probably knew Alexander better than anyone else at the office.

"What did you find?" he pushed, running his hand over his face and rubbing his tired eyes. His body screamed for rest, but his brain wouldn't allow it, not until Melanie was safe. He'd already wasted too much time sleeping tonight. So much could have happened in the last five hours.

"The forensic report on the explosion at the press conference came back."

"I don't follow." Alexander entered his office and sat behind the desk. He had hoped Simpson was calling with some sort of identification from the sketch he had sent him.

"Well, normally I wouldn't think anything of it, especially when an extremist group is involved…"

Alexander's pulse quickened. He straightened his spine, staring out the windows at the dark, snow-covered lawn, only shadowed trees visible.

"The design and chemical makeup of the bomb was pretty much identical to an explosion credited to the Islamic Union that happened one year ago."

"One year?" Alexander tightened his jaw, a sinking feeling forming in the pit of his stomach. He wanted to ward off the words he knew were about to come out of Simpson's mouth, but nothing could stop the truth.

"Yes, sir," he said reluctantly. "It could certainly just be a coincidence, but the chemical makeup of the bomb that caused the explosion at City Hall is practically identical to the bomb that destroyed the shelter in Afghanistan Mr. Tate was operating."

Alexander let out a slow breath, running his hands through his hair. All day long, he had held out hope, regardless of how small, that Melanie's abduction was completely unrelated to him and what he did for a living. That hope had been squashed in the blink of an eye. Now he knew, without a shadow of a doubt, that Melanie's abduction was tied to his company's involvement overseas and Landon's disappearance.

"Anything new on Mischa?" Alexander asked.

"I thought the same thing. I've been looking through Boston PD's files on her death. Aside from her being Landon's sister, there's nothing in her background to tie her to the shelter, so any connection to Melanie's abduction would be tenuous at best."

Alexander sighed, his mind pulled in a thousand different directions. He knew he should stay close in case the sketch of Maleek yielded new information, since he was the only concrete lead they had at this point, but he was itching to have the opportunity to rummage through Mischa's house.

He had spent the hours leading up to Melanie's disappearance looking into Mischa's background. Even with all the tricks Simpson had up his sleeve, there was nothing to tie her to his company's short-lived shelter in Afghanistan, aside from being Landon's sister. They never rebuilt after the explosion. They had done everything within their power to find the women they had provided safe harbor to, but it was as if they had disappeared off the face of the earth.

Working with NCIS, Alexander had come to the conclusion the explosion was most likely a distraction. They had found enough evidence to suggest that the women were, in all probability, returned to their families and the antiquated, barbaric traditions of the tribal communities within the country carried out. Years from now, a body may turn up that they may be able to connect to one of the women he failed to help. Until then, all he could do was assume the worst. That was the only option when someone vanished into thin air.

The idea that someone was now targeting Alexander and Mischa for their connection to the shelter seemed outlandish and improbable, especially considering a year had passed. Memories of the last time he saw Landon forced their way to the forefront of Alexander's brain. He couldn't help but wonder whether his friend's odd request was related.

"What do you think's going on?" Alexander asked Simpson.

"I wish I knew, sir. All I can tell you is what I find, and I find all of this to be too suspicious to simply be a series of isolated, unrelated events."

"I agree." He paused. "If you find anything else, let me know."

"Of course, sir," Simpson replied, then the line went dead.

Alexander slumped in his chair and rubbed his temples as he tried to collect his thoughts. He looked to the corner of his desk, his eyes falling on a framed photo of Olivia and Melanie. He needed to share this new information with her, but didn't know how. How could he possibly tell her Mischa was murdered and their daughter taken because of his company's involvement in Afghanistan?

Alexander snapped out of his thoughts when he heard a knock on the door, followed by the creak of it opening.

"I apologize for interrupting, sir," Martin said, standing in the doorway. His voice was low, exuding the exhaustion he couldn't hide on his face. They had gone days with little sleep before, but had never been put through the emotional ringer of losing a family member. And Melanie was family to him. "There's someone to see you."

Alexander furrowed his brow, eyeing the early hour on the clock. "Who?"

"O'Malley. He just came from the command center where he's been answering tip line calls."

Nodding, Alexander ordered, "Let him in." His skin

prickled with anticipation as Martin retreated from the office. In the cloud of trying to figure out what was going on, Martin had the forethought to have a few of their agents volunteer to answer tip line calls, unbeknownst to the FBI. Crises like these always seemed to bring out the humanity in people, and the command center had been flooded practically all day by neighbors and other people wanting to help. Most of them had been arranged into search parties to comb through the heavily wooded areas that made up this part of the state. However, a few volunteers came with a background in law enforcement or social services, like Alexander's agents. Fortunately, the FBI decided to put them to work on the overloaded tip line.

Alexander certainly hadn't expected any of his agents, or anyone else, to actually get any information by answering those calls. Based on his experience, tip lines were simply a way for law enforcement to make it appear like they were doing everything they possibly could to find a missing person. These days, most people barely looked up from their phones long enough to avoid getting hit by a car when crossing the street, let alone identify a rough sketch of someone.

"Mr. Burnham, sir," O'Malley said quietly as he entered the dim office. "I'm sorry for barging in at such an early hour."

"It's quite all right." Alexander gestured to the seat across from him.

He lowered himself into the chair, glancing at Alexander with a nervous expression. He was a newer agent, but Martin had appeared confident he was perfect for this task, said he could get a monk who had taken a vow of silence to talk.

"Have you found anything?" Alexander asked.

"Yes, sir. I was answering calls when I noticed a bit of

commotion. An FBI agent got a call on his cell, spoke for a few minutes, then went to get Agent Moretti."

"He's still there?" Alexander raised his eyebrows.

"Yes. There's a room with a few cots set up so the agents can get a little sleep, but are still close by in case there are any new developments."

Alexander nodded. "Go on."

"I tried to make it appear as if I wasn't eavesdropping on what was going on and kept answering calls. I'm able to read lips, though. Apparently, a man who works at a convenience store in Roxbury called, responding to the photo the FBI released of Maleek. He claimed a man matching the description of the sketch has come in at least once a day for the past several months to buy cigarettes, that he lives in a two-level house across the street from the store. At first, the clerk wasn't sure whether the sketch was the man or not, then he remembered seeing something suspicious after one in the morning on Saturday."

Alexander straightened his spine. That was in the same time frame in which Melanie had been taken.

"The clerk saw him drive up to the house and back into the driveway. Then he saw someone get out of the passenger seat."

"Did he leave a description of his passenger?" Alexander asked.

"No. He said it was dark and couldn't make out any details. He did mention his passenger was on the shorter side, maybe a few inches over five feet. They both went around the back of the SUV and opened the rear hatch. The clerk watched as they carried what appeared to be a heavy object around the back of the house. They didn't enter through the front door, so he assumed they used the back door or the storm door leading to the basement."

Alexander's heart raced in his chest as he absorbed O'Malley's report. "And how did Agent Moretti respond to all of this?"

"He put together a team to head over to the address in question right away. One of the other agents asked if they should inform you and he said no. That this may turn out to be just another caller looking for his fifteen minutes of fame. That he didn't want to get your hopes up until he was certain it was a viable lead."

Alexander slammed his fists on the desk and opened one of the drawers, withdrawing a pistol and securing it in his holster. "Bullshit. He knows damn well it's a viable lead." He bolted from his seat. "Martin." He turned to him.

"Yes, sir."

"As much as I want your help," he began with a sigh, "I need you to stay with Olivia."

"Sir," he responded, nodding, as Alexander headed out of the office and down the hallway.

"How does he know it's a viable lead?" O'Malley called after him, following him toward the front door.

"Because, O'Malley." Alexander spun around. "The FBI never said this man was wanted in connection with Melanie's disappearance. They simply said he was a person of interest wanted in connection with an ongoing investigation. This wasn't just another caller looking for his fifteen minutes of fame. This is the real deal."

TWENTY-FIVE

December 20 - 7:10 AM

Olivia's eyes fluttered open and she looked around, disoriented. The last thing she remembered was falling asleep in Alexander's arms as they sat together in Melanie's room. Now, she was in their bed… alone. Pushing back the covers, she noticed she was still in the clothes she wore the night before, but it was no longer night. The sun had risen, trying to break through the heavy gray clouds blanketing the sky.

She glanced at the clock, wondering how long she had been asleep, seeing it was already after seven in the morning. Her chest grew tight thinking about all the time she had wasted. It was selfish to sleep so soundly and comfortably when she should have been doing something…*anything*.

Jumping out of bed, she dashed into the bathroom and splashed some water on her face. After putting on clean clothes and pulling her hair back, she headed downstairs in search of an update as to what was going on.

The smell of bacon met her as she drew near the kitchen. Agent Long sat on a stool at the large eat-in island in the center of the room as Colleen fried bacon, whipped up some scrambled eggs, and toasted bread. There was already a plate of blueberry muffins, as well as trays upon trays of different kinds of Christmas cookies. Olivia wondered if Colleen had slept at all, or if she simply stayed in the kitchen, baking and cooking away her heartache.

"Olivia, dear," Colleen said when she saw her enter. She stopped what she was doing and walked up to wrap her arms around her. After a longer than usual hug, she pulled back and met her eyes. Olivia could see her pain, her fear, her unease. She looked like a woman doing everything to keep the pieces together. "How are you holding up?"

"Okay, Colleen."

"Okay?" She squeezed her arm, holding her gaze.

"Okay," Olivia repeated, drawing in a shaky breath. Would she ever be anything more than okay again? "Is Alex here?"

"No, he's not," Agent Long answered in a curt tone. Olivia whipped her head around to face her.

"Sore subject, dear," Colleen murmured into Olivia's ear.

"He left the house earlier this morning…without my approval."

"Where did he go?" Olivia pushed. "And I didn't realize we needed *your* approval to leave. It was my understanding we could come and go as we pleased, that your job here was to simply answer any questions we may have or to offer us support, not to restrict our movements."

"I also have to ensure your safety, particularly after last night's ransom demand that could have led to another abduction."

Olivia crossed her arms in front of her chest. "You really think you can do a better job at keeping my husband safe than *he* can?" she scoffed. "Not likely. Where did he go?"

Agent Long flipped the page of the newspaper. "He went out on his own, even after Agent Moretti warned him not to interfere, and is following up on a lead received earlier this morning."

"A lead?" Olivia perked up.

"Yes, Mrs. Burnham," Agent Long replied with a heavy

sigh. "It's our general rule of thumb to investigate leads before involving the family so we don't raise any hopes." She glanced up from her paper and met Olivia's rapt gaze. "But we received a call from someone who said they recognized the man in the sketch. I wouldn't put much faith into it just yet. It could be nothing."

"But it could be something, couldn't it?" Olivia asked, holding the one glimmer of hope she had left.

"Perhaps," Agent Long agreed, returning her attention to this morning's *Boston Globe* and sipping her coffee.

A million thoughts racing through her head, Olivia grabbed her cell out of her pocket and dialed Alexander, holding her breath as she listened to the call connect.

"Olivia," he answered in hushed tones after two rings.

"Alex," she breathed. "What's going on? I woke up and—"

"I'm in Roxbury," he interrupted. "One of my agents overheard a conversation at the command center about a possible lead on Maleek's location. Moretti had no intention of telling me. Thankfully, my agent knew enough to come over and inform me about what was going on."

"And what's that?"

He sighed. Olivia could sense his frustration through the phone. After living with someone for so long, you could anticipate their emotions with little warning.

"I still don't know, Olivia. A clerk at a convenience store believes the man living across the street is Maleek. Just after Melanie's abduction, he saw him pull up with another person, then carry something heavy around back."

Olivia gasped, covering her mouth with her hand. "She's there?"

"We haven't been inside yet, but she's not here. No one is."

"How can you know she's not there?" she asked urgently. "Why haven't you been inside?"

"Based on what happened at the press conference, Moretti is using an overabundance of caution and wants the bomb squad to send in a robot to secure the house before anyone goes inside. In the meantime, they used a thermal cam and there were no heat signatures, although the technology isn't exactly accurate when going through walls of a house."

"What does that mean?" she asked, his words not registering.

"Based on the readings off the camera, they don't believe there's anyone inside the house, but they want to wait to enter it until they're sure it's not rigged in any way. If this *is* Maleek's house, it stands to reason there could be explosive material here that he used to make the bomb Rayne carried into the press conference. Regardless, there's no guarantee the man the clerk saw is actually Maleek or that Melanie was ever here. Until we can get inside, we won't know anything for certain."

"But the second you get inside, you'll call and let me know what you find, right?"

"Of course."

"Okay." Olivia sighed, defeated. It felt like this was all one big waiting game. She didn't know how much longer she could survive without hearing her daughter's laugh, without feeling her small arms wrapped around her.

"The bomb squad just got on scene," Alexander said urgently, an audible commotion in the background — shouting, trucks driving by. "They're going to jam all the cell phones in the area to be on the safe side. I had Martin stay at the house. If you need to go anywhere, even at the FBI's request, he'll take you. Do you understand?"

Olivia closed her eyes, nodding. "Yes. Just be careful."

"Always," he said in a sweet voice. "I love you, Olibia."

She clutched the phone tighter, closing her eyes briefly. Listening to Alexander's breathing, she could almost picture him right beside her, whispering those words. In the midst of everything going on, that was exactly what she needed to hear to make her heart full…the nickname for her that belonged to him and only him.

"And I love you, Alex. Hurry home." She remained on the line, only to be met with dead air moments later. Checking the screen, she saw the call had disconnected.

With a heavy heart, she returned her phone to her pocket and lowered herself onto one of the barstools, staring out the window at the bleakness surrounding her.

"Hungry, dear?" Colleen asked, placing a plate of eggs, toast, and fruit in front of her.

"Thanks, Colleen, but…" She pushed the dish away.

"I know eating is the last thing you probably feel like doing right now, but it'll make you feel better. Believe me."

She met her mother-in-law's bloodshot eyes. As much as Olivia couldn't stomach the thought of eating, she did it for Colleen. She needed to feel wanted, as if she were doing something to bring Melanie back, even though they were all completely helpless at the moment, Alexander included.

A stiff silence fell over the house on that Sunday morning as Olivia pushed her breakfast around her plate. She kept looking out the window, hoping to see Alexander drive up. Colleen was just as worried, but did a better job at masking her unease. Every fifteen minutes, Olivia tried Alexander's phone, only for it to go straight to voicemail.

"He'll be fine, ma'am," Martin assured her.

All Olivia could do was nod.

After an hour, she couldn't stand it anymore. She

couldn't just sit around and wait. She needed to do something to help ward off all the thoughts circling around in her head. Grabbing her coat from the hallway closet, she headed toward the door leading to the garage, Martin jumping to his feet and following behind her.

"Where are you going?" Agent Long asked, catching up to them.

"Out," Olivia replied curtly.

"I see that. Where?"

Turning around, she sighed heavily. "Over to a friend's."

Agent Long placed her hands on her hips. "If you want to see any friends, I recommend having them come here."

"I need to get out of this house," Olivia responded through a clenched jaw. "I can't just sit here anymore. Everywhere I turn, I'm faced with another reminder of my daughter. I need to go somewhere to clear my head."

"Don't you want to be here if they find anything?"

"I'll have my cell with me. If they find anything, my husband will let me know. Goodbye, Agent Long."

Olivia headed into the garage and followed Martin to a dark SUV, hopping into the back seat. She expected Agent Long to put up a little more of a fight. Maybe she realized it was pointless, that there was no reason to keep Olivia as a prisoner in her own house.

Jumping into the driver's seat, Martin caught her gaze in the rearview mirror and nodded. No words needed to be spoken. He knew exactly where she wanted to go. After turning the key in the ignition, Martin drove out of the garage and down the long driveway, pulling onto the street. Silence engulfed them as Olivia watched the miles zoom by, acutely aware of her surroundings, worried someone would follow. Worried someone knew exactly what she had done.

Worried someone had put the pieces together and all her work had been for nothing.

As Martin merged onto the interstate and headed north, her racing heart began to slow, but she still couldn't relax completely. She felt as if the people in every car that passed stared at her, telling her with their eyes that they knew her secret, that she wouldn't be able to keep it from her husband much longer. She just didn't know how he would react.

Just before nine, Martin pulled off a residential road in Arlington. After punching a code into the gate, he navigated down a long driveway leading up to a Tudor-style home that was over a century old.

"I'll wait in here, ma'am," Martin said.

"Thanks, Martin. I won't be too long."

"Take your time."

Church bells chimed and she glanced at the tower to her right. Stepping out of the car, she could almost make out angelic voices singing a hymn as the services began. She wondered if anyone in the congregation would pray for her daughter's safe return.

A strong breeze blew through the air and she tugged her jacket closer, refocusing her attention on the house in front of her. A melting snowman greeted her as she trekked up the path to the front door. She smiled to herself, picturing one of her best friends building that creation with his three boys.

Climbing a set of concrete steps, she pulled back the screen door and inserted her key into the lock, letting herself into the house. A warmth surrounded her as she listened to the sounds of laughter emanating from the kitchen.

"Hello?" she called out, the chatter ceasing immediately.

"Auntie Olivia!" three small voices exclaimed, followed by the sound of chairs being pushed away. She was soon met with a barrage of arms wrapping around her legs.

An olive-skinned man rounded the corner to where she stood in the formal living area, a dish towel flung over his shoulder, his brown eyes awash with sympathy. His dark hair sported a touch of gray now that he was on the other side of forty, but he still had a youthful appearance about him.

"Livvy…"

She tried to retain her composure when she saw the worry on Mo's face. She bit her bottom lip, taking a quick inhale of air.

"Boys, go back into the kitchen and finish eating your breakfast," he ordered the three kids flanking her.

She gazed down at them affectionately, seeing a mixture of both their mother's and father's best features. They had dark, inquisitive eyes like their father, and light hair with a hint of red like their mother. Olivia didn't know how Kiera and Mo kept up with having three boys under the age of six, with another baby due any day now. Having one child was a lot of work, even with plenty of help. Olivia didn't know how they were going to deal with four.

Mo had taken a break from touring with his band, Groove Delay, to be here for the birth of their fourth child. He was being hounded by his record label and manager to get back on the road and promote the new album that had soared to the top of the charts in its first week. Their lives had changed almost overnight, and Olivia couldn't be happier for them, but she knew this newfound fame was diffi-cult on both Kiera and Mo, particularly when it came to having time for family. Kiera supported Mo with everything, assuring him they would find a new routine, a new normal, but Mo had recently confided in Olivia about how guilty he felt, particularly after being gone for over a month. Once Kiera hit her third trimester and had been ordered to remain on bedrest, he couldn't take it anymore, putting the tour on hold to be with his family.

"You can visit with Auntie Olivia later, okay?" He narrowed his gaze at the boys.

"Okay," they all said in unison and released their hold on her, heading back into the kitchen.

The sound of forks hitting plates echoed as Mo faced her once more, satisfied they had a brief moment to themselves. He wrapped his arms around her and pulled her tight against him, hugging her with everything he had. She took a deep breath, struggling to keep it together. She didn't know if she had any tears left to cry at this point.

"I wanted to stop by to see how you were holding up, but I couldn't leave Kiera."

"I got your message," Olivia said. "I'm sorry I didn't call you or Kiera back. It's just been a bit crazy."

"No need to apologize," he offered, pulling back and holding her at arm's length. "You have a lot on your plate. The last thing you need to worry about is calling me or Kiera. We're okay. Everything here is okay." He gave her a knowing look.

"Is that Libby I hear down there?" a familiar shrill voice boomed. Despite having to remain in her bed or on the couch, apart from showering, Kiera sounded like her normal self. "Get your a... I mean, butt up here."

Olivia allowed herself a laugh. Kiera had been a mom for six years now and still had trouble watching her language around the kids. When she first got pregnant, they often joked that the baby's first words wouldn't be "mama" or "dada". It would be "shit". Luckily, that didn't come true, although her oldest, Bryan, learned "goddammit" at one of the most inconvenient times...a funeral for one of Mo's aunts. He walked up and down the aisles of the church saying it over and over again. Kiera was horrified. Mo, along with most everyone else, laughed it off, thankful for the levity.

Shrugging at Mo, Olivia headed down the hall and up the stairs toward the master bedroom. Entering, she smiled at her friend. Aside from being bedridden, she looked like her regular self. Her fair skin contrasted with the strawberry blond hue of her vibrant hair, her bold green eyes brimming with compassion.

"Oh, Libby," Kiera exhaled, holding her arms out.

Olivia rushed to one of her closest friends and hugged her. They remained in each other's embrace for several long moments, neither one wanting to say anything or break the connection. Nearly two decades ago, Olivia had met Kiera her first week of college and they had remained friends through all of life's ups and downs.

"God, this whole thing just sucks," Kiera said through her tears.

Olivia pulled back, biting her lower lip. "Don't go getting upset," she warned, eyeing her enormous stomach.

Kiera was tiny to begin with, only hitting five-two on a good day. Each pregnancy took a toll on her body, but she insisted she wouldn't change a thing. She loved being a mom, and was about to become a mother again to either a beautiful girl or a handsome boy. They never wanted to know the gender and were happy as long as the baby was healthy. Still, Olivia held out hope that Kiera would finally get a girl.

"I don't want you going into labor just yet." Olivia winked.

"You and me both." Kiera rubbed her stomach. "You've got to cook just a bit longer, little one."

Olivia smiled at her, then caught the time on the clock. She didn't want to be gone too long, and there was still something she needed to do.

Understanding fell over Kiera's face and she nodded. "I know. Go ahead."

Mo walked into the room, sitting on a chair in the corner.

"I'm sorry for putting both of you in this predicament. I promise it'll just be maybe another day at most," Olivia assured them. "Martin is working on that whenever he can. Obviously, his priority is helping Alexander, but he's doing what he can to fix this situation without Alex finding out. Mischa would be so grateful for what you're doing for her… for everyone."

Kiera squeezed Olivia's hand, telling her in that one gesture that she would gladly do everything she could to help.

"Do you think what happened to Mischa could be connected to…?" Mo trailed off, but Olivia knew what he was getting at.

"The thought has certainly crossed my mind," she admitted, "but it doesn't make sense. No one knew of my involvement, aside from Mischa and Martin, and now you two. I've kept this from everyone for months. Even Alex has never picked up on anything going on. If *he* never put the pieces together, I doubt anyone else would be able to. There's no paper trail. There's nothing. I honestly think these were two isolated events that just happened to occur in close proximity to each other."

Mo nodded. "I hope you're right."

Olivia stood from the bed. "Me, too." She gave Kiera a kiss on the forehead, then walked out of the room.

The floorboards creaked below her feet as she padded down the hallway toward a back staircase. The original house was built by a wealthy landowner in the 1700s. Over the years, it had deteriorated and was torn down to its foundation, then rebuilt in the early 1900s. Most of the original house had been lost…except for the underground walkway the original owner had constructed so his household staff could still get to the main house from the smaller servants' quarters, which was now a guest house, even in the most brutal of snowstorms.

Grabbing her cell phone, Olivia illuminated the dark stairwell in front of her and climbed down the winding, narrow stairs. When she reached the bottom, a chill set in. Cobwebs hung from the corners of the old basement. She shined her twenty-first century flashlight around the room, searching for the wooden door. She didn't know why the tunnel hadn't been filled in over the years, but Olivia was thankful it hadn't. If it had, she didn't know what she would do. This was the only place she could think of on such short notice. If someone *had* figured out her involvement, nothing about visiting two good friends would raise any red flags.

The door hinges screamed through the silent house as she pulled it open and shined her light into the empty tunnel that probably hadn't been used in ages…until recently. With each step she took, the more her stomach churned. She didn't know why she was so nervous. She knew everything would be okay, but it didn't help settle her unease. Nothing would until she saw with her own two eyes that Mischa's legacy was still alive and well.

Reaching the end of the tunnel, a dim light illuminated a set of stairs. Olivia climbed them and opened a heavy door, emerging into the basement of the guest house. She found a staircase leading to the main floor and climbed it, stopping outside a closed door. Drawing in a long breath, she raised her hand and knocked on it in a specific pattern. *Short. Short. Long. Long. Short.*

When the door opened, she breathed a sigh of relief.

TWENTY-SIX

December 20 - 8:30 AM

"All clear," a man clad in a green bomb suit from head to toe declared, turning away from the front steps of a two-story white house with black shutters. The roof was in a serious state of disrepair, and Alexander didn't think the siding of the house had ever been pressure-washed.

He looked at Moretti, who stood to his left, and their eyes met. When Alexander miraculously showed up at the house, Moretti had made it readily apparent he was annoyed with his presence. Alexander couldn't just sit by and do nothing. Sure, Moretti had one of the highest solve rates in the bureau, but what if this was the one case he'd never be able to get to the bottom of? What if he missed something? Alexander needed to be here to make sure that didn't happen.

Exhaling in obvious annoyance, Moretti handed Alexander a set of shoe covers and gloves. "Fine, but you'd better not touch *anything*," he hissed. "I mean it. If you touch so much as a particle of dust—"

"I know. I know," Alexander cut him off. "It could compromise the integrity and admissibility of the evidence. This isn't my first rodeo. I want this fucker to burn for what he's done, so the absolute *last* thing I intend to do is give him a 'get out of jail free' card."

He pushed past him and toward the front steps of the

house, Moretti catching up to him with ease. As they approached the front door, one of the bomb squad technicians stopped them.

"Agent Moretti," he began.

"Yes?"

"I just wanted to let you know that, although the thermal cam couldn't pick up on any bodies, our robot found one inside."

"What?" Alexander's heart fell to his stomach. His legs were on autopilot as he darted into the house, frantically scanning each room, unsure of what he would find. He feared the worst. That he would stumble on a scene no parent should ever have to.

As he ran from one room to the next, all he could think was he should have been more watchful. More caring. More involved. If he had, maybe this never would have happened.

He tore down a short hallway, past a bathroom that had seen better days, and paused briefly outside a door that was ajar. Entering the room, he looked around, falling to his knees as he stared at a body slumped over a desk. He had never been so relieved, yet so distraught at the same time. Heavy footsteps echoed down the corridor, coming to a stop behind him.

Hanging his head, Alexander slowly stood and walked to the desk, careful not to touch the body. Moretti was probably anxious to get forensics in to figure out what happened, but Alexander needed this. He needed to look into those eyes.

Squatting beside the desk, he tilted his head, staring directly at the bastard's face. He had a darker complexion than Alexander had pictured, and it was evident he was of Middle Eastern descent. His eyes were blank, having long blinked their last. The through-and-through bullet wound in the center of his head confirmed that.

Straightening, Alexander stepped to the side, surveying the back of his head.

"Entry point?" Moretti asked, standing next to him.

"That's my guess. Probably never even saw it coming."

"Fucking Christ," he breathed, running his hand over his face.

Alexander felt his frustration. He didn't know how much more of this he could go through before he lost it. Every time they thought they were getting closer to finding Melanie, something would happen to bring them right back to square one.

Glancing out the window to see small snowflakes beginning to fall from the sky, dread flowed through his bones. The Nor'easter was on their doorstep, but there was no telling where Melanie was or whether she had ever actually been here.

"I want every inch of this place searched." Moretti tore his attention away from the corpse, issuing orders to his team of agents and crime scene technicians, all of them staring. "Document everything. Find out how this happened and where the hell the girl is!" His face reddened with each word he spoke. "*Now!*" he bellowed, the team jumping into action.

A chill set in when Alexander looked at Maleek's body once more, analyzing his face. He seemed familiar, and it wasn't just because of the sketch that had gone out. There was something else. He studied his features inch by inch, searching his brain for a memory he feared wouldn't come. Frustration sprouted into anger. He had been trained to memorize impossibly long combinations of numbers and letters. He could recognize someone he had seen driving alongside him during his morning commute. He could recall exactly what he was wearing when Olivia went into labor. But when it mattered, when he needed to remember something that could bring his little girl back home, he drew a blank.

He ran his hand through his hair, tugging at it, letting out a defeated groan.

"What is it?" Moretti asked, eyeing him.

"I feel like I should know this guy."

He narrowed his gaze. "Why's that?"

"I don't know. He looks familiar, and it's not because of the sketch." Alexander kept staring at Maleek, wracking his brain. He did everything he could to force a forgotten memory to return. He mentally went back in time, thinking perhaps this man was connected to Mischa. Did he work for her organization? He hadn't yet told Moretti his theory that Mischa's death was connected to Melanie's disappearance. The only people who knew were Simpson and Martin. Maybe they weren't connected. Maybe Alexander was just a desperate man at the end of his rope, grasping at straws.

"Agent Moretti," a young blonde called, out of breath as she ran toward them.

"What is it?" he replied, turning his attention away from Alexander.

She stopped in her tracks, swallowing hard when she saw Maleek's pale, cold body. It was apparent she hadn't been to many homicides.

"Agent Gibson asked me to come get you. He needs you upstairs."

"Did he find something?"

"I believe so."

"Thank you, Agent…" Moretti raised his eyebrows.

"Stocker, sir."

"Agent Stocker, please go across the street to the convenience store and ask if the clerk has seen anything suspicious over the past twenty-four hours. See if he or she remembers seeing any cars parked along the street or in the driveway, anyone coming or going from the house."

She smiled in excitement. Alexander had the feeling she hadn't been out of the academy for too long. "Yes, sir. Thank you, sir." She practically ran down the hall and out of the house.

Moretti headed toward the living room, Alexander following. "Get blood spatter in there," he ordered another agent, gesturing with his head toward the room they had just come from. "I want to know exactly where the shooter stood when he fired the weapon. I want to know what kind of bullet was used and the gun that shot it. Understand?"

"Yes, sir," a man clad in a white jumpsuit answered as Moretti and Alexander headed up a narrow staircase leading to the second floor. More agents filled each room, combing through every nook and cranny for anything that could put the puzzle together.

"Moretti!" Agent Gibson called out from the end of the hallway. "In here."

They followed the sound of his voice, curious as to what was so urgent, but neither could have expected to stumble on what awaited them.

Crossing the threshold into a square ten-foot by ten-foot room, Alexander tried to wrap his head around what he was staring at.

A desk sat in the center facing away from the door. The windows were boarded up with plywood, and there was a musty smell, probably from the lack of air and sunshine for who knows how long. Photos, newspaper articles, and hand-written notes covered the walls from floor-to-ceiling. None of it made sense until Alexander turned around and stared at the wall adjacent to the door. As his eyes fell on four rows of black-and-white passport photos, his mouth fell open.

He approached the wall, running his fingers across every photo. A name, along with a list of various offenses, was scrawled below each one — adultery, sexual promiscuity, refusal of arranged marriage, seeking divorce. Each woman had been accused of something different, but the intended end result was clear, just as it was the day Landon had convinced Alexander to finally do something good with the massive fortune the security company made. Every single one of these women was Afghani…except one.

Alexander continued along the wall, stopping in front of a black-and-white photo, her face obscured with a large red X. She was so vivid, so full of life, even in the two-dimensional photograph. It was a stark contrast to the last time he had seen her, bruised and bloody, stuffed into a metal container.

Agent Moretti approached, staring at the name below the photo. "Mischa Tate," he read. "Is this the same—"

"Yes," Alexander cut him off, swallowing hard. His theory that Mischa's murder could be connected to Melanie's disappearance was no longer just a theory. The two events were part of something bigger. "It is."

"I see," Moretti mused, staring straight ahead. "And the rest of these women?"

Alexander shook his head. "Some of their faces look familiar, I think." He scanned the rows of photos, all of them looking nearly identical. Did he really know any of them, or did he just think he did? He couldn't be sure.

"From where?"

"Afghanistan. Some of these women…" He ran his hand over the wall. "I won't know for certain until I can cross-reference my files, but I think they went missing from the women's shelter my company ran there."

Moretti grabbed his notepad from his coat pocket and

flipped through the pages. "The shelter Ms. Tate's brother, Landon, was in charge of? The one destroyed by an explosion most likely to cover up his abduction by the Islamic Union?"

Alexander nodded, not even bothering to ask Moretti how he knew so much. Of course he knew all about Landon's death. He knew everything.

"And Ms. Tate's connection to all these women?" Moretti raised his eyebrows.

Staring at the photos, Alexander let out a heavy sigh. "Apart from being the sister of the man running the shelter where these women lived, none that I'm aware of."

Maybe Moretti was right. Maybe Alexander was too invested. Maybe he needed the agent's detached brain to put the pieces together because Alexander had come up empty. The girls. Landon. Melanie. Mischa. What was going on?

He stopped abruptly as his eyes fell on one of the names. He glanced at the photo above, his breath hitching. He'd recognize that face in his sleep. It was something one didn't forget. Her scars had faded and the bruising and swelling had diminished, but those haunting eyes would stay with him forever. The last time he saw them, they pleaded with him to put an end to her suffering, as well as the suffering of all other women in her position. Now they looked at him, mocking, telling him it wasn't enough, that he should have done more.

TWENTY-SEVEN

Fourteen Months Ago

Alexander stepped out of the SUV and onto the sidewalk in front of his office building, a crisp breeze blowing through the city on the sunny October day. Entering the lobby, he nodded a greeting to Jerry, one of his security guards. He was already looking forward to the end of the day when he would get on a plane and take his daughter to Disneyland for the first time.

He'd left Olivia and Melanie in bed as he got ready to head into the office, both of them watching *The Little Mermaid* for the hundredth time. Melanie was fascinated with the movie and kept asking if she would ever be able to turn into a mermaid. Not wanting to crush her hopes and dreams, he did what any good parent would. He lied.

"Melanie, sweetie, you can be anything you want," he had told her. He truly believed that if she wanted to be a mermaid, in her mind, she would be. A child's imagination was a gift that shouldn't be broken with the dark cruelty of the real world.

Thinking of how blessed he was, Alexander smiled to himself the entire way up to the twenty-ninth floor, still in his own little dream world as he headed down the corridor and entered his office.

"A bit of a late start today, don't ya think?" a familiar voice said, snapping him out of his thoughts.

Alexander shot his head to the right, curious as to why Landon was lounging on the couch in the sitting area, his cap over his eyes. He hadn't mentioned he was heading state-side, and Alexander wondered what had brought him here, especially considering he had just been back not even six weeks ago. Maybe Rayne convinced him to finally stop drag-ging his feet and marry her. They had been engaged for longer than many people remained married.

"Landon." Alexander strode toward him as he jumped off the couch. They hugged briefly. "Good to see you, you bastard."

"You, too, you dumb prick."

Olivia always shook her head when they got together, not understanding why they would call each other such names. After persevering through something as mind-numbing and grueling as BUD/S, you formed a certain camaraderie with your teammates. And part of that included terms of affec-tion, such as "bastard" and "dumb prick".

"I wasn't expecting to see you for another few weeks," Alexander admitted.

Landon's brilliant smile faltered and he ran his hands over his pants. "Yeah, I know, but…" He trailed off.

"What is it?" Alexander sat down on the couch, Landon lowering himself beside him.

"I didn't know what else to do, Alex," he admitted, his jovial voice turning serious. "I'm in deep here and I don't know who else to turn to."

"Slow down, Landon."

Being in life or death situations with someone teaches you a lot about that person. Alexander knew all of Landon's tells. Anytime he was nervous, he would speak in vague terms. The bigger the problem, the more obscure the words. Whatever the problem this time, Alexander had a feeling Landon was in way over his head.

"Start at the beginning and tell me what this is all about."

Landon let out a sigh. "It's the girls."

"The girls?" Alexander furrowed his brow, not understanding. "I thought everything at the shelter's been manageable, aside from a few expected hiccups."

Shaking his head, Landon ran his hand over his face. In an instant, he looked years older than he was. His eyelids drooped, a forlorn weariness seeping into the lines around his eyes.

"We've been able to handle it all. Between myself and the staff, as well as some help from my buddies in the Marines and navy stationed over there, we've been able to thwart various threats."

"Then what's so important that you flew all the way here to talk to me in person?"

Landon hesitated. "Promise you'll let me finish what I have to say before you blow up."

Studying him, Alexander looked for some sort of indication about what had his friend so wound up and acting incredibly out of character. "At least you're not asking me not to get mad."

"I know you better than that," Landon replied. Turning toward Alexander, he paused, taking a breath. "It started about a month ago. As you know, we've been working with the Ministry of Women's Affairs every step of the way. And we still are."

Alexander nodded. He had met with a few liaisons in the ministry numerous times. Without their help, the shelter never would have seen the light of day.

"We're still meeting all the requirements the ministry has set forth. We're not technically breaking any protocol."

"Okay...," Alexander replied in a drawn-out voice, waiting for the punchline.

"Typically, the ministry's goal is to reunite the family

unit. They arrange supervised meetings, with a facilitator, between the girls and their families to try to make each side understand where the other is coming from. It can be a long process, sometimes taking a year or more, but in the end, the ministry wants the family unit to become whole again. As you know, our shelter's different. We take the worst of the worst, women who the ministry believe face a great risk of death or severe injury if the family members even knew their location. Our liaison handpicks these women, sending them to us for safe harbor. No one knows it's even a shelter. For all intents and purposes, it's just a medical clinic."

"Yes, I understand all of that."

"Everything was going great until…" He closed his eyes.

"Until what?"

Sighing, his shoulders fell. "A few months ago, our ministry liaison, Rahima, went missing. Her body was found a few days later, a bullet to the head." He briefly closed his eyes. "Immediately following her disappearance, the clinic was hit for the first time. I think someone figured out what's been going on and went through her to find out these women's location. Police brushed it off as just a group of locals unhappy with the western presence, but it's got to be connected to Rahima's disappearance."

"Have you spoken to your new liaison about this?"

He nodded. "Aliyah tends to agree with the local police. She says clinics get hit all the time, especially those operated by western organizations. I guess she has a point, but my gut tells me there's more to it." He drew in a long breath and met Alexander's eyes, his expression pleading. "These women have lived in fear for so long. For a second, they could finally breathe, but now…" He bowed his head. "All that's gone again. They jump at every loud noise. They're just waiting for the day our protective services aren't good enough. I thought a shelter was the best way to keep them safe, but it's not. These women are forced to live suspended between two worlds. It's not a safe haven. It's a jail. Yes, they're alive, but they're not really living. And it's only a matter of time until it all crumbles beneath us."

Alexander continued staring at his friend, waiting for him to drop the bomb. Landon rubbed his hands on his pants, his jaw clenching before he turned to Alexander once more.

"I don't know who else to go to. You're the only one I know who can pull something like this off." He ran his hands through his hair, drawing in a deep breath. "If I could just have help getting them to Ecuador, I can get them here."

"Here?" Alexander straightened his spine, disbelief covering his face. He didn't know what he thought Landon was going to say, but it certainly wasn't this. "What about the rules of engagement?!" Alexander roared.

"Fuck the rules of engagement!" Landon shot up, glaring at him. "When did you start caring more about diplomacy and bureaucracy than just saying fuck it and doing what you want? The Alex I remember from our SEAL days worked outside the box, and we did amazing things together. We can do that again! Here! We can make a difference! We can save lives!"

Alexander buried his head in his hands as he tried to reel in his anger.

"They'll never be safe there," Landon bellowed, his face turning red. "I can't just do nothing, knowing each morning they wake up may be their last. Some of them are just girls with babies of their own! One of them is pregnant from her rapist, and the family wanted her to marry him! *Marry him!* Can you imagine? I have to do something, but I need your help."

"Landon, please—"

"I know you have a lot of pull with all your contacts. I just need help getting them on a transport out of Afghanistan. Not even all of them! We'll just get one out at a time so we don't raise suspicion. If anything goes wrong, your name will never come up."

Alexander shook his head. Landon was asking him to break every rule in the book, not to mention violate federal immigration law. "How do you choose who gets to go and who stays behind? Who decided that you get to play God?"

"I'm *not* playing God. I'm just being a decent human being, helping those most at risk. Come on, Alex. You've never played by anybody's rules before. Why start now?"

"Landon, I may bend the rules," Alexander stated firmly, standing, "but I don't break them. We don't smuggle women out of the country! That's not our purpose over there. Our purpose is to provide a temporary safe haven for those who need it!"

"But it's no longer safe! There's no other option. Not anymore!"

"How do you expect me to explain the missing girls to the ministry? If they walk in and see empty beds, they're going to want to know what happened."

"I'll figure that out when the time comes."

"And you don't think the ministry will become suspicious when they notice girls start disappearing from the shelter they send their high-risk cases to?"

"And when that shelter is no longer safe for them, what am I supposed to do? Nothing?"

"Yes, Landon," Alexander argued, the vein in his neck bulging. "*Nothing.* You provide medical care. A bed. Food. Clothing. Limited protection. But what you *don't* do is smuggle them out of the country!" Alexander strode over to the wet bar and poured a tumbler of scotch, slinging it back. It was barely ten in the morning, but he needed a drink.

"What if it were Melanie?"

Alexander swung his eyes toward Landon. "We don't have those sorts of customs here, so she'll never be in that position."

"True." Landon shrugged. "But domestic violence is a big problem. What if Melanie's in an abusive relationship when she's older? What if you're not there to keep her safe? What if she seeks safety in a women's shelter, but it's not enough? Wouldn't you want someone to help her?"

Alexander drew in a breath, his eyes catching a framed photo of Melanie on one of the accent tables in the sitting area. His stomach churned at the thought of anyone harming her. He would fight for her, would do anything he could to keep her safe, would make anyone who hurt her suffer. But this was different. This was bigger. Landon was asking him to put his company's reputation on the line to help a handful of women. Alexander employed over a thousand people around the world. What would happen to their families if the company folded over his momentary lapse in judgment?

"Landon, you know I love you like a brother, and I would normally do anything to help you..." He placed his hand on his shoulder, their eyes locking. "But I just can't this time. I'll give you anything else you need. More staff. More money to do everything you can to keep those girls safe. But I have over a thousand people's livelihoods I need to consider. I can't put this company's reputation on the line for the sake of a dozen Afghan women."

A blank expression crossed Landon's face. Alexander had hoped to see some sort of emotion. He wanted Landon to berate him for being an insensitive prick, for thinking about the bottom line and the numbers in his bank account rather than acting like a decent human being. Instead, he quietly headed toward the door.

"I understand, Alex. You're right. I don't know what I was thinking. It's not our place to interfere."

Alexander shook his head as Landon walked out, quietly closing the door behind him.

TWENTY-EIGHT

Present Day

December 20 - 9:15 AM

Alexander continued scanning the photos of the women, ghosts of his past, recalling that October day. That was the last time he had seen his friend. Two months later, an explosion destroyed the shelter, and Landon's brutal death was broadcast for all to see. Except for Martin, he never spoke of their conversation to anyone. He had put it all behind him. Even when the Ministry of Women's Affairs conducted its investigation into the missing girls, Alexander never brought it up. He'd had Martin reach out to his contacts in the intelligence field, wondering if Landon had been able to smuggle the girls out, but he found nothing.

The pieces were all falling into place. After countless attacks on the clinic, Alexander had simply assumed the explosion was a way to return the girls to their families, using Landon's murder to send a message about trying to interfere with age-old traditions. Perhaps there was more to it. Perhaps someone had figured out what Landon had been able to do, using the explosion to cover his abduction. Over a week passed between his abduction and murder. Alexander imagined he spent that time being tortured, not because of his position in the shelter, but to disclose the girls' location.

Alexander doubted whether he even knew where they had ended up. Landon was smart and probably didn't want to know for that very reason.

Now, a year later, someone still wanted to find the missing girls. They went after Mischa, thinking she may know something. Rayne was most likely a victim in the whole thing, too. She was distraught and vulnerable, an easy target. They took Melanie as leverage to force him to return the girls his company was charged with keeping safe.

Unfortunately, he was clueless about where they could be. For all he knew, they could be anywhere between here and Afghanistan.

Studying the photos, Alexander knew he couldn't keep Landon's secret any longer. Regardless of the potential backlash, he needed to alert the authorities to the situation, starting with his liaison at the Ministry of Women's Affairs in Afghanistan. He supposed now was as good a time as any to inform her what Landon had apparently done.

"Excuse me," Alexander said to Moretti, pulling his phone out of his pocket. He wanted to comb through every inch of that house to see if there was a clue as to where Melanie could be, but he had another lead now. If this had to do with a dozen missing girls from Afghanistan, he could narrow the pool of suspects down substantially. With the help from his contacts overseas, he may even find precisely who was behind all of it.

He inhaled a breath of fresh air as he emerged from the house into the cool temperatures. He ignored the media circus and all the nosy onlookers snapping photos as police tried to control the crowd surrounding the house. The sky was gray, the air damp, a few light flurries falling to the ground before disappearing. Everything about the weather said it would only be a few hours until the clouds opened up and covered the city with snow.

Searching through his contacts, he found the one he was looking for, not even checking to see what time it was in Kabul. As it began ringing, he held his breath.

"Mr. Burnham," an accented voice answered almost immediately, her tone soft and full of compassion. "With everything going on, I didn't think I'd hear from you."

"Yes." He cleared his throat. "I got your email. Thank you for thinking of me and my family during this time."

"Of course. Of course. I was just beside myself when I heard the news. If there's anything I can do to help, please let me know."

Alexander paused, collecting his thoughts. He was walking a fine line. Not only did he need to tell this woman that one of his employees smuggled a dozen women out of her country, women she was charged with keeping safe, but he also needed her help in finding out if any of their family members were angry and resourceful enough to pull something like this off. He prayed she would be able to look past the wrongdoing and help him.

"Actually, Ms. Faraj—"

"How many times have I told you? Call me Aliyah. We're not as formal as you Americans, it seems."

"I apologize, Aliyah."

"That's better. Now, I'm guessing you called for a reason. Why don't you tell me what that is."

A chill bit through him as he glanced up, wondering where he went wrong, how something like this could have happened. He launched into the events of the past few days, from Mischa's death to Melanie's abduction and everything in between. He even went as far as to tell Aliyah about his last conversation with

Landon. She remained silent, listening attentively, not asking any questions. The skilled social worker she was, she knew enough to just let him talk. When he reached a point where he didn't know what else to say, he grew quiet. Seconds ticked by as he straightened his spine in anticipation of her reaction. He hoped this wouldn't tarnish his company's reputation, but none of that seemed to matter at this point. He needed to tell her everything. She could be the key to getting Melanie back.

"Well, I wish I would have known about your conversation with Mr. Tate several months ago," she finally said.

"I understand it was selfish of me to keep that to myself. I honestly believed he wouldn't actually follow through with his plan. He was upset I refused to use my connections to help him, but I figured, after he had time to cool off, he'd come to his senses. I never would have thought he'd find another way to get those girls out. I didn't think he could without my help."

"Do you have any idea where these women are now? Obviously, since it involves several Afghan women, the ministry is going to want to be involved with the investigation."

"I wish I could tell you," Alexander answered. "At this point, all I know is someone thinks I'm behind all of it."

"And the death of Mr. Tate's sister?"

"The only explanation I can come up with is perhaps they believed he may have confided in her. They were rather close, so it was entirely possible. I've combed through her background over the past few days and have found nothing to suggest she was involved."

"This man you believe is responsible for taking your daughter… What is his name?"

"When he made the ransom call, he asked to be called Maleek." The line was silent. "Does that ring a bell?"

"It's a rather common name here, Mr. Burnham, like your Mark or Michael. I have several family members with that name myself. But, if memory serves me correctly, I believe one of the women who went missing from your shelter had a brother named Maleek whom she was in fear of."

His breath hitched. Aliyah must have sensed his hope building over the phone. This was more than they had an hour ago.

"It could all just be a coincidence," she added.

"I understand that, but over the past forty-eight hours, I've stopped believing that anything is just a coincidence. It could be nothing, but it could also be everything."

"You say he was killed?"

"Yes," he answered. "Gunshot to the back of the head. One theory is he wasn't working alone and someone wasn't happy his face was blasted all over the media, deciding to cover their tracks. Do you think you could send me information about the Maleek you're thinking of?"

"I'd be happy to, as well as anything else I come up with that could be relevant. And I will await a call from your law enforcement over there to keep me apprised of the ongoing investigation."

"Of course. Thank you, Aliyah."

"No, Mr. Burnham. Thank you." There was a click on the phone and the line went dead.

Alexander turned back toward the house and took a deep breath. This case was about to blow up with government involvement. Once he relayed his suspicion that this was about smuggled girls, Homeland Security was going to want to get to the bottom of how something like this could have happened. Yes, finding these missing women was important, but it wasn't Alexander's priority. There was only one missing girl he cared about. One missing girl whose chances of coming out of this alive dwindled with each minute that ticked by.

Entering the small dwelling, it was even more chaotic than when he had walked out, FBI agents snapping photos and bagging anything and everything that could be relevant.

"We found a bunch of IDs under the sink," a voice said. Alexander turned to see Moretti and another FBI agent sorting through a tub of dishwasher pods at the dining room table. "Hid them in the bottom of this."

Alexander strode toward him as Moretti placed over a dozen IDs on the table…all from different states, but bearing the exact same photo. He picked one up. Mark Drakos from California. Tilting it, he saw the hologram and whistled.

"It's good work. It looks real."

"Sure does. But here's what we believe to be the real ID." Moretti threw a bag marked EVIDENCE across the table toward him. He peered at the photo page of an Afghan passport, all the information provided in both Arabic and English. "That's our guy. Maleek Abdar. Afghan national. I put a call in to Customs and Border Protection, but they didn't have any record of that passport being used to enter the United States. So he either snuck in or used a different passport to enter."

"Have you been able to find out how he was connected to Rayne?"

"Techs found a bunch of journals in his desk dating back months," he answered. "They're still going through them, but it looks like Maleek had been watching her for some time. Several months ago, Ms. Kilpatrick began going to a group therapy session at a church in the North End. He followed her there, gave her some sob story about how he lost someone he was close to, and was able to manipulate her." He shook his head. "This guy is one conniving bastard, preying on someone already vulnerable like that."

Alexander bit his lip and nodded, fighting off the guilt he felt about Rayne's downward spiral.

"We found some other things that may be of interest to you."

"Like what?" Alexander raised his brow, intrigued.

"This." He shoved another evidence bag at him.

"What's this? His wallet?"

Moretti shook his head. "Not his. I flipped through it. I'm sure you can imagine my surprise when I found an employee ID for your security firm. Does the name Gregory Fisher ring a bell?"

Alexander pinched his lips together, wracking his brain. "I wish it did. I can call my secretary and find out—"

"No need, Mr. Burnham," Moretti interrupted. "I already took the liberty of reaching out to your office. Mr. Fisher worked in IT. Apparently he took a leave of absence about a month ago, claiming a family emergency regarding his sister."

Alexander nodded, rubbing his chin. "I think I remember something like that."

"His sister was Jennifer Fisher. Her body was found about two weeks ago stuffed in a barrel, fingernails ripped off, throat slashed."

"Let me guess," Alexander interjected. "Another victim of the Castle Island Killer?"

"One and the same. It looks like our guy *was* the Castle Island Killer. We found a gun matching the type used in all those murders, as well as a six-inch blade. My guess is it will match the knife used to slash all those women's throats."

"So Maleek made Mr. Fisher manipulate our online

servers so he could abduct Melanie, threatening to harm his sister if he didn't."

"It appears so. My guess is we'll find Mr. Fisher's body stuffed in a barrel within a few days."

Alexander ran his hand over his face, fearing the worst. That his daughter would be found the same way. "But what about all his other victims?"

Moretti shrugged. "According to his journals, he witnessed them acting in a way he found disagreeable, so he took matters into his own hands. One man had placed illegal bets. Another had cheated on his wife. One woman drank too much."

"I guess we should be happy he's dead, but who killed him?"

"We're running every background check we can get on this guy to see if we can find out," Moretti assured him. "I'm assuming that's who has your little girl."

Alexander narrowed his gaze. "We don't know for sure she was even here."

Moretti hesitated. "Come with me." Standing from the kitchen table, he headed out the back door, Alexander following.

Blue pop-up tents had been erected in the small back yard, bags upon bags of evidence sitting on long tables, being organized. Moretti led Alexander around the corner to where a pair of storm cellar doors were propped open, permitting a subtle glow to escape. Alexander peered at a wide set of cement stairs before they disappeared into darkness.

His heart thumping in his chest, he glanced at Moretti. Alexander had come over here because he wanted answers. Now that he was on the threshold of possibly having them, he didn't want to take another step. He didn't know if his heart could handle being anywhere Melanie had been. Where she had suffered. Where she had her spirit crushed. Where she lost her belief in the goodness of people. Where he prayed she hadn't drawn her last breath.

A heaviness in his limbs, he placed one foot on the first step, then the next, the basement slowly coming into view, crime scene techs taking photos and dusting for prints. It was cold, wet, dank. Exposed pipes dripped onto the cement, and a chill set in as he tried to absorb everything with a timid curiosity. It seemed like a typical unfinished basement, but Alexander knew that wasn't all. There was only one small, boarded up window, bars mounted over it. There was no light. The only entry point was from a set of heavy metal doors most eight-year-old girls wouldn't be able to lift.

"Clear the room, please," Moretti bellowed. Instantly, all the techs finished what they were doing and retreated up the steps, leaving Alexander to take everything in.

When his gaze landed on a dingy mattress against the wall, he halted. He pulled his jacket closer to his body, needing the warmth. His breathing increased, and he could see the chill in the air every time he exhaled. He could hear the ghost of Melanie crying for help, begging for someone to warm her in the frigid night air.

Alexander took an unsteady breath, fighting for oxygen through the heaviness in his lungs and heart. He imagined Olivia's reaction if she were in his shoes. No parent should ever have to see what he was currently facing. He didn't know if he could ever share this with his wife. He wanted to protect her from the stark reality of what was happening.

Without saying a word, Moretti handed him a pair of rubber gloves. Alexander slipped them on. His feet echoed against the barren walls and floor as he walked toward the mattress. It all looked exactly as it had in the photo he received twelve hours ago.

Squatting beside the mattress, a flash of pink caught his eye. He lifted the edge slightly.

"What is it?" Moretti asked, stepping toward him.

"Her sock." He stared at the pink material, fighting the urge to pick it up and feel his daughter's warmth through that small article of clothing.

"You're certain it's hers?" Moretti pushed, glancing at him.

"Can I say beyond a shadow of a doubt that it's hers? No. It's a pink sock. It could belong to any number of young girls, but I know Melanie had socks just like that one. I've seen that sock on her foot countless times, and this was the same color sock she was wearing in the proof of life picture the bastard sent us. So, based on everything else we know, I'd say it's Melanie's sock."

Standing, he continued taking inventory of the room. Crime scene markers dotted the area, tagging the location of potential evidence. He followed a line of yellow numbered tags deeper into the basement and into a padlocked room that had been cut open.

"What the...?" he murmured, having trouble comprehending what he was looking at. A chair with leather restraints sat in front of him, dark stains of what had to be dried blood set into the wood. A lone spotlight hung overhead.

Chills ran through him as he struggled to reel in his emotions. He tried to stop himself from thinking the worst, but how could he not while looking at something so sinister and vile?

"I apologize, Mr. Burnham," Moretti said, approaching him. "I should have warned you."

"What is this?" he demanded, his voice strong, yet shaky at the same time.

A solemn look on his face, Moretti closed his eyes briefly. "We believe this is where he held his victims. According to your brother-in-law, who's on his way here as we speak, he beat his victims before killing them, except for Ms. Tate. In her case—"

"He stoned her to death."

Moretti tore his eyes from Alexander and glanced at a large white bucket in the corner of the room. Alexander didn't have to look in it to know it most likely contained the large rocks that took Mischa's life from her.

Alexander stepped toward the chair, pinching his lips together. He ran his hand over his face, unshed tears prickling his eyes as he struggled to hold himself together by a thread. He had tried so hard to remain positive and not think the worst, but as he stared at what appeared to be a chamber of torture and death, he had reached his breaking point.

A loud sob escaped his mouth. He gritted his teeth, fighting against his emotions. He needed to stay strong so he could get through this.

"Hey…" Moretti placed his hand on his shoulder.

Alexander spun around. "How am I going to tell my wife she's…" He trailed off, looking at the chair once more, thinking the worst.

"You can't think that way. We know what this guy was after, and based on what Gibson has learned from his journals, it appears he wasn't working alone in regards to taking your daughter. The only leverage this guy has over you right now is Melanie. If he no longer has that, he has no bargaining chip. She's still alive. I *know* it. And I'm not going to stop until I bring her home. I don't care how long it takes. I'll admit we may have gotten off to a rocky start, and I apologize for my unprofessional behavior, but I want you to know that I take my job *very* seriously."

Alexander nodded, not looking at him. As much as he disliked him at first, he kind of reminded Alexander of himself, which was probably why he actually cooperated with Moretti instead of did what he would normally do…conduct his own investigation outside the protective glare of law enforcement. He just prayed, between the two of them, they could find Melanie.

"I've always operated within the law," Moretti said, lowering his voice. "Without law, there is disorder, but this…" He glanced at their surroundings, hatred filling his eyes. "I *will* get the bastard who took your daughter and exposed her to this." He stepped closer to Alexander. "If you ask me, he doesn't deserve the protection of our laws." He passed Alexander a knowing look before taking a step back.

Alexander held his gaze, understanding washing over him. Moretti didn't have to spell it out for him to know what he meant.

"Agent Moretti!" a hurried voice shouted from up the stairs. They spun around to see Gibson barreling toward them, somewhat out of breath.

"What is it?"

"It's one of the computers in his office. I was going through all the journals to see if anything stood out, like you asked. All of a sudden, one of the screens sprang to life with an incoming FaceTime call. I let it ring through and, after a few minutes, the person dropped the call. But then it started again. Same person. No name in his contacts. It just says 'Number One'."

Moretti and Alexander shared a look, then sprang into action, bolting up the stairs, around the back yard, and into the house. The evidence team stayed out of their way as they dashed toward the office, slowing to a stop when they reached the computer, seeing the FaceTime call still coming through.

Without hesitation, Alexander approached the chair and sat down. He stared blankly at the screen, wondering who was on the other end. He had a feeling in the pit of his stomach this call was about to turn the case on its head.

He pulled his phone out of his pocket, glancing down at the screen and inconspicuously hitting the record button, then placed it next to him on the desk. Returning his attention to the computer, he clicked on the answer icon, everyone waiting with bated breath as a video popped up on the screen.

Alexander didn't know what he expected to see, but it certainly wasn't this.

"Daddy?" Melanie's sweet voice filled the room.

"Melanie!" he quivered, reaching for the screen, wanting to feel her, wrap her in his arms, promise her that everything would be okay.

"I want to come home, Daddy!"

Tears prickled his eyes. "I know, peanut. I'm doing everything I can." He drew in a shaky breath, collecting his thoughts. He didn't want her to see him upset, weak. He had to stay strong.

"Sweetie, can you tell me if you're hurt anywhere?" Despite her curly hair being disheveled, she looked relatively unharmed.

She shook her head. "I'm scared, Daddy. I promise, if I can just come home, I'll never bother you about making pancakes when you have to work."

He shoved his fist into his mouth, biting back a sob that wanted to escape. "I'm going to find you, Melanie. And when I do, you can have pancakes every day for every meal, if that's what you want. Do you have any idea where you are?" he asked in a bold move.

"I—"

A figure dressed in black, a ski mask over his face, approached Melanie, covering her mouth with his dark-gloved hand, muting her screams as he pulled her away.

"No! Don't you *dare* hurt her!" he fumed, his eyes rabid.

"Oh, Mr. Burnham," a voice said through a modulator as the camera shifted and a figure came into view.

It was reminiscent of television interviews where the person didn't want to be identified. A figure sat in the shadows, a dim light illuminating the area just enough so he knew someone was there. It was impossible to make out any distinguishing characteristics, apart from the ambient background noise of cars rushing by. He immediately suspected he knew this person. If he didn't, why would he feel the need to disguise not just his face, but also his voice? Alexander's mind began spinning, running through all the connections he had made in Afghanistan.

"It appears you finally figured out what I'm after. I'm rather disappointed. I thought this little game would be more fun, more exciting."

"Game?" Alexander roared, slamming his fist on the desk, causing journals, pens, and paper coffee cups to bounce slightly. "You think this is a game? You took my daughter. So help me God, if there is one strand of hair out of place on her head when I find you, which I most certainly will, you'll wish you'd never been born! I learned one very important thing during my time in the navy, and that's exactly how much pain the human body can endure. It's quite interesting how long a person can cling to consciousness while suffering excruciating, mind-numbing pain. And I can promise that you will beg for death to end your suffering when I get my hands on you!"

"You think I don't know how you feel? That I can't sympathize with what you're going through? *Wrong*, Mr. Burnham," he hissed. "I've been there! I've been in your shoes! The anger. The frustration. The regret. The second-guessing. The hopelessness. I've been there. I didn't think there was anything I could do, but I was wrong. We're not so different, you and I."

Alexander's fists clenched and unclenched repeatedly, the vein in his neck straining against the skin. He vaguely heard Moretti pleading with him not to engage any further, but he refused to listen.

"I am *nothing* like you," he spat. "I would never target an innocent little girl and use her as a pawn in whatever sick game it is you're playing. Melanie has nothing to do with this. You want me? Stop being the coward you are and come face me."

The line went silent, apart from the sound of church bells in the background of the video. "You think this is about *you*?" The voice laughed. Alexander's face flamed. "This was never about you."

"I know. I know," Alexander interrupted. "It's about the girls. But that is where you fucked up. I have no idea where they are! I didn't even know they were still alive until I walked into this house a few hours ago! Taking Melanie from me isn't going to make me suddenly have knowledge I never had in the first place!"

The more he spoke, the more he grew frustrated with the situation. What if he didn't believe him? What if finding the girls was the only way to get Melanie back? Even if he did know where the missing women were, would he be able to live with the knowledge that he most likely put their lives at risk to save his daughter? Was her life worth more than theirs? Alexander knew it wasn't, but in his mind, her life was worth more than anyone's, including his.

"Tsk. Tsk. Tsk," the voice muttered. "I really did think you were smarter than this. I'm more than aware you are absolutely clueless about the location of the women who were unlawfully taken from their families."

Alexander shook his head, bewildered. "If you know I'm in the dark here, why did you take Melanie?"

"*You* may be in the dark," the sinister voice said, "but your *wife* certainly is not."

PART III:
JUSTICE

The arc of the moral universe is long,
but it bends towards justice.
~Dr. Martin Luther King Jr.

TWENTY-NINE

Fourteen Months Ago

Fear can seep into your bloodstream, into your soul, freezing you like a human ice sculpture. You're no longer a living, breathing thing, but someone molded to behave and act a certain way through manipulation. You're held prisoner in your own head. Your thoughts become grim and dark, every noise causing you to jump and overreact. On more than one occasion, you consider ending your suffering the only way you know how. No one will miss you anyway.

Then something happens.

A smile. A kind word. A warm hug. For the first time since you can remember, you feel loved. The fear you were living with slowly drains from you, but not completely. It's always there, dormant, ready to return at any time.

Laila's fear returned the night she sat huddled in the bunker of the shelter and heard two voices she prayed she'd never have to listen to again. Her brother, Tariq, and Waleed, a sixty-year-old man with whom she had been forced into marriage at the age of thirteen. After five years of suffering mental, physical, and sexual abuse, she had enough and fled. She thought she would be safe here. Aliyah, the woman from the Ministry of Women's Affairs who had transferred her to this shelter because of her situation, assured her they would never find her.

She was wrong.

Laila didn't know how, but they had come for her…and her "husband's" unborn baby now growing inside her.

"I know she's here!" Tariq bellowed through the lobby of the shelter that actually functioned as a medical clinic.

No one was supposed to know what was really behind the locked door to the operating room…twelve women with some of the most heartbreaking and uplifting stories of perseverance. There were girls as young as thirteen and women as old as fifty-five, each of them running from a custom the elders in their respective villages held on to with everything they had. Some proudly wore the scars they suffered from the slashing of a blade. Others were quick to cover the marks left on their skin from being beaten with whips and chains. A handful of women limped around, even after receiving the best medical care possible, due to broken bones that had never properly set. Despite no longer being forced to wear a full-body burqa, one woman still donned the traditional Muslim dressing each and every day to cover a face that had been eroded by acid, an injury she had suffered from failing to wear the headdress she now wore like a shield.

Twelve women. Twelve stories of endurance. Twelve survivors of legal domestic violence. Twelve women who would be dead if their family had a say. Twelve lives that had been saved.

But for every twelve, there were thousands who wanted to defend this antiquated notion of female subservience.

And they would stop at nothing to do just that.

"Who are you talking about?" the man running the clinic, Landon, responded in Pashto.

"My sister, Laila. I know she's here!"

"There's nobody here by that name," Landon assured him. "Go ahead and take a look."

The women sat huddled together, hugging each other,

jumping at each loud noise as the two men stormed through the clinic, rummaging through each and every exam room, dumping out trays of medical supplies. Laila felt horrible, thinking this was all her fault. Her brother and husband weren't to be messed with. She was living proof of that. They would stop at nothing to bring honor back to the family after, according to them, her "actions tarnished the family name". She didn't know if she would be able to live with the guilt if something happened to any of the staff members protecting her, caring for her, smiling at her.

"It's okay," Fatima, one of the other women, comforted her. "He'll make them leave. He's a good man and won't let anything happen to us without a fight."

"That's what I'm afraid of," Laila responded, meeting her eyes, then returned her attention to the locked door, the commotion growing closer and closer.

Just when she thought they would come barreling through the door, the voices retreated. Minutes ticked by. Laila feared her brother or husband had slashed Landon's throat, just as they had threatened to do to her, just as they did to her own mother when she tried to intervene in the arranged marriage.

After her father had died at the hands of the Taliban, her brother became the patriarch of the family, making all the decisions. It didn't matter that their mother raised them, fed them, loved them. She was a woman and, according to custom, incapable of making decisions for the family.

Her father died fighting against the customs her brother was too eager to embrace.

The sound of loud footsteps grew closer, bringing Laila back from her memories. All the women tightened their hold on each other, fearful of what would greet them on the other side of the door. Keys jingled and the door opened.

Relief flooded through her when Landon stood in front of them with one of his guards, another American.

"It's okay," he assured them in their native language. "They're gone. You're all okay." He beamed his brilliant smile at them, then found Laila's concerned eyes.

The idea that anyone would put his life on the line to keep her alive was completely foreign to the way of life she had grown accustomed to over the years. She had been led to believe she didn't matter, that she didn't have any worth, that no one cared whether she lived or died.

But Landon cared. He was a complete stranger, yet he found it in his heart to keep each and every one of them safe from harm. Because of Landon, they each had a reason to keep going. If they gave up, all his effort, all his sacrifice would have been for nothing.

So they carried on, returning to their usual routine. They woke every morning before the sun, as they had been accustomed. It didn't matter they no longer had to prepare meals and clean before the men of the house rose. They did so partly out of habit…partly out of fear.

As the days stretched on, the other women assured Laila that everything would be okay, but she could see the concern in their eyes. They were worried for her, but also for themselves. If she could be found, what about the rest of them? Were they at risk, as well?

Just when they had all but forgotten about the incident and began to breathe again, Tariq and Waleed came back with more men, voices Laila recognized as belonging to people from her village. Her neighbor. Boys she grew up with who were barely old enough to be called men. Her uncles. They had all come for her.

The women crowded together, hugging each other, mumbling prayers as guns fired in the background.

"I know you're hiding the girls!" one of the men said, his voice loud, demanding, brutal.

"What girls?" Landon shot back. "You were here just a few weeks ago and found nothing! What makes you think you'll find anything this time?"

"Because, this time, you're outnumbered."

"That's still not going to make people appear out of thin air."

Shots rang out. Laila buried her head against her legs, trying to warm herself. Catching a glimpse of her stomach, she shuddered at the idea of raising a child in a world of hate.

It went on for hours. Finally, in the dark of night, silence fell over the clinic. The women held their breath, nervous expressions on their faces as the sound of footsteps grew louder and louder, just like the night a few weeks ago. They prayed it was Landon on the other side of the door again.

Tension rolled off each of their shoulders when he entered the room with another one of his guards.

"It's okay," he said. "They're gone."

But unlike a few weeks ago, there was a weariness on his face. Dried blood was caked on his boots, his knuckles scarred and dirty. His hair was disheveled, and cuts were visible on his lip and brow.

Laila hoped no one had died protecting them. Her life wasn't worth more than any of the staff who had vowed to keep them safe. She could end all of this right now. She could just go home and face the consequences of her actions, sparing the lives of the rest of the women here. It was careless of her to stay and put everyone at risk. These men wanted her. She needed to make this sacrifice to save everyone else.

Standing from the tile floor, she went to her bed and

opened the chest beside it that contained her things. She began to fill her bag with a few mementos…photos, a book, a journal and pen. She paused when her eyes fell on a tarnished gold locket. Opening it, she stared back at a photo of her mother and father, wishing with everything that they were still here. She'd do anything to feel their love surrounding her, to hear her father's stories, to listen to her mother's beautiful singing voice.

"What do you think you're doing?" someone said. Laila spun around.

"I…" She adjusted her hijab, ensuring it covered her hair, and lowered her eyes. Years of subservience had taught her to always lower her head when being addressed by a man.

"Laila, look at me," Landon said softly, his Pashto remarkably good for a westerner.

Pulling her lip between her teeth, she gradually raised her head and met his eyes. She'd only been at the shelter for a little more than a month. She'd spoken to Landon on occasion, but always avoided his eyes. Now, as she looked into the brilliant blue hue for the first time, she saw something she hadn't in months, if not years.

Compassion.

Grace.

Humanity.

"You can't give up."

"I'm not—"

"I know what you're thinking. You can't. I'm going to help you."

"How?" A tear fell down her cheek. "Those men…" She looked at the door that acted as a barrier between the girls and the rest of the world. "They're not going to stop until they get what they want. They believe I've dishonored the family name, and the only way to restore it is to kill me. They don't care how long it takes. They will keep coming for me, killing anyone who gets in their way. I can't have that on my conscience."

"So you're just going to give up after you've gotten this far? You've made it through the most difficult part. You had the courage to run, to be free. Don't stop now. You need to keep fighting."

"For what?" She shook her head, looking at her surroundings. While she was lucky to have all the luxuries in life she'd never been afforded — running water, heat, electricity, a soft bed, sufficient clothing — it was still a prison. She could never leave. "This isn't living. All of us, every single one of us, will never be safe beyond these walls. We're stuck here. We ran to save our lives, but we didn't realize the second we left, we died anyway."

"It doesn't have to be this way." He ran his hand over his face. "I can help you. I'll get you out of here. I'll get you somewhere safe. Somewhere you'll never have to worry about them finding you. Somewhere you can walk the streets and play with your baby when he or she arrives. Somewhere he or she doesn't have to worry about being subjected to the same customs you have."

"How?"

Landon placed his hand on Laila's arm and she jumped from the contact. For years, every man's touch had been unwelcome, unwanted. But this didn't cause her pain. It was warm, kind, caring. It gave her hope. Hope that her life didn't have to end. Hope that there was more out there for her. Hope that Landon would follow through on his promise.

He smiled. "You leave that up to me."

A few weeks later, Landon nudged Laila awake in the middle of the night.

"What is it?" she asked groggily.

"Come with me," he said in hushed tones, giving her a knowing look.

Wiping the sleep from her eyes, she raised herself from the bed and started to grab a few things. She knew this was it. She was leaving.

"No." Landon shook his head. "I'm sorry. You have to leave it all here. You can't bring anything that can connect you to who you were."

"Who I was?"

"Yes. From this moment forward, Laila no longer exists. Okay?"

With a heavy heart, she followed Landon out of the room in which she had spent the past several weeks. She looked over the rows of beds, all of the women sleeping as peacefully as they could. She had only known them for such a short time, but they were like family. She wondered if she would ever see any of them again.

Hours passed as Laila rode in the back of a truck, hidden by stacks of fresh produce and bread. Finally, the truck came to a stop and she heard the sound of a door opening and closing. She remained on the floor, covered with blankets. Landon had instructed her not to move. She had no problem following his orders. It was better than the alternative. She heard muddled voices and tried to make out what was being said, but they spoke English.

After what seemed like an eternity of listening to her own heartbeat and trying to steady her breathing, the door opened. A few seconds later, the blankets were pulled off and she looked into Landon's caring blue eyes once more. He held his hand out to her and she took it, allowing him to help her up.

Emerging from the back of the truck, she took in her surroundings. A one-level building sat several hundred yards away. Around her was nothing but sky and miles of paved runways. Just off in the distance was a large airplane being loaded.

Landon turned to her, placing his hands on her arms. Without saying a word, he planted a loving kiss on her head, then jumped back into the truck, peeling away, leaving her alone with a woman she'd never seen before. Her features almost reminded her of Landon's, and Laila wondered if they were related. Then again, most Americans looked the same to her.

"Where am I?" Laila asked.

"Kandahar," the woman explained, "but not for much longer." She gestured to the airplane as its engines roared to life.

"Where am I going?"

"Somewhere safe where no one will be able to find you," she answered, placing her hand on Laila's shoulder.

She looked up, knowing it would probably be the last time she ever saw the Afghan sky. She drew in a breath and basked in the aroma of tulips and jasmine. From that moment, she would always associate that scent with freedom.

THIRTY

Present Day

December 18 - 4:30 PM

L aila stood in the kitchen of her apartment in Woburn, a city northwest of Boston, when the alert came. She'd been living there for nearly a year, thanks to an angel sent from God himself. Landon's sister had done everything she could to get her out of Afghanistan and set her up somewhere safe. Somewhere she could start over again. Somewhere she could raise her son without the fear of being found.

"No one will ever find you here," she had assured Laila, whose new name was Selena, according to the American passport she was given once her plane landed in the United States. *"But if we ever believe there is a threat to your safety, we will alert you through this phone."* She handed her a small, black flip phone.

The first few months, she carried it with her wherever she went, expecting it to ring at any moment. But it never did. She went on with her life. She began taking English classes at a local community college and could now speak it with relative ease. Mischa helped her find a job at a daycare center. Once her son was born in June, she was able to return to work within a few months and take care of him, as well as the other infants she was in charge of. She planned on starting at a four-year university within the next year, in the hopes of working toward a degree in education.

The chiming of that phone cut through the sound of Mickey Mouse on the television, making her heart fall to the pit of her stomach. She almost didn't think it was real. As she peered at the screen, no information on it apart from an address, she wondered if it was a wrong number. Glancing at her son sitting on the floor, playing with his toys, she knew she couldn't take that risk.

Dashing into the bedroom, she threw a few things together — diapers, clothes, bottles, blankets, toys. She re-emerged into the living room and strapped her little boy into his car seat, glancing around her apartment one last time. Then she left.

After taking several different city busses in the hopes no one followed her, she arrived at the address on the text. She stared at the steeple of the brick building, angelic voices finding their way to her ears. It was so peaceful, so serene, at complete odds with the pounding of her heart.

Entering the church, she was greeted by a man in a dark suit.

"Come with me," he said.

Laila glanced over her shoulder, unsure of whether she could even trust this complete stranger. What if it was a trap? What if *they* had found her?

"I'm here to help. Something's happened."

"What is it?"

"I can't say, but we need to get all of you in one place to make sure you're safe."

"All of us?" Laila asked, raising her brows.

"Yes."

"You mean…" She trailed off.

"Yes." The man cracked a small smile, then turned toward a staircase.

She followed him down a narrow set of steps, having difficulty keeping up with his long strides. Stopping at the end of the hallway, he paused and knocked a peculiar rhythm on the door. After a few seconds, it opened.

Her heart filled with joy when she entered the room to see eleven women she never thought she would again.

They spent the next few hours sharing their stories. Landon had gotten each and every woman out of the shelter. Laila was grateful to see them again, but she feared something horrible must have happened to have forced them together once more. Landon had already given his life for them. How much more blood had to be shed?

As darkness fell, Laila grew more and more restless, as did the rest of the women. They were tired, confused, and scared. Finally, the man in the suit reappeared.

"Follow me, ladies. We're leaving."

"Leaving?" Laila asked. "Where are we going?"

"Somewhere else. Now hurry. We don't have much time."

"What is going on?" she demanded. "We've been sitting here for hours and have absolutely no idea what's going on, other than all of us getting a mysterious text with an address."

He let out a sigh. "I can't tell you exactly what's happened, but we need to get you to safety. There's a warm, comfortable house with food, water, a bathroom, and beds for all of you. Everything you'll need."

Laila shook her head. "I'm not going until you tell us what's going on."

"You want to know what's going on?" the man shot back, annoyed. "The woman who helped you all into this country was found dead. It could have just been a coincidence, but there's a very real possibility someone figured out what she was doing and is coming for each of you." He paused, allowing that information to soak in. "Now, come with me."

Silence fell over the women as they followed him from the room, then piled into a large passenger van painted with the logo of some airport shuttle service. Not a word was spoken the duration of the drive. Some would exchange nervous glances. Others kept their heads lowered, mouthing the words to different prayers. It was reminiscent of the uncertainty the women lived with on a daily basis in the shelter where they all met. Laila never wanted to feel that again, yet here she was.

An hour later, the van pulled up to a gated driveway. After pressing a four-digit combination into a box, the large gates opened, allowing him access to the long driveway.

"Isn't that the church we just left?" a woman named Bahara asked.

"It is," the man in the suit replied, navigating the van past the main house and toward what appeared to be a decent-sized guest house.

"Why did you drive all over the city then?" she pushed.

"In case anyone tried to follow us." He clicked a button, the garage door of the guest house opening. He drove the van inside, then turned off the engine.

The women looked at each other as he jumped out of the driver's seat and ran to open the doors for them. On shaky limbs, Laila followed the other women inside the house, carrying the car seat with her sleeping baby.

"You'll find everything you need here," the man said as they congregated in the main living area. "Keep the shades drawn and do not open the door. I'm the only one with a key. If anyone who is part of Mischa's organization stops by, they'll knock on the door leading from the basement, not the front door. There's plenty of food, water, and other amenities, such as diapers." He looked directly at Laila. "Do not contact anyone. We're going to try to get to the bottom of this as quickly as possible, but until we do, it's imperative you all remain here to ensure your safety." He paused. "Goodbye, ladies." He spun on his heels and opened the door leading to the basement.

The remainder of the night passed at a sluggish pace. The women congregated in the living room, all of them trading the semi-privacy of a shared bedroom for the security of being together. It reminded Laila of the days they spent in the shelter. She missed having that bond with another human, but she didn't miss the uncertainty. In an instant, she had been transported back to that time in her life, every sound making her jump, never knowing if the door was about to open, someone who wanted to do her harm standing on the other side.

An entire day had come and gone. The man in the suit visited a few times to check on them, still refusing to answer any further questions. They were all anxious for answers, to know how long they would have to stay here. Just as they came up with a plan to find out, a knock on the basement door tore through the living room. It was in the same pattern the man in the suit had used back at the church.

They shot their heads toward the door in unison. Laila could feel her heart thumping in her chest.

"What do we do?" one of the women asked.

"Answer it," Laila responded.

"But what if—"

"We've been waiting for answers. Whoever's on the other side of that door may have them." She jumped up, her little boy in her arms, and strode toward the door. She knew the fear each of these women dealt with right now. She had lived with that same fear for the past several years. But she had put her life on the line and escaped Afghanistan so she didn't have to live suspended between two worlds. She refused to go back to that way of life.

Glancing over her shoulder, she gave the women an encouraging smile, then faced forward, placing her hand on the doorknob. She took a deep breath and turned it.

A tall, slender brunette stepped into the room. Her brown eyes were full of compassion, sorrow, and even a hint of relief.

"Who are you?" Laila asked.

"My name is Olivia Burnham. Mischa Tate was a very good friend of mine." A few quiet voices translated in Pashto to those who didn't understand English very well.

"What happened?"

The woman took a deep breath, briefly closing her eyes before looking around the room at all the women. "As you may have already heard, she was murdered. I apologize for all the uncertainty and lack of communication, but it was imperative to get all of you to a safe house in case her death was related to her work with you." She paused. "Based on the autopsy results, I fear it is."

"How did she die?" one of the other women asked.

"The official cause of death was blunt force trauma to the head causing severe cerebral hemorrhaging. The method is what got my attention."

"Which was?" Laila asked, her skin crawling with nerves. She pulled her son closer to her.

"The police believe she was stoned to death."

Several of the women gasped. Laila shared in their horror, her stomach queasy just thinking of what Mischa had endured. She glanced at Fatima, one of the other women

Landon had helped save. She was the reason he started the shelter in the first place. She had been a victim of stoning, but she had survived, albeit barely.

"After discussing with one of the only other people who is aware of, well, all of you, he agreed it was most likely related, that Mischa was probably…" Olivia trailed off, closing her eyes before regaining her composure. "She was probably tortured by someone desperate to find one or all of you, then murdered. We didn't know whether any of your identities or locations had been compromised, so we erred on the side of caution and brought everyone to a temporary safe house. We're in the process of securing a safer option for each of you. It's best that no one return home until we can ensure there's no longer a threat to your safety."

"How long is that going to take?" Laila asked.

Olivia opened her mouth to answer, but something stopped her. She stepped farther into the room, heading toward Laila.

"You must be Selena," she said in a soft voice. "Mischa told me all about your little boy."

Laila opened her mouth to correct her, then closed it. For the past thirty-six hours, she had been living in a vacuum, all but forgetting about her new life here in the States, including her new name.

"He's my life," she said, holding her baby a little tighter against her. "I don't want his life to be tainted with the darkness that has followed me. He needs to know that good really can overcome evil."

Olivia tilted her head and gazed at the dark-skinned little boy. "What's his name?"

Laila peered at her son, then met Olivia's dark eyes. "Landon," she answered. She believed it fitting to name him after the man who saved her life. "He was born here in the

States, so he's an American. I wanted him to have an American name. I probably wouldn't be here today if it weren't for—"

"That's a beautiful name," Olivia interrupted, giving her an encouraging squeeze on her arm. "And I promise, I'm going to do everything I can to keep you, Landon, and the rest of the women here safe from harm."

"I can't go back," Laila pleaded. "Little Landon... His father..." Her body began to tremble as she was forced to face memories she would rather leave buried.

She gazed down at the boy with all the affection a mother could bestow on her child. A family should be built on love and devotion, not honor. Family should not toss a loved one out for not wanting to marry a man fifty years her senior, for not wanting to be subjected to daily abuse, for wanting to be a normal teenage girl.

"He won't find you," Olivia assured her. "I promise. Mischa swore to always keep you safe. And I promised Mischa I would carry out her wishes if anything ever happened to her. She was a wonderful woman with a beautiful heart. Looking around this room, I see her legacy, her life's work. I will not let her sacrifice, or her brother's, be in vain."

THIRTY-ONE

"My wife?" Alexander murmured in disbelief, staring at the black figure on the computer screen.

Swallowing hard, his mind. What did his wife have to do with any of this? It was *his* company that set up the women's shelter in Afghanistan. It was *his* employee who ran it, then apparently decided to take matters into his own hands and smuggle women out of the country. Olivia had never shown an interest in the workings of the shelter. Granted, she was involved with quite a few charities here in the States, but she had absolutely no connection to the shelter.

"Hmm," the man said, his voice still obscured.

The last of the church bells rang in the background. Alexander glanced at his watch to see it was just after ten in the morning. People across the city were sitting in church, praying for forgiveness for their sins, while he feared he would never have the chance to atone for his.

"It appears you do not know your wife as well as you think you do. You may want to rectify that if you want to find your daughter."

He opened his mouth to speak, but the screen went black. A flurry of activity erupted behind him as Gibson tried to get the man back on the screen. Alexander knew it was useless. He wouldn't answer. He'd given them exactly what he wanted them to know, nothing more.

Jumping to his feet, Alexander scanned the faces around him. He wasn't sure where to begin. All he knew was he needed to get to Olivia before anyone else did. He'd already lost a daughter. He wasn't going to lose his wife, too. The only thing that gave him any peace of mind was knowing Martin had stayed behind to keep an eye on her.

Pushing through the crowd of agents, Alexander stormed toward the door.

"Where do you think you're going?" Moretti asked.

He spun around. "I need to talk to Olivia, see whether any of this is true."

"Oh no, you don't." He stepped toward Alexander. "She's a person of interest in this investigation now. *I'll* be the one speaking with her."

"Person of interest? *Person of interest?*" Fuming, Alexander's skin prickled with heat. "She's my wife!"

"If you two are as close as it appears you are…" Moretti leaned into him. "How is it you claim to know nothing of her involvement in this? If this man is to be believed, she violated over a dozen federal laws by smuggling these women into our country!"

"We don't know anything for sure. Even if she *did* what that guy wants us to believe, we shouldn't treat Olivia like a criminal. She's a better person than me…than any of us." He glanced around the room, one of the black-and-white passport photos catching his attention. He stormed toward the wall. "Look at this face." He ripped the photo of Fatima off the wall and held it mere inches from Moretti's eyes. Alexander could see the anger in his fiery gaze at his disregard for the crime scene.

"It used to be covered with scars and bruises. With all the swelling, you couldn't distinguish her eyes from her nose. Thanks to my friend, Landon, she got better. She finally had a safe place to call home, and not in the shelter. Here in the United States. And you know what I did? *Nothing. Absolutely nothing!*" Alexander roared, the regret he felt from failing Landon returning with a vengeance.

"I should have done something, like he asked me to," he continued, lowering his voice. He returned to the wall, running his fingers over Mischa's photo. "I could have used my resources to make sure these girls had a better life, but I didn't." His shoulders slumping, he faced Moretti once more. "I followed the rules. I didn't engage. I walked away, even after Landon came to me asking for help. Even after the clinic had been attacked. Even after knowing these girls' lives were in danger." He drew in a shaky breath, a year of remorse leaving him as he exhaled. He couldn't turn back the clock, but he could do what was right going forward.

"If my wife played a part, we should thank her because that means these women..." He gestured to the photos. "These women are all alive today because of her, because of Landon, not because of me. If you want to treat her like a criminal, I know nothing I say is going to stop you. We don't even know what her role in all of this was, if anything. Instead of jumping to conclusions, I'd prefer to work together to bring all this madness to an end, to bring my daughter back home." He looked back at the photos. "And find these women before someone else does."

Alexander stormed out of the house, ignoring Moretti's orders that he come back and answer his questions. Rushing down the street toward his SUV, he avoided the press the best he could without seeming like a prick, repeating "no comment" over and over again as he fought off microphones and cameras. It took all the restraint he could muster not to punch a reporter in his face when he asked if they had found Melanie's body.

Finally in the relative solitude of the SUV, Alexander sped away, heading toward his house as he tried to get in touch with Olivia.

"Alex," she answered, picking up on the third ring. "Is everything okay?"

He hesitated, not sure what to say to her. Did his wife really help smuggle dozens of women out of Afghanistan and into this country? How did she keep that from him for so long? How did Mischa factor in all this? Regardless of what Olivia did or didn't do, this wasn't a conversation they could have over the phone.

"Maleek's dead," he told her. "He's an Afghan national."

"Afghan?" Her voice rose in pitch. He could sense her surprise and unease, as if she were putting the pieces together.

"Yes. And Melanie…" He drew in a breath. "She was here, but she's not anymore."

"Where—"

"I don't know, love, but…" Pausing, he glanced out the window at the snow falling at a steady clip. "I know what they want, what they're after."

"You do? What is it?"

Pulling his bottom lip between his teeth, he shook his head, his eyes drooping. "We'll talk when I get home. I'll be there in twenty minutes."

"Alex, what—"

"I love you, Olivia," he interrupted, then hung up.

She probably had a thousand questions about what he found at Maleek's house, where Melanie could be, why she was taken. He simply couldn't answer any of those questions without looking her in the eye and asking her the question he feared the answer to. If she was involved, he wanted to be angry. He should have been absolutely furious that she kept it from him for so long. Something like this could have destroyed his company's reputation.

Despite it all, he was proud to call her his wife. He should have done what she found in her heart to do. Instead, he was too concerned with keeping the lucrative contracts that had made his company as profitable as it was. He didn't care about helping people. He didn't care about doing what was right, about being a good person. All he cared about was what would make the company the most money. He was selfish, and because of that, he lost a dear friend. This was his penance, his retribution for his failure to act. But Melanie shouldn't pay the price. This was his burden to bear, and his alone.

Struggling to keep his tired eyes open, he cracked the window, allowing the chill to fill the car. For days, he hadn't slept for more than a few hours and it was starting to wear him down. He used all the little tricks he learned in the navy when forced to stay awake in some hole. One minute of sleep could mean the difference between life and death. He tried to keep his mind busy, thinking about everything from the beginning, about who could have been behind his daughter's abduction.

He swallowed through the heavy lump in his throat when his thoughts roamed to Melanie and what she could be going through at this moment. His stomach churned when flashes of her face appeared before him, begging him to let her come home. These were people who placed little value on human life. They took what was arguably one of the most peaceful religions and distorted it, waging a war against everything they disagreed with in the name of their perverted views. They preyed on the vulnerable, promising them everything a young, poor boy from a remote village in

Afghanistan could want. These young men had nothing to believe in…until now. He had seen it too many times.

Alexander ran his hand over his face, slapping at his cheeks to keep himself awake. Every time he blinked, memories from his past flashed before his eyes. Growing up in Connecticut. Moving to Boston. Going to Red Sox games with his dad. His father's vacant seat at the dinner table. His mother's excuses that he had an important job. Cutting class his first semester of Harvard and going to the navy recruitment office. Boot camp. Deployment. The last time he saw his father the night before he left for BUD/S training. Meeting Landon for the first time. The last time he saw Landon alive.

He wondered if his friend had gone to Olivia immediately after begging him for help. Would he really go behind his back and ask his wife for help, then keep it a secret from him? That didn't sound like the Landon he knew. Then again, the Landon he knew would certainly bend, perhaps even break, the rules to get what he wanted.

Alexander tried not to jump to any conclusions before he had a chance to talk to Olivia about what she did or didn't know. Despite not wanting to believe he had been so blind as to not see it, he feared his wife held the missing piece to this puzzle.

THIRTY-TWO

December 20 - 10:15 AM

"Alex?" Olivia repeated into the phone, her pulse racing, but there was no response. She glanced at the screen and saw he had ended the call. She didn't know what to think. All she knew was it had to be one hell of a coincidence that Maleek was an Afghan national.

Pulling her lip between her teeth, she straightened her spine, blinking back the tears fighting to escape. She knew the risk involved when she had agreed to help. In the final days before her murder, Mischa had warned Olivia she thought someone had figured it out. Olivia was simply a silent conspirator, for lack of a better word. She only provided the funds for Mischa to do what she needed to ensure these women landed safely in this country, then had enough financial support to begin their new lives here. She was largely ignorant of most of the details…until she went over to Mischa's for coffee at the beginning of the month and she shoved folder after folder in front of her, telling her names, cities, phone numbers, how to go about getting in touch with each and every one of them if something were to happen to her.

Never did Olivia think something would. Now she was left to carry on her legacy, but at what cost?

The instant Olivia realized Melanie had been taken, she feared her association with Mischa may have had something to do with it, but she didn't think it possible. No one could have known of her involvement. It was impossible to trace anything, even the money, back to her. They made sure of that. She had told herself it was just a series of unfortunate coincidences. Now she knew it was all connected. She had a feeling Alexander knew, too. She prayed her secrecy wouldn't be their undoing.

Dropping her phone into the pocket of her jeans, she headed into the kitchen and straight toward the coffeemaker. For the first time since this all began, Colleen wasn't in there. Instead, Olivia found her in the living area just off the kitchen, talking in hushed tones with Tyler, his wife and little boy playing on the floor.

Since getting back from Kiera's, her mind had been preoccupied after hearing all those women's stories. Now, she had to juggle that along with Alexander's cryptic phone call. She felt pulled in a thousand different directions, as if the weight of the secret she'd been keeping for so long were about to crush her.

Frozen in place, she stared at a seemingly happy family playing in front of an elaborate Christmas tree. Envy trickled through her veins. That should have been her laughing with her little girl, watching Christmas movies and talking about Santa's visit in just a few days. Instead, she was alone, unsure of whether they'd be a family again by Christmas…or ever.

"Mrs. Burnham," Agent Long said, approaching Olivia, snapping her out of her thoughts.

Colleen and Tyler looked at Olivia, finally noticing her. Their eyes were full of compassion and unease, silently asking her if she knew anything. She didn't know what to say. How could she possibly tell these people, this family who took her in and treated her like one of their own, it was her fault Melanie was taken? These were good people who didn't deserve things like this to happen to them. But Olivia? She never knew what love was until Alexander all but forced his way into her heart. These people loved unconditionally and without hesitation. Now, she wasn't sure she deserved it.

"Is everything okay?" Agent Long asked, placing a hand on Olivia's shoulder. She met her eyes, searching.

Olivia felt exposed, as if Agent Long were able to cut through the lies and see the truth of what she had done. Agent Moretti most likely told her what they found at Maleek's house. It was only a matter of time until it all unraveled.

"Alexander's on his way home," she replied, avoiding Agent Long's question. Nothing was okay. Nothing had been okay since she had heard about Mischa's death. She doubted whether anything would ever be okay again. "He called to tell me Maleek was found dead, but Melanie wasn't there."

Tyler stood from the couch and headed toward her, wrapping his arms around her. She allowed herself this one moment of sympathy. When Alexander returned and the truth revealed itself, she doubted she'd get any compassion from this group of people. They would never understand why she got involved, the importance of what Mischa was doing.

After hearing what was going on and what Landon wanted to do, Olivia felt compelled to help, to do everything within her power to give these women, women who had suffered a traumatic event at the hands of those who should have looked out for and protected them, a second chance.

"It'll be okay, Libby," Tyler comforted her. "You know Alex. He won't stop until he gets Melanie back and makes the person who's behind all of this suffer for the rest of his pathetic life."

Olivia closed her eyes, Tyler's words like a knife to her heart. He was right. Alexander wouldn't stop until he had all the answers and found Melanie. She had a feeling she was the one who held the key to getting her back. She'd always done what she thought was right, constantly giving her time to causes she believed in. Now, she feared she would have to choose between saving one life and twelve, but that one life… She treasured it more than her own.

When footsteps rang out, Olivia released Tyler, both of them turning toward the door leading to the garage. Olivia's heart caught in her throat when Alexander stepped into the kitchen, their eyes meeting. Feeling like a prisoner awaiting her sentence, she remained motionless as she stared at her husband.

Chewing on her bottom lip, she didn't know what to expect from him. Disappointment. Anger. Frustration. Instead, there was something completely unanticipated etched in the lines of his face. Respect. Admiration. Understanding.

He strode toward her, his steps deliberate. His eyes cut into her soul, ripping her open, leaving her secrets bare for the world to see. Only he could read her fears, her regrets, her personal demons, assuring her with just one look that it was okay, that he would chase them away.

Pausing mere inches away from her, the heat from his body warming her skin, he locked his gaze with hers. Their chests rose and fell in near synchronicity. In an instant, his strong hands grasped her face and pulled her toward him, his lips crushing against hers.

Olivia stilled, caught off guard by the moment of sorrow-filled passion. Then she melted into the kiss, molding her body against his, allowing them to become one. The world disappeared around them. Nothing else mattered at that moment. Not the lies and secrets of their past. Not the troubles and heartache of their present. Not the uncertainty of their future. For that one brief sliver of time, all that mattered was the love they shared. In that one kiss, Olivia knew they would get through this. That their devotion would help navigate through the stormy waters, and the sun would eventually shine on them again.

Alexander pulled away and stared down at her, not saying a word.

"You know," Olivia stated softly so no one could overhear.

Remaining mute, he folded Olivia's hand in his and led her down the hallway and into his office, pulling her onto the leather sofa in front of the large windows. When her eyes caught the snow falling, the dread and unease she'd been able to chase away momentarily returned.

Facing her, Alexander ran his fingers across her knuckles. It comforted her, reminding her of their early days together when a simple touch like this would send shivers throughout her body. Despite the passing of years, his touch still had that spark.

"Maleek killed Mischa," Alexander informed her.

She closed her eyes, allowing the truth of what she'd already assumed to wrap around her. The second he shared that he was an Afghan national, she knew he had killed Mischa.

"How do you know? Did Dave tell you?" she asked.

He narrowed his gaze at her, as if unsure how to respond. She could sense he was waiting for her to finally admit to what he already suspected, but she couldn't...not yet. She needed more information first.

"There was a room in his basement," he said in an unsteady voice, briefly closing his eyes. He bit his lip, and Olivia knew he had seen something he wished he hadn't. "There was a chair with blood on it. In the corner was a bucket full of rocks. The FBI and local LEOs are probably still there, but I'm sure we'll find a match to her blood type."

Olivia covered her trembling chin. "Why?" She shook her head. "Why would he——"

He fished his cell phone out of his coat pocket and handed it to her. "He thought she knew where these women were and tortured her to make her talk."

With shaky hands, she took the phone from him and began to scroll through images of a dozen women she had just visited. With each face, she recalled their unique story, reaffirming her belief that what she had done was right, was good, was necessary.

"All of these women lived at my company's shelter in Afghanistan at one point or another. After the explosion, they disappeared," Alexander explained when Olivia failed to show any signs she recognized them. "Landon came to see me several weeks before that."

Olivia met his eyes, remaining silent. She knew the story. She was an unspoken part of it…until now.

"It was a week or so after the first attack on the shelter," he continued. "He asked me to use my resources to help smuggle these women out of Afghanistan and establish new lives for them here in the States. He was convinced it was the only way they'd be free from their pasts."

She dropped the phone onto the couch and grabbed his hand in hers, squeezing. She didn't know if she could ever admit she went behind her husband's back to help Landon when he wouldn't.

"I refused, told him it wasn't our place to interfere."

"Landon never did like taking no for an answer, did he?" she commented, releasing her hold on his hand.

"He didn't." His eyes remained glued to hers. "When he

believed in something, he would stop at nothing to see it through to the end."

"Just like his sister," Olivia added, narrowing her gaze at him, hoping he would understand.

"His sister..." He drew in a breath. "Of course." Running his hand over his face, he turned to Olivia once more, looking at her in a way he never had before. "How...? I mean—"

"I only agreed to help with the financial side of it all," she finally admitted. "Mischa told me about your conversation with Landon. When that didn't go the way he hoped, he reached out to her. Her organization had clinics and aid workers in Afghanistan, but it didn't have much in the way of funding. To arrange something of this magnitude would pretty much deplete their resources."

"So they turned to you."

She nodded. "She didn't fill me in on the specifics, just that something else needed to be done. Up until that point, I was pretty clueless about what your company did over in Afghanistan anyway."

"I didn't tell—"

"You usually don't talk about anything work-related with me."

"Olivia, I—"

"It's okay. I understand a lot of the stuff your company does is classified. And, to be honest, I don't find it all that interesting anyway. But this... I had no idea. When Mischa told me a few of their stories, my heart physically hurt, Alex. These women had no one. They were scared to go home. They were scared to stay in the shelter. No matter where they went, they would always have to look over their shoulder to make sure no one was coming after them, always wondering if everything would come crashing back down again. Some of these women were pregnant, for crying out loud! And the person who should be keeping them safe, their husband or their father, was the one who wanted to harm them!"

Alexander's expression remained fixed, absorbing her story.

"So I agreed to help them with the financial part of it."

"All those girls who we believed were abducted from the shelter around the time of the explosion…" He looked at her, questioning.

"Landon and Mischa relocated them. There were too many to move all at once, of course. From what I was able to glean, it appears they moved one girl at a time, waiting several days between transports. I don't know where they hid them, but Mischa was finally able to get all the girls out and resettle them here."

"So you were just the money behind it? You weren't involved in any other way?"

"I—" she began, then the door opened.

"I apologize, sir," Martin said, stepping into the office and heading toward where they sat on the couch. "Agent Moretti is here and has requested to speak with Mrs. Burnham regarding what was said on the FaceTime call earlier." He raised his eyebrows.

Olivia looked at Alexander. "What FaceTime call?"

He sighed. "When we were at the house, one of Maleek's computers started ringing with a video call." He took a deep breath, placing his hand on her leg. "It was Melanie."

"What?" she cried, tears filling her eyes. "Was she…?"

"She's okay. She's alive. After seeing that room in the basement, I feared…" He swallowed hard. "But she's okay, just really scared. Before I could get her to tell me where she was, the camera shifted and I spoke to whomever is behind all this. His face was obstructed and he spoke into a voice modulator, which leads me to believe I know him somehow."

"What did he say?" She leaned closer, hanging on to every word.

"That I'd get Melanie back when I returned what he was after." He narrowed his eyes at Olivia. He didn't have to spell it out for her. She knew what this guy wanted.

Closing her eyes, she let out a slow breath. Her stomach churned at the thought of willingly handing over a dozen lives to a man she assumed wanted to return them to their families so they could carry out these barbaric traditions. She didn't know if she could live with that knowledge on her conscience, knowing she could have done something to prevent it, but sent them to their graves instead. There was no guarantee this guy would keep his promise to return Melanie. How could she be certain he would be true to his word? He'd already killed. What was stopping him from doing it again after he got what he wanted? Olivia wasn't an expert in these types of situations, but she was smart enough to know he was using Melanie as leverage. She had a purpose. But once he had what he wanted and she no longer served that purpose, Olivia didn't want to think about what he would do to her. She was certain it didn't involve returning her.

"He made it sound like you know where they are, but it appears he was wrong," Alexander said, breaking through her thoughts.

She opened her eyes, remaining stoic, her back straight.

"Or was he?" He raised his brow. "Olivia, talk to me. Was it more than just giving them money?"

"No," she exhaled, avoiding his eyes. He grabbed her chin, forcing her to meet his determined gaze. "Well, yes. At first, it was just money, but Mischa knew getting them here wasn't enough. They needed to be a completely new person on paper." She gave him a knowing look.

With wide eyes, he turned from Olivia and stared at Martin, who remained impassive, then met her gaze once more.

"I knew I couldn't go to you with it, not when you had already turned Landon down, so I guess I went to the next best thing." She shrugged and glanced at Martin, smiling slightly at their odd arrangement.

She didn't know what had compelled her to trust Martin with everything. All she knew was something had to be done and he was the first person she thought of. He'd always been fiercely loyal to Alexander and her. He knew how to get things done discreetly. When she'd approached him with her plan, she had expected some hesitation on his part, but was instead met with enthusiasm. He was a man willing to do everything within his power to keep those women safe.

"Without Martin, these girls wouldn't have been able to work, to better themselves. Some of them have started taking college courses. One of them is even in nursing school! And none of this would have been possible—"

"I know. I know," Alexander interrupted, his face turning red.

"I apologize, sir," Martin said in an even tone. "I shouldn't have gone behind your back, but these were special circumstances." He lowered his voice. "If one of these women were my daughter, I'd hope someone would stick their neck out for her."

"When I asked you to look into whether any of these girls were smuggled out of the country?"

"I withheld the truth from you, sir. Again, I believed these to be extraordinary circumstances."

"Where are they now?" Alexander sighed.

"In a temporary safe house."

"Together?"

"Yes, sir. It's not ideal, but when Mrs. Burnham raised her concerns regarding Mischa's death, we thought it best to get all the girls into a safe house until we could figure out what was going on."

"Where?"

Martin and Olivia shared a look. She had a feeling Alexander wasn't going to like this. She didn't like it much, either, but it was the best she could do on such short notice.

"Kiera and Mo's guest house," she replied sheepishly.

"Are you out of your mind?!" Alexander roared, standing from the couch and pacing the room. "They have kids! And another one on the way! Did you not think—"

"Of course I did," she shot back. "We needed someplace safe and fast while we looked into other options. Kiera and Mo were more than willing to help."

"We used every precaution to ensure we didn't raise any suspicion," Martin assured Alexander.

"They're in the guest house. Their boys have no idea the girls are even there," she added, although it didn't ease his worry.

"Why didn't you just use one of the *company's* safe houses?" he asked. "That's what they're there for and are set up for this kind of thing!"

"The thought crossed my mind, but I didn't want any of this coming back to the company," Martin replied.

"It's a little too late for that now, isn't it?"

"It appears so."

Exhaling, Alexander ran his hands through his hair, tugging at it in obvious frustration.

"What are we going to do?" Olivia asked, looking up at her panicked husband. It was clear he hadn't expected her to be this involved. She wouldn't have expected it if she were in his shoes, either.

He stopped pacing and addressed both Martin and Olivia. "We'll do the right thing," he stated. "We'll tell Moretti everything we know. From the beginning. We'll get Homeland Security involved. These girls aren't exactly here legally."

Olivia shook her head. "It's not as simple as that, Alex."

"You know as well as I do it won't end well," Martin intervened. "They'll be in the system. Anyone will be able to track them down."

"We'll make sure they get put into protective custody while all of this gets sorted out."

Martin approached Alexander. "With all due respect, sir, I understand you're willing to do anything to get your daughter back, but have you lost your mind? Protective custody? People come to us, to *your* company, because they don't feel *safe* in protective custody. A lot of these government agencies are stretched thin and have limited resources. Sure, they may feel safe for a minute, but after a while, there will be more important cases. And that's assuming Homeland Security doesn't ship them back at the first opportunity, just for them to meet the same fate Landon, your friend, your teammate, tried to save them from!" He took a breath, steadying his voice. "If you do this, it will all be for nothing. Landon's death. Mischa's death. Rayne's death. All these people you once held dear… Their sacrifice would have been useless."

"It wouldn't have been for nothing," he replied, always stubborn. "If we do this, maybe we'll get Melanie back."

"How can we get her back if we have no bargaining chip?" Olivia interjected.

"All this guy wants is to know the location of these

women. We turn the information over to the authorities and let them deal with it while we find Melanie. That should be our focus. Nothing else."

"You're right," Olivia responded. "It should be, but it's not. Does my heart ache from her absence? Of course. Have I wanted to scream and cry and wail every minute since she's been taken? Yes. She's my daughter. The love I have for her, the bond I've shared with her, no one in this room could possibly understand."

She looked from Alexander to Martin, then back at her husband. He would never be able to truly comprehend the spectrum of emotions she was going through. Yes, Alexander was a wonderful father, he grew into that role with an excitement she never expected, but he didn't have that connection to Melanie like she did.

"She grew inside me for nine months," she continued, placing her hand on her stomach. "I would do anything to get Melanie back, but I can't, in good conscience, sentence a dozen women to death in doing so." She grabbed Alexander's phone off the couch and scrolled through it, landing on a photo of a woman with dark hair, dark skin, and deep chestnut eyes.

"This woman's name is Hope." She held up the phone, forcing Alexander to stare into those haunting eyes, wanting him to see the person who would suffer from his plan. "I don't know what her name used to be, but the name she chose when she came here was Hope. Her uncle raped her. When she reported it to the authorities in her village, instead of arresting her uncle, the town elders came after her for no longer being a chaste woman. She was damaged goods and had brought dishonor on her family. Her mother helped her escape. She believes her father most likely killed her mother when he found out she was missing."

She scrolled through photo after photo, relaying each woman's chosen name and story, each one more horrifying than the last. Alexander needed to see the scars of their past on their faces, although some had faded with time. Still, the emotional scars of what these woman had endured would never fade.

"This woman…" She held up the phone. "She goes by the name Selena now. She has a son. A six-month-old little boy she named Landon, after the man who saved her life." Her fiery gaze bore holes into Alexander. "She was pregnant when she ran away from her abusive husband. Her father was a teacher who was killed by the Taliban. Her brother became the patriarch of the family and sold her to a man fifty years her senior when she was only thirteen! *Thirteen!* Melanie will be thirteen in a few years. Could you imagine anyone forcing her to marry a man fifty years older than she is? Once Selena turned eighteen, she finally had the courage to run. Now, she works at a daycare where she can spend all day with her son and not live in fear that either one of them will be killed."

Tears she had held at bay began streaming down her face. "Look at these women. Look into their eyes," she sobbed. "Look at their scars. Their bruises. The burns on their faces. This is what their future holds if we do what you're suggesting and get Homeland Security involved." She took a steadying breath. "I want my daughter back," she said through her tears. "I want to hold her in my arms. I want to tell her how sorry Mommy is and assure her I'll always be there for her." She shook her head, wiping tears from her cheeks. "But not like this. Not knowing I've sent a dozen women to their deaths."

Apart from the ticking of the clock, silence rang in the room as Olivia waited to see how Alexander would react.

After a protracted moment of uncertainty, he took a step toward her, his expression softening.

"Olivia, love…," he soothed, pulling her body against his.

Tilting her head, she looked into his eyes. These were the arms that always provided her comfort after a bad day. They showered her with love and affection on a daily basis. They were her home.

"Have I ever told you how frustrating you can be?"

She allowed a small smile to cross her lips. "Perhaps once or twice." She'd heard those words out of his mouth at least once a week for the past decade.

Alexander let out a long breath, his irritation and unease with their predicament clear in his rigid stature and distant expression.

Grabbing his cheeks, she forced his eyes back to her. "You're better than this," she reminded him. "We'll find another way to get her back, one we won't regret for years to come."

THIRTY-THREE

Agent Moretti ran his hand over his face, weariness etched in the lines around his tired eyes. Alexander had a feeling he had never been lead on as complicated a missing persons case as he had on his hands right now.

"First and foremost, I'm in agreement with Mrs. Burnham," he stated, meeting Alexander's eyes, then glancing at Olivia to his right. "We shouldn't get Homeland Security involved until we can guarantee your little girl's safety. That's our priority right now, not the illegal status of a bunch of women who ran away from home to save their lives."

Alexander nodded. At first, he wanted to jump at the opportunity to get Melanie back and didn't care who was hurt along the way, but Olivia was right. She was always more methodical than he was, always looking at the big picture when he had a tendency to act on instinct, consequences be damned. She couldn't live with the thought of being responsible for their deaths. He couldn't, either. He'd been living with the guilt of Landon's death for a year now. He didn't want any more blood on his hands.

"Now, we need to move these women to a secure location. They can't stay where they are."

"I'm already on it," Alexander informed Moretti. "I have my team arranging their relocation as we speak."

"All of them?" Moretti raised his eyebrows.

"It's risky, but it's too dangerous to keep them all together. My company has several safe houses in the area. We've split them up into groups of three or four, and are moving a few girls at a time using different agents, automobiles, and routes so as not to raise any suspicion. It's not foolproof, but it's better than not doing anything."

"Agreed," Moretti answered. "Where exactly are these safe houses located?" He grabbed his pen, about to make notes in his pad, the rest of his team also anxious for Alexander's response.

He glanced around his office, feeling as if his own personal secure space had been invaded by this team of law enforcement agents. "It's my company's policy not to give out that information. It would defeat the purpose of having a safe house."

"Yes, but it's part of *my* investigation."

"The location of where my company is keeping these women is irrelevant to the investigation. All you need to know is these houses are incredibly secure and well-protected. There will be a team of at least two agents keeping an eye on each house around the clock. No one gets in or out without an agent knowing about it. That's all I'm comfortable saying."

Pinching his lips together, Moretti flipped his notepad closed. Alexander wanted to ask him why he took copious notes of his investigations if he had a so-called eidetic memory, but stopped himself.

"Well, I suppose that's all for now then. We've received information from your contact at the Ministry of Women's Affairs in Afghanistan about a few of these girls' family members who were named Maleek. We're looking into each of them to see if it's our guy. That may get us closer to finding out precisely who put a bullet in his head and took Melanie."

Moretti stood from the couch and signaled for his team to follow him. His sudden departure caught Alexander off guard.

"Where are you going?"

"Back to Maleek's house to see if we can find anything that will give us a clue as to where your daughter could be."

Alexander sprang to his feet, ready to go with them.

Moretti held his hand up, stopping him. "Mr. Burnham, I hope you can understand that it's our policy to only allow agents working for the Federal Bureau of Investigation to visit crime scenes," he said, a smug look on his face.

Alexander opened his mouth to argue he'd already been at the crime scene, but Moretti cut him off.

"I'm just not comfortable letting someone I'm not familiar with into my crime scene where he could potentially contaminate evidence." His smug expression turned severe. "Not so much fun when the shoe's on the other foot, is it?"

He spun on his heels as Alexander's nostrils flared. He could show him he wasn't willing to back down and head over to Maleek's house anyway, but what good would that do? He doubted the FBI would come across anything that would help find his daughter. But he potentially had something that could.

"What are you going to do?" Olivia asked once she, Martin, and Alexander were alone in the room once more.

"I'm going to use what I know about this guy to find Melanie." Alexander shook his head. "There was something about that voice—"

"I thought you said he disguised his voice," she interrupted.

"And he did, but… I don't know. Something about it was

eerily familiar. I can't explain how, but it was. And the fact that he disguised his face and used a voice modulator leads me to no other conclusion than that I know him. So I'm going to listen to the audio over and over again and see if anything stands out."

"How? I thought—"

"When the rest of the FBI agents were preoccupied with how to trace the call, I made sure to record the audio with my cell phone so I could reference it later." Alexander smirked.

"You really think you'll be able to find Melanie with just that audio?" Olivia asked.

Alexander shook his head. The truth was, he had no idea, but it was better than nothing. "I'm not going to make you any promises I can't keep, but I refuse to believe this audio holds no clues as to where our daughter is."

"What can I do to help?" Olivia asked.

He placed his hands on her arms, rubbing her soft skin. "Go relax. Try to forget about all of this."

She rolled her eyes. "I'm not going to just sit here while you're off trying to save the world, Alex. I'm part of this. And I'm going to remain a part of this whether you like it or not. I know it's dangerous, but I've been putting my life on the line without you knowing for months."

"I know you want to help and I love you for that, Olivia." He brushed a curl that had fallen in front of her face behind her ear. "I thought I knew the woman I married, but I was wrong. You've surprised me today…"

She looked away, pulling her lip between her teeth.

"In a good way." He grabbed her chin, forcing her to gaze into his eyes. "You did what I was too selfish to when Landon came to me. I should have helped him. Maybe if I had, none of this would have happened. Maybe the shelter wouldn't have been attacked and Landon wouldn't have been taken—"

"You can't think like that, Alex," Olivia said, running her fingers over his cheek. "It'll eat you up if you go back and say 'what if'. Don't torture yourself like that. You don't deserve to go through that. But you can learn from it. This is no one's fault, other than whoever this guy is. I'm not to blame, and neither are you. So be the Alexander Burnham I fell in love with and do everything within your power to find our daughter." Stepping back, she grabbed the lapels of his jacket, straightening them.

"And you'll stay here?" He raised his brow.

"I don't like being a prisoner in my own house. I know you're worried about something happening to me, too, but you don't have to be. I can't just sit around and do nothing when I can do something to further Mischa's and Landon's legacies."

Alexander hesitated. The thought of Olivia leaving the house, completely unprotected, didn't sit well with him at all. He knew he'd never be able to focus on finding Melanie if Olivia wasn't safe.

Martin stepped forward. "If you don't need me, sir, I'm more than happy to accompany Mrs. Burnham anywhere she'd like to go. I will not leave her side."

Alexander looked between Olivia and Martin, an unassuming pair of co-conspirators. He was still having trouble wrapping his head around the knowledge that they had been working together on hiding these women for months and never let on. Alexander knew his wife. She was as stubborn as he was, if not more so. If she wanted to leave the house, she was going to, no matter what he did to prevent it. The best he could do was give her a way to do so as safely as possible. If Alexander couldn't be with her, Martin was the next best thing.

"Stay with Olivia," he ordered, the reluctance obvious in his voice. "I'm heading into the office to work with Simpson on this audio. The snow is supposed to pick up and become heavy after eight tonight. You'd better believe I fully intend on having Melanie in her own bed by that time." He turned and headed toward the door.

He could hear Landon's voice in his head saying, "Ninety-nine percent of achieving something is believing you can." That was what he had to do at this moment. He needed to believe he would find Melanie in the next six hours.

THIRTY-FOUR

December 20 - 2:30 PM

The parking garage beneath Alexander's building was practically vacant when he pulled his SUV into its usual spot among the fleet of company cars. After swiping his keycard for access, he stepped into the elevator and pressed the button for the twenty-ninth floor. Leaning against the wall as the car ascended, he dug his phone out of his pocket and replayed the audio of the Face-Time call. The quality wasn't great, but it was the best they had. He just hoped Simpson could work his magic and make the voice less distorted.

When the doors opened, he walked through the reception area and past the security door leading to the offices, expecting to be met by silence and relative darkness. Instead, it was a beehive of activity, agents coming and going, phones ringing off the hook.

Alexander stopped at one of the receptionists' desks outside the conference room. "What's going on here?"

The blonde receptionist jumped up from her chair, coming around to greet him. "Mr. Burnham, I apologize. I wasn't expecting you today. Your secretary didn't mention you would be here."

He furrowed his brow. "Did I miss something?"

She pulled her lips between her teeth. "No, sir. We've all been working pretty much around the clock. It's been all hands on deck."

"For what?"

A small smile crossed her face. "To help find your daughter, of course."

His mouth agape, he turned from the desk and stared at a dozen men who worked for his company in various investigative capacities. It was a Sunday, just days before Christmas. Instead of spending time with their families, all these people had come into the office…to help him.

For the first time in recent history, Alexander found himself speechless. He didn't believe he had done anything in his life to deserve having people so caring and selfless working for him. He'd never been one to get to know his employees very well. Hell, he couldn't even remember the receptionist's name and she'd worked for the company for at least a year. But none of that mattered to them. The second they heard about Melanie, they sprang into action, doing what they felt was right and just…something he should have done months ago when Landon came to him for help.

He approached one of the agents, silence falling in the halls. When he held his hand out to him, the agent took it. "Thank you," Alexander said.

"Of course, sir. If it were my daughter, I'd hope people would do the same for me."

Alexander nodded, overwhelmed by their kindness. A year ago, even a few days ago, if this had happened to one of his agents, he doubted he would have done more than offer his condolences and perhaps use of company resources. Then he would have simply headed home and forgotten about it. For too long, he had let the company's bottom line consume him. Instead of making decisions based on what he knew was the right and selfless thing to do, he had weighed that against the success and profitability of the firm. That all ended now.

He continued down the row of people, shaking hands as they offered him words of encouragement.

"We'll find her, sir."

"Whatever you need, boss."

"We'll get the bastard, Mr. Burnham."

All he could do was shake their hands and offer them his thanks, even though it was completely inadequate for what they had given him. They gave him hope in a cloud of despair.

"Mr. Burnham," Simpson called out. Alexander snapped his head up to see him rushing down the corridor. "A moment of your time, please."

Nodding, he gave his agents an appreciative smile, then turned and followed Simpson toward his office. Glancing over his shoulder, he observed his employees continuing with their work, the hallways full of commotion once more. He didn't know how he would ever repay these people for all the time and effort they were putting in to finding his daughter.

"When did all this happen?" he asked Simpson.

"What?"

"All this. Everyone working on a weekend to help find…" He swallowed hard.

"They've been here since yesterday. After the press conference, people began trickling in, offering help. They've been pulling their contacts, calling in favors. We've got eyes everywhere, sir."

He rubbed his temples, fighting off his exhaustion from running on fumes. "I hope it's enough."

"Nothing's come of it yet," Simpson said, and Alexander met his eyes, "but I think I might have something."

He narrowed his gaze at him. "From the audio I sent you?"

Simpson nodded and unlocked the door to his office, allowing Alexander to enter in front of him.

Monitors filled a large desk that took up three walls of the darkened room. Computer units were stacked against one wall, cables and wires going every which way. Simpson sat down in a chair, then typed feverishly at a keyboard in front of him. The monitor directly in the center sprang to life.

"Now, it took a bit of work, but I was able to isolate some of the background noise. The quality isn't great, but if you listen closely enough, I think you'll hear it."

He handed Alexander a pair of headphones. Sitting in the chair next to Simpson, he pulled them over his ears, the noise of whirring computers eliminated. All he could hear was his own breathing and heavy heartbeat. Simpson hit a button on the keyboard and the audio from the FaceTime call played in his ears.

Alexander listened to the sound of cars whooshing by, then his voice cut through.

"I am nothing like you. I would never target an innocent little girl and use her as a pawn in whatever sick game it is you're playing. Melanie has nothing to do with this. You want me? Stop being the coward you are and come face me."

Alexander closed his eyes, hoping it would help him focus on listening and nothing else. The *ding-dong* of church bells sounded, then he heard something he hadn't noticed before. He had been so focused on the intonation of this guy's voice, he had ignored what was going on in the background. It was barely audible, but it was there.

"JFK. UMass. Next stop: North Quincy. Transfer here for commuter rail."

He flung his eyes to Simpson, removing the earphones from his head.

"You heard it?" Simpson asked.

Alexander nodded, his mind racing.

"Good. There's more."

Alexander put the earphones back on as Simpson continued the video.

"I know. I know," his voice cut through. *"It's about the girls."* Then the sound of a train grew closer, as if passing by, before the clacking of steel against metal diminished.

Removing the headphones once more, Alexander looked at Simpson, who brought up a satellite image of the JFK/UMass stop.

"That's a red line train headed toward Braintree. They've got to be pretty much on top of the train station to hear the conductor's announcement."

Alexander nodded, scanning the map. "It looks like it's all a bunch of retail locations."

"Yes, mostly…except right here." Simpson circled a building on the map. "It's a warehouse. I got the address and did some digging. It's been vacant for the past year or so."

"Before we go in there, we need to know this is the place. It could just be a coincidence. It could be a different location close by. If they see us storm this building, they'll leave and we'll be back to square one. I need something concrete."

"How's this for concrete?" Simpson zoomed in on a white building across the street from the warehouse.

"What is that?" Alexander squinted his eyes.

"Looks like a church."

Alexander jumped up, dashing from the room. "Text me the exact address."

Running down the corridor, he brought his phone to his ear. He hated the idea of pulling Martin away from Olivia, but he needed every agent he could get, and he trusted Martin more than anyone else working for him.

The line rang several times, but Martin didn't pick up. A knot formed in his stomach, but he couldn't dwell on it, not when finding his daughter was within his grasp.

Approaching the conference room where a handful of agents pored over piles of papers, Alexander stormed in. "All of you, gear up. Let's go."

Without questioning it, they jumped into action, grabbing their jackets and checking their pistols before holstering them.

Alexander hurried out of the office and into the elevator, his agents following closely behind.

"What's going on, sir?" one of them asked.

"We have a possible location," Alexander answered. "Warehouse on Morrissey Boulevard near the JFK/UMass red line station. Two of you will come with me. The rest of you will be in a separate vehicle. We don't want to do anything to raise suspicion. No one makes a move until I say so. There's no telling what this guy is capable of."

"Sir," the agents said in unison.

Once the elevator arrived in the garage, they all filed out and into two separate company SUVs, Alexander at the wheel of one. Peeling out of the garage, he merged onto the empty streets of Boston, snow beginning to cover the pavement.

"What's the plan once we get there, sir?" one of the agents asked.

Alexander glanced at the man sitting in the passenger seat. He thought his name was Andrews or something like that, but couldn't be sure. He hated the idea of working with a team he wasn't familiar with. He picked up his phone and tried Martin again, still not getting a response.

"Sir?" Andrews repeated.

Alexander tapped the steering wheel, scanning the

streets. There were only a few cars on the road, most likely people running last-minute errands before the city shut down because of the storm. The truth was, he didn't know what they should do when they got there. He ran through a thousand different scenarios regarding what he was about to walk into. He had absolutely no idea what to expect, who was behind it. He hated the thought of walking into the unknown with a group of complete strangers, more or less, without someone he trusted.

"I don't know yet."

Pulling onto the interstate, he continued to glance at his phone every few seconds, hoping to see a message or incoming call from Martin. It wasn't like him to not answer. Hell, he could call him in the middle of the night and he'd still pick up. His gut told him something was off, so he grabbed his phone and dialed Simpson.

"Burnham here," he barked into the phone when he answered. "Run a trace on Martin's phone and his company SUV. See if you can get a location for me. He's not answering his cell."

"Copy," Simpson said. Alexander could hear him typing in the background. "It'll take a minute or two to come back, sir. In the meantime, I wanted to let you know I did some digging on Maleek Abdar."

"Anything come back?"

"Surprisingly, yes. Turns out, that's not his real name. Up until five years ago, Maleek Abdar didn't exist. No paper trail. No hospital records. Nothing. I didn't think it too strange, considering it is Afghanistan, but I ran his face through facial recognition on the off-chance I got a hit. I was surprised when one came back. Maleek was arrested five years ago for assault. Back then, his name was Aazar Faraj."

"Faraj?" Alexander repeated.

"Turns out Aazar Faraj is the younger brother of Aliyah Faraj, one of your contacts at the Ministry of Women's Affairs."

Shaking his head, Alexander furrowed his brow. "You don't think she used her position in the ministry to gain access to these girls' location, do you? Why would she put her life on the line to protect these women if she was involved?"

"Perhaps she's not, sir. Perhaps her brother used her access without her knowledge. According to information I was able to pull up about Ms. Faraj, she's spoken publicly about her brother disappearing from the jail where he was being held after he was arrested. The family had no knowledge of what happened to him until a few years later when he reappeared in some propaganda video for an extremist group."

Alexander nodded. It was a story he had heard time and time again. Extremists preying on those most vulnerable to further their twisted mission.

"You said it was five years ago?"

"Yes," Simpson answered. "According to my records, Ms. Faraj had already been with the ministry for several years at that point. My guess is someone in the Union targeted Maleek, or Aazar, because of his connection to Aliyah, figuring they could use that to their advantage."

Pinching the bridge of his nose, Alexander tried to absorb this new information. "Right. Well, we can't be sure she's not involved in some way. I'll try to get in touch with her to feel her out, but right now, I'm just a few blocks from the warehouse…" He trailed off, a sinking feeling forming in the pit of his stomach as he sped past the JFK/UMass train station and came to a stop just short of the warehouse. He swallowed hard, not wanting to believe what he saw.

"Oh, here we go, sir," Simpson said. "It appears Martin's SUV is—"

"At the warehouse," Alexander answered. "Have you spoken to him and told him where I was going?"

"No, sir," he responded gravely. "I haven't made contact with him at all."

Alexander's shoulders slumped forward as he put the SUV into park. "That's what I was afraid of. He was supposed to be keeping an eye on Olivia. Find out where she is and make sure she's okay."

Alexander hung up and opened the car door, jumping onto the street. He was torn between wanting to make sure nothing had happened to Olivia and wanting to know why Martin's SUV was suspiciously parked in front of the warehouse where he believed Melanie was being held. He tried not to worry about Olivia. He couldn't, not when he was so close to holding his daughter.

He ran to the back of his SUV and opened the hatch, unlocking a large chest containing a small arsenal of weapons. Grabbing a shotgun, he gestured for his agents to follow as he ran up the street toward the warehouse. He was flying by the seat of his pants. He had no plan, curiosity forcing him forward. Why was Martin's SUV here? Did Martin figure it out before he did? Or was he really involved from the beginning, like Moretti suspected? And where was Olivia?

Slowing to a stop outside a metal door, he held up his hand at the team of agents following him, signaling them to keep back. He brought his hand to the knob, expecting it to be locked. Instead, as he slowly turned it, the door creaked open. Adrenaline coursing through him, he looked at his agents, gesturing with his hands in which direction each pair was to go once they breached. They nodded in understanding. Alexander held up a finger, mouthing, *One, two, three*, then pushed the door wide.

They poured into the warehouse on nimble feet, two agents going left, two agents going right, Alexander and another agent pushing straight ahead toward the light. The huge space in front of them was filled with row after row of empty shelving racks. Keeping his gun raised, he headed down one row, constantly checking behind him for any sign of movement. He felt like a sitting duck with a target on his back, but he couldn't stop. He needed to push further. He needed answers. He needed to find his daughter.

Reaching the end of the aisle, he met up with the rest of the agents, all of them shaking their heads to indicate they hadn't found anything. A hand tapped his shoulder. When he looked at one of the agents, the man gestured behind Alexander toward a set of metal steps leading up to a loft, a lone lamp hanging from the ceiling.

Alexander turned toward the stairs, motioning for the rest of the team to stay where they were for the time being. His heart in his throat, he climbed the stairs, trying to subdue the sound of his shoes against the metal. Stepping onto the landing, his eyes fell on a chair beneath the lamp, a figure holding an open laptop strapped to it, bruises and cuts marring his face, arms, and hands.

When Alexander rushed toward him, the man's eyes grew wide in fear, moaning through his taped mouth. He halted in his tracks. He had spent the last few decades working beside Martin. When he indicated not to take another step, Alexander knew he needed to follow his command, no matter how difficult it was for him to see his colleague and friend so helpless and vulnerable, absolute horror etched in his eyes.

"You thought you could outsmart me?" a distorted voice cut through.

Alexander shot his eyes to the laptop, a video feed of a house he knew all too well on the screen. A line of men dressed in black with their faces covered, except for their eyes, stood against a set of bay windows. He didn't know how it happened, but they had found one of his safe houses.

"What are you talking about? What do you want from me?"

"If I were you, I'd choose my words *very* wisely, Mr. Burnham."

The camera panned down, showing a line of five girls on their knees.

"No!" he bellowed when he noticed two people who shouldn't have been at that safe house...Olivia and Melanie. He shook his head, trying to fight off the lightheaded feeling washing over him.

"I'll always be one step ahead of you, Mr. Burnham," the voice said, becoming clearer and more feminine. Then a figure came into focus.

"Aliyah," he muttered through a clenched jaw. When Simpson told him of Aliyah's relationship to Maleek, he couldn't think of any reason she would be involved, not after everything she had done for him and his company to help keep those girls safe. None of this made sense. "How...?"

"How what? How could I do everything within my power to uphold the traditions you westerners don't agree with? These women brought dishonor on their families. It's my job to make it right." She approached one of the women and held a gun to her head.

His stomach rolled when he noticed she held a baby in her arms. From Olivia's stories, he knew exactly who this woman was...Selena.

"No, please," she begged, tears streaming down her face as she knelt on the floor, clutching the baby to her, trying to shield her son from what was going on. But he knew, his cries becoming loud and desperate. Closing her eyes, she kissed the baby's forehead, then glanced at the woman to her left. Olivia. "Please, don't kill me," she begged, looking back at Aliyah.

"Oh, shut up!" Aliyah barked, her tone cold.

Without blinking, she pulled the trigger. Selena's body slumped forward. Olivia reacted quickly, grabbing the baby, as the other women screamed and cried. She stared straight into the camera, trying to soothe the baby.

During his time as a SEAL, Alexander had been through countless situations where his life was on the line. He had seen more horrific things than most people could even fathom. But this, watching a woman, a mother, lose her life in front of her own small son… This was more than he could bear.

Out of the corner of his eye, he noticed Melanie's trembling body as she held the hand of one of the women. It broke him just thinking about what she had witnessed. Parents are supposed to shield their children from the horrors of the world, but Melanie was witnessing some of the worst of the human race with her own two young eyes.

"What do you want?" Alexander hissed, his nostrils flaring.

"You know exactly what I want," she replied. "And every hour that passes that you don't bring the rest of the women your wife took from me, I'll kill one more girl. Who should be next? Your darling wife?" She smiled maliciously. "Or your daughter?" She grabbed Melanie, dragging her in front of the camera, holding a gun to her temple. Her little screams and cries forced an unbearable ache to pierce his heart.

"No!" he shouted. "Don't you dare hurt her!" His nerves were shot. He was in a vacuum. The only thing that mattered was getting Melanie back home safe and never letting her out of his sight again.

"Tick-tock, Mr. Burnham. Speaking of which, you might want to watch where you step."

Alexander's eyes widened as he looked at Martin bound to a simple metal chair, tape across his mouth. He glanced down at his feet and took a step back, noticing a plate beneath the chair. Releasing a breath, he met Martin's forlorn eyes, then looked back at the laptop.

"Guess you figured it out, huh? That's a pressure plate, but we've wired it to work in reverse. The second the weight shifts where dear old Martin is sitting, and I mean *anything* that causes him to shift in that chair at all…" A malicious smile crossed her red lips. "Boom."

The video cut out. Alexander simply stared at the laptop, wishing this were all just a nightmare he was about to wake up from at any minute.

"Boss?" one of the agents said, climbing the stairs and stepping onto the landing. "What do you want us to do?"

"Stay back," Alexander ordered. "Get out of here and go back to the cars. Call the bomb squad. Get in touch with Agent Moretti of the FBI. He should be at a crime scene right around the corner from here."

"Sir," he said, then rushed down the stairs.

Careful about where he stepped, Alexander reached for the tape and ripped it off Martin's mouth, holding his breath.

"Get out of here," Martin said firmly, sweat beading on

his brow. Alexander met his gaze. "This won't end well and you know it, Alex."

"We'll get someone up here to defuse it. It'll be okay," Alexander said, frantic.

"I'm not your priority right now. Olivia and your daughter are. So are all those women."

"But—"

"Go, Alex. I don't know how much longer I can sit perfectly still." A look of peace fell over his face as he cracked a small smile, at complete odds with the stoic man who had been at Alexander's side since the day he took over the company. "I'm an old man. I've lived my life. I don't have a wife or a daughter to make it home for. *You* do."

"But my mom…"

"Will understand."

Alexander shook his head, swallowing through the lump in his throat. He refused to believe this man was willing to give up so easily.

"Alex, stop being stubborn and get the hell out of here. I didn't do everything I should have to protect your father from getting killed on a job. I won't make the same mistake with you. So go. Now. That daughter of yours is counting on you."

He pulled his lip between his teeth, glancing between the stairs and Martin. He hated not being there for him when he needed him most, like he should have been for Landon.

Like he should be for Melanie right now.

Alexander met his eyes and paused for a moment. There was so much he wanted to say to him. Not a day had gone by over the past several decades that he didn't speak to Martin at least once. He couldn't imagine doing his job without him. He wasn't just his assistant, his right-hand man. He was his mentor, his advisor, the man he looked up to.

He was family.

"Uncle Leroy, I..." He trailed off, unsure of how to put his feelings into words.

A calmness fell over Martin's face. "I know, son."

With a heaviness in his heart, Alexander turned toward the stairs, aware that time was not his friend.

"Alex?"

"Yes?" He faced him, hopeful he had some brilliant idea that would get him out of this.

"Don't make the same mistake I've made, that your father made. Family first. Always."

Blinking back his tears, he replied, "Always."

Martin took an unsteady breath. "And tell your mom I love her. I should have told her that every day." His voice wavered and Alexander knew... He wasn't expecting to make it out of this.

"I'll let you tell her yourself," he choked out, giving him a comforting smile, then ran down the stairs, taking breath after breath to settle the tears that wanted to fall. Dashing out of the warehouse, he continued down the block, past an FBI perimeter that had been set up, and toward his parked SUV.

"What's going on here?" Moretti bellowed, running up to him. "Your men said there's someone strapped to a bomb?" He raised his eyebrows.

Alexander opened his mouth to tell him exactly what was going on just as the sound of a blast filled the air. Instinctively, everyone threw their bodies onto the ground and covered their heads. Shrapnel falling onto the pavement echoed in the distance as Alexander looked over his shoulder. He expected to see flames billowing out of the windows. Instead, there was just a little smoke, the result of a small, targeted blast. This bomb wasn't intended to do mass damage. It was just to send a message.

Alexander sprang to his feet and dashed to his SUV, racing against time.

"Where are you going?" Moretti called after him.

Stopping outside the SUV, Alexander met his confused eyes, holding his gaze. "To get my daughter and wife back," he replied, trying not to allow Martin's death to consume him. He had to stay focused on the mission. He couldn't let the sacrifice he just made be for nothing. He needed Martin's death to mean something.

Just as Moretti opened his mouth to most likely berate him for interfering with a federal investigation, Alexander asked, "Aren't you coming?"

Grinning mischievously, Moretti jumped into the passenger seat of Alexander's SUV.

"Are we good?" Alexander asked, glancing at Moretti. "I mean, with me following up on a lead and not telling you?"

"Yeah. We're good," Moretti replied. "I get it. Sometimes you need to take justice into your own hands." He gave him a knowing look, gripping onto the door handle as Alexander sped off.

THIRTY-FIVE

With shaky hands, Olivia brought the baby closer to her chest, trying to keep him from looking at his mother lying in a pool of her own blood. He cried louder. She wanted to cry with him, but she couldn't. She needed to keep it together, needed to stay strong for this sweet, innocent child in her arms and her own daughter trembling beside her. They didn't deserve to be exposed to the cruelties of this world at such a young age.

"Shh." She patted his bottom, soothing him. Her heart broke as she listened to his little cries. He had no idea what was going on. All he knew was he wanted his mommy, not some complete stranger. "It's okay, Landon," she whispered. "I'll take care of you. You're going to be okay."

She wrapped her arm around Melanie's shoulders and pulled her against her chest, snuggling her close.

"I'm scared, Mommy," she muttered.

"It's okay, baby." Olivia kissed the top of her forehead. "Daddy's coming."

"How do you know?" She tilted her head and Olivia met her eyes…those same green eyes as Alexander's.

Since she was taken less than forty-eight hours ago, Olivia wanted nothing more than to hold her in her arms, to stare into those green eyes once more, but not like this.

She didn't know how it happened. It was all a blur. One minute, Martin was driving her through the tunnel toward the Prudential Center in Boston. The next, the SUV was surrounded. She tried to fight, but they were outnumbered. The last thing she remembered was someone pointing a gun at her head, ordering Martin to tell them where they were hiding the girls. If it were anyone else, she knew he'd never disclose that information.

But it wasn't.

He would have taken that information to his grave, but he wouldn't let Olivia do the same. She had felt a stabbing pain in the back of her head, then blacked out. The next thing she knew, she was opening her eyes, staring at the living room of her old house on Commonwealth Avenue…now one of the security company's safe houses. Despite Olivia's connection to Alexander, it was impossible to trace the safe house back to either of them.

"You know your father loves you very much, don't you?" she asked her daughter. Melanie nodded. "Because of that love, he'll stop at nothing to keep you safe, even if that means putting his own life on the line."

"But I don't want Daddy to get hurt because of me."

"That's what Daddies do, princess. They sacrifice everything they hold dear to keep those they love safe."

"And Mommies, too?" She looked at Olivia.

She met her eyes, becoming more aware of the little baby in her arms. Glancing down, Olivia studied his peaceful face, having finally fallen asleep, completely oblivious to the armed men standing watch.

"Yes, sweetheart. Mommies, too."

"Are you going to be the baby's mother now?"

"No. Selena will always be little Landon's mother. But I'll try to keep him safe as long as I can."

"Just like a mother would," Melanie said.

"Yes, love. Just like his mother did."

She pulled Melanie back to her, wishing she could use her arms to shield her from all the horror she had witnessed in the past forty-eight hours.

Closing her eyes, she tilted her head back. She couldn't remember the last time she actually prayed. She couldn't say whether she believed in God or not, but she did believe there was some higher power. For the first time she could recall, she pleaded with that higher power to watch over her family. It was all she could do.

THIRTY-SIX

Alexander threw the SUV into park just outside an FBI perimeter that looked more like a construction zone. He glanced to Moretti. "Are you sure about this?"

"Do you think your wife would really want you to trade those girls' lives for hers?"

"No, but—"

"This will work," Moretti assured him, narrowing his gaze. "I'm damn good at what I do. I know you're damn good at what you do. Together, we'll take this group down, but will do so without putting any more civilian lives at risk."

Alexander nodded, taking a deep breath. He'd never felt so nervous and unsure of an operation before in his life. There was always a human factor to what he did, but this time, he could lose everything. He'd already lost Martin. He couldn't stand the thought of losing Olivia and Melanie, too.

Opening the door, he stepped onto the snow-covered pavement, the usually busy Boston street alarmingly quiet. Commonwealth Avenue was typically a main thoroughfare of the city. The lack of life was a little distressing.

"A team of agents have advanced the area and were able to evacuate all the residents within a five-block radius of the safe house. They told them some bullshit story about a gas leak," Moretti explained, walking with Alexander, handing him an earpiece and radio.

"And you weren't worried about it raising any suspicion?"

"I'm sure they expected us to evacuate. This woman wanted you to know exactly where she was, that she was able to outsmart you. The warehouse was probably a setup, probably part of her plan all along."

Alexander briefly closed his eyes, knowing Moretti was right. In investigations like this, it was sometimes difficult to see past what was a trap and what was a viable lead. He had been so anxious to finally get Melanie back, he should have known it was too good to be true. Now, Martin was dead. It was probably all part of her plan to catch him off guard, and it worked.

Trying to shake it off, Alexander followed Moretti to a staging area that had been set up in Boston Common Park, fire personnel and paramedics on standby in case it all went to shit. Moretti's plan was dangerous, particularly with no way to communicate with the girls in the house, but it was the best they could come up with on such short notice.

As they approached a pop-up tent, silence fell over the chatter between several agents armed with Benelli M3 shotguns, making it readily apparent that Moretti wasn't messing around. This wasn't an operation to simply disarm and detain. He wasn't anticipating any of the perpetrators to walk away with their lives.

Checking his watch, Moretti addressed the team. "We have five minutes. You've all been briefed?"

"Yes, sir," one of the agents responded, catching Alexander's attention. He turned, noticing Agent Long. Then he surveyed the rest of the agents. Every last one of them was female. Now it all made sense.

"Mr. Burnham will do his best to lure the captors out. Based on the video, we believe there are five heavily armed militants, gender unknown, and one woman. Once the girl is safe, I'll give the signal. Let's move out."

"What about the rest of the women they're holding captive?" Alexander asked, running to catch up with Moretti as he strode through the park.

"My priority is getting your daughter out safe and in one piece. I'm hoping if you do as you've been told, we'll be able to take down the perps, then extract the rest of the women. Your daughter needs to be our priority."

"But they have my wife, too!" Alexander bellowed over the wind.

"And I'm sorry about that. We have a plan in place to get your daughter out with no further trauma to her. If this woman takes the bait, it will increase our chances of getting the rest of them out unharmed, as well. You were given one hour, Mr. Burnham." He raised his wrist, showing him the countdown on his watch. "Time's almost up, so let's go. I sure as hell don't want to find out what happens if you don't show up." He spun around and got behind the wheel of a large passenger van, the armed female agents, along with a few emergency medical personnel, filing into the rear compartment.

Alexander hesitated, wishing there were some way to guarantee everyone would get out with no further harm, but he knew Moretti was right. His priority needed to be getting Melanie out in one piece. Then he would worry about the rest of the women.

Jumping into the passenger seat of the van, he looked at Moretti.

"Ready?" he asked, raising his eyebrows.

"Let's do this," Alexander answered.

Moretti cranked the ignition and headed toward the safe house. As they were waved into the FBI perimeter, Alexander prayed this would work. That by the time Aliyah realized the agents weren't the women in question, it would be too late for her to do anything about it.

The van seemed to move at a snail's pace, the sound of tires crunching on snow grating on Alexander's nerves. They passed block after block of darkened houses, the only lights those of Christmas decorations the homeowners hadn't turned off before evacuating. Alexander had driven down this same street countless times, even in snowstorms like this one. It had always been full of warmth. Today, in the darkness of night, it was barren and haunting, no sign of life to be found.

When the van slowed to a stop a block away from the safe house, the agents jumped out, long dark cloaks worn over their body armor, hiding their guns. They wrapped scarves around their heads, their faces all but hidden, except for their eyes. Unease crossed Alexander's face, and he felt as if he had aged years in the past two days. What if Aliyah figured out it was a trap? He prayed these women were as good a draw as Moretti claimed they were.

"It's time." Moretti glanced at him.

Alexander pulled his pistol out of his holster and made sure a round was chambered, then returned it to its hiding place.

"Even if they ask you to surrender your weapons, we'll have your back."

Letting out a breath, he opened the door to the van. "I hope so."

Making his way up the block, the team of agents followed behind him, their heads lowered. As he treaded carefully in the snow, he couldn't ignore his gut telling him this was a bad idea. From watching him work with persistence and complete disregard for anyone and anything in his search for the truth, Alexander knew Moretti was a good agent. That still didn't alleviate his fears that something horrible was about to happen. He hoped, for once, his gut was wrong.

Facing the three-story brick building, where he had kissed Olivia for the first time all those years ago, Alexander pulled his phone out of his jacket, his pulse racing as he found Aliyah's contact and dialed. He gripped Agent Long's arm as they all stayed huddled together, feigning terror, just as Aliyah answered.

"Mr. Burnham," she said in her accented voice. "I was beginning to think you would leave your wife and daughter to fend for themselves, just like you failed to come save your friend. Oh, what was his name?"

He pinched his lips together, glaring at the front door of the house with venom in his eyes. "Landon," he muttered.

"Yes. That's it. Landon." She laughed a vindictive laugh. Her voice had taken on a malicious quality, at complete odds with the warm, compassionate woman he thought her to be. He had a thousand questions about how she could have been involved with all of this, given everything she had done at the ministry, but none of that mattered. All that did was getting his family back.

"I brought the girls, just as you asked," Alexander said, not wanting to dwell on the past.

"So glad to see you finally came to your senses." He could almost hear the smile in her voice. "Send them in, then you'll get your daughter back."

"It's not going to work that way," Alexander replied. "Look out the window. You can see I brought the girls. They're all here and accounted for. Every last one of them. I've held up my end of the bargain. Bring Melanie out, then you and your men can take the girls inside."

"I'm not so sure you have a leg to stand on, Mr. Burnham. You *do* realize one of my men is holding a gun to your wife's head at this very instant."

The lights in the living room of the house sprang to life and Alexander saw Olivia standing in the bay windows, holding that poor baby. A man dressed all in black stood next to her, a gun to her temple. But she wasn't crying. She didn't look scared at all. She looked strong, fearless.

Their eyes met through the window. A thousand memories rushed back in an instant. He'd spent so many nights in his car, staring at her through those windows after an argument, wondering if he'd ruined his chances with her. But he hadn't. They'd made it through it all. Staring into those beautiful brown eyes, he knew they'd somehow make it through this, too.

"That's fine. Two can play this game." Alexander pulled Agent Long toward him. She made sure to keep her eyes down as he retrieved his weapon, holding it against her temple. "You already killed one of the girls. I have over a half-dozen out here with me. Each minute that passes that you don't send Melanie out, I'll kill one."

"Alex, what are you doing?" Moretti's voice muttered in his ear. Something just clicked. Alexander had a feeling there was more to this than just upholding age-old traditions. He was taking a huge risk, but they'd overlooked one of the biggest motivators there was…money.

"You've already shot one of the girls to make a point. I don't care if they live or die," Alexander said harshly, hating to say the words, but he had to. "Hell, until this morning, I didn't even know they were still alive. No skin off my back if they're dead." He cocked his weapon so Aliyah could hear the clicking of the gun over the phone. "Isn't that what you want anyway?"

"No! Don't."

"Interesting," he continued slyly, allowing a smile. "It appears you *do* care whether they're still alive. How much are you getting per girl? Or is each family different? Did you shoot that poor girl because she was worth less? Do you still get paid if you return them in a body bag?"

He placed his hand on the trigger, praying he was right, that he hadn't misread the signs.

"Fine! You win!" Aliyah bellowed. "I'll bring your daughter out, just as soon as you lower your weapon and throw it in the snow."

Hesitating at the thought of being unarmed, he tried to find comfort in Moretti's assurances he would have his back. Tossing his weapon to the side, he stepped away from Agent Long, their eyes meeting. He gave her a silent apology and she nodded slightly.

"Done. Now send Melanie out."

"Fine! Fine!" She shouted some orders in her native Pashto as the phone went dead. Alexander widened his stance, his eyes focused on the red door of the safe house, drawing in steadying breaths as snow fell around him.

Finally, the door opened and Melanie's frame appeared. Just as Moretti had hoped, Aliyah and one of her men stayed in the house while the rest of her militants filed out the door and down the steps, one of them pushing Melanie in front of him, his hand gripping her shoulder harshly.

Melanie's face seemed to lack the innocence it did just a few days ago, tears cascading down her cheeks. Her curls had grown limp, her vivid, innocent eyes showing the terror she had been forced to witness first-hand.

Rage filled Alexander, his face burning, despite the snow and low temperatures. He didn't care about answers anymore. He wanted Aliyah to suffer for what she had put his little girl through. It took every ounce of resolve to not pick up his weapon, march into that house, and put a bullet through her heart, but this would only work if he kept his head. He needed to focus on getting Melanie to safety. The rest would fall into place.

Melanie's shoeless feet crunched in the snow as the man kept a hand on her shoulder. Finally, after several tense moments, the man released his grasp and pushed her toward Alexander. He quickly fell to his knees, wrapping her in his arms, soothing her sobs. He kissed her head, savoring the warmth of her, not wanting to let go for anything. Despite everything he had done over the past two days, there were moments he didn't think he would ever be able to hold his daughter again. Now, he never wanted to let her go.

"Daddy, what about Mama?" Melanie cried as he cocooned her, rising and rushing down the block toward the van.

"Don't worry, princess. She's going to be okay," he assured her, opening the door of the SUV.

He glanced over his shoulder at the bay window of Olivia's old house. Aliyah's attention was entirely devoted to what was going on outside, completely oblivious to the sole FBI agent now padding lightly into the hallway from the basement entrance to the house. He remained just out of sight, hovering against the wall around the corner from the living room everyone was assembled in.

Outside, Aliyah's men approached the group of cowering women. They didn't even bother bringing to bear the automatic weapons they wore slung over their shoulders, apparently assuming the girls wouldn't put up a fight.

"How?" Melanie pushed.

He met her fearful eyes once more. "Because I'm here." He placed her in the back seat, one of the paramedics immediately wrapping her in a blanket and doing a preliminary examination. "I need you to do me a favor. You remember the fireworks we saw during the Fourth of July? How loud they were?"

She nodded. Alexander caught motion out of the corner of his eye. Aliyah's men were within arm's reach of the undercover agents.

"It's about to get just as loud, so cover your ears, sweetheart. And no matter what you do, keep your eyes facing forward. Don't look back."

He slammed the door shut. The sound of its tires turning up snow met Alexander's ears as Moretti's voice crackled into his earpiece. "Go."

A barrage of bullets erupted, the agents who had their heads down just moments ago drawing their shotguns in one swift motion, firing at the unsuspecting men. Their bodies fell to the ground like dominoes, their blood bright against the white snow.

Alexander rushed up the block toward the house just as more agents swarmed the front living room from where they had been hiding in the basement. Aliyah's only man left raised his weapon, ready to get off a shot, but he was no match for the trained agents closing in on him. Without blinking, one of them fired and the man in black fell to the floor.

Retrieving his gun from the snow, Alexander dashed up the front steps and into the house, his weapon raised, ready to take Aliyah out with no mercy. He was about to fire when Aliyah pulled Olivia back to her, holding a knife to her throat. The baby Olivia held in her arms wailed as Alexander glanced down at their feet to see Selena lying in a pool of blood.

"Don't come one step closer! Tell your men to lower their

weapons and kick them over here, or I will cut her and you can watch her bleed!" She shot her eyes from Alexander to the team of agents with their guns trained on her, then back at Alexander again. Her expression almost maniacal, a woman desperately trying to hold on to the little she had left, Aliyah pushed the long blade against Olivia's throat. "Tell them!" she shrieked.

"I'm going to put my gun on the ground." He slowly lowered his pistol, pushing it away from him. Raising his hands in surrender, he continued, "Let Olivia hand me the baby and I'll order them to lower their weapons."

Olivia met his eyes, slightly shaking her head as she pulled the bundle closer to her chest.

"Fine," Aliyah hissed.

He gave Olivia an encouraging look, trying to tell her with his eyes that it would all be okay, that no harm would fall on the baby, that she would hold him again when this was all over. Reluctantly, she pulled the baby away from her chest and Alexander took him from her arms, instinctively patting the crying baby's bottom to try to soothe him as he handed him to one of the FBI agents.

"Don't even think about it," Aliyah warned as the agent headed toward the front door. "No one is leaving this house. You take one step out that door with that baby and I slash her throat." She held the knife closer. "I've held up my end of the bargain, now tell your men to lower their weapons."

Alexander looked at the FBI agents, giving them a small nod. They immediately lowered their weapons and placed them on the floor, nudging them across the room toward Aliyah.

"Let's talk about this," he said. "I know you don't want to do this. If you did, you would have already killed her and the baby."

"Don't assume you know anything about me!" she hissed. "All you Americans are exactly the same! You think by coming into our country, trying to impose your western ideals and culture on ours, we'll all hug you and praise you with thanks? Well, I've got news for you, Mr. Burnham. Our customs were around for centuries before yours and will thrive long after yours have perished."

"Your customs?" he repeated, raising his brow. He'd witnessed those very customs first-hand. Many of the people he had met during his time overseas were friendly and thankful to have them there. But there were always those few, a very vocal minority, who had nothing but disdain for the western presence in their country. "You're not trying to protect your culture or traditions. You're trying to protect what *you* deem to be important. Your laws have evolved over the years, giving women more freedom. But, apparently, you don't like that idea, even though it's clear you've benefited from it."

"Have I benefited from it? Yes, I have, but I've only used my position to do everything in my power to protect the traditions too many people have forgotten about. Do you know how many families I've been able to reunite because of my ability to infiltrate the ministry? Countless! And it wasn't until Landon and his pal, Rahima, decided to take it one step further and hide these women, even from the ministry, that I knew I had to do more."

"So you killed Rahima and begged your superiors at the ministry to allow you to take her place?" Alexander responded, all of it making sense.

"Our cause is growing, Mr. Burnham, and you can't stop us."

"Maybe I can't. But I *can* do everything within my power to make sure these women..." He gestured to the women huddled together, watching with trepidation. "And everyone else in their shoes never have to live in fear of your traditions again."

"You don't get to play God!" she bellowed, becoming more irate, as if she were on the brink of losing everything she had worked for. There was panic in her eyes, but also fear. This was bigger than Alexander thought.

"And you do? You're just a pawn in their game, too, Aliyah," he said, his voice becoming passionate, trying to play on her own distress. "I know about Maleek." He stepped toward her. "Of course, you probably knew him best as Aazar. He was your brother, wasn't he?"

Her eyes widened, her mouth agape. "How—"

"And they made you kill him. Why? For what? They don't care about you. Or your brother. They brainwashed you, made you think you'd have everything you've ever dreamed of once the Islamic Union extended its rule around the globe. Isn't that right? Probably even guaranteed you a portion of the bounty these girls' families had placed on each of their heads, correct?" He had heard the story a few times before. People turning to a rogue extremist group to seek so-called justice in exchange for a large fee, all under the guise of some higher morality.

"They didn't—"

"It's a bit duplicitous, don't you think?" he interrupted. "You stand there and claim our western way of life is wrong, that it goes against everything you've been taught, yet what's your big motivator here? *Money*. What would have happened if you didn't get the job with the Women's Ministry in Afghanistan?" he pushed, staring into her eyes.

"You speak of these people as if they're monsters. They're not! Yes, they may have agreed to help families enforce certain traditions for a small fee, but they're still people who believe in a cause, who see the wrongs in the world and want to right them, who help people—"

"*Help* people?" he scoffed. "Tell me how terrorizing your own countrymen is helping them! Tell me how murdering innocent men, women, and children is helpful! Tell me how being forced to kill your brother, your own flesh and blood, is righting the wrongs in the world!"

"Because!" Her face grew red, the vein in her forehead throbbing as she held the knife closer to Olivia's throat. "It had to be done. He failed on his mission and needed to face the consequences. He brought dishonor on me. He was given one assignment! *One*! All he was supposed to do was find these girls by any means necessary, but my brother always had a morbid curiosity with death, even as a young boy. We could never have any pets because they all ended up dead by his hand. After recruiting him to the cause when he was arrested, I thought he would have gotten his fill of bloodlust, but I was wrong. He drew attention to himself by killing all those men and women! He needed to pay for this serious misstep. I know what I've done, but I have faith I'll be rewarded. Maybe not in this life, but certainly in the next. I've had time to make my peace with Allah." She narrowed her gaze at him, a sinister smile crawling across her lips. "Has your wife?"

In a flash, she raised the blade, swiftly bringing it back toward Olivia's throat. Without a weapon, Alexander rushed toward her. A gunshot rang out as screams filled the room. He feared they hadn't eliminated all of Aliyah's men and one had made his final stand.

Disoriented, he looked over his shoulder toward the hallway leading to the basement, letting out a small breath when he saw Moretti standing in the shadows, his pistol raised. He looked back at Aliyah, blood staining her shoulder where the bullet had entered. She had stumbled, releasing her grasp on Olivia.

Clutching Olivia's arm, he pushed her toward Moretti, keeping her out of harm's way. Able to regain her footing, Aliyah charged toward Alexander, the blade raised over her head. Reacting quickly, he bent down and ripped his own knife out of his leg holster just as she approached, running right into the blade, piercing her stomach.

Surprise crossed her face as her knife fell from her grasp, the clanging of it hitting the ground echoing in the room. Alexander lowered her to the floor, keeping his knife firmly planted in her stomach. His face reddened, his mind a rage-filled cloud. She deserved to suffer, to feel excruciating pain.

Out of the corner of his eye, Alexander caught Moretti's gaze as FBI agents escorted Olivia and the rest of the women from the house. Passing him a knowing look, Moretti nodded, then tore his eyes from Alexander.

"Clear the room!" he ordered.

The few remaining FBI agents gave him an inquisitive look, their brows furrowing.

"Now!" Moretti demanded.

Looking from their boss to Alexander, his knife still dug into Aliyah's stomach as she struggled to breathe, they nodded, then retreated from the living room and out the front door, Moretti following behind them, leaving Alexander and Aliyah alone.

Returning his attention to Aliyah, his nostrils flared, his chest heaving as he twisted the knife piercing her stomach. He grunted as her eyes widened and she let out a noiseless gasp.

"Not so much fun when the shoe's on the other foot, is it?" he hissed.

"I'm not scared of dying," she replied, her voice barely a

whisper. "I lost everything years ago. My parents. My home. Everything. Because of you Americans. You came into our country promising democracy, a world free from terror, but I have news for you. Democracy doesn't work everywhere, Mr. Burnham. There will always be people who see what's wrong with the world and will sacrifice their lives to make it better."

"Better?" He clenched his jaw. "How has anything you've done made the world a better place? All you've done is murder innocent people."

"Your friend, Landon, said the same thing before I killed him," she strained.

"That was you?" Alexander asked, his expression faltering.

She narrowed her eyes at him. "He never even expected it. Didn't even put up a fight. He was so thankful I warned him about the explosion, he willingly came with me. Stupid, stupid man."

His back tense, he trembled with hatred. "Where is his body?"

"You expect me to remember where I buried one insignificant little man?" she scoffed, the unbearable pain she was enduring evident on her face.

Alexander twisted the knife again, and she let out a grunt, gasping for air. "He wasn't insignificant. Now, tell me!"

Her face scrunched up in agony as Alexander dug the knife deeper.

"I can do this for hours. Bring you to the brink of death, then pull back. The longer you refuse to tell me what I need to know, the more pain I'll inflict on you. That's a promise," he growled.

"You wouldn't." She swallowed hard, the color leaving

her complexion. "I know you. You have too much respect for law and order to break the rules."

A rabid expression crossed his face and he leaned into her. "You don't deserve the protection of our laws," he hissed, twisting the knife, causing Aliyah to scream out.

"In the village of Malistan," she breathed finally. "At the edge of town, there's a roped off area, warning the residents of possible landmines. That's where his body is." A devious look passed her face. "If you're lucky, you may find his body *and* his head."

Ripping the knife from her stomach, he reeled back, his eyes wild. He didn't do enough to come to Landon's aid after the explosion, but he had an opportunity to make it right, to make sure justice for Landon's and Mischa's deaths would be served. He wasn't going to let it slip through his fingers again. Alexander would never forgive himself if Aliyah ever saw the light of day again, only to terrorize another innocent child.

Letting out a loud grunt, he brought the knife back down, piercing her heart. She clutched onto his hands holding the knife, blood trickling from her mouth, then her body went limp.

He remained completely still as he stared at her dark, lifeless eyes, his hands still holding onto the knife with all his strength. Taking a breath, he closed his eyes, relief that it was all over flowing through him.

"I'm sorry, Landon," he whispered, taking a moment to mourn his fallen friend.

On shaky limbs, he stood up, finally able to fully take in what had happened here over the past few hours. Two of his female agents who had been stationed to watch over the safe house lay slumped in the corner of the room, a pool of blood surrounding them. Selena was just a few feet from them, her eyes still open.

Pausing, he walked toward her body and knelt beside it. She had been through hell trying to escape the horrors she faced in her home country. This was supposed to be her new start, her chance at freedom. It wasn't supposed to end like this for her, for any of them.

With a heavy sigh, he smoothed his hand over her eyelids, closing them, then stood up and headed toward the front door. Moretti waited just outside. Without saying a word, they exchanged a look, then Alexander continued down the steps, crime scene technicians hurrying into the house to begin their work.

"Daddy!" a voice yelled. Alexander swung his head in that direction, his eyes falling on Melanie clutched in Olivia's embrace.

Relief washed over him as she dashed toward him and flung herself against him. He lifted her into his arms, kissing the top of her head, and walked toward where Olivia stood comforting Landon. Resting his forehead against hers, he closed his eyes, thankful to have his family back. For too long, he took them for granted…took everyone for granted. Never again.

THIRTY-SEVEN

December 24 - 10:30 AM

Olivia and Alexander held Melanie's hands as they walked up a cleared path. The sun was shining, and there was a happy and joyful feeling in the air all around town, children counting down the hours until Santa's big visit tonight. Alexander usually loved celebrating the holidays with his daughter and the rest of his family. However, this year, it was bittersweet knowing one very important part of their family would no longer be at the table, would no longer be sitting on the couch by the tree, would no longer be doting on Melanie as if she were his own granddaughter.

In the four days that had passed since they were able to put an end to all the ugliness, Olivia and Alexander had been asked and answered more questions by Homeland Security and the FBI than he cared to think about. Even the Secretary of Homeland Security had shown an interest in the girls' futures. Alexander didn't know what was going to happen to them, but for now, they were still safe, returning to the lives they led before Mischa's death as best they could, given everything they had been through.

He couldn't help but see his wife in a whole new light, feeling a sense of pride in everything she'd done to save these women's lives. If it weren't for her, they would have probably all perished in their home country. Instead, they led the lives they always dreamed of, all because she did what she believed to be the right thing, regardless of the consequences. Something he should have been doing all along.

"I feel like I've spent all my time lately at churches or in cemeteries," Olivia muttered, meeting Alexander's eyes as they followed the long parade of people up to the open-air chapel in the center of the cemetery swarming with people. A lot of faces were familiar, many of them agents and employees of the security company. But there were some he had never seen before — men and women Martin had served with as a Marine. Decades had passed, but they still found it in their hearts to come and pay their final respects.

"That's because we have," Alexander replied with a heavy sigh.

This marked the third funeral in so many days, having already said their goodbyes to Mischa and Rayne. The two funerals had been on opposite ends of the spectrum. Mischa's funeral had been a joyful event, a celebration of her life and accomplishments, attended by several hundred people, all lives she'd touched in one way or another during her time on earth.

Rayne's was in stark contrast to that. Besides Olivia and Alexander, her parents were the only other people in attendance. It made him realize how one event could have a devastating impact on a person's entire life trajectory. As he watched them lower her casket next to the son she had lost after only being on this planet for a few hours, he thanked his lucky stars for everything he had.

When Olivia insisted on attending the funeral, he thought she had lost her mind, given everything Rayne had done, but she reminded Alexander that Rayne wasn't to blame. She was a woman at the lowest point in her life, eager to do anything she could to be happy again. She was depressed, vulnerable, and easily manipulated. He couldn't help but think if he had pushed harder, if he had insisted on seeing her, she would have still been alive today.

"This way, Mr. Burnham," one of his agents said as they approached a police perimeter.

Several agents escorted the family through the throng of mourners, doing their best to shield them from the cameras and reporters. Alexander shook his head at the audacity. Some reporters would do anything for a story, even showing up to a funeral just to get a soundbite or a few seconds of footage to air on the six o'clock news.

Over the past few days, they hadn't been able to leave their house without another reporter shoving a microphone in one of their faces. It took all his resolve not to snap a few of their necks when they began targeting Melanie, asking her questions no eight-year-old should ever have to answer. He had always shielded her from the spotlight his position put him under. Now, she was front and center of a news story. The public wanted to hear from her, but Alexander wasn't ready for her to talk about what she'd gone through. He doubted he ever would be.

Drawing in a deep breath, he approached the front row of chairs in the small chapel. A beautiful mahogany casket sat in the center of the room, an American flag draped over it.

"Ma," he said as she stood to greet him. He wrapped her in his arms, planting a kiss on both cheeks. She met his eyes and they shared a look.

He wanted to tell her how sorry he was, how he wished he could turn back the clock and prevent this from happening, but no amount of apologies and condolences would heal her heart. For the second time in her life, his mother was forced to bury the man she loved. Alexander hated the pain he saw in her eyes. He prayed Olivia never had to experience that.

"I know, Alex," she said, her chin quivering.

He pulled a handkerchief out of his pocket and handed it to her. She dabbed at her eyes.

"He was a good man," she said with a shaky voice. "He loved you like a son." Reaching up, she tousled his hair. He caught her hand in his, squeezing it. "In many ways, he was more like a father to you than your own dad."

Alexander nodded. He never really knew his father that well. He had some memories of spending time with him during his younger years, but his work monopolized his time later on. Martin was always there when his father wasn't, checking on Alexander's mom, making sure they were all okay. Alexander knew it was his job, but after a while, even if his father never ordered him to check in on the family, Martin still would be there.

"I don't want to make the same mistakes Dad did," Alexander whispered, wondering if he already had.

After everything he had endured this past week, he was forced to come to terms with the stark reality that his job and professional responsibilities had always come first. Yes, he was physically present at his house, but even then, he seemed to spend most of his time in the office, answering phone calls, never truly just spending time with Olivia and Melanie.

He felt a squeeze on his arm and looked to his right, meeting Olivia's eyes. Then he glanced down at Melanie by her side. He never wanted her to see him the way he viewed his father. He was well aware that his father's devotion to his security firm had saved countless lives, including several lives he held very dear. Still, he shuddered at the thought of Melanie holding a grudge because her daddy was never around. He'd missed so many of her firsts because of work

— her first word, the first time she rode a bike, her first lost tooth. He didn't want to miss any more of them. He wanted to be there the first time she scored a goal in soccer. He wanted to see her first homerun in softball. He wanted to look the first boy she brought home in the eyes and remind him that she was his baby girl and no one was good enough for her.

He had devoted his life to his country, then his father's company, wanting the legacy he'd left behind to live on. Staring into his wife's and daughter's eyes, surrounded by the men and women who put their lives on the line every day to further that legacy, he knew the decision he made earlier was the right one.

"We're ready to begin, sir," one of his agents informed him.

"Thank you." He gave him a slight smile, then turned toward the podium set off to the side of the casket.

"Wait, Daddy." Melanie tugged at his arm. "Where are you going?"

Alexander crouched down to her level, meeting her concerned eyes. Ever since her ordeal, she'd suffered from separation anxiety. She didn't want to leave Alexander's or Olivia's side for fear something bad would happen. It was going to take more than just a few nights for her to come to terms with what she had been through. He was thankful to have his daughter back in one piece, even if it meant the bed he shared with his wife was just a little bit more crowded these days.

Grasping her arms, he said, "You see all the people who are here?"

She glanced over her shoulders, her brown curls springing with the motion. "Yes."

"They're all here to say goodbye to Uncle Martin, too."

A sadness washed over her face, her bright eyes growing dull. "Do we really have to say goodbye to him?"

He nodded, thinking how being a parent was a strange thing. He'd been dropped into some of the most dangerous places on earth and survived, but he hated having to teach his daughter about death. It was too dark, too bleak. She was joyful and vivacious. She deserved to keep living in her world of fairy tales and make-believe, not in a cruel world where death could take a loved one at any moment.

"Yes, princess. We do."

"Grandma said he died trying to save those girls." She looked down at her feet, fidgeting with the skirt of her black velvet dress. "And me."

"He did," Alexander answered honestly. Grabbing her chin, he forced her eyes back to his. "And he would do it again in a heartbeat. That's how much he loved you, Melanie. How much he loved all of us."

"I miss him," she choked out.

He brought her into his arms, kissing the top of her head. "I do, too, but remember what I told you the other day?"

She pulled her head from his chest and nodded, wiping her eyes. "That he's not really gone. That he'll live on."

"That he will, princess. He's touched all our lives with his devotion, his loyalty, his love." Sensing a presence hovering, he glanced up and saw his mother standing just over Melanie's shoulder, tears flowing freely down her face. "And because of him, our lives are infinitely better than had he never touched them the way he did. If you ever find yourself missing him, all you have to do is look in the mirror and you'll see him."

"How? All I'll see is me."

"And in you, he'll live on."

"Melanie, dear," Olivia said, approaching her. "Daddy has to go make a speech to say goodbye to Uncle Martin now."

She nodded slightly. "Okay, Mama." She took Olivia's hand and they walked to the front row to sit with the rest of Alexander's family.

Closing his eyes briefly, he made his way toward the casket, glancing at the large portrait of Martin that sat on an easel. Alexander paused, taken aback by the finality of it all. The past few days had been a whirlwind of interviews, phone calls, and trying to find some new normal. He never had a chance to let Martin's death really sink in…until this moment.

Stepping behind the podium, he looked at all the faces in attendance. Martin had touched each and every one of them in one way or another. He feared no words would do justice to his bravery, loyalty, and kindness.

Taking a breath, he addressed the assembled mourners. "On the day I came back to run my father's security firm, Leroy Martin had a few words of wisdom for me. He said, 'The best day in a man's life is the day he finally makes his life his own. No more excuses. No more apologies. No more acting like the world is out to get him. That's the day he finally becomes a man and proves his worth.'" He paused, remembering that day like it were yesterday. He could almost hear Martin speaking those words to him.

"He got up from behind my father's desk and walked over to me. He shook my hand, then said, 'I'm proud of you, Alex. Now it's time to prove your worth.'"

His eyes roamed the chapel, everyone dressed in dark colors and wearing heavy coats. This wasn't how he wanted to spend Christmas Eve. He should have been at home with his family baking cookies, watching Christmas movies, not saying goodbye to the person who had molded him into the man he was today.

"That was the last time he called me Alex...until recently. He'd always followed protocol, never straying, no matter what. It didn't matter that he was the person who taught me how to swim or showed me how to tie a tie. At that moment, I was no longer that little boy in his eyes. But I still looked up to him. I still needed his guidance, his advice, and sometimes his approval. And up until he took his last breath, I still did.

"He devoted his entire life to his country, then to the company, sacrificing everything so many people took for granted — friends, family, a normal nine-to-five job. Martin was a permanent fixture in my house growing up. I remember wondering why he always spent time with us when he should have been with his own family." Alexander looked down briefly, then returned his eyes to the faces in the crowd. "But now I know he *was* with his family. Blood makes you related, but loyalty makes a family, and Martin was as loyal as they come. I stand here and look around the room, able to see his influence in the face of every single one of you. He was a man of few words, but when he spoke, you damn well better listen because those words had impact. So I want to share with you some of Martin's last words."

Alexander clutched the podium, drawing strength from the sturdy wood. "He said, 'Don't make the same mistake I've made, that your father made. Family first. Always.'" He paused, allowing those words to sink in. "It's so easy to get caught up in the business of making a living that we forget to actually *live*. Our lives revolve around our work, and I know I'm not the only one who's guilty of this. When was the last time anyone here sat down to a dinner with their family, without their cell phones, and actually talked? And I mean *really* talked. Not just about work or things that needed to get done around the house, but talked about your hopes, your dreams, your fears. Because that's where the beauty of life truly lies. It's hidden in the little things. In the Saturday morning pancake ritual." He glanced at Melanie, seeing tears falling down her cheeks.

"It's in the family dinner at your ma's house where she makes enough lasagna to feed a small army." He met his mother's eyes, wishing he had the words to tell her how sorry he was that she was back here, having to say goodbye to the man she loved again.

"And it's in those quiet moments you spend with your wife." He looked at Olivia, a warmth radiating through him, despite the chilly temperatures. "It's in falling in love all over again each and every morning you wake up and can stare into her eyes. It's in the way sharing a simple cup of coffee in bed makes your day complete. It's in the way you feel like the luckiest man alive because you get to fall asleep next to the woman of your dreams every single night."

He returned his attention to the rapt crowd, men and women alike dabbing at the tears falling freely down their cheeks. "Don't take any of that for granted," he said in a soft voice, fighting back his own tears. "For too long, I took my family for granted. Never again." Clearing his throat, he continued. "From this moment forward, I will be fulfilling the promise I made to Martin. I will be putting family first. Effective immediately, I will be stepping down as President of Burnham and Associates Security Firm."

A gasp echoed from the crowd. Then he looked to Tyler, who simply nodded in agreement. "My brother, Tyler, has agreed to take over temporarily while we vet a replacement. He doesn't want the job permanently. Unlike me, he's always put family first. I will be keeping my place on the Board of

Directors, but will no longer be involved in the day-to-day operation of the company." He drew in a deep breath and looked at the portrait of Martin in a black suit sitting in front of an American flag. "Family first, Uncle Leroy. Always. Semper Fi."

A Marine appeared next to the casket and played *Taps* on his bugle, six more Marines approaching, folding the flag with meticulous precision. Outside the chapel, the boom of rifles echoed, sending chills through Alexander.

As the sound of the bugle diminished, one of the members of the Honor Guard approached his mother with the flag, slipping the traditional three rifle casings inside, and handed it to her. The Marine stepped back and saluted her.

As she stared down at the flag in her hands, sobs consumed her. Over the past few days, Alexander had wavered on whether stepping down from the company was the right decision. Now he knew it was. He didn't want his family to have to sit through another 21-gun salute any time soon.

THIRTY-EIGHT

The lights of the Christmas tree twinkled as Olivia sat on the couch, her arms wrapped around Melanie. The smell of fresh baked cookies emanated from the kitchen, the fire in the hearth warming her. From the outside, it was the picture-perfect Christmas Eve. Inside, it was anything but. A somber feeling invaded their home. Last year, this day had been filled with movies, eating, and celebrating with friends and family. This year, it was marked with uncertainty.

"Have you heard anything yet?" she murmured to Alexander as Melanie slept, cradled in her embrace. Her strong, independent girl had transformed into a child frightened of the smallest noise. It was understandable and something they knew would take time to overcome. One of the best psychiatrists in the country had been to their house every day to work with her. Olivia wasn't going to pretend what her daughter had endured wouldn't affect her. She knew it would. She also knew it was okay to need help to overcome it. Melanie was a beautiful, spirited girl. She would get through this and be stronger because of her experience. For now, Olivia was enjoying the snuggles again.

"No." He shook his head. "Moretti said he was going to try to do everything he could with the connections he has, but he has to fight the bureaucracy."

Sighing, Olivia returned her eyes to the tree in front of

her. She still found herself thinking of all the women she saved. She knew they would be okay, especially considering the Secretary of Homeland Security had taken an interest in their well-being. In the hours following the FBI's rescue, the story of why Melanie had been abducted hit the news. Despite the rhetoric of politicians wanting to ban Muslims from this country, there was much public outrage at the thought of these women going through removal proceedings and being sent back to Afghanistan, where they faced almost certain death. This pushed the Secretary of Homeland Security to grant them all asylum status just a few hours ago, even though they didn't exactly meet the standard.

Still, Olivia couldn't help but worry about Landon. He was so little and had no one left. The Department of Children and Families had to get involved, taking him into their custody, frantically trying to find a foster home to place him in right before Christmas. According to Moretti, it wasn't going well and he'd yet to leave the children's hospital. Olivia hated the thought of that poor baby being all alone. Landon needed to be surrounded by people who would love him every second of every day, not just a nurse or foster care worker who had too many other kids to tend to.

"It'll be okay," Alexander assured her. "I promised you I would never stop fighting for him, and I won't, Olivia. I failed his mother—"

"Alex, you—"

"I *did*, Olivia," he said sternly, then softened his voice. "All of this has made me reevaluate my priorities. It's no longer about following the rules or protocol. It takes a strong person to never deviate from the rules. But it takes an even stronger person to know when to bend them." He squeezed her hand, placing a soft kiss on her head as they settled in to watch Bing Crosby sing "White Christmas" against the backdrop of World War II.

"This movie again?" Melanie groaned. She stretched, then snuggled back between Alexander and Olivia.

A small smile crept across Olivia's lips, thankful for this moment. For a time, she wasn't sure whether they would be able to celebrate Christmas together. She would never take anyone for granted again.

"Yes. This movie. *Again*." Alexander nudged her. "Don't even try to pretend you don't like it. I see you moving your lips along to all the songs."

"Whatever, Dad." She rolled her eyes, then closed them.

Alexander caught Olivia's gaze and she stifled a laugh, grateful to see snippets of the Melanie they knew before all of this happened. She would never be the same again. No one would be after seeing and enduring what she had. As time went on, Olivia knew they would see more and more pieces of the girl she used to be.

"Did she become a teenager overnight?" he joked.

Olivia shrugged. "She *is* your daughter, and that includes her snarky behavior."

He reached toward the coffee table, then handed Olivia her glass of champagne. "I'd argue she got that from her mother."

Olivia rolled her eyes.

Smirking, Alexander said, "I rest my case."

The sound of a dog barking rang through the house, followed by Runner bolting from his bed in front of the fireplace, barking at the window, then at Olivia and Alexander, then the window again.

"Runner," Melanie scolded. "Where were you the night that crazy woman broke into this house? You couldn't be bothered then, could you, boy? Some guard dog you are."

He stopped his barking and came up to Melanie, placing his paw on her leg and nuzzling against her. When headlights from a car shined into the window, he raced toward the foyer.

"Did your mother change her mind?" Olivia glanced at Alexander.

"I don't think so. I told her she was more than welcome to come over, but she said the last thing any of us probably wanted to do tonight was pretend we were happy."

"Then who do you suppose is here at six o'clock on Christmas Eve?"

"There's lights on one of the cars," Melanie observed.

Olivia shot her head toward the window, able to make out a familiar silhouette trekking up the stone walkway. Seconds later, the doorbell rang, setting Runner off once more.

"I'll go see what he wants." Alexander pushed himself off the oversized couch, heading down the hallway.

"Is that the FBI agent who helped find me?" Melanie asked as she and Olivia continued to watch *White Christmas*.

"It is, sweet pea."

"What's he doing here?"

"I'm not sure." She glanced toward the foyer, then returned her attention to her daughter.

"Doesn't he have a family? Shouldn't he be with them on Christmas Eve?"

Olivia shrugged. "Some people make work their family."

"Like Daddy used to?"

"Yes." She met her daughter's eyes. "But not anymore."

Melanie snuggled against her. "Does this mean we can have pancakes every morning from now on?"

She laughed at her, always the opportunist. "You'll have to take that up with your father."

Olivia sensed rather than heard Alexander enter the room and looked toward him, seeing Agent Moretti at his side. Extracting herself from Melanie, she stood up.

"Mrs. Burnham." He nodded a greeting at her. "Merry Christmas."

"Merry Christmas to you, as well. Is everything okay?" She walked toward them, stopping in her tracks when her eyes fell on a woman accompanying him. But it wasn't the woman who surprised her. It was what the woman held in her arms. "What's going on?" she asked, swallowing hard.

"Mrs. Burnham, my name is Jacqueline Pierce. I'm a social worker at the Department of Children and Family Services."

"Nice to meet you, Ms. Pierce," she said, her eyes glued to the baby she held, trying not to get her hopes up. "What can I do for you?"

"You must have friends in very high places. The director got a call from the governor himself, telling us this child wasn't to spend another minute out of your care."

Olivia exhaled a short breath, relief washing over her. Tears welled in her eyes as she caught Alexander's gaze, a content smile on his face.

"This is certainly a huge breach of protocol, but like I said, this came all the way from the governor. It's my understanding you have everything you need? Formula, clothes, diapers, a crib?"

"Yes. Yes, of course. One of my friends seems to pop out a kid every other month. All her husband has to do is look at her and she's pregnant," she joked. "We have plenty of baby stuff here for when they stop by."

"Okay." She stepped toward Olivia and handed her the little boy.

Her heart nearly burst with happiness. For days, she'd

been living with the thought that it was her fault Landon no longer had a mother. The blame tore her apart. She hated to think she was the reason he would grow up to be just another statistic, no one to love or care for him. It ate away at her. But now, as she gazed into those dark eyes, she knew that was the furthest thing from the truth. She prayed Landon would never have to face the cruelties of the world that took his mother from him. She would do everything in her power to make sure he would only know love and happiness.

"There will be quite a few home visits while Landon is in your care," Ms. Pierce continued, "both announced and unannounced. You and your husband will have to attend regular meetings with a case worker, as well as submit to routine drug checks and psychological evaluations."

"Yes. Yes. That's all fine," she said hurriedly, caressing Landon's brow, not even looking up. She didn't care what she had to go through to keep Landon safe. She would do it and then some.

"Well, then, I guess that's all for now. We'll be in touch after the holidays to schedule an initial meeting." She handed Alexander a diaper bag, then stepped toward Olivia. "Merry Christmas, Mrs. Burnham."

"Thank you, Ms. Pierce, Agent Moretti." She nodded at him, smiling her first real smile in days, maybe even months.

"Of course, ma'am."

"Merry Christmas to both of you." Moretti gave them a small smile, then turned on his heels.

"Just one thing, Agent Moretti," Alexander called after him.

He spun around. "Please, call me Vincent."

"Okay," he answered. "Vincent. You said you have an eidetic memory. Why do you always write everything down?"

Moretti beamed a wide smile. "I can remember everything I *read*, not everything that is said, so that's why I write everything down." He allowed that to sink in. "Merry Christmas." Winking, he disappeared into the foyer.

A wiggling baby brought Olivia's attention back and she kissed Landon's forehead. For years, she had prayed for another child, but those prayers had gone unanswered. Now she knew there was a reason for all that...so she and Alexander could open their home and hearts to a little boy who desperately needed them. Like Alexander said earlier, blood makes you related. Loyalty makes you family.

THIRTY-NINE

One Year Later

Gandhi once said, "Terrorism and deception are weapons not of the strong, but of the weak."

What instills fear in someone one day only makes them stronger the next. And that was true of Melanie.

As Alexander sat on the couch, a fire burning before them, Christmas music playing in the background, the sound of Olivia in the kitchen, he marveled at how much difference a year made.

It hadn't been all good, but the happy times certainly outnumbered the bad. True to his word, Alexander stepped down from his position in the security company after overseeing an operation to retrieve Landon's body from Afghanistan. It was bittersweet to finally watch his friend's casket be lowered into the ground with an actual body inside.

It took a while to find a sufficient replacement to head the company. After turning down hundreds of qualified candidates, Alexander offered the job to Moretti. His gut told him he was the perfect person for the position, that he would run the company with his head *and* his heart, and that's exactly what he wanted. Alexander was called to consult with his firm and even the U.S. government on occasion, but spent the rest of his time with his family.

Watching little Landon grow made him realize how much he had missed when Melanie was a baby. He thought he was around a lot back then, but he realized that couldn't have been further from the truth. Even when he was physically home, he wasn't there mentally. He was always too engrossed with work issues, failing to pay attention to the thing that really mattered in life…family.

"Vroom! Vroom! Vroom!" a little voice squealed and Alexander smiled, beaming with pride as Landon stumbled into the room on unsteady legs, chasing Runner. His vocabulary consisted of three words at the moment — Dada, moo (his word for milk), and vroom. He loved everything to do with cars, and now traipsed around the house wearing a plastic fire engine hat he got when Olivia and Alexander took him to see the fire trucks a few weeks ago.

"Landon!" Melanie called, following him. Despite the nearly eight year age difference, they were two peas in a pod. Landon loved his big sister, and Melanie doted on him to no end. Her therapist believed having Landon around actually helped in her recovery from the trauma she had endured.

He spun around, shrieking with delight when he saw Melanie coming after him. "Vroom, vroom!" He pointed to the television, jumping up and down when he saw a Jeep on the screen.

"Yes, Landon," Melanie said. "That's a vroom, vroom."

"Vroom, vroom!"

Melanie picked him up, kissing him on the cheek. "Come on. Let's watch a movie with Mommy and Daddy."

"Vroom, vroom?" He looked at her.

"Yes. There's a vroom, vroom."

She brought Landon to the couch and placed him beside Alexander, then sat next to him. Olivia came out from the kitchen, carrying a tray of cookies and two flutes of champagne.

"Cookies!" Melanie jumped from the couch, running toward Olivia. She grabbed the tray and placed it on the coffee table in front of them. She shoved a few cookies in her mouth, looking at Alexander. "Can Landon have one?" she asked around a mouthful of cookie.

"Da! Da!" he said excitedly.

"I think he wants one," Olivia commented. "Go ahead and give him one, but only one. I'd like for him to get some sleep tonight." She fell onto the couch, handing Alexander a glass of champagne. "Girls are so much easier than boys." She met his eyes.

Melanie had been a dream compared to Landon. She started sleeping through the night when she was less than two months old, sleeping over twelve hours straight. Landon was a completely different baby. Up until he was about a year old, he still woke up every four hours. It made for some very long days, but Olivia wouldn't trade that time for anything. Neither would Alexander. This time around, he actually got up with Landon at three in the morning, allowing Olivia to get some rest. Being this involved in Landon's upbringing gave him an entirely new appreciation for everything Olivia had done with Melanie.

"He'll sleep," Alexander said, tousling Landon's hair. "Because Santa won't come if he doesn't."

"Da! Da!" He bounced on the couch, cookie crumbs falling out of his mouth.

"Presents! Can we open a present?" Melanie asked excitedly.

"Is it Christmas yet?" Alexander asked.

"Well, it is in England so, technically… Yes, it is." She crossed her arms in front of her chest, giving him a smirk.

He looked at Olivia, who just laughed. "She's *your* daughter."

"Fine," he conceded. "One present. It is tradition, after all."

"Yay! Can I pick?"

Getting up from the couch, Alexander shook his head. "You know the drill."

He approached the tree and grabbed three boxes, handing one to Melanie. Grinning a wide toothy grin, showing where she was missing a few teeth, she shook the box with excitement, even though she knew what was inside.

"Da? Da?" Landon slid off the couch, pointing to the box in Alexander's hand.

"Come here, buddy." He dropped to the floor, pulling Landon onto his lap, placing the box in front of him. He tore into the wrapping paper as best as an eighteen-month-old child could. Finally, he ripped all the paper off. Alexander helped him open the box, pulling out a pair of pajamas with trucks all over them.

"Vroom! Vroom!" he squealed, running around the room, his pajamas in his hand.

"Thanks, Dad." Melanie came up to him and placed a kiss on his cheek. "Pajamas. What a surprise," she said sarcastically.

"It's tradition."

"I know. I love it." She smiled. "What's that?" She nodded to the final box in his hands.

"It's a gift for your mother. Well, for everyone, but mostly your mother."

"What is it?" Olivia got up and joined him on the floor, crossing her legs in front of her.

"Open it and find out." He handed the shirt box to her.

Eyeing him suspiciously, she looked at the box and tore into the wrapping, tossing it to the side. With slow hands, she pulled the tissue back, her eyes scanning a piece of paper, her mouth moving as she read the words. Then she shot her gaze to Alexander, shaking her head.

"Is this real?" she asked in a quiet voice.

He nodded, beaming.

"But the judge said he wouldn't be making his decision until he clarified a few things in the home study."

"I guess he was able to do that."

She held the paper in her hands, tears falling down her face. Having a baby was a lot of work, the nine months leading up to the birth nerve-wracking every step of the way. Adopting a child was a whole different type of anxiety neither one of them had expected. They'd gotten to know Landon. They loved him. They couldn't fathom ever having to give up custody of him. They wanted him to be a Burnham, but for the past year, they didn't know if that would ever happen based on concerns regarding what Melanie had been through. The thought of him being taken away from them was constantly in the back of all their heads.

"What's that?" Melanie came up to them, Landon in her arms, and plopped down beside them.

"Adoption papers," Olivia answered, a smile on her face as she tore her eyes away from the papers and gazed lovingly at Melanie and Landon.

"We just have to go to court next week to make it official." Placing a kiss on Olivia's head, Alexander wrapped his arm around her and pulled Melanie to his side. He glanced at his two girls and the son he never thought he'd have, his heart filled with more love than he thought possible. It didn't come without sacrifice and heartache, though.

Regret *can* torture a man, but his mistakes don't define him. What *does* define him is how he learns from those mistakes.

Alexander Burnham had made more mistakes in his past than he cared to admit. For the longest time, he let those mistakes wear him down. But as he sat surrounded by his family and soaked in their unconditional love, all his mistakes, his failings, his shortcomings rolled off him. Life wasn't about his job, the amount of zeros in his bank account, or owning the latest gadget. It was about the little moments.

Alexander vowed to never take the little moments for granted again.

Thank you for reading VANISHED! I hope you enjoyed this story. While this is the end of the line for the Burnham Family, there's one more standalone novel in this series. Remember Cam from the Beautiful Mess Trilogy? Find out if he ever finds his happily ever after. (And there may even be a cameo by Mr. Burnham!) Pick up Heart of Light today.

A woman running from a dangerous past. A man haunted by shadows of his own. Can he bring her back from the darkness?

https://www.tkleighauthor.com/beautifulmess-world

I appreciate your help in spreading the word about my books. Please leave a review on your favorite book site.

HEART OF LIGHT

A woman running from a dangerous past.
A man haunted by shadows of his own.
Can he bring her back from the darkness?

Sex slave. Property. Disposable.

Jolene has spent the past decade of her life being paraded in front of men and sold to the highest bidder on a nightly basis, wondering when it would all end...

Until she risks it all and escapes, leaving her past behind.

Scared of being discovered, she hides away, trying to distance herself from everyone...

Everyone except a blue-eyed surfer who seems to know the secret she's hiding.

When her past closes in on her, will the truth of who she is surface in time to save her from the shadows threatening her freedom? Or will she be sentenced to live a life of darkness?

https://www.tkleighauthor.com/beautifulmess-world

PLAYLIST

I Can't Go On Without You - Kaleo
9 Crimes - Damien Rice
All My Days - Alexi Murdoch
Here With Me - Dido
Way Down We Go - Kaleo
Pendulum - Pearl Jam
Some Devil - Dave Matthews
Fire - Barns Courtney
Landfill - Daughter
Over The Rainbow - Ray Charles
I'll Follow You - Jon McLaughlin
Eavesdrop - The Civil Wars
State Trooper - Bruce Springsteen
There Will Be Time - Mumford and Sons
O Sleep - Lisa Hannigan
Oats In The Water - Ben Howard
Out Of My Hands - Dave Matthews
By My Side - Williams Fitzsimmons
Time Bomb - Dave Matthews Band
Through The Dark - Alexi Murdoch
Cat People (Putting Out The Fire) - David Bowie
In The Embers - Sleeping At Last
Better Days - The Goo Goo Dolls

ACKNOWLEDGMENTS

Wow. I don't even know how else to begin these acknowledgements but wow. It's 2017. I published *A Beautiful Mess* in August of 2013. It's been about three-and-a-half years since Mr. Burnham first made his way into readers' hands and hearts. When I first wrote his and Olivia's story in my *Beautiful Mess* series, I thought that was it for me. I honestly didn't believe I had any other stories in me. Boy, was I wrong. Not only did I have a few more stories in me involving some of the secondary characters readers met in that series, I also had an idea for a stand-alone follow up to my *Beautiful Mess* series.

I announced this book back in 2014 and I apologize it's taken this long to write it. I needed to write a few books before I could get to this one and I'm glad I waited. There's a certain element to this story I don't think I would have been able to truly capture had I not become a mother myself in December of 2015 to a beautiful little girl. Yes, at first glance, this is a story about a girl who is taken from her family and her parents' struggle to find her and bring her back home. But that's just the surface, really. At its core, this is a story about family, whether they're related by blood or not. It's a story about holding those people close and dear. Most of all, it's a story about enjoying the little things in life.

To that end, first I need to thank my wonderful husband and beautiful little girl. He's stood by my side and supported me on this writing journey since day one, not caring whether I sold ten books a day, or ten thousand. I would never be able to do this without him. (And of course a big thank you to my wonderful nannies who love and take care of little Harper like she were theirs so I could actually have time to write!)

Next, I need to thank my group of beta readers for always dropping whatever they're currently working on just for me. It's hard to find people you can trust and I'm grateful to have all of you to offer your invaluable insights and opinions… Sylvia, Lin, Melissa, Karen, Stacy, Karen, Natalie, and Victoria.

Also a big thanks to the only editor I'll ever allow to touch my babies, Kim Young. I'm so glad we share a brain and that you're able to figure out what I meant when my brain didn't. Your talent knows no bounds. I promise the next book won't be as heavy and dark.

Thanks, as always, to my admins who help me manage my social media presence: Melissa, Victoria, Lea, and Joelle — you girls make me look good.

I wouldn't be where I am today without my ever growing group of women who volunteer their precious time to help spread the word about my books online and on the street. When I first started this book adventure, I had no idea what a street team was. I'm glad I found out. They truly are my "angels".

A special shout out to my #BurnhamBitches. Thanks for being my go-to girls with, well, everything!

Last but not least, thank you to YOU, my readers. Thank you so much for your patience while I've been working on *Vanished*. So many authors are able to pump a book out every other month. I've never been able to do that so I thank all of you for standing by my side and waiting while I work to give you all the best possible book I can. I hope you have all enjoyed this final installment of the Burnham family saga… or is it?

ABOUT THE AUTHOR

T.K. Leigh is a *USA Today* Bestselling author of romance ranging from fun and flirty to sexy and suspenseful.

Originally from New England, she now resides outside of Raleigh with her husband, beautiful daughter, rescued special needs dog, and three cats. When she's not writing, she can be found training for her next marathon or chasing her daughter around the house.

9 780998 659602